I0579849

MYSTERY OF THE BLUE DRAGON (ENRICHED EDITION)

MYSTERY OF THE BLUE DRAGON (ENRICHED EDITION)

A NEO-NOIR DIVE INTO CRIME, PASSION & THE ABYSS

DARCY KIERAN

WWW.BUZZWINX.COM

Copyright © 2023-2024 by Darcy Kieran. All rights reserved.

Published by Buzzwinx Media.

All pictures purchased from Shutterstock.

COPYRIGHT: The purpose of copyright is to encourage authors to produce works that enrich our culture and society. Uploading or distributing any content from this book without prior authorization is theft of the author's intellectual property. Please respect the author's work as you would your own.

For permission requests, quantity sales, and special orders, please email: publisher@buzzwinx.com. *Thanks for your support of the author's rights.*

WORK OF FICTION: This book is a work of fiction. While references may be made to actual historical events or existing locations, the names, characters, places, businesses, and incidents are either the product of the author's imaginations or are used fictitiously. Any resemblance to actual persons, living or dead, business establishments, events, or locales is entirely coincidental.

Mystery of The Blue Dragon (Enriched Edition): A Neo-Noir Dive Into Crime, Passion & The Abyss

ISBN 978-1-7390198-4-6

Version 1.3b

CONTENTS

CHAPTER 1
BARRACUDA

*"You're an ocean, beautiful and blue.
I wanna swim in you."*

A KALEIDOSCOPE of vibrant blues and greens danced with the sunlight as it filtered through the water's surface, casting shimmering patterns on the seabed below. Nollaig Durand, dive center owner and seasoned underwater enthusiast floated weightlessly below a group of scuba divers who had come aboard his Barracuda dive boat. A school of silver jacks darted past him, their streamlined bodies effortlessly gliding between the coral formations below.

Nollaig had Lady Antebellum's song in his head while he watched the divers intently, taking in every detail of their movements and equipment. "You're an ocean, beautiful and blue. I wanna swim in you." As the proprietor of Seize the Deep, he was responsible for not only providing an unparalleled underwater experience but also ensuring the safety and well-being of each client. Though he had long ago handed over the daily operation of his boats to his skilled captains and divemasters, Nollaig still made occasional dives to monitor his crew's performance. He took pride in knowing that his team consistently delivered the high-quality experience he had built his business on.

As much as these dives served a practical purpose, they were also a balm for Nollaig's soul. After countless hours beneath the waves, the allure of the underwater world had never faded for him. The weightless serenity, the symbiosis of myriad species, and the ever-changing landscapes of coral and algae, filled him with a sense of wonder unmatched by anything on dry land. In the midst of a dive, his disillusionment and frustration towards an increasingly dysfunctional society seemed to melt away, if only for a little while.

Observing his clients exploring the stunning underwater environment, Nollaig couldn't help but feel a pang of envy for new scuba divers. Their eyes wide with amazement, they reveled in the novelty of this alien world, unburdened by the knowledge of the darker side of the dive industry. They were blissfully unaware of the corners cut and risks taken by less scrupulous operators.

For Nollaig, it was a constant battle to maintain his high standards amidst an increasingly cutthroat market. Every decision he made, from the sustainable refreshments on board, the banning of plastic water bottles and requiring that sunscreen lotion be reef-safe, to the meticulously maintained dive equipment, set him apart from competitors like Vanilla Dive Shop, the other large dive boat operator in Key Largo. But with each choice came a financial cost, and the temptation to follow the path of greed was ever-present.

NOLLAIG'S EYES darted through the water as he scanned for signs of trouble. It was then that he noticed a diver some distance away, separate from the group. She was thrashing about in a state of near-panic, her breathing rapid and unsteady, her eyes wide with terror. Her buoyancy was all over the place, causing her to sink rapidly, damaging the reef with her fins before briefly swimming back up. Nollaig's heart clenched at the sight; clearly, this woman needed help.

Without a moment's hesitation, he swam towards her with strong, determined fin kicks, closing the gap between them. As he approached, he could see that she was young, her long blonde hair floating behind her like a banner of distress. He did not recognize her as one of his Barracuda divers.

"Easy, take it slow," Nollaig thought as he reached her, hands outstretched. He attempted to communicate calm through a series of scuba diving hand signals. He caught her gaze, trying to evoke a sense of reassurance. He gestured for her to breathe slowly, demonstrating the technique with exaggerated breaths. The woman hesitated, her fear-stricken eyes searching his face for trust before she began to mimic his deep, slow inhales and exhales.

"Good, now let's get you stable," Nollaig signaled, adjusting her buoyancy control device as he held onto her arm firmly. All the while, his mind raced with concern for this stranger who had been left to fend for herself in an environment so unforgiving to the inexperienced. What kind of dive operator would allow someone like her into these waters without proper guidance?

Once the woman's buoyancy was relatively under control, Nollaig stayed by her side and guided her along the mooring line, his firm grip steadying her as they ascended together. His eyes never left her face, searching for any signs of distress. She seemed to be fumbling with her regulator before she finally managed to get on the path of catching her breath. Her eyes were still a bit wide and terrified; he could see remnants of rapid breathing despite her best efforts to control it.

"Almost there," Nollaig thought. They moved slowly towards the surface, each inch bringing them closer to safety. He watched as Lucy's expression gradually shifted from fear to relief and, finally, determination.

As their heads broke through the water's surface, Nollaig immediately inflated both buoyancy compensator vests before removing his regulator. Lucy gasped for air, taking several deep breaths before turning to him with watery eyes.

"Thank you," she croaked, her voice hoarse from the strain of her underwater ordeal.

"Are you okay now?" Nollaig asked, concern etched across his features. "What happened? How did you end up down there alone?"

"I'm Lucy," she said, swallowing hard before continuing. "I was with a group from Vanilla Dive Shop, but they just... I don't know... I ended up alone. I panicked when I realized I couldn't find them, and then my buoyancy went all wrong."

Lucy shivered, both from the lingering chill of the water and the realization that she had been so easily abandoned by those she had trusted. Nollaig saw her discomfort and tried to reassure her while guiding her towards the boat ladder.

"Let's get you out of the water and warmed up," he said gently.

Once aboard, he provided her with a towel to help her regain her composure.

"Thank you," Lucy murmured again, her gaze shifting from her dive gear to Nollaig's kind face. "I don't know what I would have done without you."

"Don't mention it," Nollaig said, his voice tinged with bitterness.

As they sat on the side bench together, Lucy's fear subsided, replaced by a sense of gratitude for the man who had selflessly come to her aid. As she regained her composure, Nollaig stepped back, allowing his team to take care of her while he scanned the water for the other divers.

"Dive's almost over," he mused, watching as, one by one, members of the group emerged and clambered onto the boat, shedding fins and masks with joyous laughter. The camaraderie was evident among them.

As Nollaig's staff efficiently helped the divers get back on board, the sun caught on the glistening water droplets that clung to their wetsuits. They ushered clients to their seating spots, offering fresh fruit and water in reusable containers, ensuring each person had what they needed after their dive.

"Here you go," one of the divemasters said to Lucy, handing her a mango slice with a warm smile. Lucy took it gratefully, still shaken from her earlier ordeal, but Nollaig's crew did their best to make her feel at ease.

"Thanks," she murmured, briefly meeting the divemaster's eyes before turning her attention to the fruit. It tasted sweet and refreshing, the perfect antidote to the salty seawater that lingered on her lips.

Nollaig stood nearby, overseeing the scene while keeping an eye on Lucy. He noticed one of his young divemasters, Marco, studying the young woman's gear with a frown.

"Her equipment is in terrible shape," Marco commented, gesturing toward Lucy's worn-out BCD and regulator. "It's amazing she didn't have more problems down there."

Nollaig nodded grimly.

"GASI needs to do something," Marco continued. "You will file an incident report, right?"

Nollaig raised an eyebrow. "I will file a report, but that's for the insurance company. Just in case."

"And GASI?" Marco insisted.

"Training agencies never do anything unless there's a death, and even then, it's often just a slap on the wrist," Nollaig replied bitterly. "It's all about immediate, short-term profits, Marco. Especially the dive training agencies owned by private equity firms."

"Damn," Marco muttered, shaking his head.

"But we'll keep doing our part," Nollaig added, "making sure our clients are safe and well taken care of. That's all we can do. And let's not talk about that in front of clients, please."

As Nollaig walked away to attend to other matters, he couldn't help but think about the state of the world – extreme capitalism running unchecked, the environment ravaged for short-term profit, social values crumbling under the weight of selfish desires. It was a bleak picture, one that seemed to grow darker with each passing day.

A scuba diver who had been observing Nollaig's conversation with Marco from the corner of her eye approached Nollaig as he prepared a new tray of fresh fruit to offer the divers. Her curiosity was piqued by his passionate words about the dive industry and its shortcomings.

"Hey, I couldn't help but overhear you talking about the dive industry," she said, leaning against the boat railing. "Is it really that bad?"

Nollaig looked up, meeting her gaze, and nodded. "Unfortunately, it is. The lack of proper quality assurance processes allows for a lot of negligence and unsafe practices."

"Like what happened with Lucy?" she asked, glancing back at the now recovering diver.

"Exactly," Nollaig confirmed. "But I'm sorry you heard that. It's our problem."

A frown crossed her face as she digested this information. Despite her tough, punk appearance, her concern for others was evident. "That's messed up," she stated bluntly.

"It is," Nollaig agreed, his frustration apparent in both his voice and the tense set of his shoulders. "But there are people like our staff who still care about doing things the right way, prioritizing safety and protecting the environment. We just have to keep fighting the good fight, even if it feels like swimming against the current."

Her eyes flashed with determination, and she extended her hand. "I'm Sierra, by the way."

She was an experienced diver. Noll had seen her around the dive boats multiple times but never so close. An air of danger surrounded Sierra with her vibrant hair and body decorated with numerous piercings and intimidating tattoos.

"Nollaig," he replied, shaking her hand firmly. From the moment their eyes met, an undeniable connection was formed. A kindred spirit seemed to course through them both—a unified sense of ethics and purpose, a relentless drive to oppose the mainstream and swim against the current.

As they continued their conversation, diving deeper into the issues plaguing society at large, Nollaig couldn't help but feel a renewed sense of drive. In Sierra, he saw a fellow concerned citizen, someone who understood and shared his values. They were both warriors in their own way, fighting against the insidious effects of unchecked capitalism and lack of ethics.

As they stood side by side on the boat, their words flowing easily between them, Nollaig knew that despite the darkness and uncertainty of the world around them, there was still hope—in the connections forged and in the battles waged by people like him and Sierra, who refused to let greed and selfishness destroy everything they held dear. After all, he wanted his kids to have a planet to live on.

THE BARRACUDA SLICED through the waves, its powerful engines roaring as it began its journey back to shore. Nollaig stood next to his captain, eyes scanning the horizon – an old habit from when he was the captain on his first dive boat years ago. The adrenaline from rescuing Lucy was still coursing through his veins, although he couldn't shake the nagging feeling that there was more to her story than met the eye.

On the bow of the boat, Lucy stretched out on a towel, her bronzed skin glistening under the sun as she lay topless, soaking in the golden rays. Her provocative display was impossible to ignore, and Nollaig felt a familiar pang of guilt and desire tugging at his conscience. He loved his wife deeply, but the sight of Lucy's half-naked body stirred something primal within him that he struggled to repress.

The captain grinned, elbowing Nollaig playfully in the ribs. "Quite a view, eh, boss? Seems like she's got her sights set on you."

"Me? Why me?" he replied gruffly, his cheeks reddening slightly.

"Look at her. Her eyes… She's on to you!"

A sense of unease settled over him as Nollaig watched Lucy absent-mindedly toy with her long blonde hair. He knew he was a happily married man and should not indulge in such distractions, but Lucy's targeted behavior stirred something within him – an unsettling mix of lust and suspicion.

"Hey, I'm not judging," the captain added, raising his hands defensively. "Just making an observation. There's definitely something… intense about that girl. Can't quite put my finger on it, though."

Lucy seemed otherworldly, somehow, as if she belonged to a different realm altogether. And although he couldn't quite pinpoint the source of his disquiet, Nollaig had the feeling that beneath her carefree facade, there was a hidden depth – a secret waiting to be uncovered.

"Her face is familiar," the captain breathed, squinting his eyes in an attempt to remember. "It's like… I've seen her before, somewhere."

"You mean her face… or… hmm..." Nollaig muttered, but their conversation was quickly cut short when Sierra approached with a strange glint in her eye.

"Everything okay?" she asked with a smirk.

"Fine," Nollaig replied, forcing a smile. "Just… thinking."

"About Lucy?" Sierra's gaze flicked towards the bow, where Lucy continued her sultry sunbathing.

Nollaig hesitated, unsure how to reply to this woman he had only just met and who seemed to have no boundaries. But something about Sierra—her fierce intelligence and shared sense of purpose—made him want to trust her.

"Captain," Nollaig called out to the weathered man at the helm of the Barracuda, "Can you keep an eye on that one?" He gestured discreetly towards Lucy. The captain nodded, "We'll bring everyone back safely."

With a deep breath, Nollaig turned his attention to Sierra, who had taken a seat nearby. Her piercing gaze was locked onto Lucy, seemingly lost in thought. As Nollaig approached her, the wind picked up, causing her vibrant blue hair to dance around her face like tendrils of fire.

"Mind if I join you?" he asked, while a mysterious force made him want to rekindle their earlier conversation. Sierra glanced up at him, her eyes softening with a hint of vulnerability.

"Please," she replied, motioning for him to sit beside her. Settling down, Nollaig couldn't help but notice how the sunlight created a halo effect around Sierra, giving her an almost otherworldly appearance.

"Where were we?" Nollaig began, his voice low and earnest.

"We were on the world crumbling under the weight of greed," Sierra answered, her eyes dark with frustration.

Nollaig felt a surge of empathy for Sierra – this stranger who seemed to understand his deepest concerns in a way that few others ever had. Their shared passion for justice and environmental protection created an unspoken connection between them, an immediate bond that transcended the confines of the dive boat.

"Maybe," he ventured cautiously, surprising himself, "we can do something about it."

Sierra's gaze snapped to his, her eyes wide with surprise and hope. For a moment, they simply held each other's gaze, the unspoken promise of a rebellion against a corrupt system hanging heavy in the air.

"Maybe," she whispered, her voice barely audible over the roaring engine. "Maybe we can."

As the Barracuda cut through the water, its powerful engines purring like a well-fed cat, Nollaig felt a strange sense of hope blossoming within him. Though Lucy's mysterious allure still cast its shadow over his thoughts, it was Sierra – a kindred spirit in their fight against avarice – who truly captured his heart.

THE MID-DAY SUN cast a golden glow on the water, reflecting off the wet dive gear that adorned the Barracuda. As it came to a halt at the dock, Nollaig's crew sprang into action with the precision and professionalism instilled in them by their leader.

"Easy there, ma'am," the young Marco said, extending his hand to help a middle-aged woman off the boat. He took her arm and guided her onto the dock with practiced ease, careful not to let her slip on the slick surface. Meanwhile, another crew member, a young woman named Jasmine, hoisted wet dive gear over her shoulder and carried it ashore. The clients watched in silent appreciation as their equipment was handled with care and respect.

Lucy stood near the edge of the dock, clutching her smartphone with a furrowed brow. As she scrolled through her phone to order an Uber, her long blonde hair dripped water onto the screen, making it difficult to navigate. She bit her lower lip in frustration, her warm eyes focused intently on the task at hand.

Nollaig noticed Lucy's struggle and approached her with a friendly smile. "Hey, Lucy," he said, trying to get her attention. "You don't have to worry about getting an Uber. I'll give you a ride back to Vanilla."

She looked up from her phone, her face breaking into a relieved grin. "Really? That would be amazing, Sir. Thank you so much."

"Of course," he replied, his voice calm but firm.

Lucy nodded, her eyes filled with genuine gratitude.

As they prepared to leave, Nollaig glanced back at his crew, who continued to work diligently on the dock. He knew that their collective dedication to excellence set them apart from their competitors – a fact that made him both proud and more resolute than ever to uphold the highest standards of professionalism in the face of an industry that seemed hell-bent on self-destruction.

The sun blazed overhead as Nollaig led Lucy to his car. Her long, wet blonde hair dripped down the back of her white T-shirt, which clung to her body like a second skin. As they got in, she shot him a flirtatious smile, and he could feel the heat rise to his cheeks.

"Thanks again for the ride," she said, leaning closer. "I don't know what I would've done if you hadn't found me out there."

Nollaig shifted uncomfortably in his seat, trying to focus on the road. He couldn't deny that Lucy was gorgeous – but something about her forwardness made him uneasy. Was it merely gratitude, or was there more to it than that?

"Really, it's no problem," he replied, forcing a smile. "It's just... part of the job, you know?"

Lucy's eyes twinkled mischievously. "Well, you're very good at your job," she said, her hand brushing against his arm. "You must have a lot of experience."

He swallowed hard, attempting to steer the conversation in a safer direction. "Experience is important in this line of work, especially when it comes to safety."

"I'm sure it is," she agreed, her fingers still lingering on his arm. "But gaining experience can be... exciting too, don't you think?"

As Nollaig pulled up to Vanilla Dive Shop, he felt relieved to finally have a reason to put some distance between them. He stepped out of the car and helped Lucy carry her dive gear inside, all the while wondering how much of her behavior was genuine and how much was an act.

"Here we are," he said as they entered the Vanilla Dive Center, his voice strained. "Let's get you sorted out."

"Thank you," she whispered, her eyes never leaving his.

Inside the dive shop, Nollaig tried to ignore the lingering sensation of Lucy's touch and focused on helping her with her gear. Nollaig approached the counter with Lucy at his side, her dive gear slung over his shoulder. The staff member on duty, a disheveled young man with a bored expression, glanced up from his phone.

"Hey," Nollaig said, setting the gear down with a thud. "You left one of your divers behind at the dive site. We picked her up."

The staff member stared at them for a moment before bursting into laughter. "That's a good one! Nice try, though." He returned his attention to his phone, dismissing their claim.

Nollaig's jaw tightened. "I'm serious. Your crew left her in the water. It's lucky we were still there."

The laughter stopped abruptly, and the staff member frowned, looking from Nollaig to Lucy. "Wait, you're not kidding?"

"Does it look like we're kidding?" Lucy snapped, frustration etched across her face. She crossed her arms tightly against her chest, trying to preserve what little warmth she had left after the icy gusts of air conditioning assaulted her drenched clothes.

"Uh... let me get Steve," the staff member said, suddenly flustered. He disappeared into the back room, leaving Nollaig and Lucy standing awkwardly at the counter.

As they waited, Nollaig's mind raced, churning through thoughts of negligence and the dangers that came with it. He couldn't help but think of how vulnerable Lucy had been out in the open sea, abandoned by those who should have protected her.

"Is everything okay here?" Steve, the owner, emerged from the back, his tone indicating annoyance.

"Your boat left her behind," Nollaig stated bluntly, gesturing to Lucy.

"Of course not," Steve scoffed, waving a hand dismissively. "We knew she was on your boat. We didn't leave her behind."

"Are you serious?" Lucy interjected, her voice incredulous. "You were gone by the time I surfaced!"

"Maybe you should have stuck with your dive buddy," Steve suggested, his tone patronizing.

"Or maybe you should actually roll call your divers before leaving the site," Nollaig countered, his anger rising.

"Look, it's not a big deal. She's fine now, right?" Steve said, attempting to diffuse the situation. It only served to infuriate Nollaig further.

"Fine? You think that's fine? This is negligence, plain and simple.

You're supposed to be responsible for the safety of your divers!" Nollaig could feel his face growing hot with indignation.

"Hey, we do our job. You don't need to come in here and tell us how to run our business," Steve snapped back.

Nollaig bit back a retort, realizing that arguing would get him nowhere. He exhaled slowly, trying to regain his composure.

"Before I go," Nollaig began, trying to offer a helpful suggestion despite his irritation. "There's a simple method to manage a roster of scuba divers, ensuring no one gets left behind."

"Save your breath, Noll," Steve interrupted, rolling his eyes. "We've got it covered. Mind your own damn business."

Nollaig clenched his jaw, the muscle in his cheek twitching with suppressed anger. He wanted to drive home the point, but Steve's stubbornness made it clear the conversation would only devolve into another heated argument.

"Fine," he muttered, finally stepping away from the counter.

"Wait, Noll!" Lucy called out, catching up to him. Her wet blonde hair clung to her shoulders, framing her beautiful face as she looked up at him with gratitude shining in her eyes. "I just wanted to say thank you again for rescuing me. I don't know what I would have done without you."

"Of course," Nollaig replied, his anger momentarily dissipating as he met her earnest gaze. "Just... be careful out there, alright? The world isn't safe… It's full of humans!"

Lucy nodded, her smile bittersweet as she acknowledged the truth in his words. "I'll do my best," she promised before returning to Steve at the counter.

As Nollaig walked away, his thoughts returned to the grim reality of the world he lived in. What had happened to Lucy was just a symptom of a much larger issue – an issue that seemed insurmount- able. But as long as he could make a difference, even to just one person like Lucy, he would do everything in his power to fight against the tide of darkness threatening to engulf them all.

Nollaig took a detour through the dive shop on his way back to his car, his keen eyes scanning the disheveled space. The sight of a greasy pizza box, its contents seemingly abandoned since the day before, further fueled Nollaig's disdain for the establishment. Even worse, he noticed open files of student divers strewn across a table – their personal information, including addresses, dates of birth, and credit card numbers, exposed for all to see.

"Unbelievable," Nollaig muttered under his breath, his fists clenching with outrage at the blatant disregard for privacy and professionalism.

"Hey, can I help you with something?" a staff member called out, eyeing Nollaig suspiciously.

"Thanks, but no," Nollaig replied tersely, his jaw set as he continued walking. There was nothing here that was new to him.

He made his way towards the compressor and fill station, the hum of machinery filling his ears. Nestled against the wall, partially hidden under a blue tarp, Nollaig spotted a pile of waterproof boxes – a model he had never seen before despite selling a variety of such items in his own dive store.

The sight of the waterproof boxes tugged at Nollaig's curiosity, drawing his attention away from the disarray of Vanilla Dive Shop. He stepped closer to the pile. His fingers traced the smooth surface of a waterproof box, searching for a brand or any indication of where it had come from. But there was nothing, save for the face of a blue dragon adorning each box. Its fierce gaze seemingly dared him to uncover the secrets within.

"Hey!" Steve's voice boomed through the shop, startling Nollaig. "What do you think you're doing nosing around here? We don't go snooping through your stuff!"

Nollaig straightened up, meeting Steve's glare with a calm, unwavering gaze. "I was just admiring these waterproof boxes," he said, gesturing to the pile. "They look quite impressive, but I couldn't find a brand on them. Are they custom-made?"

"None of your damn business," Steve snapped, his face reddening with anger. "Now get out of here and stop poking around where you don't belong."

Nollaig frowned, feeling a wave of unease wash over him. What could be so secretive about a few waterproof boxes? Nevertheless, he chose not to push the issue further. After all, he had already caused enough trouble by revealing their negligence in leaving Lucy behind.

"Fine," Nollaig said, raising his hands in mock surrender. "I'll leave you to your... business." As he turned to walk away, he couldn't help but wonder what secrets lay beneath the surface of this seemingly ordinary dive shop.

Why did the dive center owner react so aggressively to a simple inquiry about waterproof boxes? Did it have anything to do with the general unprofessionalism of Vanilla Dive Shop?

These questions swirled in Nollaig's mind as he walked back to his car. The relentless Florida sun beat down on him as he climbed into his vehicle, beads of sweat collecting on his brow. He couldn't shake the image of the Blue Dragon waterproof boxes from his mind – they seemed to hold some sinister secret that Steve was desperate to keep hidden.

As the ignition roared to life and the car lurched forward, Nollaig's thoughts turned to Lucy and Sierra. His palms grew sweaty as he thought about how their unexpected appearance had made this day so much more than just an ordinary day of scuba diving. Little did he know that these two women would forever alter his life.

CHAPTER 2
MAKSYM

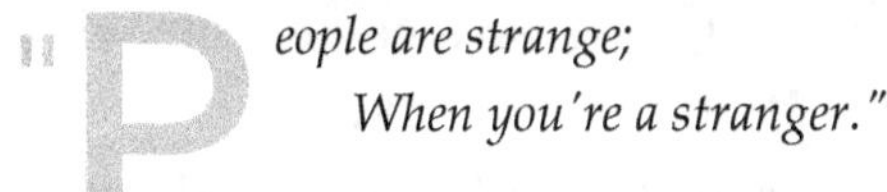

THE SUN HAD BARELY RISEN, and the Durand household was a flurry of activity. Nollaig stood at the kitchen counter, skillfully flipping pancakes while his kids, Daniel and Jane, chattered excitedly about everything and nothing. His wife, Susan, sipped her coffee elegantly, watching the scene unfold with a mixture of amusement and impatience.

"Daniel, tell me more about that science project you're working on," Nollaig said, his eyes never leaving the frying pan.

"Sure, Dad! We're learning about marine life, and I chose to research sea turtles! Did you know they can live for over a hundred years?"

His son's excitement was contagious, and Nollaig smiled warmly at his enthusiasm.

"Jane, how about you? What are you looking forward to in kindergarten today?" Nollaig asked as he slid a pancake onto her plate.

"Ms. Johnson said we're going to paint pictures of our families today!" Jane beamed, her blue eyes sparkling with anticipation.

"Make sure you use lots of bright colors for me, sweetheart," Nollaig said, ruffling his daughter's hair affectionately. He glanced at Susan, who was checking her nails, seemingly uninterested in the conversation.

After breakfast, Nollaig bundled the children into the car and drove them to school. After dropping them off at school, they waved goodbye as they disappeared into the building. The warmth of the morning sun on his face reminded him of the importance of being there for his kids, and he pushed thoughts of Susan's unconcern out of his mind.

Arriving at his Miami dive store, Nollaig found Leo, his general manager, already immersed in work. They exchanged pleasantries before diving into a discussion on customer satisfaction, employee engagement, and overall quality control in the shop.

"Leo, I want to ensure we keep up the level of quality our customers have come to expect from us, both in-store and underwater," Nollaig said firmly. "Let's set up a meeting with the staff to discuss ways we can continue to improve."

"Of course, boss," Leo responded, already making a note in his planner. "And I'll make sure everyone knows that their opinions and input are valued."

Nollaig nodded approvingly, his mind already racing with ideas for maintaining the high standards his business was known for. In a world where trust and security were increasingly scarce, it was vital to him that his dive store remained a beacon of reliability and excellence.

As he walked to his office, the weight of responsibility heavy on his shoulders, Nollaig couldn't help but reflect on the fragile balancing act of his life – providing for his family, nurturing his children's growth, and striving to keep his business afloat amidst an uncertain future. It was a struggle, but one he would face head-on, driven by love, determination, and an unwavering commitment to doing what was right.

Throughout the morning, Nollaig juggled phone calls and paperwork in his cluttered office at the back of his Miami dive store. He spoke with suppliers, negotiated deals on equipment, and checked in with his Key Largo staff to ensure that everything was running smoothly.

"Hey, just wanted to touch base with you guys," he said into the phone, the lines on his forehead creasing with concern. "How are the dives going today? Any issues with the gear or the boats?"

Nollaig listened intently as his Key Largo manager filled him in on the day's events, offering suggestions and troubleshooting solutions when necessary. His commitment to helping his team was unwavering, a testament to the passion and dedication he brought to his business.

As he hung up the phone, Nollaig frowned, wondering if there was more he could do to support his staff. He knew that in an industry as cutthroat as theirs, it was crucial to maintain a high level of morale and unity among the team members.

* * *

JUST BEFORE LUNCHTIME, Nollaig stepped out of his office, rubbing the stiffness from his neck as he headed for the front of the store. The scent of saltwater and neoprene greeted him, a familiar comfort amidst the chaos of his day.

He was surprised to see Lucy standing by the counter, chatting animatedly with a man he didn't recognize. Her eyes met his, and for a moment, there was a spark of lust between them – a silent acknowledgment of the physical attraction simmering beneath the surface.

"Ah, Nollaig! I'd like you to meet Maksym," Lucy said, gesturing toward the man beside her. "I told him about how you rescued me in Key Largo last Saturday."

Maksym extended a hand, his grip firm and confident. "Nice to meet you, Nollaig. Lucy mentioned that your dive store offers better quality services than others, so I thought I'd come and see for myself."

Nollaig nodded, curious about the unexpected visitor. He wondered what Maksym's connection to Lucy was. Glancing around at the meticulously organized shelves and equipment, he couldn't help but feel a surge of pride in the business he had built – a business that prioritized quality and safety above all else.

"Welcome," Nollaig said. "I hope you find what you're looking for here. We strive to provide the best possible experience for our customers, both in-store and underwater."

"Well, Nollaig," Maksym said with a friendly smile, "why don't you join us for lunch at the sushi place next door? My treat."

Nollaig hesitated, glancing between Lucy and Maksym. He had work to do, but there was something about the invitation that intrigued him – not to mention the undeniable chemistry he felt with Lucy. She looked back at him, her eyes pleading as if to say she wanted him there, too.

"Come on, Noll," Lucy chimed in, giving him an encouraging smile. "It'll be fun, and you have to eat, no?"

"Alright," Nollaig agreed, unable to resist the pull of their combined persuasion. "Just let me grab my things."

As they walked toward the sushi restaurant, the South Florida sun beat down on them, casting dappled light through the swaying palm trees overhead. The heat was almost oppressive, but the vibrant energy of the city around them seemed to counterbalance it, creating an atmosphere of excitement and anticipation.

"So, how long have you two known each other?" Nollaig asked, trying to make sense of their relationship dynamics. He watched as they exchanged glances and shared a secretive smile before Lucy answered.

"Only a few weeks," she replied casually. "I started working part-time at Maksym's nightclub recently. The HeatWave Lounge."

"Ah, I see," Nollaig said, nodding thoughtfully. But still, he couldn't shake the feeling that there was more to the story than they were letting on.

Over lunch, the conversation flowed easily, touching on various topics like travel, hobbies, and life in Miami. Yet, despite the casual nature of the discussion, Nollaig couldn't help but notice how Lucy's gaze would occasionally linger on him. Her eyes were filled with a mix of desire and something else – an internal conflict he couldn't quite decipher.

"Lucy's been a great addition to the team at the nightclub, but we're not dating or anything like that," Maksym clarified as if he sensed a question Nollaig didn't ask. "We're just friends."

"Right, just friends," Lucy echoed, her voice laced with a hint of regret that only Nollaig seemed to detect.

As the meal continued, Nollaig found himself increasingly intrigued by Lucy and Maksym's enigmatic connection. "People are strange when you're a stranger, " the old song by The Doors, was in his mind, as he knew there was more to their story than they were revealing. But for now, he was content to enjoy their company and the brief respite from his busy day.

Nollaig leaned back in his chair, studying Maksym across the table. "So, tell me about your nightclub, Max," he said, his curiosity evident in his voice. "Is Max fine? Or Mak?"

"Either!" Maksym replied with a grin. "HeatWave Lounge is the most trendy nightclub in South Beach, if I may say so myself. We have the hottest DJs, the best drinks, and, of course, the most beautiful dancers."

Nollaig glanced at Lucy, who blushed slightly under his gaze. "So, you're a dancer at the club?" he asked her.

"Uh, yeah," she stammered, tucking a strand of blonde hair behind her ear. "But it's not what you think. I'm not a stripper or anything like that. We dance on stage next to the DJ or sometimes on platforms throughout the club. It's more like... creating an atmosphere, you know?"

"Exactly," Maksym chimed in, nodding in agreement. "Our dancers are there to entice our male customers and keep them coming back for more. And Lucy is one of our best. But it's not a strip club!"

"Ah, I see," Nollaig said, trying to hide his surprise. "Kind of like when nightclubs leave your Ferrari and other expensive cars out front to impress their clientele."

The moment the words left his mouth, he realized his mistake. The silence that descended upon the table was almost palpable, and he could feel his face growing hot with embarrassment. "I'm so sorry, Lucy. I didn't mean to compare you to an object. That was thoughtless of me."

Lucy waved away his apology with a good-natured laugh. "No, it's fine, really. In a way, you're right. We are like those fancy cars – we're there to be admired but not touched. Just part of the scenery."

"Well," Nollaig pressed, "your beauty is most certainly a magnet for men at the nightclub. That much I can see."

"Thank you," she replied, her cheeks pink with a mix of pleasure and discomfort.

Sensing it was time to change the subject, Maksym steered the conversation back toward scuba diving. "So, Lucy tells me she was really impressed with your dive operations in Key Largo. She said they were far superior to the ones at Vanilla Dive Center."

"Is that so?" Nollaig asked, his interest piqued.

"Yes," Lucy confirmed, nodding emphatically. "Your attention to safety and quality was really remarkable. Max, you were the one who recommended Vanilla Dive Center to me in the first place, right? Shame on you!"

Maksym shifted in his seat, looking slightly uncomfortable. "Yes, I did. I apologize if it wasn't up to par. You see, I use their services regularly for... group dives with... friends."

"Really?" Nollaig said, intrigued. "What kind of dives do you usually organize with your friends?"

"Uh, just casual outings, you know? Nothing too serious," Maksym replied evasively, avoiding eye contact with Nollaig.

"Night dives, mostly," Lucy clarified while Maksym seemed annoyed that she said it.

"Sounds like fun," Nollaig said, trying not to push too hard. He couldn't shake the feeling that there was more to this story than Maksym and Lucy were letting on, but for now, he decided to let it go. After all, everyone had their secrets – and Nollaig had more than enough on his plate without getting tangled in someone else's web.

Nollaig leaned back in his chair, the sun casting a warm glow on their table as they enjoyed the last few bites of sushi. He glanced at Maksym and Lucy, both seemingly relaxed and enjoying their lunch. But something about Maksym's evasive answers regarding Vanilla Dive Center nagged at him.

"Hey, Max," Nollaig ventured, "you know... I have to say it... If you ever want to try something different from Vanilla, you should consider my dive center in Key Largo, Sea Spell Diving. We have six boats, and I'm confident you'll enjoy the experience."

Maksym raised an eyebrow, a flicker of interest igniting in his eyes. "Interesting proposition, Noll. But you know... Tell me more about the dive industry. Lucy mentioned something, but..."

Nollaig hesitated for a moment, unsure how much he wanted to reveal to this enigmatic man. But he took a deep breath and decided to be honest. "I believe that scuba diving should be a safe and enjoyable experience for everyone involved. Unfortunately, many dive centers cut corners and compromise safety to save money. I refuse to do that."

"Commendable," Maksym replied, his gaze never leaving Nollaig's face. "What would it take for you to expand your business so that more divers could benefit from your quality services?"

At first, Nollaig offered the usual excuses—a lack of time and resources—but eventually admitted that financial constraints were the main obstacle to expansion. "Running a dive operation with high-quality standards and a real quality assurance system is expensive, and we can't fully pass on the cost to our clients because most scuba divers don't understand the difference between a good dive center and a bad one. As a result, our profit margins are smaller than other dive centers, which makes it difficult to secure financing from banks."

Maksym nodded thoughtfully, his fingers tapping rhythmically on the table. Nollaig sensed that there was a hidden agenda at play but still couldn't quite put his finger on it.

Finally, Maksym said, "Your commitment to quality is impressive. I would be willing to invest in your business and help you expand if you're interested. Open more professional dive centers."

Nollaig's eyes widened in shock. He had not expected such an offer. He hesitated, unsure of what to say. Maksym simply smiled and added, "Sleep on it, and let me know if you're interested."

The lunch came to an end, and they all got up to part ways. As Nollaig walked back to his dive shop, he watched Maksym and Lucy stroll towards a sleek McLaren parked nearby. The sight of the luxury car fueled Nollaig's suspicions. Yet, there were plenty of dive businesses financed by rich people "investing" play money in the dive industry. So, maybe this was an opportunity.

Back in his office, as Nollaig mulled over the unexpected proposal, he couldn't help but feel uneasy. Why was Maksym so quickly interested in his business? What were his true intentions? And what secrets did both he and Lucy hold? Deep down, Nollaig knew he had to tread carefully—after all, even the warmest, sunniest days in Miami could hide dark clouds just beyond the horizon.

THE EVENING SUN cast a warm glow through the kitchen windows as Nollaig scrubbed at the remnants of dinner on their plates. Suds clung to his forearms as he wordlessly tackled the task, lost in thought. His wife lounged at the kitchen table, swirling her glass of white wine and taking dainty sips. She seemed content, but Nollaig could see the wheels turning in her head as she picked at the label on the bottle.

"Met an interesting guy today," Nollaig said, breaking the silence. "Maksym Byrne – he owns that famous nightclub, HeatWave Lounge."

Susan looked up, curiosity piqued. "Oh? What did he want?"

"Actually, he's interested in investing in my business," Nollaig replied, setting down a now-clean plate. "Wants to help me expand."

"Expand?" Susan frowned, her brow furrowing. "But isn't our business already doing well?"

Nollaig nodded and hesitated before continuing. "It is, but Maksym thinks there's potential for more growth. He was impressed by our commitment to quality and safety, especially compared to other dive centers."

Susan eyed her husband warily, her grip tightening around her wine glass. "And what would that mean for us, Noll? If you expand the business, won't you need to keep more cash in the company? We have our own expenses, you know."

Nollaig paused, dishwashing brush in hand, sensing the tension building. "I understand your concerns, Susan. But think about it – if we can grow the business, it could benefit all of us... in the long run."

"Benefit us how exactly?" Susan shot back, her voice sharp. "I've been wanting to remodel this kitchen for years, and now you're talking about sinking more money into the business? I don't see how that's going to help me."

Nollaig sighed, feeling the weight of his wife's words on his shoulders. He knew his stay-at-home wife had a point – she had her own financial needs to consider. But he also couldn't shake the feeling that Maksym's offer could be a game-changer for his dive centers. And perhaps, the industry.

"Look," Nollaig said, trying to keep his voice even, "I promise I'll think it over carefully. I won't make a decision without talking it through with you first. Just... let me mull it over, okay?"

Susan's gaze didn't waver, but she finally nodded. "Fine. But do not cut the amount of money you bring home... to me... ever!"

Nollaig forced a smile as he returned to washing the dishes, the sound of water running and clinking glassware filling the room once more. As he worked, he felt torn between his desire to grow his business and his loyalty to his wife. What was best for his family? And what secrets were Maksym and Lucy hiding behind their charming smiles?

As the sun dipped below the horizon, casting long shadows across the kitchen floor, Nollaig knew that this decision would test the strength of his marriage and his commitment to his values. The future loomed before him like an ocean full of possibilities – some alluring, others treacherous – and he knew he would have to navigate these waters with care.

CHAPTER 3
SIERRA

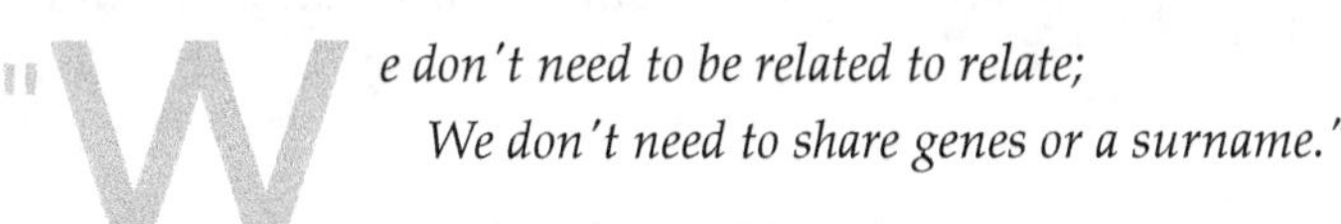

"*We don't need to be related to relate;
We don't need to share genes or a surname.*"

SATURDAY, around lunchtime, Noll exited his Miami dive store and walked to his car. He left the store in capable hands, trusting his well-trained employees to manage it while he drove to Key Largo to check on his dive boat operations in the Florida Keys. As he pulled out onto i95 and then US1, his thoughts were occupied by two opposing forces: Max's offer to invest in his company for expansion and his wife's objections to the idea.

Noll gripped the steering wheel tighter, feeling the weight of the decision he had to make. He knew that taking Max's money would mean giving up some control over his business, but the potential benefits were also significant. Meanwhile, his wife's concerns echoed in his mind. Expanding a business could mean reinvesting the cash instead of taking it home, and his wife wanted a lot of cash to come home. The potential damage to their marriage could be real.

Then, his thoughts wandered off track as he considered his dive store and the brands he carried. A memory surfaced from a couple of weeks earlier when he had seen dry boxes with a blue dragon logo at Vanilla Dive Center in the Florida Keys. They had appeared well-manufactured, and he had been unable to find a supplier. It was a small thing, but it nagged at him like an itch he couldn't quite reach.

Arriving in Key Largo, Noll decided to stop at Vanilla before going to his own dive operations. He hoped to find some indication of who the supplier of the Blue Dragon dry boxes might be, despite Steve's warning not to look into them. Walking into the dive shop, he carefully avoided engaging with any of the employees, not wanting to draw attention to himself.

He headed directly to the area near the fill station where he had last seen the boxes. The spot was empty, yet very wet, as if wet gear had been stored there just moments before. The absence of the waterproof dry boxes only deepened the mystery, and Noll's curiosity grew stronger.

In the afternoon, Noll stood on the deck of one of his dive boats, Manta, the salty breeze ruffling his salt-and-pepper hair. The sun cast a warm glow over the calm waters surrounding them, and the turquoise sea appeared to stretch endlessly towards the horizon. It felt like paradise above water, but he knew that the true beauty lay beneath the surface.

"Alright, everyone! We've arrived at our dive site," a divemaster in Noll's crew announced as another crew member secured the boat to a mooring. "Make sure your gear is ready, and later, double-check your buddy's equipment before we start the descent."

As Noll scanned the group of divers, he noticed Sierra standing alone near the stern of the boat, her bright-colored blue hair contrasting with her dark wetsuit. She seemed to be scanning the group for a partner but found none.

"Hey, Sierra," Noll called out as he approached her. "It looks like you don't have a buddy for this dive. Would you like to pair up with me?"

Sierra looked him up and down, seemingly sizing him up. After a moment, she nodded. "Sure, why not? Just don't rush me," she said with a hint of challenge in her voice.

Noll grinned, appreciating her spirit. "No worries, I'll do my best to be slow."

With their gear checked and their dive plan discussed, Noll and Sierra took the plunge into the water. As soon as they hit the cool embrace of the sea, it was as if a whole new world opened up to them. Schools of brightly colored fish danced around vibrant coral structures while the shadows of massive sea fans swayed gently in the current.

Underwater, Noll and Sierra moved in perfect harmony. They seemed to instinctively understand each other's movements, matching their pace and buoyancy with ease. Their slow, deliberate approach allowed them to get closer to the reef and its inhabitants without startling the delicate ecosystem.

Noll marveled at how well they clicked as dive buddies, especially considering this was their first time diving together. He had dived with countless partners over the years, but few had matched his style so seamlessly. While they explored the underwater landscape, he couldn't help but feel a connection with Sierra that transcended their shared passion for diving.

As they approached the end of their dive, Noll caught Sierra's eye and gave her the signal to ascend. She signaled in agreement, her eyes reflecting a mutual appreciation for their time beneath the waves. Together, they began their ascent towards the surface, leaving behind the mesmerizing world below.

As the dive boat cruised back to shore, Noll kept busy assisting his staff with their tasks. He coiled ropes and stowed gear, his hands moving with practiced ease. Sierra watched him for a moment before joining in. Her actions mirrored his as they worked together seamlessly, like an extension of their underwater connection.

"Thanks for your help," Noll said, smiling at Sierra as they sat down for a brief rest. The wind tousled their damp hair while the sun warmed their skin, casting golden highlights over their features.

"Of course, I'm always happy to lend a hand," Sierra replied, returning his smile. "That was an amazing dive, by the way."

"Indeed, it was," Noll agreed, feeling a warmth inside that had little to do with the sun. "You know, if you're not in a hurry to go anywhere, would you like to join me for a drink?"

Sierra hesitated, her eyes searching Noll's face as if trying to decipher his intentions. Finally, she nodded. "Sure, I'd like that."

Later, at the dock, Noll and Sierra helped the crew unload the boat and prepare it for the night dive. Their camaraderie was evident as they laughed and joked with the staff, making quick work of the necessary tasks.

With the boat secured and ready for its next adventure, Noll led Sierra to a nearby oceanside bar nestled under swaying palm trees. They found a table close to the water, where the soft lapping of waves provided a soothing soundtrack to their conversation.

Noll ordered a mojito, while Sierra surprised him by requesting a scotch, neat. As they sipped their drinks, they exchanged stories and learned more about each other. When Noll asked about her work, Sierra revealed that she was in IT.

"Really?" Noll raised an eyebrow, intrigued. "So, you're a computer nerd?"

"Guilty as charged," Sierra admitted with a grin. "I'm pretty good at it, I believe. But I prefer to talk about anything else."

Noll couldn't help but notice the mysterious glint in her eyes as she spoke, hinting at secrets he had yet to uncover.

As the sun dipped below the horizon and twilight crept in, Noll found himself more captivated by Sierra than he'd been by any woman in a long time. She was rough around the edges, like the scotch she favored, but there was an undeniable connection between them.

Sierra leaned in, curiosity brimming in her eyes. "So, tell me something, Noll. How do you ensure consistency and quality across your dive boats... centers... and instructors...? I mean, it must be quite a challenge."

"Ah, that's the million-dollar question," Noll sighed, placing his mojito on the table. "Truth is, there isn't a real quality assurance system in the dive industry. Each dive operator has to figure it out for themselves – reinventing the wheel, so to speak."

"Really?" Sierra raised an eyebrow, clearly surprised. "I thought training agencies like G.A.S.I. provided standards."

Noll shook his head. "About that. The Global Association of Scuba Instructors… They set the standards for scuba diving skills, of course. How to remove and replace your mask underwater. But when it comes to managing quality, customer experience, or staff, they don't really provide any guidance. It's up to each dive center to find its own way."

Sierra took a slow sip of her scotch, her gaze never leaving Noll as she mulled over this information. "That seems inefficient. So, if you want more divers to have access to a good experience, shouldn't you, yourself, open more dive centers?"

Noll couldn't help but chuckle. "You know, that's exactly what an investor told me not too long ago." He paused, taking another sip of his mojito. "I've been thinking about expanding, actually. But it's not as simple as just opening new locations."

"I suppose not," Sierra agreed, her tone half-joking as she added, "But hey, if you ever need help setting up computer and quality systems for your future network of dive centers around the world, I could always lend a hand."

Noll looked at her, considering her offer. "You know, all jokes aside, I could really use some help with that."

For a moment, the air between them felt charged with possibility, as if they were on the precipice of something new and exciting. Their shared values and desire to help others seemed to create an unspoken bond that was only just beginning to form.

"Let's see where life takes us," Sierra said, raising her glass in a toast. "To new adventures and unexpected connections."

Noll smiled, clinking his mojito against her scotch. "To new adventures and unexpected connections."

Although no deal had been struck, the seeds of collaboration had been sown – waiting for the right time to bloom into something much greater.

Noll and Sierra lingered at the bar, enjoying the last sips of their drinks. The conversation flowed with surprising ease, and they found themselves reluctant to say goodbye. As the sun dipped lower in the sky, casting long shadows across the sand, Noll glanced at his watch.

"Wow, time flies," he remarked, draining the last of his mojito. "I should probably get going."

"Me too," Sierra agreed, finishing her scotch. "But this was really nice, Noll. We should do it again sometime."

He smiled, genuinely touched by her words. "I'd like that."

They stood up from their seats and headed towards the exit, the balmy ocean breeze lifting strands of Sierra's wild hair as they walked side by side. Outside, they paused for a moment, taking in the beauty of the setting sun before heading to their respective cars.

"Take care, Sierra," Noll called out as he unlocked his car door.

"Same to you, Noll," she replied, giving him a quick wave before disappearing into her own vehicle.

Alone once more, Noll slid behind the wheel and let out a deep breath. He started the engine and jumped onto US1 as he began the drive back to Miami. His mind raced with thoughts, each one vying for attention as the miles rolled by.

Maksym's offer to invest in his company and help him expand weighed heavily on him, but so did his wife's objections. How could he find a balance between his ambition and his married life? Sierra's intriguing personality and her offer to help with computer and quality systems added another layer of complexity. Could he trust her?

And what about the Blue Dragon dry boxes? It seemed like such an insignificant issue, but it bugged him that a low-quality competitor had special waterproof boxes he couldn't even find a supplier for.

As the road stretched before him, the darkness of night swallowing the last vestiges of daylight, Noll found himself consumed by these thoughts, the seeds of doubt and uncertainty taking root in his mind. What would the future hold?

But for now, Noll focused on the hum of the engine and the steady rhythm of the road beneath his tires, driving through the night with an uneasy heart and a world of possibilities waiting just beyond the horizon.

Otherwise, no matter what the future held, he was grateful to have met Sierra, potentially a new friend. Rina Sawayama was singing in his head, "We don't need to be related to relate. We don't need to share genes or a surname."

CHAPTER 4
A DANCE PARTNER

 "*Rip it up, move down;*
Rip it up, move it down to the ground."

NOLLAIG GRIPPED the steering wheel of his car, his knuckles white as he navigated through the rush of traffic on i95. The sun had set, and the darkness swallowed up the long stretch of highway ahead. Maksym's proposal consumed his thoughts: an investment in his dive business that could lead to expansion and improvement in an industry that desperately needed it. The prospect excited him – the chance to make a difference, to leave a mark in the world. But the question remained: could he trust Maksym, a man he'd only recently met?

He decided to stop by HeatWave Lounge, hoping to catch a glimpse of the man's management style. It was a slight detour on his way home from Key Largo, where he had spent the afternoon scuba diving.

As Noll pulled up to the entrance, the sight of Maksym's McLaren parked alongside a MacLaren and a Lamborghini caught his attention.

The vehicles exuded power and wealth, much like Maksym himself. A line of eager patrons snaked around the building, waiting for their chance to enter the exclusive club. Nollaig grabbed his phone and sent a quick text to Lucy, asking if she could help him get in.

"Wait at the door," came her swift reply.

Noll stepped out of his car, scanning the faces in the line; they were young, beautiful, and full of anticipation. He approached the entrance, feeling the weight of their gazes on him, questioning who he was and why this seemingly ordinary man warranted special treatment.

Lucy appeared at the door, her stunning figure drawing even more stares from the crowd. With a nod to the guards, she beckoned Nollaig. The sense of exclusivity was palpable as those left waiting outside continued to scrutinize him, their expressions caught between envy and curiosity.

"Thanks, Lucy," Noll said, his voice barely audible over the pulsating music that filled the club.

"Of course," she replied, her eyes locked onto his for a moment longer than necessary before disappearing into the throng of dancers and partygoers.

The atmosphere inside Maksym's HeatWave Lounge was electrifying. Nollaig followed Lucy through the pulsating crowd, the vibrant techno music reminiscent of the Miami Ultra Music Festival he had attended years ago. The club was filled with attractive young people, their bodies moving in sync with the hypnotic beat that seemed to take over every cell, every fiber of their being.

A DJ perched high on a platform commanded the room, orchestrating the energy and movement of the crowd below. The vibe was intoxicating – a celebration of life that made the outside world feel distant and irrelevant.

While they weaved through the sea of dancers, Nollaig found it impossible not to steal glances at Lucy. Her model-like figure was barely concealed by the fancy dress she wore, its wide-open back revealing the tantalizing curve of her spine. He couldn't help but wonder if his excitement stemmed more from seeing her again than from visiting Maksym's nightclub.

Upon reaching the VIP section, Lucy signaled to the guards, who promptly opened the velvet rope to let them pass. As they entered, Noll noticed curious eyes following them, once again questioning his connection to this stunning woman, well-known among the regulars.

Inside the VIP area, the ambiance shifted to an air of exclusivity and quiet indulgence. Luxurious couches lined the perimeter, offering a retreat from the chaos of the dance floor. They had barely settled into their seats when a waiter appeared, presenting them with a bottle of Crystal champagne without any prompting. It was clear that Lucy had perfected this routine, and the staff knew exactly what she desired.

Nollaig couldn't help but marvel at the scene unfolding around him – the opulence, the extravagance, all bathed in the pulsing glow of neon lights. For a brief moment, he had entered the world of the rich and famous and felt as if he belonged.

"Cheers," Lucy said, raising her champagne flute in a toast.

"Cheers," Nollaig echoed, clinking his glass against hers. As the bubbles tickled his throat, he couldn't help but wonder what the future held – for him, for his business, and for the enigmatic woman sitting beside him.

"Lucy, tell me more about Maksym," Nollaig asked, swirling the golden liquid in his glass. The bubbles danced to the beat of the music, reflecting the dizzying lights above.

"Max is... a very interesting man," Lucy replied hesitantly, her eyes darting around the VIP area as if searching for an escape. "He's ambitious and knows how to get what he wants."

"Is that so?" Nollaig prodded gently, trying to gauge her true feelings on the topic.

"Absolutely," she said, avoiding eye contact. "His nightclub is the talk of Miami, after all."

Before Nollaig could ask another question, Maksym himself appeared, sliding onto the couch next to Lucy with an air of confidence that seemed to fill the room. Lucy's demeanor shifted instantly, her evasiveness replaced by a radiant smile. She leaned in close to Max, praising him enthusiastically. "Maksym has really outdone himself with this place! It's absolutely amazing!"

"Ah, thank you, Lucy," Max replied, grinning broadly. "I always strive for the best – both in business and pleasure."

Nollaig couldn't help but notice the change in Lucy's behavior. Her sudden admiration for Max felt forced, but he couldn't quite put his finger on why. He decided to play along, raising his champagne flute in a toast. "Here's to your success, Maksym. You've built something truly extraordinary here."

"Thank you, my friend," Max said, clinking glasses with Nollaig. "It's only the beginning."

As they sipped their champagne, Nollaig complimented Maksym on the well-run nightclub, impressed by the attention to detail in every aspect. Max beamed at the praise and extended an invitation. "Would you like to see the nerve center of this operation? I think you'll find it quite fascinating."

"Sure, I'd love to," Nollaig agreed, curiosity piqued.

Maksym led Noll to his office, with Lucy following. The room, high up behind the DJ with one-way windows, offered a bird's-eye view of the nightclub yet remained invisible to those below. Inside, the music was muffled, allowing for conversation without shouting over the pulsating beats.

"Welcome to my sanctuary," Maksym announced, gesturing at the sleek furnishings and state-of-the-art equipment. Nollaig couldn't help but be impressed by the setup; it was both functional and aesthetically pleasing, a testament to Maksym's attention to detail.

"It's incredible," Nollaig admitted, taking in the panoramic view of the dance floor below. "From up here, it's like watching a living, breathing organism."

"Exactly," Max said with a grin. "It's where I come to observe my creation – and make sure everything runs smoothly."

As they stood in the dimly lit office, Nollaig felt a newfound respect for Maksym. Despite Noll's reservations about the man, there was no denying that Max had built something truly remarkable. And perhaps, just perhaps, this could be the start of a fruitful partnership.

"Excuse me, gentlemen," Lucy said as she stepped toward the door, "I need to get back to work." She offered them a quick smile before leaving the office, the door closing gently behind her.

Nollaig couldn't help but be drawn to the sight of Lucy dancing on the platform next to the DJ. Her movements were fluid, graceful, and utterly captivating. He watched as she swayed to the rhythm of the music, her body seeming to become one with the beat.

"Beautiful, isn't she?" Maksym remarked, following Noll's gaze. Nollaig nodded in agreement, unable to tear his eyes away from Lucy.

"Anyway, about our earlier conversation," Max continued, steering their discussion back to business. "I'd love to help you expand your dive operation. With my investment, we could offer a consistent, high-quality experience to more scuba divers."

Nollaig looked at Maksym, still intrigued by the proposal. It was true that the extra funds could do wonders for his business. And there was something about the way Maksym spoke that made it seem like this was just a fun venture for him, a chance to indulge his passion for scuba diving. Still, Nollaig remained cautious.

"Your offer is tempting, Max," Noll admitted. "But I'd need to see what the shareholder agreement would look like before making any decisions. And the equity split."

"Of course!" Maksym enthusiastically agreed. I'll have my lawyers draft something for you to review. Take all the time you need – I want you to feel comfortable with our partnership."

With that, the two men shook hands, the beginnings of a tentative alliance forming between them. As they left the office, Maksym handed Nollaig a card. "Show this at the door whenever you come here. You'll never have to wait in line."

"Thanks, Max," Nollaig said, pocketing the card. As he made his way toward the exit, he paused a few times to gaze at Lucy dancing next to the DJ. Her lithe form and graceful movements held him captivated, a magnetic pull that was difficult to resist.

Despite the potential risks of partnering with Maksym, Nollaig couldn't deny the allure of the opportunity – or the undeniable attraction he felt for Lucy. The world around them seemed to pulse with life and energy, drawing them ever deeper into its embrace. And for better or worse, Nollaig found himself unable to turn away.

THE HUM of the tires on the asphalt beneath him melded with the muted roar of the i95 traffic. The thrill of the night's events still coursed through his veins, but as the adrenaline waned, his thoughts turned to the dive industry and the possibilities that Maksym's investment could bring.

A small smile played at the corners of Noll's mouth as he imagined a fleet of state-of-the-art boats around the world, each one gleaming with polished chrome and capable of providing a quality diving experience for his clients. He envisioned an army of skilled instructors and divemasters, each one dedicated to the safety and enjoyment of their charges, guiding them through the hidden treasures beneath the waves.

Noll's heart swelled with pride at the thought of raising the bar for the entire industry. Caught up in his dreams, Nollaig barely noticed the sleek silhouette of a black SUV pulling up alongside him. The window rolled down, revealing a grizzled man with a scar running down his cheek. The stranger's dark eyes bore into Noll, an unspoken challenge lingering in the air between them before the SUV sped ahead.

Noll's heart raced as he watched the SUV disappear in the darkness, quickly brushing it off his mind.

He knew that Maksym's wealth could propel his business to new heights, but he also understood that there would always be those who sought to undermine his success. The weight of responsibility settled on his shoulders.

With each mile that slipped away beneath his tires, Noll's dreams grew bolder and more expansive. Glimpses of Lucy's alluring form danced within his thoughts, intertwining with visions of a brighter future for the dive industry. As the headlights sliced through the dark night, Nollaig felt an undeniable pull – toward both the promise of success and the treacherous allure of desire. At that moment, he knew that the path before him was fraught with peril, but he was determined to navigate the treacherous waters ahead. What was life without a bit of risk?

In a sudden burst of energy, Noll cranked up the music in his car and began to sway his body in tune with the rhythm. His fingers tapped away on the steering wheel as he hummed along with an old Wang Chung song. He felt like dancing away into the future. "Rip it up, cool down. Rip it up; get out what's inside of you. Everybody have fun tonight. Everybody have fun tonight."

CHAPTER 5
A DIVE BUDDY

NOLLAIG PACED THE LIVING ROOM, his hands clenched into fists. His wife watched him with a mixture of concern and annoyance, her arms crossed over her chest.

"Are you really going to let Maksym invest in our business, Noll?" she asked, her voice tight with worry. "We're doing fine on our own. We don't need his money."

"Fine? Is that what you call it?" Nollaig snapped, his frustration boiling over. "The dive industry is suffering, Susan. We have a chance to make a real difference here, and you just want to sit back and watch it all go to hell?"

"Who cares about the industry?" Susan retorted, her eyes flashing. "It's about us, our family. If Maksym becomes an investor, we'll lose control. You won't be able to make decisions without consulting him first. You may bring less money home."

"Damn it, Susan," he growled, running a hand through his salt-and-pepper hair. "It's not like I'm selling my soul. Maksym trusts me. He believes in me. I'll still be the one in charge. This expansion will help improve my business and the industry, and that's all I want."

"Is it, though?" Susan challenged, her brow furrowed. "Or are you just so desperate to save your precious industry that you're willing to risk everything we've built together?"

"Improving the dive industry is part of my legacy," Nollaig replied, his voice firm but calm now. "I can't do that without taking some risks. Maksym may not be perfect, but he's offering us an opportunity we can't pass up."

"Fine," Susan huffed, uncrossing her arms and turning away from him. "Just never cut my money down. Ever!"

"Trust me," he said quietly. "I know how important your shoes are."

"Fuck you!"

"Ya! I love you, too!"

THE NEXT DAY, Nollaig sat in his office at the back of his Miami dive store, poring over the documents Maksym had proposed. Maksym leaned against the desk, watching him with a patient smile.

"Your lawyers really did their homework," Nollaig remarked, nodding in approval as he scanned the pages.

"Of course," Maksym replied, his tone smooth and reassuring. "I want this to be a mutually beneficial partnership, Noll. I love scuba diving just as much as you do, and I believe in your vision for the industry. That's why I want to invest in you."

"Thank you, Max," Nollaig said, looking up from the documents. "But I need to know that you won't interfere in the day-to-day operations. I've been running this business for years and know what's best for it."

"Relax, partner," Maksym reassured him, his grin never faltering. "You'll remain President & CEO. I'll be Chairman of the board, but I don't intend to meddle in the nitty-gritty. You have my word."

Nollaig hesitated only a moment before nodding, his eyes filled with determination. He knew the risks involved in partnering with Maksym, but he also believed in the potential benefits. For the sake of the industry he loved, he was willing to take that gamble.

A COUPLE OF DAYS LATER, Nollaig leaned back in his chair, the weight of the signed documents heavy on his desk. The amount Maksym was investing seemed like play money to the wealthy nightclub owner, and Noll felt reassured that Max would trust him to manage the business without interference.

When the door to his office opened, Sierra stepped inside, a smile playing at the corners of her lips. She looked around the small room, taking in the dive gear and posters adorning the walls.

"Nice place you've got here," she commented, raising an eyebrow.

"Thanks, Sierra! So, did you think about what we talked about last time? About working together to develop better IT and quality systems?"

Sierra studied his face for a moment, weighing her options. Finally, she nodded. "Yeah, I did. And I think it could be a good fit. But can the business afford it? How much will you invest in this project?"

Noll crossed his arms, his gaze never leaving her.

"Well, actually, I won't be investing any money myself," Nollaig explained, gesturing to the stack of legal documents on his desk. "I've found an investor who's willing to put up the cash for our project. I'm just investing my time and expertise."

"An investor?" Sierra asked, her curiosity piqued. "Who?"

"His name is Maksym Byrne," Nollaig replied, watching her reaction closely. "He owns a popular nightclub in Miami, and he has a passion for scuba diving. He believes in my vision for the industry and wants to help me make it a reality."

Sierra considered this for a moment, then shrugged. "Well, as long as he's not going to interfere with your plans, I don't see a problem. But are you sure you can trust him?"

Nollaig hesitated for a second before answering. "I think so. He's given me his word that he won't meddle in the day-to-day operations, and I believe him."

Nollaig studied Sierra's face, trying to gauge her reaction to his proposal. Her piercing brown eyes seemed to be analyzing every word he said.

"Well," she finally replied, a slight smile tugging at the corners of her lips. "I can work part-time for your business, Noll. But I have one condition."

"Name it," Nollaig said, eager to secure her cooperation.

"Give me free rein to develop complete IT systems we'll need to control and ensure consistency in the quality of the experience at various locations beyond your current dive operations in Miami and Key Largo."

"Done," Nollaig agreed without hesitation. He had confidence that Sierra's expertise would be invaluable in achieving his vision for the future of the dive industry.

"Great," Sierra said, her smile growing wider. "Now, let me share an idea with you."

"Go on," Nollaig encouraged, intrigued by the enthusiasm in her voice.

"Instead of opening new dive centers, what if we offered our operating standards and quality assurance system to other dive operators who would be authorized to operate under your Seize The Deep brand?" Sierra suggested, her eyes sparkling with excitement. "It would require less capital than owning new dive centers while satisfying your goal of providing more places where scuba divers can trust that they will receive a good and safe diving experience."

Nollaig leaned back in his chair, considering Sierra's proposition. The idea had merit, and it would undoubtedly make their expansion plans more feasible. His fingers drummed against the armrest as he weighed the pros and cons.

"Sierra, that's brilliant," he finally admitted, his expression serious. "By doing it that way, we could focus on maintaining high standards across our affiliated dive centers without the burden of owning and managing each location ourselves."

"Exactly," Sierra said, clearly pleased that he understood her line of thinking. "And we could still grow your brand and reach, giving divers more options for safe and enjoyable experiences."

"Let's do it," Nollaig decided, his voice filled with determination. "We'll revolutionize this industry together, Sierra."

"Okay," she replied, her eyes gleaming with anticipation. "I promise you won't regret this, Noll. We're going to make a real difference in the world of diving."

"Okay, but what about the money?" Nollaig then asked. "How much for you?"

Noll was surprised by Sierra's reaction. She smirked and shrugged as if money was no issue for her. "Your call, Noll! Whatever you think is fair."

As if she wanted to end the discussion about her remuneration, Sierra extended her hand. They shook hands, and Nollaig felt a surge of optimism course through him. With Sierra's innovative ideas and their shared dedication to improving the dive industry, he knew they were on the precipice of something extraordinary. The future was uncertain, but one thing was clear: together, they would face whatever challenges lay ahead and emerge stronger for it.

A couple of weeks later, Nollaig leaned against the doorframe, watching as Sierra unpacked her impressive array of computers and monitors. The room next to his office was quickly transforming into a high-tech lair.

"Wow, Sierra, this is quite the setup," Noll commented, raising an eyebrow. "Are you sure you're not some kind of hacker?"

Sierra paused in the middle of connecting a tangle of cables. Her eyes darted to him, then back to her task at hand. Silence hung in the air like a heavy fog.

"Look, Noll," she finally said, sighing. "I need you to promise that what I'm about to tell you stays between us."

"Of course," he replied, nodding solemnly.

She took a deep breath. "I am a hacker. But not just any hacker. I go after the rich and powerful who exploit the rest of us." She glanced at him nervously. "You can't tell anyone, got it?"

Nollaig was stunned by her revelation. But who doesn't hate abusing, planet-destroying billionaires? "Your secret's safe with me," Nollaig eventually assured her. "Why share this with me, though?"

"Because we're going to be working closely together, and... you know," she said, looking him straight in the eye. "Don't look over my shoulder when I'm on my keyboard. But we've got a chance here to make a real difference in the dive industry and maybe even beyond."

Nollaig swallowed, his mind racing as the reality of her confession sunk in. He had heard about hackers, of course—those elusive figures who navigated the digital shadows—but he never expected to find one working beside him. Yet, as he studied Sierra's determined expression, he couldn't help but feel intrigued by this unexpected aspect of her character.

"Well, how does your hacking... you know, fit into all this?"

"Let's just say it gives me an edge when it comes to developing the systems we need," she explained, a mischievous glint in her eye. "Trust me, Noll, I can make our IT infrastructure bulletproof."

"Okay," he conceded, trying to wrap his head around the revelation. "Just be careful, alright? I don't want the FBI knocking on our door!"

"Of course," she assured him, her tone laced with sincerity. "I've always been careful. I genuinely believe in what we're trying to accomplish here. I want to use my skills to help make the dive industry better instead of the race to the bottom we see everywhere in this immoral society."

Nollaig studied her face, searching for any signs of deceit. But all he saw was passion and conviction, a fierce determination that mirrored his own. Maybe, he thought, this unlikely partnership was exactly what they needed to bring about real change.

"By the way... Kim... one of our part-time dive instructors... she's an FBI agent. But, whatever. Welcome aboard," he said, extending his hand. "Let's do this. Together, we'll transform the dive industry and give people the safe, quality experiences they deserve."

IN THE DAYS THAT FOLLOWED, Nollaig found himself spending more time than ever with Sierra, even though she was technically only supposed to be working part-time. Together, they dove deep into data analysis and quality assurance systems. Their collaboration was seamless as if they had been partners for years.

"Sierra, I've got to say, I'm really glad you're on board with this," Nollaig confessed one evening in her office.

"Me too, Noll," she replied, a smile playing on her lips.

"It feels like we're diving into the future together."

"We make a great team, both underwater and above it."

Their partnership solidified over time, and soon enough, their weekend trips to Key Largo became the highlight of their week. One day, Noll played the Bad Religion song "I Love My Computer" on the way to the Florida Keys, to tease Sierra. "I love my computer. For all you give to me. Predictable errors and no identity."

But as they descended beneath the waves, the weight of the world seemed to lift from their shoulders. The beauty of the underwater world can even make a hacker forget about her keyboard. In those moments, it was just them, the ocean and the vibrant life that called it home.

Together, they explored the depths of the sea and the challenges facing the dive industry. Bound by their shared passion and unwavering trust, Nollaig and Sierra were determined to make a difference in a world where nobody could be trusted. They knew they had a long journey ahead, but they faced it side by side, ready to tackle whatever obstacles came their way.

CHAPTER 6
THE BAHAMAS

NOLLAIG "NOLL" Durand sat behind his desk, reviewing the latest invoices for his dive businesses. The calm air of the office starkly contrasted with the turmoil he felt inside. On the surface, everything seemed perfect. He and Sierra worked well together, their partnership solid and productive. Maksym had transferred all the money he'd promised, and the business bank account was brimming with funds.

Furthermore, Maksym didn't get involved in the day-to-day operations, leaving Noll to run the business and work with Sierra on the expansion.

"Hey, Noll," Sierra called from her desk. Her bright blue hair glowed under the fluorescent lights, and her piercings glinted as she turned to face him. "You okay? You seem a bit tense."

Noll forced a smile. "Just focusing on these bills. We've got a lot to pay out this month."

"Right." Sierra nodded, her eyes searching his face for any hint of deeper unrest. She returned to her work, tapping away at her computer with a quiet intensity that Noll admired.

A FEW DAYS LATER, Noll decided to have a sit-down with Maksym to update him on the progress of the dive business expansion. He found Maksym lounging in one of the VIP areas in his nightclub, sipping what looked like an expensive cocktail.

"Max, I wanted to talk to you about how we're spending your invested money," Noll began, trying to keep his voice steady. "I feel it's important that you know where your funds are going."

Maksym waved a dismissive hand, a sly smile playing on his lips. "Noll, I trust you to do what's right. I don't need the details; just make it happen."

This response left Noll feeling both relieved and disconcerted. He was grateful for Maksym's trust. Yet, he couldn't help but wonder why Max seemed so uninterested in the details. Was it possible that this man, who appeared to be the perfect business partner, had ulterior motives? The thought gnawed at Noll, even as he tried to focus on the positive aspects of their partnership.

"Alright, if you're sure," Noll said slowly, trying to ignore the nagging unease that settled in the pit of his stomach. "I'll see you around."

"We sure will," Maksym replied with a smirk, his eyes never leaving Noll's face. There was something unsettling about the intensity of his gaze, as though he were searching for a weakness to exploit.

Noll excused himself from Maksym's presence and returned to the office, where Sierra was still hard at work.

A WEEK LATER, the sun had long since dipped below the horizon as Noll and Sierra strolled along the beach in The Bahamas, their shoes sinking into the powdery sand. They had spent the day meeting with a local dive operator, discussing their vision of a worldwide scuba brand built on consistency in the quality of the experience.

"Can you believe it?" Sierra asked, her voice filled with excitement. "We might actually make this happen."

Noll couldn't help but smile at her enthusiasm. "Yeah, it's starting to feel real, isn't it? I'm glad we're doing this together, S," he said, using a new nickname affectionately. He felt a sense of camaraderie with her that he hadn't experienced in years. It was a refreshing change from the cutthroat world of business and finance he had grown so weary of.

They continued to walk, enjoying the salty scent of the ocean air and the gentle lapping of the waves against the shore. As they neared their destination, the sound of laughter and clinking glasses drifted toward them. An elegant restaurant perched on the water's edge beckoned, its warm light spilling out onto the sand.

"Here we are," Noll said, holding the door open for Sierra. They stepped inside, the atmosphere shifting from the casual ease of the beach to the intimacy of the candlelit dining room.

"Wow, this place is beautiful," Sierra remarked, her eyes taking in the floor-to-ceiling windows that offered a panoramic view of the ocean.

"Only the best for our celebration," Noll replied with a grin. They took their seats, the plush cushions enveloping them like a comforting embrace.

As they perused the menu, the conversation flowed effortlessly between them. They discussed the details of their recent meeting and shared anecdotes about past diving experiences. Each story, each laugh, drew them closer together, revealing new facets of one another that only served to strengthen their bond.

"Let's make a toast," Noll suggested, raising his mojito. "To new partnerships and to changing the world of diving for the better."

Sierra lifted her glass of scotch, her eyes meeting Noll's as they clinked their drinks together. "Cheers," she whispered, her voice barely audible above the hum of conversation around them.

They shared an expensive sushi platter, savoring each delicate bite as they continued to talk about their shared passions and dreams. As the evening wore on, it became increasingly apparent that this was more than just a business celebration. The line between their professional and personal relationship blurred until it was impossible to distinguish one from the other.

"Sierra," Noll began, hesitating as he searched for the right words. "I don't know how to say this, but... I feel like we're more than just business partners. We share the same vision, the same values. It's not just about the dive industry; it's about how we see life in society. You understand me in a way no one else does."

Sierra looked down at her hands, her fingers playing with her glass.

The air between them crackled with unspoken tension. Their emotions were laid bare as they dared contemplate what these revelations meant for their future. They were treading in dangerous waters, but perhaps it was a risk worth taking. For now, they allowed themselves to bask in the glow of their newfound understanding. The world outside faded away as they sat side by side, their hearts beating in tandem.

LATER, as Noll and Sierra walked into the hotel lobby, the night air was cool and heavy with the scent of the ocean. Sierra's eyes reflected the excitement of their successful meeting earlier in the day. "We should have a final toast before calling it a day," she suggested, her punk-colored hair shimmering in the dim light.

"Sounds like a plan," Noll agreed.

Noll and Sierra stepped onto the elevator, neither of them uttering a word. Exiting the elevator, they wandered in eerie silence down the dark hallway until Noll stopped at his hotel room door. He quickly pushed it open and gestured for Sierra to enter inside. With an unnerving sense of trepidation, she followed him in, and he called for a bottle of champagne and two glasses from room service.

The tension was palpable, and the room was filled with shadows.

"Here's to us," Noll said, raising his glass after pouring the bubbly liquid.

"To rebuilding the world," Sierra replied, clinking her glass against his. They drank, savoring the delicate taste of the champagne as it danced on their tongues.

As the minutes turned into hours, they talked about everything and nothing, finding solace in each other's company. Their laughter filled the room, echoing off the walls and mingling with the distant sound of the waves crashing on the shore. At that moment, it seemed as if the world outside had ceased to exist, leaving just the two of them adrift in their own private universe.

Eventually, exhaustion began to creep in, and they found themselves lying side by side on the bed, still fully clothed. Noll felt the weight of Sierra's body next to his, her warmth radiating through the thin fabric of their clothes. His heart raced despite his tiredness, torn between the desire to be close to her and the knowledge of the consequences that would follow.

NOLL JOLTED AWAKE, his heart racing as he felt a warm weight resting across his chest. He opened his eyes to find Sierra still and silent beside him, her breaths tickling his neck like whispers in the night. He was enthralled by the sight, feeling an unfamiliar stir of emotion deep within his soul. With a single gaze, they were both motionless for a moment, their eyes saying more than words could ever express.

The world around them became a distant memory as the fire of their attraction blazed to life. Their bodies remained intertwined, hugging with an intensity that burned hotter and brighter until the morning sun said hello.

BACK HOME, Noll found himself seated at the kitchen table across from his wife, Susan. "So, how was your trip to the Bahamas?" she asked, her voice deceptively calm.

"Uh, yeah," Noll replied, his fingers tapping nervously against the tabletop. "We had a successful meeting, and we may have a deal for the first affiliated dive center."

"Did you sleep with... what's her name?" Susan's question was sharp and direct, cutting through the air like a knife.

"Of course not!" Noll lied, trying to sound indignant. But Susan saw right through him, her eyes darkening with suspicion. He shifted in his seat, attempting to change the topic. "The important thing is that our business is expanding, and it's all thanks to Sierra."

Susan's gaze remained fixed on her husband, unyielding and cold. He wished he was still in the Bahamas, and Might Good Road played "I Want To Go To The Bahamas" in his head. "I want to go to the Bahamas today. Take it slow in the Bahamas today." Instead, he feared a storm had arrived at his home – one he had created.

THE TENSION in the office was palpable as Noll avoided making eye contact with Sierra. He shuffled through the dive center's financial reports, his fingers shaking ever so slightly. The guilt from their night together in the Bahamas weighed heavily on him, and he couldn't shake the feeling that he had betrayed not only his wife but also himself.

"Listen, Noll," Sierra finally broke the silence, her voice strained. "I can tell something's changed between us since the trip."

Noll sighed and ran a hand through his salt-and-pepper hair. "It's just... I'm married, Sierra. What happened shouldn't have happened. It's affecting our working relationship, and I don't know how to fix it."

Sierra looked away, hurt flashing across her pierced features. "Nothing happened. Not really. We didn't even undress. What's wrong with hugging a friend? But maybe you should find someone else to replace me. Someone who won't be a distraction."

"Replace you?" Noll frowned, the thought of losing Sierra causing a sharp ache in his chest. His business expansion was happening thanks to her, and he couldn't imagine continuing without her by his side. Slowly, an idea began to form in his mind. "How about we take a break from the office? Let's go diving in Key Largo and clear our heads. Maybe that will help."

She hesitated, considering his offer. After a moment, she nodded. "Alright, let's give it a shot."

As they drove down US1 toward Key Largo, the ocean shimmering beside them, Noll wrestled with his conflicting emotions. He wanted Sierra in his life, needed her for the expansion of his business, but he couldn't forget that he was a married man. He clenched the steering wheel, the weight of his choices pressing down on him like the crushing depths of the sea.

CHAPTER 7
THE CUBE

"*Mystery, mystery, mystery, mystery;*
mystery, mystery, mystery roach!"

NOLLAIG STEPPED out of his car, the salty air of Key Largo filling his lungs as he gazed upon the familiar sight of Sea Spell Diving. He knew every inch of the place. Beside him, Sierra Fleming stretched her tattooed arms above her head, the piercings in her ears glinting in the sunlight.

"Ready for some therapeutic diving?" Noll asked, a small smile playing on his lips.

"Definitely," she replied, excitement shining in her eyes.

As they walked toward the dive center, Noll's brow furrowed at the sight of a cube truck occupying several parking spaces meant for customers. It seemed out of place, like a foreign object disrupting the harmony of the dive center.

"Jon!" Noll called out to the general manager of Sea Spell Diving, who was busy arranging scuba cylinders outside the shop. "What's with this truck?"

Jon looked up, surprise flickering across his face. "I thought you knew, Noll. Maksym uses that truck."

"Max? What does he need it for?" Noll asked, his curiosity piqued.

"Beats me," Jon shrugged. "A guy takes it out and brings it back before and after their night dive charter."

"Night dive charter?" Noll echoed, taken aback.

"Really?" Jon eyed him skeptically. "I assumed you were aware since he's your new business partner and all. He goes out with friends on Tuesday nights."

Noll furrowed his brow as he mulled over Jon's revelations about Maksym's mysterious Tuesday night dives. He couldn't shake the feeling that something was amiss, yet at the same time, he was sure there was a good explanation.

"Let me check the bookings," Noll said, pulling out his phone to access Sea Spell Diving's records. As he scrolled through the bookings and payments, he noticed a significant cash deposit on each of the last two Tuesdays. "Jon, can you explain these cash payments?"

"Sure," Jon replied, sounding puzzled. "Maksym pays cash for everyone on those night dives. I thought it was all good with you since he's your partner. And it's good money."

"Good money... ya... he's paying almost ten times the usual rate for these dive outings!" Noll observed, his voice tinged with suspicion.

"Really? I don't check him," Jon admitted, scratching his head. "I just assumed everything was okay since you two..."

Noll clenched his jaw, annoyed with himself for not being more vigilant about his company's dealings. "I'll need to talk to Maksym about this," he muttered under his breath, making a mental note to contact Max.

Before heading to the dive boat with Sierra, Noll walked over to the cube truck parked in the lot. The back door had a padlock – the industrial unbreakable kind. He tried the driver's door handle, but it was locked. Pressing his face against the window, he squinted, trying to see what lay inside. But the shadows within remained stubbornly secretive, revealing nothing.

"Damn," Noll sighed, frustration mounting within him.

"Is everything okay?" Sierra asked, approaching him with a concerned look.

"Maybe," Noll replied, forcing a smile. "Just some business stuff I need to figure out. Let's focus on the dive for now, alright?"

"Alright," she agreed, though her eyes still held a hint of worry.

Noll hoisted himself onto the dive boat, followed closely by Sierra. The afternoon sun glinted off the water, casting a shimmering light over their surroundings. They had chosen to blend in as clients for this trip, not wanting to cause any disruptions or draw attention to themselves. However, their experience and familiarity with Sea Spell Diving's operations made it impossible for them not to lend a hand to the staff on the way to the dive site.

"Starboard side clear!" Noll called out, his voice mingling with the hum of the boat's engine.

"Thanks, boss," a crew member replied with a knowing grin.

The boat cut through the waves, leaving a foamy trail in its wake. Noll stood beside Sierra at the railing, their eyes locked on the horizon. He could feel her presence like an electric current, the air between them thick with unspoken tension.

———

"READY?" Noll asked, turning to face Sierra.

"Always," she replied, flashing a smile that made his pulse quicken.

Descending into the depths, their bodies moved in tandem—two shadows gliding through an underwater world shrouded in mystery. The weightlessness of their body in the water cocooned them, making it easier to forget the troubles that bubbled beneath the surface of their lives. There, among the vibrant coral and darting fish, Noll found himself increasingly drawn to Sierra. They communicated through hand signals, their eyes never straying too far from one another.

As they explored the ocean floor, Noll became lost in memories of the Bahamas—their bodies sleeping together in a tight embrace. The memory was intoxicating, and he felt an overwhelming desire to reach out and touch her. But he knew that now wasn't the time or place.

Instead, he focused on the beauty surrounding them, trying to keep his thoughts from straying too far down that path.

Back on the boat, Noll and Sierra helped the staff secure the equipment and prepare for the return trip. They exchanged glances, their eyes sparkling with a shared secret. Their chemistry was undeniable, and it seemed to grow stronger with each passing moment.

"Thank you," Sierra murmured as they disembarked from the boat onto the dock. "That was incredible. Best therapy, ever."

"Anytime," he replied, his voice rough with emotion.

The drive back to Miami was a quiet one, the roar of the highway filling the silence between them. As the sun dipped lower in the sky, casting long shadows across the road, Noll's thoughts drifted back to Maksym and the unanswered questions that haunted him. He gripped the steering wheel with his left hand, feeling the weight of his responsibilities pressing down on him like an anchor.

Sierra reached over, her fingers intertwining with his. The simple act of connection offered him a lifeline—a reminder that he wasn't alone.

"Sierra," Noll whispered, his voice barely audible over the engine's hum. He raised a finger to his lips, signaling her to remain silent. With a nod, she understood. Noll pressed the button on the steering wheel to dial Maksym, his heart pounding in anticipation.

"Hey, Noll," Maksym answered, his smooth voice filling the car. "What's up?"

"Max, hi. I hope I'm not interrupting anything," Noll said, trying to keep his tone casual. "I wanted to talk to you about your private dive outings on Tuesday nights."

"Ah, yes. My friends and I enjoy the underwater world just like you do," Maksym replied, his voice dripping with arrogance. Noll's jaw clenched at the change in Max's demeanor.

"Right," Noll said, swallowing the bitterness that bubbled up inside him. "But I can't help but wonder why there's a cube truck in our parking lot."

Maksym chuckled, something cold and calculating in his laugh. "You worry too much, Noll. That's not like you."

"Max, you know how much I appreciate your investment. But I

need to know what's going on with my businesses, especially when it involves my dive boats and parking lot." Noll's voice tightened, betraying a sense of urgency.

"Listen," Maksym said, his voice taking on an edge Noll had never heard before. "You should be happy I'm paying far more than any other customer would for a private charter. Those few parking spots for my cube truck are nothing compared to the money I'm putting into your business."

Noll's grip on the wheel tightened, knuckles turning white. He didn't like where this conversation was going, but he couldn't back down now. "Max, it's not about the money. It's about transparency and trust."

"Then trust me, Nollaig," Maksym snapped, his tone icy. "And mind your own business."

Noll's pulse hammered in his ears, the silence in the car thickening as he struggled to find words. He couldn't let Maksym walk all over him, but he also had to tread carefully. The future of Sea Spell Diving and Seize The Deep depended on it.

"Maksym," Noll finally said, forcing a steadiness he didn't feel into his voice. "I understand you pay more for your private charters, but there's something else you need to know. For insurance purposes, an authorized Sea Spell Diving captain must be in charge of the boat on Tuesday nights, not one of your friends."

There was a pause on the other end of the line, and Noll held his breath. Sierra glanced at him, her eyes betraying a mixture of curiosity and concern. She reached out to touch his arm, offering silent support.

"Fine," Maksym barked, the venom in his words making Noll flinch. "I'll take care of it. Happy now?"

"Max, I just want to make sure everything is above board and safe. This is important to me, and I thought it was important to you, too."

"Of course, it's important, Nollaig," Maksym replied, his voice dripping with sarcasm. "You win. I'll fix the captain issue. Goodbye."

The call disconnected abruptly, leaving a hollow ringing in Noll's ears. He stared at the blank screen on the dashboard, stunned by the coldness of Maksym's words. It was as if he'd been speaking to a stranger, not the gentleman who had invested so much into his business.

As if on cue, Frank Zappa's song, "Mystery Roach," started to play on his smartphone he had connected to the car sound system. "Mystery, mystery, mystery, mystery; mystery, mystery, mystery roach!"

Sierra squeezed his arm gently, drawing him back to the present. "What now?" she asked, her voice soft and genuine.

Noll shook his head, trying to shake off the shock that had settled over him like an icy shroud. "I don't know, Sierra. I thought Max and I were on the same page, but I'm not so sure anymore."

"Maybe he's just under a lot of stress," she suggested, her fingers tracing comforting circles on his arm. "People can act out of character when they're feeling overwhelmed."

"Maybe," Noll conceded, though he couldn't shake the nagging feeling that there was more to Maksym's behavior than simple stress. There was a darkness in his voice that Noll had never heard before, something that unsettled him deeply.

He shifted gears, focusing back on the road as they continued their drive back to Miami. But instead of finding comfort in the familiar landscape, Noll felt a seed of unease take root in his chest.

As the miles slipped by, Noll's thoughts churned relentlessly. He knew he couldn't ignore what had happened, but confronting Maksym might jeopardize everything he'd built. It was a risk he wasn't sure he could take. But the alternative—turning a blind eye and allowing whatever Maksym was hiding to fester unchecked—was equally unthinkable.

For the first time in a long while, Nollaig Durand was at a loss. Caught between loyalty and integrity, he faced a choice that threatened to tear him apart. And as the sun dipped below the horizon, casting the world into darkness, Noll couldn't help but wonder if this was just the beginning of a far greater storm.

CHAPTER 8
NO CHAPERONE

As Noll entered the Sea Spell Diving Center in Key Largo, the sun cast a warm glow on his tan skin and salt-and-pepper hair, a testament to his life by the ocean. He found Jon, the general manager, organizing some paperwork at the front desk.

"Hey, Jon," Noll greeted him with a friendly smile.

"Hey, boss," Jon replied, looking up from his papers.

"How are things going? Anything you need from me to keep delivering those legendary dive experiences for our customers?"

"Everything's running smoothly, but I could always use more help during peak hours."

"Understood. I'll look into it." Noll knew that maintaining the high-quality experience he prided himself on was essential in an industry increasingly defined by cutthroat competition. "By the way, did Maksym go out for a private dive charter last night with his friends?"

"Yep, they went out as planned. You can see the large cash payment in yesterday's sales results," Jon confirmed, pointing to a row of numbers on one of the papers before him.

Noll nodded, recalling Max's penchant for grand gestures. "Who was the captain?"

"Max still used the same guy he did before."

"Wait, what?" Noll furrowed his brow in frustration. "I had a conversation with Max about this very thing—no matter if it's a private outing, the captain must be an authorized Sea Spell Diving captain for insurance purposes!"

Jon looked surprised by Noll's reaction. "Max brought all the necessary paperwork for his captain, so I added him to our list of insured captains. I thought you'd be okay with it."

Noll sighed, rubbing his temples as he tried to make sense of the situation.

THE OCEAN BREEZE carried the scent of salt and seaweed as Noll and Sierra settled into their seats at an outdoor table of a small beachside restaurant. The sound of waves crashing against the shore provided a soothing soundtrack to their conversation. Sierra took a sip of her unsweetened iced tea before raising her eyebrow inquisitively.

"So, how did your meeting with Jon go?" she asked, stirring her beverage.

Noll sighed, the weight of his earlier conversation still lingering. "It was fine, mostly. But I found out that Max's captain-friend was added to our list of authorized captains. I wanted to question one of our regular captains about what's going on during those private charters." He shook his head, frustration etched on his face. "And that cube truck is still in our parking lot. Taking spots from our customers."

"Maybe you're overthinking it," Sierra offered, her tone soothing. "Why don't you join them on their night dive next Tuesday? You might get some answers or at least put your mind at ease."

Noll laughed, the tension draining from his shoulders. "You know, that's such a simple idea; I can't believe I didn't think of it myself.

Maybe I'm just seeing problems where there aren't any. After all, Max is paying good money for these dives."

"Exactly," Sierra agreed, her lips curving into a smile that hinted at something more than just friendship.

LATER THAT EVENING, after Noll had tucked his kids into bed and made sure they brushed their teeth, Susan called him to join her in the living room. She sat elegantly on the couch, swirling a glass of white wine. Noll couldn't help but notice that she hadn't helped with dinner or bedtime, leaving him to handle the everyday tasks alone.

"Sit down," Susan beckoned, her voice icy and detached.

Noll obeyed, sitting on the edge of the couch, his hands resting on his knees, unable to shake off the unease that had settled in the pit of his stomach. The dim light from the table lamp cast a soft glow on Susan's face, emphasizing her sharp features and the cold expression in her eyes.

"Tell me, Noll," she began, her voice icy and unforgiving. "In which motel were you and Sierra all day?"

He blinked, taken aback by her question. "What are you talking about? We went to Key Largo for business."

Her laugh was bitter, devoid of any warmth. "Business? Is that what you call it now? I went to see you at the Miami dive shop today, and neither you nor Sierra were there. My friend on the staff told me you two are always together."

"Sierra is my colleague, Susan," he said defensively. "And yes, we went to Key Largo to check on our other location. That's all."

"Really?" She leaned forward, her eyes narrowing. "You expect me to believe that you didn't spend the day indulging in skin-related activities?"

"Of course not!" Noll protested, feeling his face heat up with indignation. "We're friends, nothing more."

"With good benefits, I bet," Susan spurted out mockingly, then sighed dramatically. "Well, you'll be happy to know that from now on, you can have the guest room all to yourself."

"What?" Noll stared at his wife, his confusion quickly turning to shock.

"Exactly what I said. I don't care what you do anymore, Noll, as long as you keep bringing home the cash I need." She stood up, her movements fluid and graceful despite the bitterness in her voice.

"But, Susan—"

"Save it," she cut him off, her gaze unwavering. "It shouldn't be a surprise to you. Our sex life has been dead for years anyway." She turned away, ready to leave the room, but paused by the door. "Oh, and just so we're clear—it's a two-way street. I expect you not to create any problem if I bring a male friend into our… my bedroom one day."

Noll watched her walk away, his heart pounding in his chest, feeling as though he had just been slapped in the face. The reality of their marriage crumbling around him left him breathless, unsure of how to respond or what to do next.

ON THE FOLLOWING TUESDAY, Noll found himself at the Key Largo dive center with Sierra, the warm Florida sun casting long shadows on the ground. The hum of activity buzzed around them as they helped the staff wrap things up after another busy day of diving at Sea Spell Diving. When Maksym pulled up in a giant F350 pickup truck, Noll couldn't help but feel an undercurrent of tension.

"Look who's coming for a night dive," Sierra muttered, her eyes narrowing as she watched Maksym step out of his gas-guzzling vehicle.

"No McLaren today!" Noll mumbled.

The cube truck was conspicuously absent from the parking lot when they'd arrived earlier that morning, but soon after, a tough-looking guy drove it into the lot. As if on cue, a few strangers appeared at the same time.

"Friends of Max?" Noll asked, his curiosity piqued.

"Seems so," Sierra replied, her voice tinged with suspicion.

Maksym strode into the dive center, an envelope of cash in hand, clearly ready to pay for the charter. He looked surprised to see Noll there. "What are you doing here?" he asked, a hint of annoyance in his tone.

"Thought I might join you guys on your night dive," Noll said casually, trying to play it cool. "I've been itching to get back in the water at night."

Maksym's arrogance became palpable as he handed the cash envelope to Noll. "I pay good money not to have a chaperone," he sneered.

"Come on, Max, we're all just here for a good time, right?" Noll persisted, trying to maintain a friendly demeanor.

"Take a hike," Maksym shot back, his voice cold and final.

Stunned by Maksym's refusal to let him join them on his own dive boat, Noll stood there, momentarily speechless. Sierra stepped in, her hand on his arm, offering both physical and emotional support, her touch sending a calming current through him.

As they watched the preparations unfold, Noll noticed that there were ten people boarding the dive boat but only enough scuba gear for four divers. It made no sense. Why would Maksym pay top dollar for an outing with friends if more than half of them wouldn't even be diving?

"Something's off," Noll murmured to Sierra, unable to shake the feeling that they were witnessing something much larger than a simple night dive among friends.

Noll's attention was drawn to the cube truck as a team of tough-looking men began unloading dry boxes onto the dive boat. His eyes widened in surprise as he recognized the mysterious boxes from Vanilla Dive Center, each adorned with the head of a blue dragon but no other marks. He'd tried to find the supplier of these well-made waterproof boxes before, but his efforts had been fruitless.

"Sierra, look," Noll said, pointing at the dry boxes. "Those are the same ones I saw at Vanilla Dive Center. Why are they here with Maksym?"

Sierra squinted at the boxes and then back at Noll. "I don't know, but it's definitely strange."

As they watched the men move the boxes, it was clear that they were heavy. The effort the men exerted to load them onto the boat only deepened the mystery. "Why so many waterproof boxes?" Noll muttered, his brow furrowing. "And why do they need them on a night dive?"

Before Sierra could respond, another surprise arrived: Lucy. As Noll approached her, her shock was evident, and she seemed uncomfortable when he started talking to her.

"Lucy, going diving with Max? Do you know anything about those Blue Dragon boxes?" Noll asked, trying to keep his voice casual despite his growing concern.

"Uh, no, I don't know anything, Noll," Lucy stammered, avoiding eye contact and trying to sidestep him. But Noll persisted, desperate for answers.

"Come on, Lucy, you can tell me. What's going on?"

"Look, Noll," she said, frustration creeping into her voice. "I'm just a hired diver, okay? I don't know anything." And with that, she hurried onto the dive boat to get away from him.

Noll stood there, his mind racing with questions. If Lucy was some 'hired' help instead of a friend joining Max for a night dive, then what was really going on with this supposedly friendly night dive?

Noll's mind churned with questions as he and Sierra retreated to the shadows, deciding to stick around and see what Maksym's group would do when they returned from their dive. Nollaig moved his car into a dark alley nearby, then led Sierra across the canal, binoculars in hand. From this vantage point, they would be able to observe without being seen.

"Something doesn't add up," Noll murmured, his voice low and tense. "If Lucy was hired as a diver, then this isn't just a casual outing for Maksym and his friends."

"Maybe it's some kind of underwater operation," Sierra suggested. "Smuggling, perhaps?"

"I don't know, but we'll find out soon enough," Noll replied. As they settled in to wait, the close proximity between them seemed to amplify the attraction that had been simmering beneath the surface since they met. Noll could feel the heat radiating off Sierra's body, and he knew she could feel his gaze on her.

"Hey," she said softly, turning to face him. "We're in this together, right?"

"Of course," Noll responded, surprised by the sudden vulnerability in her voice.

"Good," she whispered, her breath warm against his cheek.

There was an undeniable pull between them, Noll thought.

"Sierra, I—" he started but stopped himself before he could say anything more. He couldn't allow himself to give in to temptation, not when he was still married, even if his wife had sent him to the guest room and threatened to bring male friends to sleep over.

"Never mind," he muttered, focusing his attention on the dock. He sensed Sierra's frustration, but he couldn't allow his personal feelings to cloud his judgment or distract him from the task at hand.

As they continued to wait in silence, Noll's mind raced with questions about Maksym, Lucy, and the mysterious Blue Dragon dry boxes. What was really going on beneath the surface of this seemingly innocent night dive? And would he be able to unravel the tangled web of deceit before it was too late?

With each passing minute, the weight of uncertainty grew heavier on Noll's shoulders.

THE SOUND of the approaching dive boat cut through the night air, and Noll's heart raced with anticipation. He gripped the binoculars tightly, ready to observe every detail as Maksym and his group returned from their mysterious outing.

"Here they come," Sierra whispered, her breath warm against Noll's ear.

As the boat docked, Noll focused his attention on the activity unfolding before them. The tough-looking guys wasted no time unloading the Blue Dragon dry boxes from the boat and transferring them back into the cube truck, except for two boxes they threw in the bed of Maksym's pickup truck before pulling a cover over it. The waterproof boxes still seemed heavy, but they were dripping wet this time.

"Something's not right," Noll muttered under his breath, his eyes narrowing as he tried to make sense of the situation.

"Definitely," Sierra agreed. "But what?"

Noll racked his brain, searching for answers that eluded him. He couldn't shake the feeling that there was more to this than met the eye, something sinister lurking beneath the surface.

"Maybe they're smuggling something," Sierra suggested again, her voice tense. "Drugs?"

"Could be," Noll conceded, though he couldn't help feeling that even those possibilities didn't quite fit the puzzle. "But the boxes are heavy at the beginning and at the end. Sierra, we need to find out what's going on. This could impact my business."

"Right," she simply replied, her eyes glinting with resolve in the dim light.

After loading the last of the dripping wet boxes into the cube truck, a man left with the truck while the group dispersed, leaving Noll and Sierra to ponder the enigma they had just witnessed.

Back in Nollaig's car, Glenn Frey's "Smuggler's Blues" song gave the night a Miami Vice feel: "There's trouble on the street tonight. I can feel it in my bones. I had a premonition."

The night sky, speckled with stars, offered no clues or answers, only a vast emptiness that echoed the void in their understanding.

CHAPTER 9
TIE WRAPS

'm gonna get me a gun;
I'm gonna get me a gun."

NOLLAIG WATCHED as Sierra expertly maneuvered from one dive boat to another, installing small, unassuming devices on each vessel.

Jon, the general manager of Sea Spell Diving, raised an eyebrow at her handiwork. "What are these for?" he asked, suspicion creeping into his voice.

"Fuel efficiency," Sierra replied smoothly, a hint of mischief in her eyes. "We will just keep an eye on gas consumption to spot any issues with the engines."

Noll observed their exchange from a distance, noting the captains' unease. Trust was rare in a world where everyone had their own agenda, and Nollaig knew that they needed to tread carefully. As Sierra completed her task, he admired her skill and dedication, all while keeping the true purpose of the trackers hidden.

TWO DAYS LATER, as Wednesday afternoon waned, Nollaig and Sierra approached Jon at the dive center. With a conspiratorial smile, Noll draped an arm around Sierra's waist.

"Hey, Jon, we're going to take one of the boats out tonight," Nollaig informed him, his tone suggestive.

Sierra leaned into Noll, feigning infatuation. The two played their roles convincingly as if embarking on a clandestine love affair. Jon eyed them curiously but didn't question their intentions; he simply nodded.

"Have fun," he said, smirking as he walked away, oblivious to their actual plan.

Once out of earshot, Nollaig and Sierra exchanged a knowing glance, their connection deepening as they prepared to uncover the truth behind Max's late-night excursions. In a world where love rarely lasted and trust was scarce, they found solace in their shared mission – even if it meant putting on a convincing performance for those who might be watching.

"Ready?" Nollaig asked, his voice barely above a whisper.

"Always," Sierra replied, her piercing dark brown eyes locking onto his as they stepped aboard the boat. Noll thought that her tone indicated she was ready for more than a boat ride, but now was not the time for distractions.

Under a sky painted with orange and pink hues, Nollaig and Sierra left the dock aboard the dive boat, a quiet determination settling over them. The steady hum of the engine accompanied their journey, while the gentle rocking of the boat created an almost soothing atmosphere that belied the tension coursing through them both.

"Alright," Nollaig murmured, his fingers tapping lightly on the steering wheel as he guided the boat toward open waters. "Let's see what Max has been up to."

Sierra leaned in, checking the tracking technology she had installed earlier in the week. "I've got the coordinates from Tuesday evening. It's a remote location, outside of any popular diving or fishing spots."

"Strange," Nollaig mused, furrowing his brow as he considered the implications. "Why would he take a dive boat out there, especially at night?"

As they continued their journey, Sierra nestled herself between Noll and the steering wheel, her body pressed against his. He couldn't deny the magnetic pull he felt towards her, but he remained focused on the task at hand.

"Looks like we're getting closer," Sierra said, her voice low and breathy as she peered at the device in her hands. "You'll need my help navigating around the reef up ahead. There's no marked channel."

The sun dipped lower in the sky as Nollaig slowed the boat, his eyes scanning the water for any signs of danger. Sierra stepped towards the bow, bracing herself against the railing as she guided him through the treacherous waters. Noll marveled at her fearlessness and the trust they had built in such a short time.

"It must be a weekly challenge for his captain to navigate here," Nollaig thought aloud, his voice tense as he focused on avoiding the jagged edges of the reef lurking beneath the surface.

"Indeed," Sierra agreed, her voice carrying over the wind. "But we're almost there. Hope we find something."

As they approached the mysterious location, Nollaig couldn't shake the feeling that something sinister awaited them. Yet, with Sierra by his side, he knew they were prepared to face whatever challenges lay ahead, no matter how dangerous or betraying they might be.

Nollaig's brow furrowed with concentration as he carefully maneuvered the dive boat into its final position. The water was deceptively calm, but he knew that just beneath the surface lay a treacherous reef waiting to tear the hull apart. He glanced over at Sierra, who stood poised on the bow, her eyes scanning the water for any signs of danger.

"Drop anchor now," Noll called out, and Sierra complied, lowering the heavy metal device into the depths below. They watched as the chain rattled and strained against the weight of the anchor, their hearts pounding in anxious anticipation. If the anchor hit the reef, it could cause irreparable damage not only to the delicate ecosystem but also to their mission.

"Easy... easy..." Sierra murmured, her breath hitching as the anchor finally settled without incident. Noll exhaled in relief, wiping the sweat from his brow. "We did it," he said quietly, and Sierra nodded in agreement.

With the boat secured, they wasted no time in preparing for their dive. Although protocol dictated that someone should always remain on board while divers were in the water, Noll and Sierra had no choice but to break the rules. There were only two of them on this mission.

As they geared up, Nollaig couldn't help but admire Sierra's determination and grit. Despite the possible risks involved, she remained focused and unwavering in her pursuit of the truth. It reminded him of why he had been drawn to her in the first place – her passion for justice and her unwillingness to bow to the corrupt forces that threatened to destroy everything they held dear.

With one last glance at each other, Noll and Sierra made a giant stride entry into their mission.

Nollaig's heart raced as he and Sierra started by swimming along the surface, their eyes scanning the seemingly desolate dive site with strong underwater flashlights. The ocean stretched out around them, its vastness a reminder of how small they truly were in this world. Despite the beauty that surrounded him, Nollaig felt an undercurrent of tension – something about this place was off, and he couldn't quite put his finger on it.

"Anything?" Sierra's bright-colored hair clung to her face, her multiple piercings glinting in the moonlight.

"Nothing," Nollaig replied, frustration rising within him. He'd hoped they would find some clue as to what Max had been doing here, but so far, they'd come up empty-handed.

Sierra signaled for them to dive to search more closely, and Nollaig nodded in agreement. They submerged beneath the surface, leaving the world above behind.

As they swam, Nollaig marveled at the alien world that surrounded them, a world where Max had chosen to conduct his mysterious operations.

The ocean floor was a maze of coral and rock formations, their shadows casting eerie patterns across the sand. Nollaig and Sierra moved carefully, navigating the obstacles with practiced ease as they searched for any sign of what brought Max and his cohorts to this desolate place.

While they continued their search, Nollaig couldn't help but feel a growing sense of unease. The more he thought about Max's secretive behavior, the more questions he had. Why would Max risk coming to such a dangerous location every Tuesday evening? What could be so important that it warranted these covert meetings with suspicious characters?

As they searched the ocean floor, Nollaig found himself increasingly aware of the dwindling air supply in his scuba cylinder. Time was running out, and still, they had found nothing. Frustration bubbled up in him as they swam through the labyrinthine coral formations, each twisting path leading to yet another dead end.

Sierra caught his eye and gave him a questioning look. Nollaig hesitated for a moment, then reluctantly signaled for them to ascend. Disappointment weighed heavily on them both as they prepared to leave the mysterious dive site behind.

But just as they were about to begin their ascent, Sierra's eyes widened. She grabbed Nollaig's arm and pointed towards a mini-cavern hidden beneath a coral ledge. There, nestled in the shadows, was a waterproof box emblazoned with the head of a Blue Dragon.

Nollaig's pulse quickened as they swam closer, cautiously extracting the box from its hiding place. They discovered two more similar boxes concealed nearby, but their air supply was dangerously low. Realizing they had no choice, Nollaig and Sierra surfaced, the mystery of the Blue Dragon boxes burning within them.

Back on the dive boat, they hastily switched scuba air cylinders, eager to investigate their findings further. As they prepared to return to the ocean depths, Nollaig couldn't shake the feeling that they were on the brink of uncovering something much larger than they'd anticipated – something that could change everything.

Noll had seen Max's crew leaving the dock with Blue Dragon dry boxes and coming back with them. So, what were these boxes still doing here?

With fresh scuba cylinders strapped to their backs, Nollaig and

Sierra plunged back into the water, their hearts pounding with anticipation. Nollaig clutched a lift bag in one hand, his eyes scanning the underwater terrain as they retraced their path to the concealed dry boxes. The weight of their discovery hung heavy between them, an unspoken tension that neither could ignore.

They located the first box once more. Noll handed Sierra the lift bag, and she swiftly attached it to the handle of the waterproof box. With a nod from Sierra, Nollaig took his alternate air source – his octopus – and began slowly filling the lift bag with air.

The dry box rose, buoyed by the expanding lift bag. Nollaig gave Sierra a thumbs-up signal, and they started their ascent, carefully guiding the suspended box towards the surface. As they broke through the water, Nollaig's thoughts raced, wondering what secrets might be locked within the Blue Dragon-emblazoned container.

"Help me get this onto the dive platform," Nollaig shouted, his voice strained with effort as they struggled against the weight of the heavy box. Sierra grunted in agreement, her muscles straining as she pushed from below while Nollaig pulled from above.

Finally, with a grunt of effort, they managed to lift the box out of the water and onto the dive platform at the back of the dive boat. Sweat dripped down Nollaig's face as he caught his breath, his mind racing with the implications of their discovery.

"Remember those tough-looking muscular guys we saw with Max on the night boat rides?" Nollaig asked, his voice tense. "I guess we know why they were there now."

"No kidding!" Sierra nodded solemnly, her eyes locked on the Blue Dragon logo adorning the cover of the box. Nollaig clenched the cutters in his hand, hesitating for a moment before snipping through the tie wraps securing the dry box.

"Ready?" Nollaig asked, meeting Sierra's gaze.

She nodded, her eyes narrowing with determination. Together, they lifted the lid of the waterproof box, revealing its shocking contents.

Inside, neatly stacked and secured, were rows of guns – big guns. A few lead weights, like those used by scuba divers, were also tucked inside the box, likely to prevent it from floating away while underwater. Nollaig's breath caught in his throat as the gravity of their discovery hit him.

"Jesus Christ," he muttered under his breath, staring at the weapons. "Max is smuggling guns."

Sierra's expression mirrored his own shock and disgust. "These are semi-automatic 50 caliber rifles. Heavy shit!"

Nollaig stared at Sierra. How did Sierra know so much about guns? He had never seen guns like these before. But without saying another word, they both sat down on the platform at the back of the dive boat, the waterproof box full of heavy guns between them. Their minds raced, trying to piece together what this meant for them and the dive business Nollaig had built from the ground up.

"Whatever Max is involved in could put us in danger," Nollaig said finally, his voice low and tense. "Not just us, but my entire business."

Sierra looked over at him, her piercing gaze sympathetic. "You couldn't have known, Noll."

"Maybe not," he admitted, frustration seeping through his words. "But I should've done better due diligence before accepting his money."

"It's my fault!" Sierra declared, which puzzled Noll. "I should have checked him out. That's what I do for Gator."

"What do you mean? Who's Gator?"

But Sierra appeared to regret what she had just said and quickly changed the topic. "It seems Maksym wanted to invest in your dive business because he wanted easy access to a dive boat for smuggling."

Nollaig nodded slowly, the pieces of the puzzle falling into place. "It makes sense. I guess he was doing it with Vanilla Dive Center before. But why change to us?"

"Regardless, we need to figure out how to get him out," Sierra said firmly, her resolve solidifying. "We can't let him destroy everything you've built, Noll. Not to mention the danger his operation poses... legally."

Nollaig looked at her, gratitude shining in his eyes. "I couldn't agree more, Sierra. We'll find a way to stop him."

Nollaig clenched his jaw, his eyes darting between the waterproof box and Sierra. "We can't leave it like this," he said, his voice barely audible over the gentle lapping of the water against the dive boat. "If Max finds out we were here, if he knows we've seen what's inside these boxes..."

"Agreed," Sierra nodded, her expression determined. "For now, we have to put it back where we found it, but we need to make sure it looks untouched."

"Right," Noll muttered, his mind racing. "We need tie wraps to secure the box again." He searched the dive boat, rummaging through compartments and equipment bags, but came up empty-handed. Frustration bubbled in him as he realized they had no choice but to close the box and return it as is.

"We'll just have to be extra careful not to attract attention to us," Sierra offered, her voice soft yet firm.

Together, they lowered the box back into the water and, with the lift bag, swam it to its original hiding spot beneath the mini-cavern. As Noll let go of the box, he couldn't help but wonder if they were making a mistake—one that could cost them dearly.

The boat ride back to Sea Spell Diving's dock was tense and silent, both Noll and Sierra lost in their thoughts. The weight of their discovery hung heavy in the air, the implications far-reaching and dangerous. They knew they were on the precipice of something much larger than either of them had anticipated.

While they were busy securing the boat back at Sea Spell Diving's dock, a cube truck pulled into the parking lot. A tough-looking guy stepped out, his cold stare fixed on Noll and Sierra. Panic simmered under the surface, threatening to bubble over.

"Act natural," Noll whispered, praying his voice didn't betray the fear gripping him. "As if we didn't see him."

Sierra nodded, leaned in, and pressed her lips against Noll's, their kiss a desperate attempt to convince the driver that their boat ride had been nothing more than a romantic tryst. When the driver continued to stare, Sierra took it a step further, pulling her black t-shirt over her head and exposing her firm breasts adorned with nipple piercings.

As they clung to each other, the truck driver finally seemed to believe he was witnessing an intimate moment between lovers. He turned away, walked off the property, and jumped into a car waiting for him.

Noll and Sierra remained entwined for a while, their hearts pounding in sync. Later, as they got into Noll's car, an old Cat Stevens song played. "Gonna get me a gun. Gonna get me, get me, get me a gun."

CHAPTER 10
LUCY

THE WEIGHT of their recent discovery hung heavy in the air as Noll and Sierra sat across from each other in Noll's Miami office, sipping their morning coffee in silence. The once-comfortable space felt cold and unfamiliar now that they knew about Maksym's gun smuggling activities.

"Damn," Noll muttered, breaking the silence. "How am I supposed to focus on expanding my dive operations, knowing Maksym's dirty money is behind it all?" His hands were shaking with a mixture of frustration and fear.

Sierra locked her dark brown eyes on his, her blue hair a stark contrast against her pale skin. "We have to be careful, Noll. If Maksym realizes we know, there's no telling what he'll do."

Noll clenched his jaw, every fiber of his being yearning for justice, but he knew she was right. "We could go to the police. But there's no proof. If they tie the illegal operations to my business, they could seize the business or something. Maybe. I don't know. So, what? We just pretend everything's fine and hold our tongues?"

"For now, yes," Sierra said firmly. "We keep up appearances while we figure out our next move. If we tip him off, it could put us both in danger." Her gaze softened, a hint of vulnerability breaking through her tough exterior. "I don't want anything to happen to you, Noll."

"Thanks, Sierra," Noll replied, feeling a sense of camaraderie between them. The resolve in her voice reassured him that they would find a way to deal with Maksym eventually. But for now, they had to play along.

ON THE FOLLOWING TUESDAY EVENING, Noll stood at the kitchen sink, washing dishes in an attempt to distract himself from the situation in Key Largo. His wife sat at the kitchen table, a glass of white wine in front of her as she chatted away on the phone.

"Of course, I love dancing," Susan cooed into the receiver. Noll's ears perked up, and he couldn't help but listen to her conversation. She giggled, twirling a strand of her hair between her fingers. "You're such a good dancer, too. I had so much fun the last time."

As Noll scrubbed at a stubborn stain on a plate, he felt his stomach knot with anger and hurt. Was his wife really flirting with another man while he was right there in the same room, doing family chores? He struggled to keep his emotions under control as he listened.

"Maybe we can go dancing again soon," Susan continued, her voice sultry and inviting. "I know just the place. It's very private."

Noll slammed the frying pan onto the drying rack, unable to take it anymore. The sound echoed through the kitchen, causing Susan to flinch and shoot him a warning glance. But she didn't stop her flirting, nor did she try to hide it from her husband. And as Noll stood there, feeling betrayed and powerless, he couldn't believe that this was his life – his marriage crumbling before his eyes and his business tied to a dangerous criminal.

LATER THAT EVENING, Noll stepped out of his house, the night air heavy with humidity. He could feel the sweat beginning to form on his brow as he climbed into his car and started the engine. As the vehicle rumbled to life, he pulled out his smartphone and opened an app that displayed a map with a single red dot. With a deep breath, Noll punched the address associated with the red dot into his GPS.

Soon, the neighborhood he found himself in was nothing like the Miami he knew – it was a place he had heard of but had never seen despite his decades in the city. The streets were poorly lit, casting long shadows across the cracked pavement. Abandoned buildings loomed menacingly, their dark windows staring down at him like empty eye sockets. Noll parked a few blocks from the red dot, his heart pounding in his chest as he glanced around nervously.

"Get it together, Nollaig," he chastised himself under his breath. Swallowing hard, he exited the car and began walking toward the destination.

As he approached the building, Noll stayed close to the nearby structures, trying to be as inconspicuous as possible. He circled the building, examining it from different angles until he found what he was looking for – large garage doors, big enough to let a truck through. Taking a deep breath, he settled into a dark corner near the garage doors and waited.

The oppressive heat of the Miami summer night clung to him like a second skin, making him uncomfortably aware of the beads of sweat trickling down his back. There was no breeze to offer even the slightest reprieve from the stifling heat, and the smells of garbage and decay hung heavy in the air. Noll fought the urge to gag, instead focusing on the task at hand, although he couldn't help but wonder how he had ended up in this situation.

"Is this really worth it?" Noll thought to himself, his mind racing with doubts and fears. But as he stood there, hidden in the shadows, he knew that he had no choice. He had to see this through – for himself, for his business, and for those he cared about. So, despite the heat, despite the smell, and despite the ever-present danger lurking just out of sight, Noll waited. And as the night wore on, he couldn't help but feel that his life would never be the same again.

The streets of this forgotten part of Miami were eerily empty, the darkness swallowing them whole as Noll leaned against a grimy brick wall. He mused that nobody in their right mind would willingly walk through such a dangerous area at night. The unsettling silence was only broken by the distant hum of city life and his own shallow breaths.

"Is this really what it's come to?" Noll thought, anxiety gnawing at the edges of his resolve. Shadows danced around him, threatening to expose his presence, but he held his ground. He knew he had to see this through, no matter the cost.

Suddenly, the sound of a garage door grinding open pierced the silence. Noll's heart leaped into his throat as he watched the same cube truck he'd seen in Sea Spell Diving's parking lot drive out with the same tough-looking driver behind the wheel. The tension in the air thickened, and Noll's instincts screamed at him to run, but he remained rooted to the spot.

"Stay calm," he told himself, trying to steady his breathing. "You've come this far."

As the truck disappeared from sight, Noll felt something cold and metallic press against his back. A gruff voice snarled in his ear, "Don't move." It took every ounce of willpower Noll possessed not to flinch, his body frozen in place as countless movie scenes of men killed in situations like this flashed through his mind.

"Shit," was all he could think of as the adrenaline coursed through his veins.

Suddenly, a gunshot rang out, and Noll's knees buckled as he nearly passed out from the shock. But, to his surprise, he was still alive. Before he could react, a familiar female voice urged him, "Hurry up! Follow me!"

Noll turned around, his eyes wide with disbelief. There, standing next to the lifeless body of the man who had just threatened him, was Lucy, her gun still smoking. Blood pooled around the dead man's body, staining the pavement a dark crimson.

"Come on!" she yelled, snapping Noll out of his shock. "We need to get out of here before they come looking for him!"

Without waiting for a response, Lucy sprinted off, and Noll stumbled after her, his legs shaking with fear and adrenaline.

Noll's heart pounded in his chest as he trailed behind Lucy, their footsteps echoing off the grimy walls that lined the narrow alleyways. He didn't dare look back, focusing only on keeping up with her as they weaved through the labyrinth-like streets. His legs felt like jelly, and sweat dripped down his face, but he forced himself to keep running.

Finally, they reached a black SUV with heavily tinted windows. It looked menacing, something you'd expect to see in a movie about crime lords and secret agents. Lucy leaped into the driver's seat, and Noll quickly followed suit, sliding into the passenger side.

As soon as the doors slammed shut, Lucy floored the gas pedal and sped off, tires squealing against the pavement. Noll gripped the door handle, his knuckles turning white as he tried to steady himself.

"Who the hell are 'they'?" Noll asked, his voice shaking. "You said we needed to run before 'they' came to check on the dead guy. And what the fuck were you doing there? Who are you?"

Lucy remained silent, her eyes focused on the road ahead. Noll's frustration grew, but before he could press her further, she pulled into the parking lot of a rundown motel. The flickering neon sign cast an eerie glow on the cracked asphalt, and the shadowy figures lurking in the corners sent a shiver down Noll's spine. This was not a place one would willingly choose to stay.

Lucy parked the SUV in the back alley and got out without a word. Noll hesitated for a moment, then followed her, unable to shake the feeling that he was stepping into a world he didn't belong in.

They reached a door at the far end of the motel, and Lucy unlocked it, gesturing for Noll to follow her. As he stepped inside, he was confronted with a sight that left him speechless: Lucy, standing by the bedside table, gun in one hand and a DEA badge in the other. She held it up for him to see, her expression stern.

"D.E.A.?" Noll choked out, his mind racing as he tried to process this new information. "You're a fucking agent?"

Lucy didn't answer, her silence only heightening Noll's disorientation. He stared at her, a thousand questions racing through his head, struggling to reconcile this revelation with the woman he thought he knew.

Noll stared at Lucy for a while, his mind a whirlwind of confusion and anger. The dim light from the motel's bedside lamp cast shadows on her face, making her expression unreadable.

"Alright," he demanded, his voice trembling with fury. "What the hell is going on? And why were you at that warehouse?"

Instead of answering, Lucy shot him an irritated look. "I should be asking you the same question. What were you doing there, Noll?"

"Me?" Noll scoffed. "I was following up on the truck I saw last week when you went on that dive with Max. You know, the one where you and Maksym... You used my goddamn boat to smuggle guns?"

Lucy rolled her eyes, clearly unimpressed. "Congratulations, detective."

"But what do guns have to do with the D.E.A.?"

"Drugs in, guns out," she replied flatly as if it were the most obvious thing in the world.

"Jesus Christ," Noll muttered, trying to process everything. His hands clenched into fists, and he fought the urge to lash out at Lucy. "You're the one who introduced me to Maksym! You knew he was a criminal, and yet you let him invest in my business!"

"Keep your voice down," Lucy snapped, her tone authoritative. "Yes, I knew. You were the target."

"Target? So, this whole thing... You left behind in distress, underwater... All a fucking act?"

Lucy simply shrugged.

"Oh, great. So I'm just a pawn in your little game, is that it? You throw me into bed with a drug lord... gun smuggler... whatever, then expect me to be grateful when you swoop in to save the day?"

"Look," she said, her voice softening slightly, "I understand you're upset, but..."

"Upset?" Noll's voice cracked, the weight of the situation beginning to settle in. "My entire fucking life is at risk, Lucy! And it's all because of you!"

"My boss," she clarified. "Because of my boss. I don't call the shots.

But the D.E.A... we will take care of Maksym. Once he's dealt with, your business will be all yours again."

Noll couldn't help but snort derisively. "I should trust you, now? So, you were using Vanilla before. Why me, now?"

For a moment, Lucy looked like she might apologize, but her expression quickly hardened. "Steve is crooked. The FBI is looking into him. For something else. We... My boss... Wanted a clean dive operator."

"Oh, for fuck's sake!" Nollaig was pissed. "I get screwed because I am an honest citizen with a clean business? Great fuckin' government we have!"

"You need to calm down and trust me, Noll. I'm on your side."

Noll let out a bitter laugh. "Trust you? That's rich!"

Noll clenched his fists, his nails digging into his palms. The pain grounded him, though it did little to quell the anger that boiled in his veins. He glared at Lucy, unable to comprehend the mess she'd dragged him into. And for some weird reason, Ariane Grande's song, "Dangerous Woman," came to his mind. "Nothin' to prove, and I'm bulletproof and... Know what I'm doing."

"Can I trust you?" Lucy's voice was steady, but her eyes betrayed a flicker of fear. "The D.E.A. can't afford Maksym finding out who I am. My life is on the line here."

"Fuck off," Noll spat, his heart pounding in his chest. "My life is at stake, too, not to mention my business."

"Listen," she warned, her expression hardening. "If my boss has any doubts about my loyalty... and your ignorance... there will be consequences."

"Are you saying you'd kill me too?" Noll demanded, his voice shaking. He couldn't believe this was happening, that the small blonde woman he had rescued at sea was capable of something like this.

"Grow up, Noll," she snapped. "You're not the only one with something to lose here."

Lucy seemed to deflate slightly, her shoulders slumping as she sighed. "No one, not even my boss, can know what happened tonight. Understand?"

"Are you serious?" Noll laughed nervously. "What, the D.E.A. doesn't have carte blanche to just go around killing people in Miami?"

"Ah, fuck off," she barked, irritation flashing across her face. "That guy wasn't a person; he was a hired goon who would've killed you if I hadn't taken him out. You should thank me and play along."

Noll's laughter died, replaced by a cold, hollow feeling in his chest. He stared at Lucy, trying to reconcile this hardened agent with the woman he thought he knew. How could he ever trust her again after all this?

The silence in the motel room was suffocating, broken only by the erratic rhythm of Noll's breathing. The gunshot echoed in his mind, a chilling reminder that he had come so close to losing everything – his life, his business, and any semblance of control. He began to tremble, the shock finally setting in, and Lucy looked at him with concern.

"Hey," she said softly, her voice carrying a note of sympathy. "It's normal for the rush to be delayed like this and for the shaking to happen later."

"Play along," he grumbled, defeated. "So, you came on your own. And you don't want your boss to know. Why? How?"

"I... We..." Lucy hesitated.

But Noll insisted. "Tell me... if you want me to play along!"

"We... I... placed trackers on your car. And, so, I noticed you near the warehouse."

Noll managed a weak laugh, trying to steady his pounding heart. "Tracker? Uncle Sam... Is this legal? You have a warrant or something?"

"That tracker just saved your life. So, grow up! And... Did you have a warrant for the tracker you put on the cube truck?"

Lucy's eyes took on an unreadable expression as she turned away from Nollaig. She began to undress, her movements relaxed and unhurried, as if they were simply having a casual conversation in a normal coffee shop rather than a life-and-death one in a seedy motel room.

Despite his anger, Noll's gaze was drawn to her like a magnet, unable to look away from the graceful curve of her neck, the perfect slope of her shoulders, and the flawless expanse of her skin.

His situation was serious. Yet, Noll's mind was somewhere else. He remembered seeing Lucy topless on the bow of one of his dive boats, but witnessing her full nudity was even more breathtaking. He knew he should leave, that staying in this room with Lucy would only complicate things further, but his car was far from the motel, and the adrenaline pumping through his veins held him captive.

As if sensing his turmoil, Lucy headed to the bathroom without a word. Noll listened to the sound of the shower running, his mind racing with a thousand thoughts and questions he couldn't quite articulate. Eventually, Lucy emerged from the bathroom, her hair wrapped in a towel while the rest of her body remained bare. The sight of her, so vulnerable yet so powerful, shook him to his core.

He wanted to say something, anything to break the heavy silence that had settled over them, but no words would come. Instead, he focused on the rise and fall of her chest as she breathed, the water droplets clinging to her skin like tiny diamonds, and the way the dim light of the motel room cast shadows across every curve and hollow of her exquisite form.

At that moment, Nollaig Durand was utterly lost. Subdued.

His eyes remained fixed on Lucy's naked body, unable to tear himself away from the sight. He coughed, trying to clear his throat and regain some semblance of composure. "Should I, uh, order an Uber to get back to my car?" he asked awkwardly, hoping that mentioning the car would remind him of the danger he was in and help him focus.

"Absolutely not," Lucy replied decisively, her tone leaving no room for argument. "Taking an Uber would leave a trace. This" – she gestured around at the dingy motel room – "is a hideout. Officially, I have a nice apartment near Maksym's nightclub. You're just going to have to sleep here tonight. It's late, and I'll drive you back to your car tomorrow morning when I swap this D.E.A. S.U.V. for my own wheels."

The mention of the D.E.A. sent a jolt through Noll, grounding him back in reality. But the thought of spending the night with Lucy, especially given their current sleeping arrangements, made him uneasy. "I don't think I can stay here, especially with only one bed. I'm married, you know."

Lucy laughed, clearly amused by his discomfort. "Oh, please. You sleep in the guest bedroom at home, and your wife already has a boyfriend – or, maybe, a boy toy." She smirked, enjoying the shocked expression that crossed Noll's face.

"How do you know that?" he demanded, feeling exposed and vulnerable. "I never told anyone about… Are you tracking her, too?"

Lucy simply rolled her eyes.

"And what boyfriend?"

Lucy ignored his questions. Instead, she pulled back the bedsheets and slid her naked body into bed without a hint of self-consciousness. She patted the empty spot next to her, the corner of her lips turning up in a teasing smile. "Good night, Noll."

Noll hesitated, torn between his loyalty to his fledging marriage and the allure of Lucy's presence. But as he weighed his options, his mind drifted. The night's events replayed in his head – the gunshot, the dead man, and the secrets he now shared with Lucy. He realized that, for better or worse, he was tied to Lucy, at least for the time being... or... the night being.

With a resigned sigh, Noll climbed into the bed beside her, his clothes on, acutely aware of every inch that separated them. His heart pounded in his chest, and his thoughts raced with unanswered questions and unspoken desires. As he lay there, sleep far from his grasp, he knew that tonight would change everything — and that there was no turning back.

CHAPTER 11
MILE MARKER

"*T*ake *me to church;*
I'll worship like a dog at the shrine of your lies."

NOLL FLIPPED the pancakes on the griddle, his hands steady despite the turmoil brewing inside him. Lucy's words echoed in his mind: "Act normal..." and "The D.E.A. will arrest Maksym soon..." He glanced at the calendar on the kitchen wall – three months had passed since that fateful night when she'd shot a man to save him. What did "soon" even mean? The uncertainty gnawed at him, but he couldn't let it show.

"Morning, Daddy!" his son chirped, bounding into the kitchen with youthful energy.

"Good morning, buddy," Noll replied, forcing a smile as he plated the pancakes. His daughter trailed after her brother, rubbing sleep from her eyes. Noll was grateful for their presence, the love and innocence they brought into his life. It grounded him and reminded him why he needed to stay strong. Without them, he probably would have made a dozen bad decisions by then.

"Morning," Susan drawled, sauntering into the kitchen. She settled into a chair at the head of the table, eyeing her husband expectantly. The kids dug into their breakfast, oblivious to the tension between their parents.

"Here," Noll said, handing Susan a cup of coffee and placing a plate of pancakes before her. She accepted them with a haughty nod as if he were nothing more than a servant attending to her whims.

As the kids finished eating and scampered off to play, Noll prepared to leave for work. "I'm heading to Key Largo today," he told his wife casually. "Big groups of divers scheduled."

"Really?" She arched an eyebrow, skepticism etched on her face. "With Sierra, no doubt?"

Anger flared within Noll, and he snapped back, "Sierra left the company a month ago, remember? The expansion's on hold."

"Whatever you say, Nollaig." Susan rolled her eyes and took another sip of her coffee.

"Believe what you want," he muttered, grabbing his keys and heading out the door.

Noll's anger towards Susan quickly dissipated as he drove towards Key Largo. His thoughts drifted to Sierra, and an ache settled in his chest. He missed her presence in his life and couldn't help but blame Lucy for the mess he found himself in.

"Damn you, Lucy," he cursed aloud, gripping the steering wheel tightly. His mind played back the night he had spent with Lucy, their bodies entwined, her model-like figure pressed against him. The memory stirred a mix of guilt and longing within him.

It felt strange to Noll; he didn't feel like he had cheated on Susan that night. Instead, it felt as if he had betrayed Sierra – the one person who had truly understood him and shared his beliefs. And he missed her deeply.

When Noll arrived at the parking lot of Sea Spell Diving in Key Largo, he parked next to the cube truck used by Maksym for drug and gun smuggling. Glancing around to ensure nobody was watching, Noll got on his back and slid under the truck. His heart raced as he searched for the tracker he had placed there three months earlier.

"Where the hell is it?" he whispered, panic setting in when he realized the tracker was gone. Sweat beaded on his forehead at the thought of Maksym's men discovering the device. "Idiot!" he chastised himself. "Lucy took it off, obviously."

As he crawled out from under the truck, Noll knew he needed to tread carefully going forward. His future, and perhaps even his life, depended on it.

"M.M. 92.8" – the cryptic message awaited Noll on a piece of paper tucked under his windshield wiper at the end of the day. He furrowed his brow, puzzled by its meaning. His initial thought was that it could be a trap set by Maksym to kill him. But as he considered the possibilities, he reasoned that Maksym wouldn't choose such a public location along a busy highway to carry out a murder.

With a mixture of curiosity and trepidation, Noll climbed into his car and drove south to Mile Marker 93, then continued another two-tenths of a mile. The landscape consisted of little more than a small church nestled among swaying palm trees. He pulled into the empty parking lot, scanning the area for any signs of life.

"Is this some sort of joke?" he muttered, frustrated with the lack of answers.

Deciding to investigate further, Noll exited his car and cautiously approached the church. He smirked as Hozier's song, "Take Me To Church," played in his head. "Take me to church. I'll worship like a dog at the shrine of your lies."

He pushed open the heavy wooden doors, revealing a dimly lit interior. As his eyes adjusted to the darkness, he spotted a familiar figure sitting in one of the pews, with a smartphone in hand and earbuds in her ears.

"Sierra?" he breathed, his chest tightening with surprise and relief.

He approached from behind and heard part of the phone conversation. "Yes... I know you don't do it on U.S. soil, Gator... Florida, I mean... I just thought... Yes, an exception... Guns and drugs... Fine! I'll find another way. Thanks for nothing!"

She looked back over her shoulder and noticed Nollaig. Her bright blue hair contrasted sharply against the somber surroundings. For a moment, they simply stared at each other, their eyes locked in silent recognition. Then Sierra rose from the pew, crossed the distance between them, and wrapped Noll in a warm embrace.

"Hey," she said softly, her voice tinged with emotion.

"Hey," he replied, holding her tight. "How are you? What's going on?"

They separated and sat side by side on the church bench, their hands brushing against each other like old friends. Noll glanced around the quiet sanctuary, then turned back to Sierra.

"Seriously, what's with the cloak and dagger stuff?" he asked, his voice low but insistent.

"Sometimes," Sierra replied cryptically, "you need to meet in the shadows to bring things to light. I found information about your business partner."

Noll studied Sierra's face, noting how the dim church lighting seemed to accentuate the determination in her eyes. "Sierra, you really shouldn't be risking your life investigating Maksym and his businesses. It's not safe."

"Someone has to do it, Noll," she replied, her tone resolute. "Besides, I'm careful about how I dig for information."

"Careful?" he scoffed, remembering his own brush with death. "I almost got shot when I followed that cube truck to a warehouse."

Sierra's eyes widened in shock. "What? When did that happen?"

He sighed, recounting the harrowing experience. "A few weeks back. A man pointed a gun at me, and Lucy… she killed him. Right there, on the spot."

"Lucy? As in the same Lucy that works for Maksym and the D.E.A.?" Sierra asked, her voice a mix of disbelief and concern.

"Wait! You know she's an undercover D.E.A. agent? How? I didn't know that until that night. I don't get why she hasn't arrested Maksym already."

"Well, how did you find out about Lucy's true identity?" Sierra pressed, her curiosity piqued.

"From Lucy herself," Noll admitted, feeling the weight of the secret lift slightly as he shared it with Sierra. "But tell me, how did you find all this information?"

"Let's just say I have ways," Sierra said with a faint smile. "I don't have to follow trucks into shady parts of town. I can find what I need from a safe distance."

Noll couldn't help but feel a mixture of admiration and concern for Sierra's tenacity. "So, what did you uncover about Maksym's activities?"

"His primary business is laundering money for drug cartels and other criminal organizations. He's been doing that for years. He only recently got into smuggling drugs into the U.S.A."

"Is smuggling guns out of the country payment for the drugs he imports, or is it a separate business?" Noll wondered aloud.

"I'm not sure yet, but I'll keep digging," Sierra promised. "I contacted you because I'm worried about you, Noll. If Maksym's main activity is laundering money, maybe he has plans for your dive business beyond just using the boats for smuggling."

Noll felt a chill at the thought. He had already lost so much to Maksym's machinations; the idea of losing his livelihood, too, was overwhelming. "Thanks for looking out for me, Sierra. I don't know what to say. Or do, for that matter."

A heavy silence filled the church as Noll and Sierra were done sharing their information. Noll found himself unable to shake off the feeling of guilt from that night with Lucy. His heart ached for Sierra, and he couldn't help but feel like he had betrayed her.

"Sierra," Noll began, his voice barely above a whisper. "I need to tell you something."

She looked at him with concern, her dark brown eyes searching his face. "What is it?"

Noll hesitated before admitting, "On the night Lucy saved my life, we... we ended up sleeping together."

Sierra's expression didn't significantly change. Instead, she remained silent, giving him room to continue.

"In a safe house. Sort of. Ever since then, I haven't been able to stop thinking about you," Noll confessed. "I feel like I cheated on you, even though we were never... you know..."

The air between them was thick with tension as they locked eyes, their unspoken feelings laid bare. Noll wanted nothing more than to reach out and hold Sierra, to assure her that she was the one he truly cared for.

"Sierra, I don't want you to disappear again," Noll pleaded. "But I understand that it's safer for you not to be seen with me, especially now that we know how dangerous Maksym is."

"Lucy's dangerous too," Sierra added, bitterness creeping into her tone. "She killed a man in cold blood on a Miami street without batting an eye. And like you said, I don't understand why Maksym hasn't been arrested yet."

"Maybe she's still gathering evidence," Noll suggested, momentarily trying to remain rational. "But you know, she killed one of his goons. Why doesn't she just kill him?"

They stood there, their gazes locked, the connection between them both undeniable and fragile. Slowly, Noll reached out to pull Sierra into a hug, but she put a hand on his heart to stop him.

"Promise me you'll be careful, Sierra," he whispered.

"I promise," she murmured back.

Reluctantly, Noll headed back to his car, his heart heavy with the knowledge that he might not see Sierra again for some time. She remained in the church, ensuring they would not be seen leaving together, but the memory of their initial embrace lingered with him as he drove away.

CHAPTER 12
A PERFECT STORM

"*L*ike a dog without a bone;
An actor out on loan;
Riders on the storm."

THE CHEAP DINER'S worn leather seats squeaked beneath Lucy as she shifted her weight, sipping bitter coffee. Across from her, a stern-looking man in a suit picked at his breakfast. His eyes periodically darted to the two black SUVs parked outside, their dark windows concealing any occupants.

"Tell me again why we haven't arrested Maksym yet?" Lucy asked, her voice low and tinged with frustration.

The man glanced up, his expression hardening. "We don't have enough evidence."

"Are you kidding?" Lucy countered, her patience wearing thin. "I've given you everything you need in that D.E.A. file – drug trafficking routes, names of associates, hell, even photos of him handling the merchandise! It's the thickest D.E.A. file I've ever seen."

For a moment, the man seemed caught off guard, fumbling for

words. Then he abruptly said, "Well, you have been on the job only two years… And we want more information on his money laundering activities."

"Since when does the D.E.A. care about money laundering? I thought our focus was drugs," Lucy said, her frustration evident.

"Uh, well…" He hesitated again, clearly uneasy. "We got a request from the F.B.I."

"Fine," Lucy sighed, trying to reel in her frustration. "So, when do I get to meet this F.B.I. contact and the A.T.F. rep, might as well, to review the gun trafficking info?"

The man didn't answer, choosing instead to stab at his eggs with a fork.

"Look," Lucy continued, leaning forward, "I was supposed to be undercover for two months. It's been six. What's going on?"

The man's jaw clenched, and his impatience bubbled to the surface. "I'm the boss, Lucy. You just need to shut up and do your job."

With that, he tossed some cash onto the table and stormed out of the diner, leaving Lucy to sit alone in the dimly lit booth. She watched him climb into one of the black S.U.V.s and drive away, her gut churning with unease. Something didn't add up, and she couldn't shake the feeling that her D.E.A. boss was a far shadier character than she'd initially thought.

An hour later, Lucy pulled her D.E.A. SUV into a parking spot outside a Starbucks. The aroma of freshly brewed coffee wafted through the air as she walked in, locking eyes with Sierra, who sat at a corner table. Sierra offered a small smile and waved Lucy over.

"Hey, Sierra," Lucy began as she took a seat across from her. "Thanks for meeting me."

"Sure thing," Sierra replied, her piercing gaze never wavering.

"So, did you manage to reassure Noll?" Lucy immediately inquired.

Sierra hesitated before answering, her voice laced with sarcasm: "No. Quite the contrary. But why do you even care about him? Government agents usually don't give a damn about the little people they're destroying."

Caught off guard, Lucy fumbled for words. Sierra smirked, sensing her discomfort.

"Is it because you slept with him?" Sierra prodded. "Or because you killed a man in Miami without doing the proper paperwork?"

Lucy's eyes widened in shock. She hadn't expected Sierra to know about that. Sierra leaned back in her chair, her smirk still plastered on her face. "Pretty obvious Noll would tell me, no?"

Lucy remained silent for a while and then laughed. "Well, why do you think I approached you when I needed a hacker?"

Sierra was puzzled by Lucy's question, although she had wondered about that herself.

"Noll speaks in her sleep," Lucy smirks. "I just don't know why he needed a hacker in his dive businesses."

"He doesn't." Sierra quickly clarified. "But why do you? Don't you have access to an army of overpaid geeks in mysterious government offices?"

"Look," Lucy said defensively, "that's why I'm here. My D.E.A. boss wants information on Maksym's money laundering operations. I specialize in drugs, not finances. I thought maybe you could help. And the official channels are too slow."

Sierra studied Lucy for a moment. "None of what I do is admissible in court."

"Let me worry about that. First, I need to know what is going on. Then, I'll find the legal proofs."

Sierra nodded slowly. "Alright, I'll help you. But only because I hope it will help Noll if this case is closed sooner rather than later."

"And because I have a big discretionary budget," Lucy smirked.

"I don't give a shit about your dirty government money!" Sierra snapped back.

"Even better," Lucy breathed a sigh of relief.

"D.E.A.," Sierra countered, her voice dripping with disdain. "You approached me to help the D.E.A., not the FBI. But all government agencies are corrupt anyway, so the alphabet doesn't really matter, I guess."

After the meeting she just had with her boss, Lucy wondered if there wasn't some truth in Sierra's words but felt compelled to defend her position. She knew her role in this case was essential, and she had to see it through, no matter how complicated the case became.

Lucy studied Sierra for a moment, her brow furrowed in curiosity. "Why are you working part-time for the D.E.A. if you hate all government agencies?"

"I hate drugs!" Sierra's gaze hardened. She leaned forward and said, "I'll help you with Maksym's money laundering operations, but I need you to plant something on his computer."

"Plant something?" Lucy echoed, unsure of what Sierra was proposing.

"Yes," Sierra replied, her voice low and serious. "And Maksym must be receiving loads of cash somehow to launder through his nightclub. Be on the lookout for any delivery of boxes, briefcases, or anything that could carry cash so I can match it to his financials."

Lucy nodded, listening to the instructions Sierra gave her. She understood the importance of gathering information on Maksym's finances, but the thought of planting something on his computer made her uneasy. However, she knew she had to trust Sierra, who seemed to have Noll's best interests at heart.

NOLL PULLED into the parking lot of his doctor's office, repeating the words the doctor had told him on the phone: "It's better we do this face to face." He swallowed hard, his hands gripping the steering wheel tightly as anxiety churned in his stomach. It was never reassuring to hear those words from a doctor.

Noll stepped out of his car and walked into the doctor's lobby. The place looked more like a V.I.P. spa than the cheap doctor's offices he visited with his parents when he was young. A friendly receptionist greeted him with a warm smile. "Welcome back, Mr. Durand. Would you like your usual espresso?"

"Uh, sure," Noll replied, forcing a smile despite his nerves. He couldn't shake the feeling that he was about to receive bad news, but at least he could appreciate the top-notch service at the doctor's office.

Noll shifted uncomfortably in the plush leather chair, his heart pounding while he waited for the doctor's arrival. The scent of espresso and disinfectant hung in the air, creating an odd contrast that seemed to embody Noll's current state of mind — a blend of dread and luxury.

"Mr. Durand?" A voice called out, breaking his train of thought. Dr. Thompson entered the room, his face wearing a professional yet empathetic expression. "Sorry to keep you waiting."

"Uh, no problem." Noll forced a tight smile, his hands clasped together in his lap. "You're 2 minutes late for crying out loud. Don't mention it!"

Dr. Thompson took a seat across from Noll and glanced down at the medical file in his hand. After a brief pause, he looked up and met Noll's gaze. "Your recent blood tests showed a significant increase in your PSA level. Last year, it was close to zero, but now it's at 4.1."

"PSA?" Noll asked, his stomach twisting with anxiety. He knew it couldn't be good news.

"Prostate-specific antigen," Dr. Thompson explained. "It's a protein produced by the prostate gland. Elevated levels can be a sign of prostate cancer. However, I want to stress that it's just a sign, not a certainty. Some men have PSA levels between 4 and 10 without having cancer, while others with a score lower than four may have it. I'd like you to undergo a biopsy as soon as possible so we can know for sure."

The room seemed to close in on Noll, the weight of the information crushing him. Cancer. The word rang in his ears, its implications suffocating. Dr. Thompson continued talking, outlining the next steps and offering reassurances, but Noll's thoughts were elsewhere.

After leaving the doctor's office, Noll got into his car and slammed his palms against the steering wheel. "Damn it!" he shouted, tears pricking at the corners of his eyes. He was convinced that the biopsy would confirm he had cancer. The stress of the past few months – Maksym's illegal activities involving his dive boats, Lucy's deception, and his crumbling marriage – felt like a malignant growth, slowly consuming him.

"Lucy, this is all your fault!" Noll yelled, cursing her for introducing him to Maksym and setting off this chain of events. His anger then shifted to his wife, Susan. She had turned their home into a toxic environment, forcing him to sleep in the guest bedroom and treating him with disdain. Their relationship had become another form of cancer, one that was eating away at his happiness and well-being.

As Noll drove towards his Miami dive store, his hands shook on the wheel. He couldn't escape the feeling that everything was spiraling out of control, a perfect storm threatening to consume him entirely.

LATER, Noll pushed open the door to his Miami dive store, shoulders slumped, head down, and heart heavy. The scent of saltwater and neoprene filled his nostrils as he made his way to the back office. He couldn't shake the dark cloud that hung over him, the potential cancer diagnosis casting a pall on everything else in his life.

As he entered his small office, Noll spotted a large envelope on his desk emblazoned with the G.A.S.I. logo — the Global Association of Scuba Instructors. He frowned and ripped into the package with apprehension. What he found inside shocked him: a stack of quality assurance complaints against both of his dive businesses. His jaw clenched as he scanned through them, each one like a slap in the face.

"Unbelievable," Noll muttered under his breath, anger bubbling up within him. He prided himself on safety and high standards, constantly striving for excellence in an industry that seemed content to cut corners and put lives at risk. He thought of Vanilla Dive Center, the competitor in Key Largo that routinely flouted regulations while he did everything by the book.

"Damn it all," he growled, tossing the complaints onto the desk. The weight of Maksym's illegal operations with his dive boat, the sour state of his marriage, the looming possibility of cancer, and now these accusations... It was too much.

In a haze of depression, Noll stepped out of the office and walked towards a local Irish pub. He needed a drink, some space to breathe and think.

Once there, he settled onto a barstool and ordered a beer, then another, and another. Each bitter sip only served to fuel his growing despair. Was it even worth trying to fight against all of this? The odds were clearly stacked against him, and he felt suffocated by the mounting pressure.

"Perfect storm," he muttered. "George Clooney dies at the end of that movie."

As if on cue, the old song by The Doors, "Riders on The Storm," started to play in the bar speakers. "Riders on the storm. Riders on the storm. Into this house, we're born. Into this world, we're thrown."

"Everything all right, mate?" the barman asked, polishing a glass with a disinterested air. Noll could tell the man didn't really care, but he tried anyway.

"Feels like my life is falling apart," Noll admitted, staring into his beer. "My business, my marriage... and now I might have cancer."

"Rough deal," the barman replied, setting down the glass and moving on to another task. His lack of empathy only served to deepen Noll's sense of loneliness.

Noll continued to nurse his drink, pondering the wreckage of his life. The world around him swirled like a whirlpool, threatening to pull him under. And as much as he wanted to fight, he couldn't shake the feeling that it was all for naught.

CHAPTER 13
GLOBAL ASSOCIATION OF SCUBA INSTRUCTORS (GASI)

"Everybody knows that the dice are loaded;
Everybody rolls with their fingers crossed."

NOLL'S HEAD throbbed as he stood in the kitchen, flipping pancakes for his two kids. The weight of last night's binge at the Irish pub clung to him like a damp blanket, suffocating any semblance of happiness or hope. His hands shook slightly, a side effect of both the hangover and the stress that had been mounting with each passing day. His eyes were bloodshot, and his face pale, a clear sign of his rough night.

"Ugh, you look terrible," his wife said, entering the kitchen in her expensive silk robe, her voice dripping with disdain. "Were you out partying with some half-naked dive instructor?"

"Morning to you too, Susan," Noll muttered, doing his best to ignore her jabs. He wanted to tell her about Maksym and the illegal activities threatening to destroy everything he'd built. He wanted to tell her about his possible cancer diagnosis, but he knew she wouldn't care. She would just blame him for it all like she always did for everything.

LATER THAT DAY, Noll found himself in his office at the back of his Miami dive store. With a heavy sigh, he picked up the phone and dialed his G.A.S.I. representative. As soon as the call connected, he launched into an angry tirade.

"Listen, I received a pile of quality assurance complaints yesterday, and I'm not happy about it. I'm probably the only GASI dive center that hasn't violated any scuba diving standards!"

"Mr. Durand, I understand your frustration," the GASI rep replied, his voice placid and bureaucratic. "But you should know the process by now: whenever we receive a complaint, we have to deal with it. Just answer the complaints, send your responses back to G.A.S.I., and forget about it."

"Easy for you to say," Noll snapped. "I've got so many complaints here that I'd need to take a week off just to address them all! This is pure B.S.—I have two high-quality dive centers to manage!"

"Mr. Durand, please try to understand—" the rep began, but Noll had already slammed the phone down in frustration, his anger boiling over.

"Damn GASI and their bureaucracy!" he muttered under his breath. They didn't care about quality or safety; they only cared about paperwork and covering their own backsides. And now, it was left to him to deal with the fallout.

He put on some music and started filling out forms to answer GASI quality assurance complaints. In the background, Leonard Cohen was singing. "Everybody knows that the dice are loaded. Everybody rolls with their fingers crossed." Every part of that "Everybody Knows" song seemed accurate to Nollaig on that day.

THE DOOR to Noll's office creaked open, and Kim Banks walked in. She was a trusted part-time instructor on his team, as well as a U.S. Marshal. Her short red hair and lean, athletic frame gave her an air of authority that was hard to ignore.

"Hey, Noll," she said, eyeing the stack of paperwork on his desk. "What's all this about?"

"Quality assurance complaints from GASI," he replied, rubbing his temples. "A whole bunch of them."

"Really?" Kim looked genuinely surprised. "I've never seen anything like this before. What's going on?"

"Anyone can file a complaint against us, and then GASI just forwards it to me after removing the name of the person who sent it," explained Noll, frustration seeping into his voice.

"Seems like a pretty lousy system," Kim remarked, frowning. "Do you think it's that Vanilla Dive Center causing all this trouble? They're always jealous of our nearly five-star reviews."

Noll nodded, considering the possibility. "I wouldn't put it past them. But right now, I just need to find a way to deal with all these complaints."

"Maybe I could help?" Kim suggested hesitantly. "With my legal background, I might be able to make some sense out of this mess and help you respond appropriately to them."

"Really?" Noll's eyes lit up with hope for the first time that day. "That would be amazing, Kim. But don't you have your hands full with your Marshal duties?"

"I do," she admitted, "but I can help you part-time. It might take a while, but we'll get through it."

"Thank you," Noll breathed a sigh of relief, suddenly feeling less alone in his struggle. "GASI can wait for their useless paperwork, anyway. Fuk'em."

"Speaking of help," Kim continued, "would you be okay with me asking my friend Harper to lend a hand? She's an FBI Agent and also works part-time as an instructor here."

"Absolutely, the more the merrier!" Noll agreed, grateful for the support. Together, they split the pile of complaints into two, one for Noll and the other for Kim and Harper.

"Thanks again, Kim," Noll said, shaking his head in disbelief at the stack of papers. "I really appreciate it."

"Of course, Noll. We're a team, right?" Kim smiled and patted him on the back before leaving the office to start tackling the complaints.

Noll leaned back in his office chair, the weight of the world pressing on his shoulders. The door had barely closed behind Kim when the thought occurred to him: why was it that a busy full-time US Marshal and part-time scuba instructor was willing to help him sort through this bureaucratic nightmare while his own wife, also a scuba instructor, sat at home doing nothing?

He stared at the pile of paperwork, letting the bitterness seep into every crevice of his thoughts. How had their marriage come to this? Noll remembered when he first started dating Susan. She was fun, full of life, and always ready to help him, whether it was with their dive business or taking care of their kids. But now? It felt like they lived in separate worlds, bound together only by a shared roof and their children.

"Damn it," Noll muttered under his breath, feeling the heavy cloud of depression settling over him. He needed a break, a chance to clear his head and escape from the never-ending problems that seemed to be plaguing him.

THE NEXT DAY, on impulse, Noll decided to take the afternoon off and go diving on one of his dive boats in Key Largo. Maybe being immersed in the underwater world would help him find the clarity he so desperately sought.

As he drove down the sun-drenched highway, Noll couldn't resist stopping at Vanilla Dive Center. As he walked around the dive center and onto their dock, Noll noticed at least a dozen GASI standard violations. The realization brought a mix of anger and satisfaction; perhaps it was Steve who had filed those complaints against him out of jealousy.

"Hey!" Steve's voice rang out across the dock, startling Noll from his thoughts. "Get the fuck out of here!"

"Excuse me?" Noll raised an eyebrow, meeting Steve's furious gaze.

"Get out!" Steve repeated. "I never want to see you around here again. You're a goddamn customer thief, stealing business away from my dive center."

Noll frowned, unsure of what to make of Steve's accusation. He hadn't stolen any customers; his success was built on providing consistent high-quality experiences for his clients. Perhaps Steve was referring to Maksym. But he wasn't in the mood for a confrontation, so he wordlessly turned and left, Steve's threat ringing in his ears.

As he drove away, Noll wondered again if Steve had been the one behind the GASI complaints. It seemed like a possibility, especially given Vanilla's own issues with safety and standards. But regardless of who had filed them, the complaints still needed to be addressed, and Noll knew he'd have to face that challenge head-on.

For now, though, he just wanted to dive and let the underwater world envelop him, offering a temporary respite from the chaos above.

***

DESCENDING into the depths of the ocean, Noll felt an overwhelming sense of calm wash over him. The weight of his worries seemed to evaporate as he submerged himself in the cool, clear waters off the island of Key Largo. The muted blues and greens of the underwater world enveloped him, providing a much-needed escape from the chaos above.

Hovering in mid-water, Noll marveled at the sensation of weightlessness, akin to an astronaut floating through space. It was a magical feeling, one that reminded him of why he'd fallen in love with diving in the first place. Surrounded by vibrant coral formations and darting schools of fish, he felt a sense of harmony that had been sorely lacking in his life lately.

As Noll drifted through the water, he was captivated by the delicate dance of a couple of angelfish weaving their way around a sunken shipwreck. Their elegant movements were mesmerizing, their colorful scales shimmering like precious gems beneath the surface. He watched as a sea turtle glided gracefully overhead, its powerful flippers propelling it through the water with ease.

All the while, Noll used hand signals to communicate with his fellow divers, exchanging silent messages of awe and appreciation for the beauty surrounding them. This unspoken language was familiar and comforting, a reminder of the camaraderie he found among fellow divers that was often missing in other aspects of his life.

Noll pushed all thoughts aside, focusing instead on soaking up the tranquility of the ocean floor. This temporary reprieve from the challenges of his life on the surface was a balm for his weary soul, reenergizing him in much-needed ways.

As Noll gradually made his way back to the surface, he felt a renewed sense of determination. He knew he would have to face his problems head-on, but this brief escape had given him the strength and clarity to do so. The underwater world had given him a glimpse of peace and harmony, and it was up to him to carry that feeling back into his everyday life.

CHAPTER 14
CHANGING OF THE GUARD

"*Everybody knows the war is over;*
Everybody knows the good guys lost."

THE TIRES of Noll's car crunched on the gravel as he pulled into the parking lot of his Miami dive shop. He parked and stepped out, taking in the familiar sight of the storefront with a deep breath. As he walked toward the entrance, he noticed two big guys standing on either side of the door. They were wearing security guard outfits and had the build of football players. Noll narrowed his eyes at them, wondering what they were doing there.

"Stop," one of the men said, raising his hand in a halting gesture. "Name and ID."

Noll laughed incredulously. "Are you serious? This is my business. What the hell are you guys doing here?"

"Name and ID," the man repeated, unfazed by Noll's frustration.

"I'm Nollaig Durand, the owner of this place. I didn't ask for any security guards, so why don't you just step aside?"

The other man glanced down at a list and shook his head. "Sorry, Mr. Durand, but you're not allowed inside."

"What?" Noll's face reddened with anger. The man handed him a letter and stated that Noll had been served.

"Are you kidding me? What is this?" Noll waved the letter in front of the guard.

The guard shrugged, clearly uncomfortable. "I have no idea, sir. Just doing my job."

Noll clenched his jaw as he gripped the envelope. In front of the two guards, he tore it open and scanned its contents. It was a formal notice from Maksym, the Chairman of the Board, informing Noll that he had been terminated for cause from his position as President and CEO of both of his dive businesses in Key Largo and Miami.

He looked back up at the security guards, his eyes burning with a mix of fury and disbelief. They stood there, stone-faced, just doing their job as they had said. There was no point in arguing with them.

"Fine," Noll muttered through gritted teeth, stuffing the letter back into the envelope. He stormed back to his car and slammed the door shut, the sound echoing through the parking lot.

His hands trembled on the steering wheel as he pulled out his phone and dialed his corporate lawyer's number. "I need an emergency meeting," he demanded, his voice shaking with anger. "Now."

As he hung up, Noll felt the weight of everything crashing down on him: Maksym's betrayal, the possibility of cancer, his crumbling marriage, and now this. It was enough to make anyone feel lost, adrift in a sea of uncertainty and despair. But for Noll Durand, whose entire life had been tied to his dive businesses, it was like being ripped away from the only thing that made him feel anchored in this world.

NOLL SAT across from his lawyer in the well-appointed office, the letter in question spread out on the polished mahogany desk between them. The lawyer, a middle-aged man with graying hair and a sharp gaze, carefully read the words, his lips pursed in thought.

"According to this," the lawyer said, looking up at Noll, "you've received a number of quality assurance complaints from GASI recently. Is that correct?"

Noll nodded, feeling the weight of each complaint like a lead anchor around his neck. "Yes, I got a pile of them earlier this week."

The lawyer sighed and rubbed his temples. "Alright, Mr. Durand. I'm going to need you to gather every document you've ever signed with Mr. Byrne. Bring them all to me so I can review everything and advise you on the best course of action."

"Of course," Noll agreed, desperation creeping into his voice. He needed answers, and he needed them fast.

Leaving the lawyer's office, Noll felt as if the entire world had been pulled out from under him. He climbed into his car, his hands gripping the steering wheel tightly, but he couldn't bring himself to turn the key in the ignition. Where could he go? His life had always been tied to his dive businesses in Key Largo and Miami. Without them, who was he?

His mind raced through his mounting problems – the possibility of prostate cancer, his disintegrating marriage, Lucy's failure to arrest Maksym as she had promised – and it all felt suffocating, like the crushing depths of the ocean closing in on him. He closed his eyes, took a deep breath, and tried to steady himself, but the sense of loss remained.

"Get it together, Noll," he muttered to himself, but the words rang hollow. Everything he had worked for, everything he believed in, was slipping through his fingers like sand, and there seemed to be nothing he could do to stop it.

At that moment, Noll realized that he wasn't just fighting for his businesses – he was fighting for his very identity. But with the tide of misfortune rising against him, he felt as though he was drowning, alone and adrift in a vast and uncaring sea.

LUCY'S HEART pounded in her chest as she stood in Maksym's office behind the DJ stand in his South Beach nightclub, HeatWave Lounge. The dim lighting cast eerie shadows on the walls, amplifying her sense of urgency. She fumbled with a small USB key, her fingers slick with sweat. Finally, she managed to insert it into the side of Maksym's laptop and pressed the power button.

The whirring sound of the laptop coming to life seemed deafening in the tense silence that enveloped the room. Lucy held her breath, straining her ears for any sign of Maksym's approach. Just as the screen flickered to life, she heard the distinct sound of footsteps approaching the office door. Panic surged through her veins, and she hastily removed the USB key, dropping it into her purse before scrambling to find an escape route.

But it was too late. The door swung open, revealing Maksym's imposing figure. He froze when he saw Lucy sitting in his office chair, his eyes narrowing in suspicion. "What are you doing here?"

Thinking quickly, Lucy forced a flirtatious smile and leaned back in the chair, trying to appear casual. "Just imagining what it'd be like to be the boss," she said, her voice surprisingly steady despite the fear threatening to overwhelm her. "Do you think I could ever be in charge of something one day?"

Maksym's gaze remained suspicious for a moment longer before he smirked and crossed the room, taking a seat in the visitor chair opposite Lucy. "Why not?" he replied, his voice smooth and unsettling. "In fact, your dream could come true today if you wanted."

Lucy swallowed hard, her mind racing to decipher his cryptic words. "What do you mean?" she asked, struggling to maintain her composure.

Maksym leaned back in the chair, his eyes fixed on Lucy. "I've taken care of the problem with Nollaig nosing around our Tuesday night dive charter boat activities. Our partners found a waterproof box with no tie wraps the other week. So, anyway... I need someone to run Seize The Deep and Sea Spell Diving."

Lucy's heart skipped a beat, and she felt her blood run cold. She stared at Maksym, stunned and speechless, wrestling with the gravity of what he was proposing.

"Max," Lucy began hesitantly, her voice trembling slightly. "I can't run Noll's businesses. I'm only 24 years old and don't know the first thing about running a business."

She paused, searching Maksym's face for any sign of understanding. "Besides, you need me as a scuba diver on Tuesday evenings to switch the Blue Dragon boxes underwater."

Maksym leaned forward, his gaze sharp and authoritative. "Lucy, you're a scuba diver. You'll figure out how to manage the dive businesses." His tone softened for a brief moment. "The only part of your job that I care about is how you'll manage the cash deposits I'll provide to you."

He straightened up in his chair, lifting a hand to silence any further protests from Lucy. "For the rest, just find someone internally and make that person executive vice-president. That E.V.P. will actually run the dive activities I don't care about."

Defeated, Lucy nodded, unable to formulate any response. Maksym pulled out his phone and dialed a number without breaking eye contact with her.

"John, it's Maksym," he spoke into the phone. "I need you to do whatever paperwork is necessary to make Lucy Grayson the new President and CEO of Seize The Deep and Sea Spell Diving. Also, notify the staff at these two dive businesses, including the security guards, that she's the new boss."

As Maksym ended the call, he stood up, and Lucy mirrored his movements. Smirking, he extended his hand to her, and she hesitantly shook it.

"Congratulations, Miss Grayson," he said, his voice cold and calculating. "You're now the boss of something."

"Thank you," Lucy stammered, her mind reeling from the sudden turn of events.

"Now, get out of my office," Maksym ordered, and she obeyed without question.

As Lucy left the room, her mind raced with thoughts of the immense responsibility now placed upon her shoulders. She thought about Noll's predicament, his life crumbling around him, and her own role in it all. The weight of her new position pressed down on her, threatening to crush her spirit. But then a smile showed up on her lips.

"Cash deposits? I guess I'll have first-hand knowledge of money laundering. Finally!"

Noll slumped into the plush leather chair in his lawyer's office, his face a picture of despair. The room was still dimly lit, casting ominous shadows across the polished mahogany desk that separated him from his legal counsel. He could hear the relentless ticking of the clock on the wall, each second seeming to echo the mounting pressure he felt.

"Look, Mr. Durand," the lawyer said, shuffling through the pile of documents in front of him. "I wish you'd consulted me before signing these agreements with Mr. Byrne."

"Tell me what it all means," Noll pleaded, his voice cracking with anxiety.

"Simply put," the lawyer began, adjusting his glasses as he scanned the shareholder agreement, "Maksym Byrne is the Chairman of the Board, and he has sole and final authority over who gets appointed as President and CEO of both companies."

Noll's eyes widened, his breath hitching in his throat. The crushing weight of this revelation threatened to suffocate him. His life was falling apart around him, and this news seemed like the final straw.

"Fine, so let's change the Chairman?" Noll asked, desperate for even a glimmer of hope.

The lawyer shook his head, his expression somber. "It can only be done by a majority vote of the board. Considering the board consists of you, Maksym, and his lawyer, I'm afraid you don't stand a chance of removing him from his position."

Noll clenched his jaw, a wave of despair washing over him. He shifted gears, now focused solely on the financial implications of his situation. "What about my share in the companies? Will I still receive money? I have a family to feed."

"Dividends are paid at the board's sole discretion," the lawyer explained, his tone apologetic. "In other words, you'll only get dividends if Maksym and his lawyer want to pay them to the shareholders. I wouldn't count on it."

Noll felt a cold shiver run through him, his heart pounding in his chest. The enormity of his predicament was almost too much to bear.

His business partner, Maksym, had betrayed him, and now he faced losing everything he had worked so hard to build.

"So what can I do? Sell my shares?" Noll asked, his voice barely above a whisper.

Noll slumped in his chair, feeling the weight of the world on his shoulders. His lawyer leaned back in his own seat, shaking his head. "Mr. Durand, considering that dividends are at Mr. Byrne's discretion, your shares are essentially worthless. No one would buy them knowing they might never see a return."

The words stung like salt in a fresh wound, and Noll couldn't help but feel even more defeated. The lawyer, sensing Noll's despair, continued with a stern tone. "I can't stress this enough – in the USA, you should never, ever sign anything without consulting a lawyer first."

Noll remembered wanting to consult a lawyer, but the documents seemed perfect. Then he thought about his dive boats being used for drug and gun smuggling and how Maksym likely wanted to use the businesses for money laundering. He opened his mouth to bring this up again with his lawyer but hesitated. He didn't have any solid evidence – anything tangible to show.

"Look," the lawyer said, seeing the frustration etched on Noll's face. "You mentioned Mr. Byrne using your dive businesses for illegal activities. If you find proof, take it to the authorities. But that's beyond corporate law. I can't help you there."

"Alright," Noll muttered, his voice barely audible. He knew it wouldn't be easy to gather evidence against Maksym, but it was the only option left. Rising from his chair, Noll thanked the lawyer and left the office, his thoughts spinning like a whirlpool, pulling him deeper into the abyss of despair and uncertainty.

The first thing Noll did once in his car was put Leonard Cohen's song on. "Everybody knows the war is over. Everybody knows the good guys lost. Everybody knows the fight was fixed. The poor stay poor, the rich get rich."

But it didn't have to be this way. "Lucy needs to arrest this guy. That's all!"

CHAPTER 15
SUSAN

NOLL'S KNUCKLES turned white as he gripped the steering wheel of his car, pulling into the parking lot of HeatWave Lounge. The warm Miami evening was thick with humidity, intensifying the storm brewing inside him. He needed to confront Maksym, to regain control over his life and protect himself and his family.

Exiting his car, he approached the club's entrance. A line of young people snaked around the building, their laughter and excitement a stark contrast to Noll's turmoil. With determination, he showed the security guard the pass Maksym had given him months ago – a promise that he would always have access without waiting in line.

The burly security guard looked at the pass and then back at Noll, his eyes narrowing. "The boss doesn't want to see you," he said gruffly, snatching the pass from Noll's hand and pocketing it.

"Wait, what?" Noll stammered, feeling the weight of the guard's indifference. "I need to speak with Maksym."

"You heard me." The guard turned back to face the queue, effectively dismissing Noll.

Frustration bubbled up like lava in his chest, but Noll bit back any further words. He returned to his car, slamming the door behind him. He dialed Maksym's number, only to be greeted by an impersonal voicemail system. His voice cracked as he left a message, the anger barely contained. "Maksym, I don't care about your illegal activities anymore. We can find a way to help each other, right? Just call me back."

Hanging up, Noll's thoughts raced. A moment later, he called back, leaving another message. "If you noticed tie wraps cut on an underwater Blue Dragon box full of 50 caliber guns, that was me. So, it's best for both of us if you meet with me before I bring that info to the authorities."

Noll ended the call, the silence in the car feeling like a suffocating blanket. He knew Maksym held all the power, but desperation forced him to play his hand. He just hoped it would be enough to protect himself and those he loved from the consequences of Maksym's dark empire.

Noll sat in his car, the engine idling softly as he stared at the unfamiliar vehicle parked beside his wife's. The streetlights cast an eerie glow on the quiet suburban neighborhood, shadows playing tricks on his mind. He knew he should go inside, but a nagging feeling held him back. Memories of Susan's words echoed in his ears, telling him she expected him not to have any issue if she ever brought another man into their marital bed.

The crushing weight of Maksym's betrayal and the uncertainty surrounding his health made it impossible for Noll to think straight. With a heavy sigh, he switched off the engine and stepped out of the car. The night air was still thick with humidity, suffocating him as he walked towards the house.

As he entered, the silence that greeted him offered no comfort. He crept past the master bedroom, straining to hear any sounds from within. Hearing nothing, he hesitated before making his way to the guestroom, where his wife had banished him. He collapsed onto the bed, still clothed.

THE NEXT MORNING, Noll woke up feeling groggy and disoriented. He rubbed his eyes, trying to shake off the lingering tendrils of his restless dreams. With a deep breath, he got up and headed for the bathroom, hoping a shower would wash away the fog clouding his mind.

As he approached the bathroom, the door swung open, revealing a naked man smirking at him. Noll froze, his eyes briefly drawn to the man's impressive endowment before getting a wild feeling that he recognized the man from somewhere. Their eyes locked, but no words were exchanged as the man sauntered past him.

Tension coiled in Noll's stomach as he took his shower, his thoughts racing. Who was this man, and why did he look so familiar? He hurriedly dressed and went to the kitchen, determined to make breakfast for his two kids as always.

"Morning, Daddy!" his children chirped as they entered the kitchen. He forced a smile onto his face, trying to hide his turmoil from them.

"Good morning," he replied, focusing on preparing their breakfast. Just as he was setting the plates on the table, his wife and her boyfriend walked into the kitchen.

"Morning," Susan said casually, as if nothing was amiss. Her eyes flicked between Noll and the man, a hint of satisfaction in her gaze.

"Morning," the man echoed, his smug grin never leaving his face.

Noll clenched his jaw, struggling to keep his emotions in check. For now, he had to play along and pretend everything was normal – at least, in front of the kids. Susan stood by her boyfriend, a smug expression on her face. "Two coffees, please," she said, with a hint of condescension.

"Sure," muttered Noll, clenching his jaw and doing his best to maintain his composure. He handed them their coffees before turning his attention to cooking eggs. He could feel their eyes on him, scrutinizing his every move.

"Scrambled for me," Susan requested. "And make sure they're fluffy."

"Of course," Noll replied, swallowing his pride. He focused on the eggs, whisking them vigorously as he tried to ignore the man's presence.

"Nothing for me, thanks!" the stranger declared as casually as if he were talking to a waiter in a diner.

Once everyone had been served, the kids finished eating and left the table to play in another room. Noll finally allowed himself to look at the stranger who had invaded his home, the man who had slept with his wife in his bed and now sat comfortably at his kitchen table. As their gazes met, a flicker of recognition passed through Noll's mind.

It hit him like a tidal wave – this was the man driving Maksym's cube truck the night he followed it, the man he'd seen moments before Lucy saved his life by killing another. And, oh my god, it was the same man who had followed him on i95 after his first visit to the HeatWave Lounge. What the hell was he doing in his house?

"Enjoying your breakfast?" the man asked nonchalantly, seemingly entertained by Noll's obvious internal turmoil.

"Delicious, thank you," Noll managed to say without choking on the words.

Susan got up from the table, leaving her half-eaten meal behind. "I'm going to get ready for Blindcreek Beach," she announced, planting a lingering kiss on her boyfriend's lips before disappearing down the hallway.

"Listen," the man began, leaning in closer to Noll. "Mr. Byrne doesn't want to hear from you ever again. Got it?"

Noll's anger boiled within him, but he couldn't bring himself to lash out. The man was built like a football player, and any attempt at violence would be futile. Instead, he held his tongue and clenched his fists beneath the table, seething with rage and frustration.

Susan's boyfriend leaned back in his chair, studying Noll with a predatory gaze. "You know, a real man would accept when he has lost," he said in a low, menacing tone.

Noll clenched his jaw, trying to suppress the rage boiling within him. "So, you followed me here after my first meeting with your dirty scumbag of a boss?"

The man smirked. "Your wife was a fun target! Hope I don't need to have... other targets, you know?"

Noll didn't dare respond, suddenly fearing that any sign of defiance might put his children at risk.

And sure enough, after a brief silence, Susan's boyfriend continued, "Otherwise, you could lose even more." His eyes flicked toward the hallway where the kids had disappeared, and Noll's heart twisted painfully in his chest. The threat was clear.

"Your kids are charming, though," Susan's boyfriend added with a smirk. "Well-brought-up. She must be a good mother."

Before Noll could find the words to reply, Susan re-entered the kitchen, her short, thin sundress leaving little to the imagination. It was obvious she wasn't wearing a bra – something Noll hadn't seen her do in years. He also remembered suggesting a visit to a nude beach once, only for Susan to shoot down the idea without hesitation. Now, she was going to Blindcreek Beach with her new boyfriend, a well-known nude beach destination. The irony stung.

"Are you two done chatting?" Susan asked, her voice dripping with condescension. She looked between Noll and her boyfriend, a cruel smile playing on her lips.

"Of course, darling," her boyfriend replied smoothly, standing up from the table. He placed an arm around Susan's waist and pulled her close, pressing a lingering kiss to her temple.

"Good," Susan said, her gaze never leaving Noll's face. "You'll have to babysit today, Noll."

Noll swallowed hard, feeling the weight of humiliation settling over him like a suffocating shroud. It was becoming increasingly difficult to see a way out of the darkness that enveloped his life.

In the doorway, Susan's eyes locked onto Noll's, a wicked smile playing on her lips as she leaned in and pressed her mouth against her boyfriend's again. The kiss was long and passionate, clearly designed to provoke Noll and remind him of what he had lost. As they kissed, Susan's boyfriend casually reached down and grabbed her ass, his fingers digging into the fabric of her sundress. Without breaking their embrace, he lifted the hem of her dress to reveal that she was not wearing any panties, his hand now gripping her bare flesh.

Noll stood there, speechless and fuming, unable to tear his gaze away from the blatant display of dominance. He couldn't understand how his life had spiraled so far out of control, each day delivering another crushing blow to his already battered spirit.

When the kiss finally ended, Susan's boyfriend released her, his smug expression never leaving his face. He walked over to Noll's kids. "Hey, you two," he said, his voice dripping with false warmth. "Be careful today, okay? I really hope nothing bad happens to you."

The thinly veiled threat hung in the air like a cloud of poison, making Noll's heart race. He knew Susan's boyfriend was there to keep an eye on him, to ensure he didn't interfere with Maksym's plans. But to use his own children as leverage – that was a level of cruelty Noll hadn't anticipated.

"I guess there's no honor left in this world."

With no other option, Noll spent the day with his kids. While it was a welcome distraction from the chaos that had enveloped his life, it also painfully reminded him of everything he stood to lose.

As he prepared lunch for them, he found himself thinking about the cost of groceries and the mounting bills he would struggle to pay without a steady income. His net worth had plummeted to zero with the loss of his dive businesses, and he had no idea how he would provide for them in the days, weeks, and months to come.

The only asset Noll still owned was the house, but even that felt like it was slipping through his fingers. He wondered what Susan would say when he would tell her they had no more revenue, that their comfortable life was crumbling around them.

As Noll's mind raced with worries and fears, he held onto the one thing that kept him going – the love he had for his children. It was a light in the darkness, a reason to keep fighting, even when it seemed like every force in the universe was against him. But as the sun moved down and the shadows lengthened, Noll couldn't help but feel that the light was growing dimmer, and the darkness was closing in.

Susan breezed through the front door, a satisfied smile plastered on her face. Noll watched as she kicked off her sandals and spun around, her sundress swishing around her legs.

"God, that was fun!" she exclaimed, her eyes twinkling. "I never thought I'd enjoy a nude beach so much! You were right, honey! But I guess a well-hung man... You know? Nice scenery!"

Her words were like daggers, but Noll refused to let them penetrate his resolve. He clenched his jaw and remained silent, tightening his grip on the back of the couch.

"Speaking of which," Susan continued, her tone shifting from gleeful to accusatory, "who is Lucy Grayson?"

Noll's heart stuttered in his chest, and he struggled to find his voice. "What do you mean?"

"Lu. Cy. Gray. Son," she repeated slowly, enunciating each syllable with disdain. "You didn't think I'd find out you appointed her as President and CEO of your precious dive businesses? What, is she giving you a hell of a blowjob or something? Why else would you nominate a 20-something blonde bimbo for such a position?"

The accusation left Noll reeling, but he couldn't muster a response. His situation was so desperate that he almost laughed as he started to hum "I Heard It Through The Grapevine" by Creedence Clearwater Revival. "Ooh-ooh, I heard it through the grapevine. Not much longer would you be mine. Ooh-ooh, I heard it through the grapevine. And I'm just about to lose my mind. Honey, honey, yeah."

Susan didn't understand why he was humming that song. Instead, she laughed at him. And without another word, she dropped her sundress to the floor, revealing her naked MILF body underneath. With an air of triumph, she sauntered toward the bathroom, leaving Noll standing there in his own world.

His mind raced as he sank to the floor, staring blankly at nothing. Lucy had been the one to introduce him to Maksym, the man who had taken everything from him. And now, she was running his beloved dive businesses. Was it all just an elaborate con? Was Lucy even a D.E.A. agent?

Noll clenched his fists, his knuckles turning white. The possibility that he'd been played by both Maksym and Lucy was almost too much to bear. He could feel the walls of his life closing in around him, suffocating him with betrayal and loss.

"Damn it," he muttered under his breath, his voice cracking with despair.

CHAPTER 16
THE B WORDS

THE DOOR to the diner creaked open as Lucy stepped inside, scanning the dimly lit room for her boss. She spotted him in a dark corner, nursing a cup of black coffee, his eyes flicking up to meet hers before returning to some papers spread out before him. Lucy approached with a mixture of apprehension and determination, her blonde hair catching the faint light from the neon signs.

"Good morning," she greeted, sliding into the seat opposite him in the booth. Her boss looked up again, offering a tight smile.

"Morning, Lucy. So, what's new?"

"Something came up." Lucy's voice was low and urgent. "Maksym named me President and CEO of Noll's two dive businesses. So, that's fucked up. I can't continue being an undercover agent at his nightclub."

Her boss let out a hearty laugh, shaking his head. "Well, this is great news! It'll be much easier for you to find all the information we need about Maksym's money laundering activities."

Lucy furrowed her brow, considering his words. "I guess you're right. Maksym did specifically say he'd use me for that."

"See? It's perfect," her boss said, taking a sip of his coffee. "Now, relax. You've got this under control."

"Except I have no idea how to manage a business," Lucy admitted, frustration creeping into her voice.

"Relax," her boss repeated, leaning back in the booth. "You should only worry about managing the money laundering activities. Promote someone internally to executive vice-president to actually manage the two businesses."

Lucy's eyes widened; Maksym had used those exact words. For a brief moment, she wondered if her D.E.A. boss had direct contact with Maksym, but she quickly brushed that thought aside. She was young and eager to make her mark in the D.E.A.; she had to play the game, whatever it was.

"Alright," Lucy sighed. "I'll do what I can."

Lucy's boss chuckled, stirring his coffee. "You know, Lucy, you're going to have a great life for a while. With another monkey actually managing the businesses, you'll only have to worry about the money laundering side of things. That means plenty of free time for you to enjoy."

"Except," Lucy interjected, "I'll be getting an official salary as President and CEO of these dive businesses, and Lucy Grayson is just my undercover name. How will that work with my real D.E.A. salary?"

Her boss paused, tapping his fingers on the table before replying. "Well, for now, I want you to give me a resignation letter for your job at the D.E.A. It'll make it easier to manage all this."

"Wait, what?" Lucy frowned, trying to process his words. "Why do I need to do that when my D.E.A. job is under my real name?"

"Trust me, Lucy. It's just temporary," her boss assured her with a smile that didn't quite reach his eyes. "As soon as Maksym's case is closed, I promise I'll re-hire you officially in the DEA. It's normal, kiddo!"

Something about her boss's insistence didn't sit right with Lucy, but she was determined to prove herself within the agency. She swallowed her doubts and nodded hesitantly.

"Alright, if you say so, boss."

As they finished their breakfast, Lucy's boss leaned closer and lowered his voice. "Now, go treat yourself to a nice, expensive car to match your newfound position. You deserve it."

"Really?" Lucy raised an eyebrow, feeling a mix of excitement and suspicion.

"Absolutely." Her boss handed her a business card. "This guy's a friend. He'll make sure the paperwork matches your undercover name. And he'll accept cash when you have some later."

"Hmm... Okay... Thanks," Lucy murmured, taking the card from her boss' hand. She couldn't shake the feeling that she was being played somehow, but for now, she had to trust her boss and play the game.

A FEW DAYS LATER, Lucy sat behind the mahogany desk in the office at the back of Seize The Deep – the office that used to belong to Noll. The room still carried traces of his presence, like the faint scent of his cologne lingering in the air. As she organized some papers, the door creaked open, and an old man with a weathered face and kind eyes entered, carrying a zipped bag.

"Ms. Grayson," he said, his voice gravelly from years of smoking, "why do you still insist on making the daily bank deposits? I could take care of that for you."

Lucy looked up at him and smiled warmly. "You already do so much as Executive VP, Leo. The least I can do is take the risk of carrying cash with me."

Fred shook his head but didn't argue further. He placed the bag on her desk and left the room, gently closing the door behind him. Lucy sighed, her mind racing as she considered the implications of her new daily routine. She opened a closet, revealing a Blue Dragon dry box nestled among wetsuits and dive gear. Her hands trembled slightly as she unlocked the box and lifted the lid, exposing a stack of cash inside.

She took a pile of money from the box and slipped it into the zipped bag before closing the box and relocking it. The weight of her actions settled heavily on her chest, but there was no turning back now. She was in too deep, playing a role that she never envisioned herself taking on.

***

SIERRA AND NOLL sat across from each other at a nearby cafe, the tension between them palpable. Noll's eyes were bloodshot, and his hands shook as he gripped his coffee cup.

"Sierra," Noll began, his voice tense, "you did some work for the D.E.A... for Lucy. Are you still working for that bitch?"

Sierra shifted uncomfortably in her seat. "Yeah, not much. But she had me dig out some stuff about Maksym yesterday. Money laundering stuff."

"Right! Sure! Sounds more like an elaborate con by Lucy and Maksym to steal my dive businesses. And you were part of it. How much did they pay you?"

"Look, Noll," Sierra said, clearly offended. "I only do odd computer... you know, digging... jobs for Lucy. And I don't give a shit about being paid. I was hoping to help get Maksym arrested, fast. To help you. I had no part in anything else."

Noll stared at her, his eyes narrowing as he searched her face for any sign of deception. But Sierra held her gaze, her dark brown eyes filled with sincerity. Despite this, he couldn't bring himself to trust her. He slammed his coffee cup down on the table and stood up abruptly.

"Sure," he spat, his anger boiling over. "Don't expect me to believe a word you say." With that, he stormed out of the cafe, leaving Sierra stunned and hurt.

As he sat in his car, gripping the steering wheel until his knuckles turned white, a single thought echoed through his mind: Had anyone in his life not betrayed him?

AT THE END of the day, Lucy clicked the alarm on and locked the doors of Seize The Deep, glancing around the now-empty parking lot. With a sigh, she made her way to her 911 Sport Classic Porsche, her heels clicking against the asphalt. As she approached her car, another vehicle's door opened nearby, and a man stumbled out, nearly collapsing onto the pavement.

"Lucy! You bitch. Cunt!" Noll slurred, his face contorted with anger and pain. He was very drunk, his breath reeking of alcohol as he staggered towards her.

"Hey, Noll, let's just calm down, okay?" Lucy tried to soothe him, but he wasn't having it.

"Do you even work for the D.E.A.? You were just playing me this whole time?" he accused, his eyes wild. "You and Maksym, stealing my dive businesses… That was a great con! Congrats!"

"Please, Noll, I can explain," Lucy pleaded, hoping to find a way to calm him down.

"Explain? Explain what? That you played me like a fool? That you never intended to arrest that mother fucker?" Noll's voice rose with every word, attracting attention from passersby.

"Look, Noll," Lucy expressed, desperation creeping into her voice, "things are more complicated than they seem. I promise I'll tell you everything, but not here."

"Was sleeping with me part of the con, too?" Noll spat, his face inches from hers. "The night you killed that man to save me… did you even kill him? You were just acting to play me and steal my dive businesses?"

"Of course not, Noll! I saved your life because I care about you," Lucy insisted, her eyes filling with tears. "But I need you to trust me, please."

"Trust you?" Noll scoffed, swaying dangerously on his feet. "You don't know the meaning of that word, fuckin' blonde slut."

Noll's face contorted as he continued his drunken tirade, spitting out his words like venom. "And now Susan, that cold-hearted bitch… must be your twin sister… she's divorcing me! Kicked me out of my own house, and I can't even see my kids!" His voice broke, a raw vulnerability shining through the anger. "I've been sleeping in my car. My damn car!"

Lucy felt her heart twist at the pain in Noll's voice. She knew about his troubles with Susan but hadn't realized how dire the situation had become. "Noll, I'm so sorry," she said softly, reaching out to touch his arm in a futile attempt to offer comfort.

"Sorry?" Noll snarled, flinching away from her touch. "You think 'sorry' will fix everything? You ruined my life! My entire life, gone, because of a blonde bitch!"

"Please, just let me help you," she implored, her eyes pleading. "I didn't want any of this to happen, Noll. I never meant for things to get so out of control."

"Control?" Noll laughed bitterly, his eyes wild as they darted around the dimly lit parking lot. "There is no control anymore. My accountant told me today I have no choice but to file for bankruptcy. Bankruptcy, Lucy! Because of your sick little game!"

With those words, Noll's legs gave way beneath him, and he crumpled onto the asphalt, a broken man. Lucy hesitated for a moment before crouching down beside him, her heart heavy with guilt.

"Come on, Noll," she said gently, trying to coax him back to his feet. "You can't stay here. Let me take you someplace safe."

"Safe?" Noll scoffed, making no effort to move. "There's no such thing as safe on this planet."

"Please, Noll," Lucy persisted, her voice soft but insistent. "You're in no condition to drive. Just let me help you."

It took several more moments of pleading, but eventually, Noll relented. With Lucy's assistance, he staggered to his feet and stumbled over to her 911 Sport Classic Porsche, collapsing into the passenger seat.

"Nice car," he slurred, glaring at her through bleary eyes. "Guess crime really does pay, huh?"

Lucy winced at the accusation, knowing it had some truth to it. But she said nothing, simply starting the car and pulling out of the parking lot, determined to get Noll to safety, even if he hated her for it.

Soon after, Nollaig sang Bon Jovi out loud in Lucy's passenger seat, although he could barely pronounce words in his advanced state of drunkenness.

"Shot through the heart, and you're to blame; Darling, you give love a bad name; An angel's smile is what you sell; You promised me heaven, then put me through hell."

The headlights of Lucy's Porsche illuminated the dingy motel sign as she pulled into the parking lot. She could feel the weight of Noll's drunken stupor in the car, his head resting against the window, his breath heavy and labored.

"Here we are," Lucy said, her voice tense with concern.

Noll stirred, blinking groggily at the familiar surroundings. The shady motel where they'd spent that fateful night together loomed before them. He grimaced, a combination of alcohol-induced nausea and bitter memories threatening to overwhelm him.

"Come on, let's get you inside," Lucy urged, helping Noll out of the car and wrapping his arm around her shoulders for support.

"Didn't wanna come back here," Noll slurred, his words barely coherent. "Too many goddamn memories. With a dirty slut."

"Right now, it's the safest place for you," Lucy said quietly, her heart aching with regret.

They stumbled together toward the room where their lives had become so irrevocably intertwined. Lucy fumbled with the key, finally managing to unlock the door and guide Noll inside. The room was musty and dim, an oppressive air of despair hanging over it like a shroud. With great effort, Lucy eased Noll onto the bed, where he collapsed into the lumpy mattress.

Seconds later, his snores filled the air, his body surrendering to the alcohol's sedative effects. Lucy stood there for a moment, looking down at the man she once admired, now lost and broken by the very world she was supposed to be fighting against.

She knew she shouldn't leave him like this, but staying meant putting both of them in danger. Gazing out the window at her gleaming Porsche, she realized the car would attract unwanted attention in this shady part of town. With a heavy heart, she made her decision.

"Goodbye, Noll," she whispered, her voice barely audible over his snores. "I'm sorry."

With one last look at the man who had unwittingly become a pawn in a much larger game, Lucy slipped out of the room and back to her car. As she pulled away from the motel, she couldn't help but wonder just how much more they would all have to sacrifice before their fight was finally over.

CHAPTER 17
A TOOTHBRUSH

NOLL'S EYES FLUTTERED OPEN, the throbbing pain in his temples threatening to split his skull in two. He squinted against the light filtering through the thin curtains of a cheap motel room, its sickly yellow walls peeling and stained, a musty smell permeating every corner. The bed beneath him creaked with every movement, the rough sheets scratching against his skin. His stomach churned, and he clutched it, groaning from the sheer intensity of the hangover.

"Fuck," he muttered under his breath, trying to sit up despite the nausea and dizziness that accompanied each motion. Blinking through blurred vision, he noticed Lucy's naked body sprawled beside him on the bed, her golden hair fanned out across the pillow. She stared at him, her blue eyes sharp and calculating.

"Morning, sunshine," she said, her voice dripping with sarcasm. "You look like hell."

"Jesus Christ, what the fuck happened?" Noll asked, his mind racing as he tried to piece together the events of the previous night. He remembered drinking – heavily – but beyond that, everything was a hazy blur.

"And smell like shit." Lucy laughed, a wicked smile playing at the corners of her mouth. "Well, you got absolutely plastered, called me every name in the book… you couldn't decide if I was a bitch, a cunt, or a slut… and then passed out. Real charmer, you are."

"Shit, I don't remember any... most... some..." Noll rubbed his face with both hands as if trying to wake up his memory. "But it sounds about right, considering you ruined my fucking life."

Despite the harsh words, Noll couldn't help but be momentarily distracted by Lucy's beauty: her smooth, tanned skin, the curve of her hips, the swell of her breasts. It was infuriating how effortlessly attractive she was, even in such sordid surroundings.

"Whatever helps you sleep at night, Noll," Lucy retorted, her voice cold and unapologetic. "Just be glad I didn't leave you to drown in your own vomit."

"Thanks for the fucking favor," he snapped, his anger mingling with an unwelcome surge of desire. He turned away from her, trying to focus on anything else – the stained carpet, the peeling wallpaper, the buzzing neon sign outside the window – but her presence was impossible to ignore.

"Get over yourself, Noll," Lucy said, rolling her eyes as she slid out of bed, not bothering to cover her naked body.

Lucy's gaze remained steady on Noll, unflinching as his anger and accusations bounced off her like harmless pebbles. "You need a shower," she simply stated, her voice devoid of emotion. "You seriously stink."

"Thanks for the update," Noll replied sarcastically, the tension between them thick in the air.

"Look, I bought you a toothbrush and toothpaste. They're in the bathroom. Use them," Lucy added, her tone softening slightly as if to ease the heavy atmosphere.

Still pissed off but unable to deny the truth in her words, Noll begrudgingly accepted her suggestion and made his way towards the cramped bathroom. As he turned on the shower, he couldn't help but feel a confusing mix of emotions – anger at Lucy for turning his life upside down, yet an undeniable attraction to her beauty and the fact that she seemed to care about him. The tepid water cascaded down his body, washing away the grime and sweat from the previous night, but not the frustration that lingered within him.

When Noll emerged from the shower, a towel wrapped around his waist, he found Lucy fully dressed. She stood by the window, sunlight casting a halo around her perfect blonde hair. Her jeans hugged her hips and legs like a second skin, while her bare feet were adorned with sexy sandals. A braless tank top accentuated her curves, making it impossible for Noll to look away. For a moment, he forgot the animosity between them, stunned by her radiant beauty.

"Enjoyed your shower?" Lucy asked, a hint of amusement in her voice.

"Better than smelling like a dumpster, I guess," Noll grumbled, realizing he had no choice but to put on the same dirty clothes he'd been wearing the night before. "You could have bought me some deodorant, too, you know."

"Next time," Lucy replied with a nonchalant shrug, her eyes holding a challenge that Noll couldn't decipher.

As he reluctantly dressed, Noll couldn't deny the effect Lucy had on him. Her beauty was almost infuriating, and despite everything, she still managed to make his heart race. But as he pulled on his smelly shirt, the anger resurfaced, reminding him of the chasm that lay between them.

Stepping out of the dimly lit motel room, Noll squinted against the harsh glare of the outside world. The air was thick with the stench of stale cigarettes and rotting garbage, a constant reminder of the filth that surrounded them.

"Should we return the key to the front desk or something?" Noll asked, pausing halfway out the door.

"This is my permanent hideout. Comes in handy sometimes. You know... slut and all!" Lucy replied, her eyes scanning the area. "Use it for now, Noll. Here's the key!"

Noll grunted in response while they made their way across the cracked asphalt toward a beat-up old car parked nearby. As he took the motel room key from Lucy's hand, he looked at her car and hesitated for a moment, trying to recall something from the hazy fog of the previous night.

"Wait! Didn't you have a Porsche?"

Lucy giggled, gesturing at the rough neighborhood around them. "It got stolen," she said, smirking.

Noll's face fell, but before he could say anything, Lucy burst into laughter. "I'm just kidding. I had remorse for leaving you all wasted last night, so I drove the Porsche away and brought back this unique beauty." She patted the rusty hood of the cheap car affectionately.

"Very funny," Noll muttered as they climbed inside. The interior of the car smelled like mold and stale fast food, making him wrinkle his nose in disgust. But it was better than being on the streets, he supposed.

While Lucy drove them to a nearby diner, Noll couldn't help but steal glances at her. Despite everything she'd put him through, she still managed to captivate him. It was maddening.

They slid into a booth in a dark corner of the diner, ordering breakfast and sipping on hot coffee. The warm liquid helped clear some of the cobwebs from Noll's mind as he listened to Lucy speak.

"We're close to closing the file on Maksym, thanks to all the money laundering information I've gathered since becoming President & CEO of your dive businesses," Lucy said, her eyes locked with Noll's.

"Sounds like a light at the end of the tunnel," Noll replied cautiously, stirring his coffee. "But you told me the same thing years ago."

Lucy sighed, her shoulders sagging slightly. "I wasn't working at the D.E.A. years ago! But, yes, I know what you mean. Still, this time, it's different. We're closer than ever."

The future seemed uncertain, but if they could finally put an end to Maksym's reign of terror, maybe there was still hope for something better.

Noll drained the last of his coffee, bitterness lingering on his tongue as he stared at Lucy. "So, let me get this straight," he said, voice heavy with skepticism. "I'm supposed to just trust that you and Maksym didn't con me out of my businesses?"

Lucy's face softened, her eyes filled with understanding. "Noll! I can't change the past. All I can do is try to make things right."

"Right," Noll scoffed. "And how am I supposed to know you're not still in bed with Maksym? How do I know this isn't all just some... I don't know. You getting off stringing me along or something?"

"Because I'm here, trying to help you." Lucy's gaze held his, earnest and unwavering. "We're close, Noll. We just need a little more time."

"Time?" Noll shook his head, frustration mounting. "When will everything be back to normal?"

"Another couple of weeks, at least," Lucy replied, her voice cautious. "My boss told me he needs that much time, even though he already has all the information he needs."

"Two more weeks of this hell?" Noll sighed, running a hand through his salt-and-pepper hair. "I don't know if I can take it any longer."

"We'll get through this together," Lucy said softly, her hand reaching across the table to cover his.

The silence that followed their heated exchange seemed to linger, thick and heavy in the air. Noll found himself staring at the empty cup of coffee before him, lost in his thoughts about Maksym, Lucy, and the tangled web they had woven together. The diner's dim lighting and worn vinyl booths added to the weight on his shoulders, making it nearly impossible to shake off the feeling that he was sinking deeper into a world he couldn't escape.

"Hey," Lucy said finally, her voice soft but insistent. "I had an idea… last night… while listening to a snoring orchestra."

Noll looked up, meeting her earnest eyes. "What?"

"Let's go on a dive trip together, just for a week or so," she suggested, her gaze holding his. "I don't really have any more information to gather on Maksym, anyway. Just gotta wait for my boss. For something."

"Are you crazy?" Noll scoffed, shaking his head. "I'm not in the mood for a fun vacation, Lucy. I have no place to sleep, and my life is falling apart around me. A dive trip won't fix any of that."

"Exactly," she replied, her words carefully chosen. "You need a break, Noll. You need to clear your head and just breathe for a little while. And why not a bed in a tropical paradise? On me."

He hesitated, wanting to resist her logic but finding it increasingly difficult. The thought of escaping the chaos, even for a short time, was undeniably tempting. But there were still too many unanswered questions.

"How would that work out with your bosses? Maksym and the D.E.A. – the two mother fuckers?" he asked, his eyebrows furrowing as he considered the potential complications.

"Let me worry about that," Lucy assured him. "But neither of them should know we went on a trip together. We'll book flights from an airport on Florida's west coast, and I'll travel under a different name."

"An alias?" Noll sighed, running a hand through his hair. "What if we get caught?"

"Caught by who?" she asked. "Nobody really cares about you anymore. I mean... Sorry! Just the way it is. And I simply need to be careful with my cover."

He sat back in the booth, considering her proposal. The weight of everything that had happened pressed down on him, making it difficult to breathe. Maybe a week away from it all would help clear his mind.

"Alright," he finally agreed, though his voice was still laced with hesitation. "Let's do it. But remember, Lucy, I don't trust you."

"Understood," she nodded, a hint of relief in her expression. "Nothing will go wrong, I promise. We'll get out of here, clear our heads, and come back ready to face whatever challenges are waiting for us."

Noll started humming a U2 song. "It's all right, it's all right, it's all right; She moves in mysterious ways, yeah." He could only hope she was right.

THE NEXT DAY, the shadows cast by the towering buildings enveloped Maksym's sleek McLaren, which was parked in a dark back alley. Inside, Maksym drummed his fingers impatiently on the steering wheel as he listened to Lucy's D.E.A. boss, who sat in the passenger seat.

"Lucy is under control, Max," the D.E.A. boss said, trying to sound confident. "You've got nothing to worry about."

Maksym's eyes narrowed, not entirely convinced. "I don't like uncertainties, especially when it comes to my business."

"Listen," the D.E.A. boss leaned in, his voice low and steady. "Lucy isn't even an official D.E.A. employee anymore. If the F.B.I. or A.T.F. gets too close, we can blame everything on her. She'll be our scapegoat."

He let out a chuckle, which sounded more like an ugly cough. "How do you think she can afford a Porsche, Sir?" he asked as if talking to a third person who wasn't there. "She's a dirty ex-D.E.A. agent. And you still have her on camera, killing your man, right? Lucy is our get-out-of-jail-free card, Max."

Maksym smirked at the thought, but his suspicion lingered. "Fine, but why is she taking a week off? What's she up to?"

The D.E.A. boss hesitated, then admitted, "I don't know, but I'll find out. Just give me some time, Max. I promise I'll keep her in line."

"Make sure you do." Maksym's voice was laced with warning and menace. "You know I don't like... tolerate... surprises."

"Understood." The D.E.A. boss nodded, his face a mixture of fear and determination.

As the engine of the McLaren roared to life, Maksym couldn't shake the feeling that there was something he wasn't being told—an unease that gnawed at him beneath his carefully cultivated confidence. He glanced at the man beside him, wondering how far he could trust a government agent tangled in webs of corruption and deceit.

In this dark, oppressive world, trust was a luxury that few could afford.

CHAPTER 18
BONAIRE

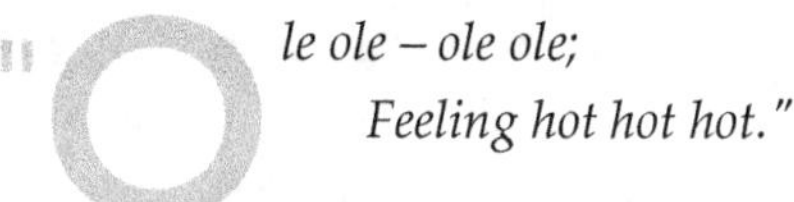

le ole – ole ole;
  Feeling hot hot hot."

NOLL EYED the bustling Orlando airport as he stood in line for check-in, feeling a pang of annoyance at the chaos surrounding them. When it was finally their turn, Noll glanced over just in time to catch Lucy identifying herself as Mia something—her words drowned out by the surrounding chatter. His brow furrowed, trying to piece together her name and intentions.

Noll couldn't shake his curiosity as they made their way through security. "Is Mia your real name?" he asked, searching her blue eyes for answers.

"Who I am is who I am," she replied with a coy smile, flipping her long blonde hair over her shoulder. "A name is just a name."

Noll wasn't sure what to make of her response, but he didn't have much time to dwell on it as the boarding had already started, and they had to run. As they settled into their seats, he couldn't resist questioning her choice of airports. "Why Orlando? I thought we were leaving from the West Coast… of Florida, that is."

"More tourist traffic here," Lucy said, shrugging nonchalantly. "Easier to blend in. And more flights, obviously."

Later, after they landed in Bonaire, the shuttle from Bonaire Pink Scuba — a dive resort — picked them up. Lucy and Noll checked into an apartment on the resort grounds, and the staff assigned them a pickup truck for the week. A friendly staff member explained the diving arrangements: their package included unlimited scuba cylinder refills at the fill station, unlimited shore diving around the island, and four half-days of boat diving.

"I always loved Bonaire," Noll remarked, forcing a smile despite the turmoil inside him. He knew he needed this escape, but as he looked at Lucy, he felt a mix of attraction and distrust. The more time they spent together, the more Noll found himself questioning her motives and wondering what secrets she was hiding.

As they unpacked in their apartment for the week, Noll noticed that it had only one bedroom and one bed. He raised an eyebrow but didn't have time to question it because, barely a second after they were inside, Lucy stripped completely naked, tossing her clothes carelessly on the floor. Only then did she open her suitcase and pull out a tiny bikini.

"Get in your bathing suit," she urged Noll with a mischievous grin, "We're going for a night dive from shore."

Noll hesitated for a moment as he took in Lucy's confident nudity. He wanted to hate her, to blame her for his current misfortunes, but there was something about her free-spirited nature that he found undeniably sexy.

"Alright," he agreed reluctantly, changing into his bathing suit while trying not to stare too obviously at the perfect body of a young blonde woman.

Once they were changed, Lucy and Noll loaded two full sets of scuba gear and cylinders into the back of the pickup truck assigned to them. Noll couldn't help but notice that she was driving barefoot. For some inexplicable reason, the sight made his heart race, and he felt a thrill of excitement that he hadn't experienced in a long time.

They drove along the road following the shoreline, looking for a dive site marked by a yellow stone on the side of the road. This method identified all the shore dive sites, making it easy to find a suitable spot for their night dive.

"This one sounds good," Lucy said suddenly, steering the truck toward a small beach access point. The sun had just slipped below the horizon, casting the world around them in a soft, twilight glow.

The pickup's tires crunched over the sand as Lucy parked on the beach, the salty air caressing their skin. She jumped out of the driver's seat and hopped into the back with Noll to prepare for their dive. With a carefree grin, Lucy removed her bikini and began to put on her full wetsuit.

"Wait, why are you taking off your bikini?" Noll asked, trying to keep his voice steady.

Lucy laughed as she zipped up her wetsuit. "I don't like a wet bikini, and since it's evening, there's no sun to dry it after the dive." Her casual attitude about being nude momentarily disarmed Noll's frustrations, and he found himself smiling at her candidness while humming a tropical song by The Merrymen. "Ole ole – ole ole; Feeling hot hot hot."

They both geared up and walked towards the shoreline, fins in hand.

As they entered the water, Noll couldn't help but be taken aback by the beauty that surrounded them. The underwater world was like a paradise compared to the hell he faced on land – a welcome escape from the turmoil of his life.

Swimming side by side, they descended through the crystal-clear water, a vibrant tapestry of marine life unfolding before them. Coral gardens teemed with colorful fish while sea turtles lazily chewed on seagrass nearby. Rays glided gracefully across the sandy floor, and schools of shimmering fish darted through the crevices between coral formations.

Noll marveled at the underwater spectacle, a sense of peace washing over him. Here, in this realm mostly untouched by human greed and corruption, he could forget about Maksym, his legal troubles, and the heartache that awaited him on the surface.

As they swam deeper, Noll caught sight of an octopus camouflaged against a rocky ledge. It shifted its colors and texture, blending seamlessly with its surroundings. In that moment, Noll felt a connection to the creature – both of them trying to adapt and survive in an ever-changing, hostile world. Lucy, sensing Noll's fascination, gestured toward the octopus with a hand signal, her eyes full of excitement. Noll nodded in appreciation, grateful for this temporary reprieve from his problems.

They continued exploring the underwater realm, exchanging hand signals to communicate as they swam through a labyrinth of coral archways and swim-throughs. Mesmerized by the world beneath the waves, Noll allowed himself to be immersed in the magic of the ocean, embracing the solace it offered him.

As they drifted deeper into the underwater world, Noll felt a sudden tug on his hand. Turning to see Lucy beside him, her eyes twinkling with mischief, he realized she had taken hold of his fingers. They swam hand-in-hand, exploring the vibrant coral reefs and observing the myriad of marine life that called it home. At this moment, their connection transcended words as they communicated solely through touch and subtle gestures.

At one point, Lucy caught Noll's gaze and motioned towards her regulator. He watched in confusion as she removed it from her mouth and edged closer to him. It dawned on him that she intended to kiss him, and without hesitation, he followed suit, pulling out his own regulator. As their lips moved closer together, however, their masks proved to be an obstacle.

Chuckling silently at the situation, they each took a breath from their regulators before carefully removing their masks. Eyes locked, they leaned in once more, finally allowing their lips to meet amidst the saltwater. The taste of the ocean mingling with the warmth of Lucy's lips sent shivers through Noll's body, igniting a spark within him that had been dormant for far too long.

When their night dive came to an end, they reluctantly surfaced and made their way back to shore. As they removed their fins and walked toward the pickup truck, Noll couldn't help but feel a sense of loss at leaving the sanctuary of the ocean behind. Climbing into the back of the truck, they began the process of changing out of their scuba gear, making sure to keep the sand away from their equipment.

"Man, that was incredible." Noll's voice was tinged with awe as he peeled off his wetsuit. "I can't remember the last time I felt so… alive."

Lucy grinned at him, her eyes filled with genuine happiness. "That's what diving does for me, too, Noll. It's like an escape from everything else in life. For a little while, it's just you, the ocean, and all its amazing creatures."

Noll nodded, understanding completely what she meant. For all the problems and uncertainties that awaited them back in Miami, those precious moments underwater had given them both a brief, much-needed reprieve.

After shedding their dive gear, Lucy and Noll proceeded to remove their wetsuits. Once she was free of the neoprene, Lucy stood naked in the back of the pickup, her body glistening with seawater. She laughed, a sound that echoed through the still evening air.

Noll couldn't help but stare at her, captivated by the sight of her perfect form and feeling a surge of desire course through him. "Why are you laughing?" he asked, trying to keep his voice steady.

"Because," Lucy replied, gesturing to her damp skin, "I took off my bikini so it would be dry for when we went to have drinks after our dive. But we forgot to bring towels, and now I'm all wet with no sun to dry me off."

Noll chuckled, understanding her predicament. He removed his own wetsuit, letting it fall to the truck bed, and then looked around for a solution. "Here, use my t-shirt," he offered, handing it to her.

"Such a gentleman," Lucy teased as she took his shirt and began drying her body. Noll couldn't tear his eyes away from the sight, watching as she meticulously dried every inch of her skin. When she finished, she handed the now-wet shirt back to him with a smirk. "Guess you'll have to be wet."

"Fine with me," Noll replied, pulling the damp fabric over his head. Lucy slipped her tiny bikini back on, and they climbed into the front seat of the truck. As they drove back to the dive resort, Noll's thoughts continued to drift back to the image of Lucy's naked body in the moon-light, the way her laughter had filled the night, and the undeniable attraction between them.

He wondered if this vacation might just be the escape he desperately needed, even if only for a short while. Away from the chaos of their lives, the dark secrets, and the impending danger, they could find solace in each other's company and the beauty of the underwater world that had brought them together in the first place many months before.

After they parked the pickup truck near their apartment in the dive resort, Lucy stretched her arms over her head and grinned at Noll. "I'm in the mood for a drink. Let's hit the bar," she said, her eyes sparkling with excitement. "On me, of course! I'm your sugar mamma! Wait... I didn't mean... to make fun of..."

"It's okay," Noll interrupted her, unable to resist her enthusiasm. They walked into the open-air resort's bar by the pool, and the atmosphere was buzzing with conversation and laughter. Noll couldn't help but notice that the crowd was mostly old white men like him, and Lucy stood out like a beacon in her tiny bikini and radiant smile. As they stood at the bar, many of the men openly flirted with Lucy, who seemed to take it all in stride.

"Tequila for me, please," Lucy ordered, leaning against the bar counter as she scanned the room. Noll, meanwhile, asked for a mojito, trying not to dwell on his complicated feelings for Lucy.

"You know you're the star of the evening here, right?" Noll remarked, nodding toward the men who were still stealing glances at her.

"Of course," she replied, a playful grin spreading across her face. "You should leave me alone, so I have a chance to pick up a man for the night."

Noll's heart skipped a beat, and he stared at her, shocked by her words. But then Lucy laughed, her eyes twinkling with mischief. "I'm just kidding, old man. Relax."

He shook his head, forcing a smile. He took a sip of his mojito and tried to focus on the present moment, to enjoy this brief respite from the chaos that had become his life. As they sipped their drinks, Noll found himself watching Lucy – the way she interacted with others, the ease with which she drew people in. It was undeniable that she was captivating, but he couldn't shake the nagging feeling that there was so much more to her than met the eye.

"Cheers," Lucy said, raising her tequila-filled glass. "To a week of forgetting our troubles and just enjoying life."

"Cheers," Noll echoed, clinking his glass against hers. As they drank, Noll tried to focus on the moment, on the laughter in Lucy's eyes and the warmth of their companionship. He knew that they couldn't escape the darkness waiting for them back home, but for now, they could pretend – even if it was just for a little while.

"Hey, Noll," Lucy said playfully, leaning in closer to him. "You know what would really show these guys that they're welcome to hit on me?" Her blue eyes sparkled with mischief.

"Uh? What?" he asked, curiosity piqued.

"If you made it clear, you're just... a servant or something. You could, I don't know, kiss my feet right here at the bar?" She giggled, clearly enjoying the outrageous idea while wiggling her sexy bare feet.

Noll raised an eyebrow, then chuckled. "Uh? You're kidding, right?"

"Of course I am," she replied, laughter still dancing in her eyes. "Wait! Maybe not? I'm a goddess, right?"

As Noll looked around the bar and saw the various men eyeing Lucy with interest, he felt a strange sense of freedom wash over him. This was a week away from his troubles, a week where he could forget about his crumbling life and simply be present.

With a shrug, he got down on his knees beside Lucy's barstool. The murmurs of conversation around them died down as people turned to watch. Noll hesitated for a moment, then pressed a slow, deliberate kiss to the top of Lucy's right foot.

As he moved to repeat the action on her left foot, the silence in the bar was palpable. He could feel every eye on him, but for once, he didn't care. This was a moment between him and Lucy, a moment of shared levity amidst the darkness of their lives.

He finished the second kiss and stood up, brushing sand off his knees. Picking up his mojito, he took a sip, a smile playing on his lips.

Lucy's eyes sparkled with excitement as she grabbed Noll's hand

and pulled him along as they left the bar. She walked quickly, her grip firm but gentle, leading them to their apartment. Noll tried to speak, his mind buzzing with questions and confusion, but Lucy silenced him with a finger pressed gently against his lips.

"Shh," she whispered, her voice soft and commanding at once. "No more words for now."

As soon as they stepped inside the apartment, Lucy wasted no time in shedding her bikini, leaving it in a small heap on the floor. Her movements were fluid and graceful, a testament to her comfort in her own skin. Noll couldn't help but wonder if Lucy had grown up in Europe. He had never met an American woman so comfortable in the nude.

At the same time, he felt his heart race, torn between his attraction to Lucy and the lingering darkness of his recent past.

In a smooth motion, Lucy yanked Noll's wet t-shirt over his head, tossing it aside. Her hands reached for his bathing suit, pushing it down until he stood completely naked before her. The air felt cool against his exposed skin, heightening his awareness of every touch and sensation.

Lucy guided Noll onto the bed, urging him to lie on his back. He obliged, watching as she climbed atop him, her body silhouetted against the dim light from the window. Noll opened his mouth to say something, but Lucy silenced him again, her lips pressing softly against his lips as she positioned herself above him.

He could feel the heat of her body as she lowered herself onto him, her vaginal lips devouring his manhood with an intensity that sent a surge of pleasure coursing through him. Noll struggled to contain a moan, biting his lip to obey Lucy's command for silence.

As they moved together, Noll found himself surrendering to the moment, the weight of his troubles temporarily lifted. His thoughts focused solely on the connection he shared with Lucy, the raw passion igniting between them. It was a reprieve from the darkness, if only for a short while.

They communicated through touch and movement alone, their bodies entwined in a dance of unspoken words and shared under-standing.

The world outside their apartment, with all its pain and uncertainty, seemed to fade away as they lost themselves in each other. And for that brief moment, Noll allowed himself to forget the hardships he faced, immersed in the passion that burned between him and Lucy.

CHAPTER 19
THE S WORD

"*No need for confessions now;*
'Cause now you've got the fight of your life."

THE DIM LIGHT of the room cast eerie shadows on the walls as Noll sat in a chair facing the only bed in the apartment he shared with Lucy at the Bonaire Pink Scuba Resort. In the silence, his thoughts swirled like a dark storm cloud. He glanced over at Lucy, her naked body barely covered by the thin sheet. Her peaceful expression was a stark contrast to the turmoil inside him. He stood up and pulled the cover sheet down to Lucy's feet, exposing her completely. The sight of her should have brought him comfort, but instead, it fueled his growing despair.

"Is she a demon hiding in the body of an angel?" Noll thought bitterly. They'd spent a week diving in paradise, yet Lucy had been getting paid the entire time as President & CEO of his two dive businesses – the very businesses Maksym had stolen from him with her help. The realization gnawed at him, and he couldn't shake the question: why the fuck had he spent a week having fun with her instead of killing her?

Memories of their diving adventures around Bonaire played back in his mind. The vibrant colors of the reefs, the fascinating marine life, and the envious stares of other men who wished they could be with the tantalizing blonde. For a brief moment, he'd escaped reality, submerged in a magical underwater world with a model by his side.

But now, as their last night at the resort drew to a close, the cruel truth of what awaited him back home resurfaced. Bankruptcy, no money, no job, no revenue. And having to sign the final papers for a divorce that would leave him without a house while his ex-wife prevented him from seeing his kids. It felt like a slap in the face, pulling him out of the fairy tale and back into a nightmare.

Noll's chest tightened as the weight of his troubles pressed down on him. He stared at Lucy, her beauty a cruel reminder of everything he'd lost and the pain that was still to come. In this murky moment, he couldn't see a way out.

Sitting in the dark, Noll's thoughts continued to spiral, each darker than the last. He couldn't shake the image of his wife cozying up to one of Maksym's thugs, using his own children as pawns in their twisted game. The thought of going through with the biopsy for prostate cancer loomed over him like an executioner's blade; it was yet another cruel reminder that life seemed to be conspiring against him.

"Sierra," he muttered under his breath, his former trusted friend. A bitter taste filled his mouth as he recalled her betrayal, helping Lucy and the D.E.A. screw him. How many more people would stab him in the back before everything was said and done?

His gaze flicked back again to Lucy, her beautiful naked form a sharp contrast to the mounting darkness within him. She would continue to work in his former position at his dive business, driving a Porsche and pocketing a fat salary while he had been sleeping in his car before this trip to Bonaire. It felt like the world was laughing at him, playing a sick joke on his already tattered life.

"Bankruptcy," Noll whispered, the word heavy with despair. It was a dark cloud that would hang over him for the rest of his life. Lucy kept insisting that the D.E.A. would arrest Maksym soon, but how could he trust her assurances? She had been singing the same song for so long. And what would he do without his businesses? He'd never done anything else professionally, and the idea of starting over felt impossible.

Everybody in the industry would point at him as proof that high quality was a dead-end road.

"Dead-end," he murmured, summing up the seemingly endless list of problems that lay ahead. Each issue appeared insurmountable, a fatal blow to any hope he had left. As he stared into the abyss of his future, Noll's depression deepened, and the temptation to give in to his darkest thoughts became almost unbearable.

"Everything's so fucked," he mumbled, his voice barely audible even to himself.

Noll's thoughts swirled like a storm inside his head, dark and unrelenting. He couldn't see any point in flying back home to Miami. Besides, it seemed that nobody needed him anymore.

Driven by despair, he stood up, put on his bathing suit, and left the apartment without a word.

Outside, the tropical paradise of Bonaire was as beautiful as ever, yet it only served to mock him. The gentle breeze, the turquoise waters – they all felt like a cruel joke when contrasted with the turmoil within Noll's heart. He walked towards the pickup truck assigned to them for the week, not caring how much air was left in the scuba cylinder he grabbed.

With his dive gear in tow, Noll continued to the beach. The pristine sand gave way to warm waves lapping at his feet. He waded into the inviting water, fins in hand, ignoring the breathtaking surroundings as if they were nothing but an irritating distraction.

Once the water reached waist-deep, Noll slipped his fins on and began swimming away from shore. The colors of the reef shimmered beneath him, alive with a vibrant underwater world that usually would have enchanted him. But today, the natural beauty held no appeal for him.

As he reached the drop-off – a wall that descended into the dark abyss – Noll submerged himself and hovered just above it. Looking down, he could no longer see the bottom, only darkness. Despite the multitude of colors present on the reef at the top of the wall, the black void below seemed to call out to him, echoing the emptiness he felt within.

Noll's thoughts spiraled further into despair, sinking deeper into the abyss that mirrored his own heart. The swirling currents of self-doubt and hopelessness threatened to pull him under, and he found himself wondering if there was any reason to keep fighting at all. For a moment, he felt the urge to simply let go and allow the darkness to consume him, as it seemed to be doing already.

Noll's thoughts drifted to the one thing he still owned: a large life insurance policy that would benefit his kids, not his wife, if he were to die. The idea settled into his mind like a dark cloud, suffocating any lingering hope. His children would be better off with a million dollars each for college and university than having a useless father sleeping in a car. With that final thought, Noll began his descent into the abyss.

As he looked down, he kept the wall in the corner of his eye to gauge his progress. The darkness loomed larger and more menacing with every meter he sank. But just as he succumbed to the pull of the void, something stopped him from behind. Startled, Noll glanced up and saw Lucy gripping the valve of his scuba cylinder, her eyes wide with determination.

Noll's first instinct was to push her away, but he immediately realized doing so would threaten her safety. She had put air in her buoyancy control vest, known as a BCD, to offset Noll's negative buoyancy, creating a delicate balance between them. If she were to lose her grip on him, her positive buoyancy would send her rocketing to the surface like a cork, putting her life in grave danger. Noll had only wanted to take his own life, not someone else's.

"Lucy..." he thought, his mind racing with confusion and guilt. How had she known what he intended to do? And why on earth was she risking her own life to stop him?

Their eyes locked through their scuba masks, and without words, they shared an understanding. Noll begrudgingly acknowledged that he couldn't go through with his plan while putting Lucy in harm's way. He glanced down at the abyss one last time before nodding his consent to ascend.

With Noll's agreement, Lucy gestured upward, urging him to

follow her lead. They began their ascent together, the darkness below slowly receding as they returned to the vibrant world above.

Just before they broke the surface of the water, Noll was struck by the vibrant colors of the tropical paradise that surrounded them — even in the middle of the night. It was a stark contrast to the dark abyss he'd been so drawn to moments before.

It wasn't until they were swimming back to shore that Noll noticed Lucy's shivering form, her naked body exposed to the elements under her BCD. She had clearly rushed after him without a thought for her own comfort or safety. As they reached the shallows, Noll couldn't help but feel a mix of gratitude and guilt wash over him.

"Lucy," he muttered, barely audible above the sound of the gentle waves lapping at the shore.

"Save it," she spat back, her eyes stormy with anger and concern. They walked in silence towards the pickup, the wet sand squishing beneath their feet.

Once they'd dropped their dive gear into the truck bed, Lucy rounded on Noll, her fury unleashed. "How dare you?" she hissed, her palm connecting with his cheek in a sharp slap. "You selfish bastard! Did you really expect me to go back to Miami with your corpse?"

Noll winced, both from the sting of the slap and the truth behind her words. He hadn't considered the impact his actions would have on her. In his own twisted way, he'd convinced himself that his death would be a gift to those he left behind. But now, with Lucy's tear-filled eyes boring into his, he saw the error in that thinking.

"Lucy, I—"

"Shut up," she cut him off, her voice trembling with emotion. "Just… shut up."

And so he did. He stood there, taking in her anger and disappointment, chastising himself for the pain he'd caused her.

Back in their apartment, Noll stared at the floor, trying to reconcile the searing accusation of selfishness with his own perception of self-sacrifice.

As Lucy's words echoed in his ears, he realized that his intentions had perhaps not been as noble as he'd thought, even though they seemed logical at the time. He was silent, mulling over the disconnect between the reality of then and the reality of now.

"Get your shit together, Noll," Lucy snapped, bringing him back to the present. It was already around 5 AM. Instead of going back to bed, Lucy began packing her belongings, her movements swift and efficient. Noll figured she wanted to stay awake and keep an eye on him.

"Look," she said, her voice authoritative but laced with a hint of vulnerability, "I brought you to Bonaire for a week to help you. So you better be ready to face all your issues when we get back to Miami." She paused, clenching her jaw. "I'm willing to help you, Noll, but you have to want to help yourself first. Fight for what you think is worth fighting for. Am I worth fighting for?"

Her words struck a chord within him, and he found himself at a loss for words. He watched her move about the room, and something inside him shifted. He couldn't just give up—not when someone like Lucy was fighting for him. The weight of everything he faced still pressed down on him, but now, there was a glimmer of hope the universe had communicated to him through a young woman.

As they continued to prepare for their departure, Noll remained silent, reflecting on Lucy's words and the profound impact they'd had on him. Suicide had always been a taboo topic, one that people shied away from discussing openly. And yet, here was Lucy, confronting him head-on about his intentions and forcing him to confront the reality of his actions.

Lucy started singing. "You have been dying since the day you were born. Now you've got the fight of your life."

"Metallica?"

Lucy simply nodded.

"You're skipping verses!"

For the first time in a long while, Noll felt seen, understood, and cared for. It wasn't going to be easy to untangle the mess his life had become, but with Lucy by his side – ready to slap his face if he needed it – he found himself willing to try. He owed it to her—and to himself —to face his demons and fight for a better future.

CHAPTER 20
TWO BEDROOMS

"*Money, money, money;*
Always sunny;
In the rich man's world."

THE BAGGAGE CLAIM area in Orlando was a sea of weary travelers, their faces etched with stress and exhaustion. Noll stood by the carousel, waiting for his suitcase to emerge from the conveyor belt. He glanced over at Lucy, the young woman who had saved his life twice already. Her golden hair framed her face, making her look like an angel among the harried masses. She seemed so out of place among them, as if she belonged to a different world entirely.

Noll couldn't help but notice the unhappy expressions on the faces of those around him. It was as if they were all caught in some relentless cycle of misery, unable to find happiness in their lives. The thought saddened him, and he wondered what it would take for these people – and himself – to find contentment.

As he pondered this, Lucy's phone rang, its shrill tone cutting through the ambient noise. She stepped aside to answer it, her voice barely audible above the din of the airport. Noll strained to hear what she was saying but could only catch fragments of the conversation. He heard her last words while she walked back toward him: "I'll be there with him in five hours or so. See you soon."

Noll felt a flicker of curiosity as to whom Lucy had been talking about but was reluctant to question her. He assumed she meant him and that the estimated five-hour timeframe referred to driving from Orlando to Miami. A self-mocking thought crossed his mind: perhaps Lucy was planning to deliver him to Maksym and had only saved his life in Bonaire because Maksym wanted the pleasure of killing Noll himself. Yet something within him acknowledged the absurdity of such an idea, and he silently chided himself for not thinking more positively.

"Everything okay?" Noll asked as Lucy rejoined him.

"Yep, just checking in," she replied with a casual shrug, her eyes not betraying any hidden motives or information. Noll decided to trust her, for now, focusing on the task at hand – retrieving their luggage and moving forward with whatever awaited them in Miami.

WALKING across the sun-bleached asphalt of the parking lot, Noll glanced at Lucy's Porsche. He hadn't paid much attention to it before, but on that day, he couldn't help but marvel at its sleek design and gleaming paint job. The car practically screamed wealth and power.

"Is this not the most expensive limited edition Porsche ever?" Noll asked, unable to contain his curiosity any longer.

Lucy smirked and nodded in confirmation. "It is."

Noll shook his head in disbelief. He still couldn't fathom how this young woman, who had saved his life twice already, was now the president and CEO of his former dive businesses – all thanks to Maksym's machinations.

"I guess you are making more money than me with my dive businesses!"

Yet, as he stared at the luxurious car, he reminded himself to think positively. This was just another challenge, another obstacle for him to overcome.

"Come on," Lucy said, unlocking the car with a beep. "We've got a long drive ahead of us."

As they cruised down the turnpike from Orlando to Miami, their conversation drifted toward their shared passion for scuba diving. Noll found solace in discussing the various dive destinations they had visited, though he couldn't help noticing the difference in their experience. Being younger, Lucy hadn't ventured to as many exotic locations as he had, but she was determined to catch up.

"Before the ocean starts boiling, I want to visit Tonga and the Great Barrier Reef in Australia," Lucy declared, her eyes sparkling with excitement.

"Those are both fantastic places," Noll agreed, recalling his own adventures beneath the waves. "Tonga has some amazing underwater small, fun caverns, and the Great Barrier Reef... well, it speaks for itself. Although, there are so many tourists..."

"Definitely sounds like a dream trip," Lucy mused, her hands solidly set on the steering wheel.

"Absolutely," Noll said, forcing a smile. He had to admit that the sudden idea that he could travel with Lucy to explore new diving spots was enticing, even in the midst of all the chaos surrounding them. It was a small glimmer of hope, a reminder that life was still worth living – even if it felt like everything around him was falling apart.

"Let's make a pact," Lucy suggested, her voice filled with determination. "No matter what happens, we'll keep pushing forward. We'll explore the world's oceans together and defy the odds."

"Deal," Noll agreed, sealing their pact with a firm nod. This wasn't the end; it was just another chapter in their lives, and they would face it head-on.

While they continued to drive on the turnpike through Fort Lauderdale, Lucy suddenly switched the topic.

"Listen, Noll," she began, her voice firm but gentle. "There are three reasons I'm driving you to Sierra's place."

Noll raised an eyebrow and glanced over at her, intrigued by the change in conversation, but remained silent, opting to hear her out instead of interrupting.

"First, you need a place to sleep that isn't the back seat of your car."

This was true – Noll remembered his muscles protesting from days of uncomfortable rest.

"Second, you shouldn't be mad at Sierra. It was my idea to hire her for the D.E.A., and she only did it to help you – to help get Maksym arrested. She never accepted any payments."

At this revelation, Noll frowned. He had known that Sierra was a hacker who did side gigs. He wondered how Sierra and Lucy got to meet. But he chose to stay quiet and listen to what Lucy had to say.

"Get over it, Noll," Lucy continued, a hint of frustration creeping into her voice. "Sierra is one of the few friends you have left, so don't push her away just because your ego is hurt."

Noll clenched his jaw, replaying in his mind the memory of Lucy slapping his face. The sting of the slap had faded, but its effect lingered. He decided to swallow his pride and accept her words, even if they stung.

"Alright," he muttered, forcing himself to nod in agreement. "I'll try."

"Good," Lucy replied, seemingly satisfied. "Now, the third reason you should be staying at Sierra's place is more important. We... you, Sierra, and me... we need to work together to figure out what the fuck is going on with Maksym, my D.E.A. boss, and our lives."

Noll's curiosity was piqued, but he remained silent, urging her to continue with a simple nod.

"Before we left Orlando's airport, I checked a message from my boss," she said, her voice lowering in intensity. "He told me he needed at least another month before he could do anything about Maksym. In the meantime, he wants me to keep laundering money for that bastard and enjoy my fat salary with little work involved."

Noll couldn't help the anger that bubbled within him at the thought of Maksym continuing his dirty business unchecked. He clenched his fists but remained silent, waiting for Lucy to finish her thoughts.

"Obviously, that doesn't sit well with me," she added, her eyes darkening with determination. "We can't just stand by and let this happen, Noll. There's something fishy. We have to figure things out ourselves."

He looked into her determined eyes and nodded slowly, realizing the gravity of the situation and their shared responsibility to confront it.

"Alright, fine," Noll finally conceded after Lucy finished outlining her reasons for bringing him to Sierra's place. "Yes, ma'am!" he added with mock formality, a wry smile pulling at the corner of his mouth.

Lucy rolled her eyes but couldn't suppress a small grin. For a brief second, their eyes locked, and they shared a moment of amusement at the irony of Noll addressing her as if she were his boss. Then Lucy looked back at the road ahead of them, her expression turning serious once more.

"Y'know, we're pretty progressive; you'll be my boss, I guess, in this venture," Noll joked, trying to lighten the mood. "A young woman like you, in charge of an old guy like me. We're smashing sexism and ageism left and right. Or is it reverse ageism? I don't know."

"Sure," Lucy agreed with a chuckle. "And I suppose it's just a bonus that you could be my father, age-wise. Daddy!"

"Hey now," Noll protested with feigned indignation, though he couldn't help but laugh. "No need to rub it in."

As they drove down A1A, Lucy pulled up to the valet parking in front of a luxurious condo building right on the beach, just a bit north of Miami. Noll's eyes widened in shock as he took in the opulent surroundings. He couldn't believe Sierra lived here – this was a place for millionaires and billionaires, not the friend he thought he knew.

"Is this really where Sierra lives?" he asked, glancing over at Lucy with disbelief.

Lucy hesitated, seemingly unsure whether to answer his question. She finally opted to ignore his question, leaving Noll to wonder what else he didn't know about Sierra and how she had come to afford such a lavish lifestyle.

As they exited the car and Lucy handed the keys to the valet, Noll couldn't help but feel a growing sense of unease.

Lucy led Noll to an exclusive penthouse elevator, and he felt his shock deepen as they stepped inside. The elevator whirred to life, effortlessly carrying them up to the top floor of the luxurious building.

"Get ready," Lucy said with a knowing smile as the doors opened directly into Sierra's penthouse. "I think you're going to be even more surprised."

Noll couldn't have prepared himself for what he saw. Light poured through wall-to-wall, floor-to-ceiling windows, illuminating the vast space before him. In front of his eyes, taunting him, was a gigantic terrace with its own private pool. It was as if he had entered another world – one where opulence and extravagance knew no bounds.

"Welcome," said Sierra, her voice warm yet laced with an edge that hinted at the secrets she kept hidden. She stood near the sparkling pool, her blue hair vibrant against the pale interior.

"Sierra, this place is... incredible," Noll managed, unable to find words that could do justice to the breathtaking view and the sheer luxury surrounding him.

"Thank you," she replied, her eyes twinkling with a mixture of pride and amusement. "All paid for by my daddy!"

"Generous dad," Noll observed.

"Oh! He doesn't know he paid for it!"

Noll opened his mouth to ask what that meant, but something told him to stay quiet. Clearly, Sierra had some secrets, but who didn't?

After they walked through the spacious living area and past the state-of-the-art kitchen, Sierra guided them toward the bedrooms. There were three in total. The first one had been converted into a computer room filled with a variety of computer towers, laptops, and a series of monitors on a giant desk. The next one was decorated in Sierra's unique style, complete with a full bathroom and jacuzzi.

Sierra opened the door to the third bedroom, and Noll couldn't help but let out a low whistle. It was just as luxurious as Sierra's bedroom, with a king-sized bed draped in sumptuous linens and an en-suite bathroom complete with a jacuzzi. The room was bathed in warm light from a chandelier above, casting a cozy glow on the plush carpet below.

"Wow, this is amazing," Noll murmured. "I'd love to stay here."

"Actually, Noll, I'm sorry, but this room isn't available for you," Sierra said apologetically. "You should find one of the many living room couches to be comfortable." She turned to Lucy, who had been quietly observing them, and addressed her directly. "Lucy, you should use this room so we can work more actively on our project."

Lucy stared at the opulent space, her eyes wide with disbelief. "No, no, I can't stay here. I can't have them find out I'm with you and Noll," she objected. But Sierra ignored her protests, determined that her new friend would have a comfortable place to sleep and work during their time together.

"The only thing is," Sierra added, "you shouldn't come here with your Porsche anymore. The D.E.A. and Maksym could easily track you that way."

Lucy's face paled as she realized her mistake. "You're right. I shouldn't have taken it to Orlando's airport, either. I'll go get rid of it now."

As Lucy left to take care of the car, Noll seized the opportunity to ask Sierra about her wealth. "So, your dad is so rich that he didn't even notice paying for this?" he inquired, gesturing to the stunning penthouse around them.

But Sierra remained evasive, her eyes flicking away from his. "It's complicated," she replied cryptically. The air between them was thick with unspoken secrets, making him wonder what else she was hiding from him.

"Alright," he said slowly, not wanting to push her too far. "I guess we'll have plenty of time to catch up on each other's news while we're working together. And thanks for your help!"

Sierra simply nodded. And as Noll searched her face for any hint of the truth behind her mysterious fortune, she offered no further clues – only a tantalizing enigma that would continue to haunt him in the days to come.

THE SOUND of the elevator door closing echoed through the penthouse as Lucy returned, her face weary from the long day. "Got rid of the

Porsche," she announced, collapsing onto one of the luxurious armchairs.

"Good girl," Sierra said, glancing at the clock. It was late, and they all looked exhausted. "We should get some sleep."

Noll nodded in agreement, surveying the spacious living room. He selected an oversized couch near the floor-to-ceiling windows and began arranging the cushions into a makeshift bed. Sierra quickly handed him a pile of bedsheets and a pillow.

"Night, Noll," Lucy called softly, heading to her new bedroom. Sierra followed her, and soon, the sounds of hushed conversation drifted from behind the closed door.

As Nollaig settled down, the twinkling city lights outside seemed to mock his current situation—once a successful businessman, now reduced to sleeping on a friend's couch. Looking around, he started humming along with an old Abba song: "Money, money, money; Always sunny; In the rich man's... woman's world."

Meanwhile, in Lucy's room, the two women sat on the edge of the plush bed, their voices low. Lucy giggled, a mischievous glint in her eyes. "I wonder how long Noll will last on that couch before trying his luck in one of our bedrooms?"

Sierra laughed, shaking her head. "You think so? I don't know..."

"Come on, boys will be boys," Lucy said with certainty.

"Well, men have a thing for blondes—you'll probably have a visitor before I do."

"Maybe you're not entirely right about that," Lucy countered, her tone more serious. "When Noll looks at me, I see lust. But when he looks at you... I see love."

Sierra raised an eyebrow, incredulous. "Love? You've got to be kidding."

"Trust me, there's a difference," Lucy insisted, her expression earnest.

"Well," Sierra sighed, "he's got enough problems on his plate without adding love to the mix."

"Maybe, but sometimes love has a way of sneaking up on you when you least expect it." Lucie yawned and stretched, signaling the end of their conversation. "Goodnight, Sierra."

"Goodnight, Lucy." Sierra stepped out into the dimly lit hallway. She couldn't help but ponder Lucy's words as she closed the door behind her. Love? She didn't want that to become an issue. But as sleep beckoned, she pushed those thoughts away for another day, leaving only the enigmatic dance of shadows on the wall.

CHAPTER 21
THREE DOWN

NOLL LAY in a sterile hospital room, his arm tethered by the IV drip. The antiseptic smell filled his nostrils as he stared at the featureless ceiling. The door opened, and Lucy and Sierra stepped inside, their faces lighting up with relief.

"Thank god you're okay," Lucy said, leaning down to place a gentle kiss on Noll's forehead. Sierra followed suit, a genuine concern etched on her punk-rock face.

"Hey, it wasn't life-threatening," Noll chuckled weakly, trying to lighten the mood. "It's just that now, I won't be able to create life."

The friends exchanged glances, knowing that Noll was attempting to mask the deeper pain and vulnerability he felt.

At that moment, the doctor entered the room, his white coat billowing behind him like a cape. He hesitated when he saw Lucy and Sierra, wondering if they should leave for privacy.

"No secrets here," Noll insisted, nodding towards the two women. "They know everything."

The doctor smirked at the implication of Noll's living arrangements. Clearing his throat, he got down to business. "The operation went well. We took samples all around the prostate to check for cancer, and there was no sign of it anywhere else. I'm pretty confident that we got all of it."

Everyone in the room exhaled a collective sigh of relief, gratitude washing over them. Noll looked between Lucy and Sierra, appreciating the unwavering support these two women had given him throughout this tumultuous journey.

The doctor adjusted his glasses and studied Noll for a moment before speaking. "You know, you're quite lucky," he began, causing Noll to let out a strange, mirthless chuckle.

"Feels like a strange thing to say," Noll remarked, still reeling from the emotional rollercoaster of the past few months.

"Men usually have prostate cancer at a much older age," the doctor continued. "Because you got it at a younger age, it was easier to operate on you and remove the prostate. You should be back on your feet in no time." He glanced at the chart in his hand. "In fact, you can be discharged from the hospital this afternoon."

Noll's eyebrows raised in surprise. "Wow, that's... sooner than I expected."

"Your body is resilient," the doctor assured him. "Just make sure you take it easy and follow the post-op instructions."

As if sensing something else was coming, Lucy and Sierra exchanged glances, their concern palpable. The doctor hesitated, looking at the two women again before turning back to Noll. "There's one last piece of information I need to share with you."

Noll reassured him, "These two know everything. There's no reason to hold anything back."

"Alright," the doctor sighed. "Before the operation, I mentioned to you that the nerves responsible for erections pass close to the prostate gland. If one or both of those nerves are damaged during surgery, it can lead to erectile dysfunction." He paused for a moment, allowing the weight of his words to sink in. "I think we didn't touch those nerves much during the procedure, but only you will be able to find out if you can still have erections."

An awkward silence filled the room as Noll processed the news. Lucy and Sierra remained quiet, respecting the intimate nature of the information. Noll, however, broke the silence with a wry smile.

"Guess I'll find out... maybe... one day," he said, attempting to inject some humor into the situation. But his eyes betrayed the uncertainty that gnawed at him beneath the surface.

"Take care of yourself and give your body time to heal," the doctor advised before excusing himself from the room.

The moment the door closed behind the doctor, Sierra's eyes twinkled with mischief. She and Lucy exchanged glances as they stifled giggles.

"Say, Noll," Lucy began, her voice laced with feigned innocence, "how will you test out if your... equipment is still functional?"

"Right," chimed in Sierra, her grin widening. "It seems like quite a conundrum."

Noll shook his head, fully aware of their teasing. The tense atmosphere was lightened by their playfulness. Yet, he couldn't help but feel a mixture of apprehension and gratitude for these two women who had become so important in his life.

"Very funny, you two," he said dryly, rolling his eyes. "I think I can handle that particular experiment on my own, thank you very much."

"Isn't your wrist too old for that," Lucy replied with a shrug, though her eyes danced with amusement.

Noll changed the topic, his voice a hoarse whisper. "You know, you two are the only real friends I have nowadays."

He stared at the bland ceiling tiles, his mind swirling with thoughts of betrayal and abandonment. "It's sad how all those so-called friends I had quickly turned their backs on me as soon as... I couldn't give them a rebate on a scuba regulator."

Sierra shifted in her seat, her bright blue hair falling over her dark brown eyes. She reached out and squeezed Noll's hand, offering silent support. Her punk aesthetic belied her fierce loyalty to her friends.

"Hey, people can be pretty shitty sometimes," Lucy chimed in, her warm smile wavering for a moment. The beautiful blonde's empathetic heart was evident in her every action. "But look at us—we're here, and we're not going anywhere."

"Lucy's right," Sierra added, her tone firm. "We've got your back, Noll. Screw those fake friends of yours. They don't deserve you. And screw the whole moral-less self-centered society, for that matter."

Noll sighed, his chest tightening with emotion. Despite being an undercover D.E.A. agent investigating Maksym, Lucy had somehow found it in her heart to care for him. And Sierra—a brilliant hacker who despised extreme capitalism—had opened up her luxurious penthouse to him when he had nowhere else to go.

"Thanks. Both of you," Noll murmured, his throat tight. He couldn't help but think about the downward spiral his life had taken since Maksym had betrayed him and taken control of his businesses.

"Listen, Noll," Lucy said, her voice firm but gentle. "I'm going to tell you this once more: focus on the future. If I hear you getting all mopey again, I'll slap your face just like I did in Bonaire when I saved your life. Again."

Noll managed a small smile, grateful for Lucy and Sierra's unwavering support. He knew he couldn't change the past, but with friends like these, maybe there was hope for his future after all.

NOLL AND SIERRA stepped off the private elevator into her luxurious penthouse. The sun cast warm, golden rays across the room, accentuating the plush furnishings and modern decor. Noll took a deep breath, inhaling the familiar scent of their shared sanctuary.

"Too bad Lucy had to get back to work," Sierra remarked, leading Noll towards the terrace. "Wouldn't want Maksym or her D.E.A. boss getting suspicious."

"True," Noll agreed, following her outside. They settled into the long chairs beside Sierra's private pool, the sparkling water reflecting the azure sky above. Despite the heavy thoughts that weighed on him, Noll couldn't deny the beauty of the moment.

Sierra studied him for a moment, concern etched on her face. "You seem to be walking just fine and looking relatively good, considering everything you've been through."

"Thanks to you and Lucy," Noll commented, his voice tinged with emotion. "I don't know where I'd be without you two."

"Probably still sleeping in your car," Sierra quipped, but her eyes softened. "But seriously, Noll, we're here for you. We're a team."

Noll smiled at her, the warmth of their friendship seeping into his bones.

The terrace's cool breeze brushed against Noll's skin as he leaned back in the long chair, letting his thoughts drift. Sierra, ever observant, watched him for a moment before speaking up.

"You know, Noll, you've really come far these past couple of months since Bonaire," she began, her voice soft and contemplative. "I mean, your bankruptcy is finalized, your divorce is done – though I'm sorry your ex-wife still won't let you see your kids. And she moved up North with them. But anyway, now, it seems like your prostate cancer is in the past, too."

Noll nodded, feeling the weight of Sierra's words. It was true; so much had changed recently, and despite the lingering pain from his surgery, there was a glimmer of hope shining through the darkness. He looked at her, his eyes filled with gratitude.

"Plus, you've got a place to stay here in my penthouse for as long as you need," Sierra continued, offering him a reassuring smile.

"Sierra, I can't thank you enough for everything. For paying those ridiculous prices for the best medical care and for being here when I had no one else," Noll said sincerely, his voice thick with emotion. "I mean no one else besides Lucy. You and Lucy are my saving angels."

"Hey, we're all in this together," Sierra replied, her tone lightening. "Stick it to the man."

"But speaking of Lucy, what have you two found out about Maksym? I know you guys wanted me to focus on my health and all the other stuff while you investigated him, but I want to be part of that team now. I've got three issues down, and I don't want to lose momentum."

"Of course," agreed Sierra. "We wouldn't want to leave you out of the loop forever. We'll fill you in next time Lucy comes over. Just remember that we need to tread carefully. Maksym's dangerous, and we don't want to make any mistakes."

"Understood," Noll said, determination etched on his face. Despite the trials he'd faced, Noll knew he could rely on Sierra and Lucy as they navigated through the treacherous waters of their shared enemy. And for the first time in a long while, he felt a renewed sense of purpose.

"Right now, though, you need to focus on healing," Sierra continued, her piercing dark brown eyes locked onto his. "We may need to go scuba diving for Blue Dragon dry boxes soon, and you won't be much help if you're not in good shape."

Noll nodded, knowing she was right. He couldn't let his eagerness to confront Maksym overshadow the importance of his recovery. The thought of diving again after everything he'd been through both excited and terrified him.

"By the way," Sierra added, tilting her head slightly as she studied him, "you should take Lucy's bed tonight. You've been sleeping on that couch long enough, and you need proper rest to heal."

"Are you sure?" Noll asked hesitantly, not wanting to impose further on her hospitality. "Is Lucy okay with that?"

"She suggested it," Sierra said with a warm smile. "It's the least we can do after all you've been through. You need a comfortable night's sleep."

"Alright then," Noll conceded, grateful for the offer. It had been a while since he'd slept in an actual bed, and the prospect of a peaceful night's rest sounded like heaven.

While they sat on the terrace, Noll felt a renewed sense of hope. With Sierra and Lucy's support, he was ready to face whatever challenges lay ahead. He had been surfing on dark waves, going with the flow for too long. It was time for action.

Meanwhile, on Sierra's fancy sound system, Katy Perry was singing. "I got the eye of the tiger, a fighter; Dancing through the fire; 'Cause I am a champion, and you're gonna hear me roar."

CHAPTER 22
THE INFLATABLE

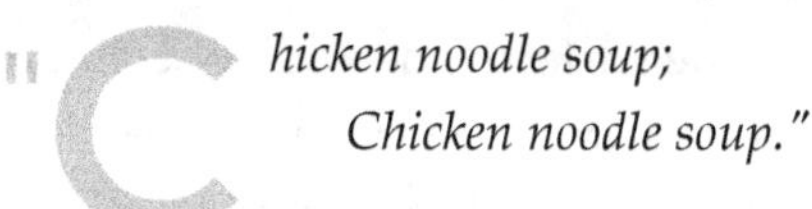

"Chicken noodle soup;
    Chicken noodle soup."

NOLL HOVERED WEIGHTLESSLY UNDERWATER, the vibrant coral reef below him teeming with life. Fish of every hue darted in and out of the swaying tendrils of the sea fans while a massive, slow-moving grouper lumbered past. The world beneath the surface held a magic unlike any other, an enchanting escape from the harsh realities above.

But Noll's attention was drawn to the Blue Dragon waterproof box lying incongruously on the ocean floor. It was a stark reminder that this beautiful underwater sanctuary was tainted by human greed and corruption. The contents of the box — either drugs or guns — symbolized the evil that had permeated his own life as well.

He shook off the thought and focused on the task at hand. With practiced ease, Noll attached a lift bag to the dry box. He took his octopus, the alternate air source, and slowly filled the lift bag with air until it was just buoyant enough for it to lift the box. As he looked up, he watched the lift bag carry the box toward the surface, the air inside expanding as it ascended.

Noll's heart pounded, not out of fear but out of determination. This underwater world had always been his sanctuary, where he felt most at home. Now, it would become the site of his resistance against Maksym's dark empire.

His eyes followed the lift bag, watching as the underbelly of a zodiac positioned itself next to it. The inflatable boat outfitted with a small outboard motor, signaled the next phase of their plan. Confidence surged through Noll, fueling him for the battles yet to come.

Noll watched intently as the lift bag and box were pulled out of the water by the crew of the zodiac, disappearing from his sight. His determination surged like a current through his veins, prompting him to swim towards the second Blue Dragon dry box.

This time, his movements were even more efficient. He attached the lift bag securely and filled it with just enough air from his octopus. He glanced up, tracking the box's ascent to the surface. The zodiac seemed to appear almost instantly, ready to collect its sinister cargo. Despite the gravity of their mission, Noll couldn't help but marvel at the ease and precision with which they executed each step.

With only one lift bag remaining, he swam toward a third box. As he repeated his actions, the underwater world around him seemed to fade into the background, replaced by a singular focus on the task at hand. Once the inflatable boat appeared next to the third lift bag and box, Noll knew it was time to ascend.

He released some air from his buoyancy compensator device and slowly rotated, scanning the area for any signs of approaching boats. The outboard engine of the zodiac fell silent in anticipation of Noll's arrival, making his ascent safer. As he moved closer to the surface, his thoughts turned to the people waiting for him above – Lucy and Sierra – and the battle they were facing together.

The weight of Maksym's dark empire and the destruction it wrought loomed heavily over Noll's heart. But in this underwater sanctuary, where he had always found solace and strength, he knew they could succeed. This was not only a fight against a powerful criminal; it was a fight for the values and lives that had been torn apart by greed and self-centered ambition.

As Noll rose to meet the early morning rising sun, determination and confidence filled every fiber of his being. He was ready for whatever lay ahead – even if it meant diving into the deepest, darkest depths to bring an end to Maksym's reign.

The moment Noll broke the surface, the beauty of the underwater world was replaced by a different kind of allure. Sierra and Lucy had just pulled the third dry box into the zodiac, their sun-kissed skin glistening under the early morning heat of the Florida Keys. Both women wore bikinis that barely covered their bodies, but the contrast between them was striking.

Lucy, her golden hair cascading freely down her back, sported only the bottom half of her bikini, leaving her young, firm breasts to bask in the sunlight. Her body was smooth and unmarked by tattoos or piercings. At first glance, she appeared angelic—a stark contrast to Sierra's punk-inspired aesthetic. Sierra's blue hair, multiple piercings, and intricate tattoos created an image of a rebellious spirit, yet Noll knew that beneath her rough exterior, she possessed the most generous heart.

As Noll admired the two women in the inflatable boat, he couldn't help but think that this was almost paradise: beautiful scuba diving in a magical world with two amazing women by his side. But this wasn't paradise—not when they were fighting against Maksym and his drug and gun smuggling ring.

With his thoughts firmly anchored on the task at hand, Noll removed his scuba unit from his back and handed it over to Sierra, who effortlessly hauled it into the boat. As if mimicking a seal leaping onto a dock, Noll climbed over the side of the zodiac and slid inside with practiced grace.

For a fleeting moment, surrounded by the enchanting ocean and the company of Lucy and Sierra, Noll allowed himself to believe that maybe—just maybe—they could find a way to restore order to the lives that had been shattered by Maksym's greed. But until that day came, there would be no true paradise, for him, anyway.

The outboard engine roared to life as Sierra steered the inflatable boat back toward shore. Noll, still soaked from his dive, squinted against the wind and spray, his thoughts racing as fast as their vessel.

"Should've used a bigger boat," he grumbled, shaking his head. "Taken all the boxes at once. It's gonna be more dangerous now—they'll be on their guard."

Sierra glanced back briefly, her blue hair whipping around her face. "Our goal is to create chaos between Maksym and his partners – whoever they are, not steal everything ourselves. Remember?"

Lucy laughed, her sun-kissed skin glistening. "Besides, what would we do with that much cocaine – I presume – or 50 caliber guns anyway?"

Noll felt a hint of a smile tug at his lips, but he remained silent. The girls were right, of course. Their mission was calculated mayhem, not outright theft.

As they neared an informal landing at the end of a street in Key Largo, Sierra expertly maneuvered the boat into position. The early morning sun cast a golden glow over the coastal town, and for a moment, Noll was struck by its picturesque beauty.

"Almost there," Sierra called out as they neared the shore. "Are you ready, Noll?"

"Always," he replied confidently and jumped off of the boat, still wearing his wetsuit boots. "I wouldn't want those sexy feet of yours getting damaged on rocks or dead corals."

"Such a gentleman," Lucy teased, her laughter ringing like a silver bell.

Noll waded through the shallow water, grabbing hold of the boat's front rope and pulling it towards the shore. He glanced back at Sierra and Lucy, acknowledging their teamwork with a nod. He then jogged over to the nearby pickup truck parked with a trailer hitched to it.

"Alright, ladies," Noll said after he backed the trailer up to the inflatable boat. "Let's get this beauty on the trailer."

Together, they worked in near silence, each knowing their role and moving with efficiency. With the boat secured on the trailer, they turned their attention to the Blue Dragon waterproof boxes.

"Quick thinking with the tarp," Noll praised Sierra, who was covering the boxes.

"Can't be too careful," she replied, tying everything down with bands. "These streets are filled with prying eyes. Well, the whole world is, I guess."

"True," Noll agreed, feeling the weight of the danger lurking in the shadows.

With the boat and its cargo secured, the trio climbed into the pickup truck – Noll behind the wheel and Sierra in the passenger seat, while Lucy sat in the backseat. As they drove away, an uneasy quiet settled among them. Noll's thoughts raced, considering their next moves and the risks involved.

"Stay focused," he reminded himself. "We're one step closer to bringing Maksym down."

The pickup truck rumbled along the coastal road, the morning sun still low in the sky, casting elongated shadows on the pavement. Noll's stomach growled loudly, breaking the silence in the cab. He glanced over at Lucy and Sierra.

"Anyone else hungry?" he asked. "We left before sunrise and skipped breakfast."

Sierra nodded. "I could eat."

"Same here," Lucy agreed.

"Alright, there's a place up ahead called Mrs. Mad Max's Kitchen. We can stop there."

Soon after, Noll turned into the parking lot of a small diner.

"Mad Max's?" Lucy laughed. "Let's hope it's not related to our Max."

"God, I hope not," Noll muttered under his breath.

They entered the diner, the smell of coffee and bacon wafting through the air. They slid into a booth by the window and quickly scanned the menu. As they waited for the waitress to take their order, Noll leaned in close to Sierra and Lucy, whispering conspiratorially.

"Isn't it ironic? We're sitting here while our truck outside is probably loaded with guns or cocaine worth millions."

Lucy's face paled as she realized the gravity of their situation. "We shouldn't have stopped together. If Maksym or the D.E.A. finds out I went diving with you, Noll, we're all screwed."

"Damn, you're right," Noll admitted, frustration creeping into his voice. Sierra nodded in agreement.

"Let's forget breakfast and get out of here," Sierra suggested, her eyes scanning the diner for any suspicious activity.

They moved with purpose, but not too quickly, so as not to draw more attention to themselves.

As they climbed back into the pickup truck, Noll couldn't help but feel the heavy weight of their dangerous situation bearing down on them. With each passing moment, the stakes grew higher and the risks greater, but there was no turning back now.

On the way to Miami, Noll glanced at Lucy and cleared his throat. "I'm sorry for suggesting we stop for breakfast. I should've known better."

Lucy looked at him with a small smile. "It's alright, Noll. I'm the bad one. I'm the federal agent here – sort of; I should be smarter. Never listen to your stomach!"

Noll nodded, gripping the steering wheel tighter.

Lucy giggled and started singing. "Chicken noodle soup; Chicken noodle soup; Chicken noodle soup; Wit' a soda on the side."

Sierra shook her head. "What the hell is that song?"

"Webstar & Young B," Lucy answered. "It's rap."

Noll shook his head next. "I guess I'm too old for that one."

"It was 15 years ago!" Lucy laughed.

"Really? Oh well, there you have it. I'm not a rap fan. There are not songs. It's like a talk show."

"Okay, old man!"

"In any case," Sierra interrupted. "No more reference to food, please!"

As they drove, Noll thought about how, for a brief moment, he had felt like he was in paradise – scuba diving in crystal-clear waters, surrounded by two women he adored. But reality had come crashing down around him, reminding him of the danger they were all in.

"None of us should let our guard down until Maksym is behind bars," Noll said quietly, more to himself than anyone else. Sierra and Lucy exchanged glances, both understanding the gravity of their situation.

"Or dead," Noll added after a beat, his jaw clenched as he stared out at the road ahead through the windshield.

"Dead?" Lucy asked, raising her pierced brow.

"Harsh, but maybe necessary," Noll replied, his voice tinged with bitterness. "Maksym has ruined countless lives, including mine."

Lucy sighed, shifting uncomfortably in her seat. She knew Noll was right. Maksym was a dangerous man who would stop at nothing to protect his criminal organization – even if it meant eliminating those who dared to stand against him.

While the pickup sped down US1 towards Miami, their minds raced with thoughts of the dangers that lay ahead. They knew they were playing a dangerous game, but they were determined to see it through to the end, no matter the cost.

CHAPTER 23
HIDDEN

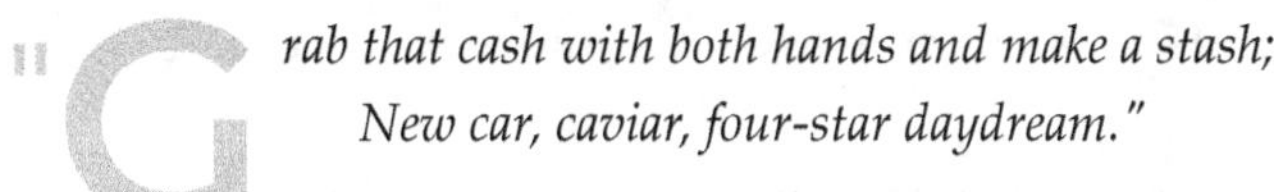

THE WAREHOUSE DISTRICT was a monochrome landscape of concrete and steel, punctuated by the occasional graffiti tag. Noll maneuvered the pickup truck through the bleak surroundings, trailer in tow with their stolen cargo on it. Lucy sat behind him, her expression unreadable, while Sierra stared out the window from the passenger seat, her blue hair contrasting sharply with the drab scenery. The end of the morning cast a dull light over everything, emphasizing the grayness of their environment.

As they reached the self-storage facility, Noll slowed down and pulled up in front of a nondescript warehouse door. He put the truck in park. Without a word, Sierra climbed out of the vehicle and opened the large door. Noll drove the entire pickup and trailer inside the dark warehouse. The heavy door closed behind them, plunging them into near darkness.

"Thanks for helping me out financially, Sierra," Noll said, his voice echoing slightly off the metal walls. "But I can't help but think this might be a bit excessive. A storage unit big enough to fit the whole truck and trailer?"

"You'd be surprised how easy it is to spot a vehicle these days," Lucy interjected, her tone serious.

"Exactly," Sierra chimed in, her eyes meeting Lucy's. "And I made sure to deactivate the manufacturer-installed tracking system. It's not under my name, on top of that. A fake ID."

Noll sighed, running a hand through his salt-and-pepper hair, and glanced at both women before speaking. "I guess I owe you both my life. Literally." His voice was thick with gratitude but also laced with the weight of all that had transpired recently.

The warehouse was dimly lit, casting eerie shadows upon the walls as Noll, Sierra, and Lucy climbed into the inflatable boat still on the trailer. As they worked together to remove the tarp covering it, their movements were efficient and calculated, like those of a team practicing secrecy. The first blue dragon box came into view, secured tightly with tie-wraps.

With a snip of a pair of wire cutters, Noll sliced through the tie wraps and lifted the box's lid. The sight inside made him pause: bundles of cocaine, meticulously wrapped and stacked, filled the entirety of the container. He glanced at his companions, their expressions a mix of anticipation and dread.

"So our guess was correct. Still want to go ahead with your crazy plan, Noll?" Sierra asked him, her voice low and serious.

Noll stared at the drugs for a moment longer before nodding firmly. He was now a man on a mission. There would be no turning back. They needed to make Maksym pay for what he'd done, and this was their chance.

As they moved on to the second box, their hands shook slightly from nerves and adrenaline, but they didn't hesitate to open it. Inside, they found something they never expected: stacks upon stacks of US$100 bills. Their eyes widened in surprise as they looked from the money to each other.

"Did any of you expect this?" Noll questioned, astonishment lacing his voice.

"Of course not," Lucy replied, her brow furrowed in confusion. "Hell, my boss said Maksym was smuggling drugs but never even mentioned the guns. And money? What the fuck?"

"Damn," Sierra murmured, her eyes locked on the cash. "This is a whole new level of danger we're dealing with now."

For a moment, the three of them stood there, staring at the unexpected fortune, unsure of how to proceed. But one thing was clear: Maksym had plenty of secrets.

Noll leaned back, his eyes fixed on Lucy as he tried to make sense of their discovery. "Lucy, can you confirm what you've told me before about how Maksym gets paid for the cocaine?"

Lucy brushed strands of her blonde hair away from her face. "Assuming we can believe my boss, Maksym, is essentially just a transporter. He's responsible for moving the cocaine boxes from underwater to a warehouse. He doesn't actually get paid the value of the drugs – it's more like a fee for his transportation services."

Noll nodded, taking in the information. "Okay, so if Maksym's role is limited to transporting cocaine, then how does he get paid for smuggling guns out of the USA? Is it the same process?"

Lucy shook her head. "Well, it has to be for the same party. It's the same boxes. I guess Maksym brings the cocaine in... maybe for a South American cartel... and then ships guns out of the USA using the same boxes. I mean... Cartels love their guns!"

"Could be," Noll mused, rubbing his chin thoughtfully. "But what about the money?"

"Fuck if I know," Lucy commented, her brow creasing slightly. "Cartels usually have too much money in the U.S.A. they need to launder. So why bring more in? Maybe it's being shipped out like the guns? And, damn! My D.E.A. boss never mentioned any of that. And he's slower than a turtle."

Noll glanced at the opened boxes once more, his mind racing with possibilities and unanswered questions. One thing was clear: Maksym had entangled himself in a dangerous web of crime and deceit. And now, Noll, Lucy, and Sierra were caught in the crosshairs, fighting to bring him down.

Noll stared at the money, his mind racing as he tried to piece together the implications of their discovery. "Well, maybe the money's coming in with the cocaine," he began, thinking out loud, "perhaps as payment for the guns Maksym ships back in the boxes."

"Could be," Lucy agreed, her eyes flicking between Noll and Sierra.

Suddenly, Sierra laughed, a sardonic smile crossing her face. "Well, Noll, you had a plan for the cocaine, but now we need a plan for millions of US dollars!" Her tone was light, but there was an undercurrent of tension beneath her words. And on that, she started singing.

"Grab that cash with both hands and make a stash; New car, caviar, four-star daydream; Think I'll buy me a football team."

"Thank you, Miss Pink Floyd! But first things first," Noll said, trying to organize his thoughts. "We need to make sure this money is real."

"Good point," Lucy replied, picking up a small stack of hundred-dollar bills. "I'll get these checked by a friend at the F.B.I. You know her. Harper."

"Harper?" Noll's eyes widened slightly in recognition. "Of course. She used to be a part-time scuba diving instructor in my dive centers." He paused, curious despite himself. "Are Kim and Harper still part-time dive instructors at Seize The Deep?"

"Kim and Harper are not teaching much there anymore," Lucy established, "they've been very uncomfortable with the changes that happened after you were pushed out."

"Can't blame them," Noll murmured, rubbing the back of his neck.

"Okay," Sierra interjected, "but if it's not fake bills, what are we gonna do with all this cash."

"Let's deal with one problem at a time," Noll said firmly, the fire of determination burning in his eyes. "Isn't counterfeit a Secret Service thing?"

"Harper will figure it out," Lucy snapped.

As they stood there, united in their purpose, Noll felt a renewed sense of hope. He knew that with Lucy and Sierra by his side, they would have a fighting chance against Maksym and the dark world he had dragged them into.

Sierra raised an eyebrow, her piercing glinting in the dim warehouse light. "Why didn't we just open all the boxes underwater? We could've checked them all."

"Impossible," Noll shook his head. "The pressure underwater would make it too difficult to open the boxes."

As they spoke, Lucy was already working on the third box, her blonde hair falling over her face as she concentrated. With a final tug, she pried the lid open, revealing more stacks of $100 bills. Her eyes widened, and she looked up at Noll and Sierra.

"Again? This one, too," she said, her voice a mixture of disbelief and excitement.

Noll rubbed his chin thoughtfully, his mind racing with the implications of their find. Sierra leaned against the side of the inflatable, smirking at the situation they found themselves in.

Lucy glanced between the two of them, biting her lip. "I think we should leave the cash here for now. I'll take a few to check if the bills are fake, but beyond that, we need to know if these numbers are tracked by the U.S. Secret Services or the F.B.I."

"Well, have fun with that," Noll joked, feeling a renewed sense of comfort by having Lucy with him. They were not only dealing with drugs and guns but also a large amount of dirty money. He knew that they had to tread carefully.

"This is a lot more money than what Maksym has me launder for him through Seize The Deep and Sea Spell Diving... even if I would be there over a year!" Lucy observed. "It's going somewhere else. It seems like a lot even for his nightclub."

Together, they placed the tarp over the three boxes once more, shrouding the content from view even though it was inside their warehouse. After unhooking the trailer, Sierra drove the pickup out of the warehouse while Lucy locked it up securely. The trio then climbed into the F150 that Sierra had purchased just for this project.

As they drove away, Noll couldn't help but feel a strange mix of adrenaline and dread coursing through his veins. The stakes had risen even higher now, and every moment counted.

As the pickup truck maneuvered through the sun-dappled streets, Noll couldn't help but mention again Sierra's recent expenditures. "You've spent a lot of money to help me out," he said, glancing at her from the passenger seat. "The warehouse, the pickup and trailer, the inflatable... Where do you get all that cash?"

"In our warehouse," Sierra joked, keeping her eyes on the road. "But seriously, let's just say it was evil money I converted into good money, all right?"

Noll raised an eyebrow, intrigued by her cryptic response, but he left it at that. Lucy, seated in the back, leaned forward, resting her arms on the center console. "Sierra, I think it's time we tell Noll about that other thing we did while he was recovering from his operation."

Sierra nodded, her expression serious. "Yes, it's time."

Noll looked at them, puzzled, wondering what they were keeping from him.

Approaching the penthouse, Sierra dropped Lucy off a few corners away, then did the same for Noll, ensuring they arrived separately. As Noll walked toward the luxurious building, he felt a growing mixture of curiosity and unease, wondering what else had transpired during his convalescence.

Upon reaching the penthouse, he found Sierra waiting for him with a cold drink in hand. She handed it to him, her blue hair shimmering in the late morning light. "We'll talk once Lucy gets here."

As they waited, Noll gazed out at the ocean, feeling the weight of all the secrets and betrayals that had led them to this point. He knew that whatever Lucy and Sierra had to reveal would be significant, and he braced himself for another twist in their ongoing battle against Maksym and his dirty activities.

Soon after, Lucy strolled into Sierra's penthouse, her long blonde hair swaying gently as she moved. Noll had been waiting on the expansive terrace by the private pool, his eyes still adjusting to the dazzling display of wealth and opulence that surrounded him.

"Alright, Noll," Lucy teased, walking up to him with a grin, "Your convalescence is officially over. Next time, you'll have to be a gentleman and let me be the one who gets dropped off closer to the penthouse."

Noll chuckled softly, feeling a warmth in his chest that he hadn't experienced in quite some time. He had to admit that having these two strong, intelligent women by his side gave him a strong sense of purpose and determination.

"Fine," he agreed playfully, "But only because you saved my life— twice."

Sierra appeared from inside the penthouse, her blue hair glinting in the gentle breeze that swept across the terrace. She gestured for Noll and Lucy to join her by the sparkling pool, where an array of comfortable chairs awaited them.

"Come on, you two," she called out, her voice confident and full of energy, "We've got something important to discuss."

As he took a seat next to Sierra, Noll felt a mixture of anticipation and unease. The three friends sat in silence for a moment, with the sound of waves crashing against the shore below. He glanced at Lucy, whose expression had turned serious, then back at Sierra, trying to gauge what was coming.

"Alright," Sierra began, her piercing dark brown eyes meeting Noll's, "We've got news for you, Noll. But first, I want you to know that everything we've done, we did it because we believe in you and your cause."

The intensity of her gaze sent a jolt of electricity through Noll, igniting a fire in his chest that burned with curiosity and resolve. He looked from Sierra to Lucy, bracing himself for the revelation to come.

CHAPTER 24
CUBAN COFFEE

LEO LEANED back in the chair, sipping his Cuban coffee with a contented sigh. Lucy sat opposite him at her desk, her own cup in hand, the rich aroma of the strong coffee mingling with the scent of paperwork and the faint hum of office equipment.

"Thanks for the cafecito, boss," Leo said, setting down the empty takeout cup and getting up from his seat. "I love this stuff."

"Anytime, Leo," she replied with a warm smile, raising her cup in a small toast. "Enjoy the rest of your day."

Leo waved goodbye as he walked out the door, leaving Lucy alone in the office and walking into the retail area while Karina Magallon sang in the speakers of the dive shop. He tried to sing along. ""Pienso en ti, como un cafecito; en la primavera; se siente tan rico. Damn! I badly need Spanish lessons. Maybe a Spanish-speaking girlfriend..."

Alone in her office, Lucy glanced around at her mostly empty desk and sighed, wondering what she could do with her day. Leo and Jon, her two general managers, and Fred, her executive vice-president, were the ones who really managed the business. The hefty pay she received for doing very little was certainly nice, but she knew it couldn't last. Maksym would eventually end up in jail, and then she would go back to being an underpaid federal agent.

Shaking her head, Lucy decided to make the most of her free time. Grabbing her phone, she called a nearby spa and booked a 90-minute deep tissue massage. A small part of her felt guilty for indulging in the luxurious treat, knowing that it was financed by dirty money. But she shrugged off the feeling – why not enjoy the good life while it lasted?

Just as Lucy was getting up to leave for her massage appointment, her smartphone rang. Glancing at the screen, she saw it was the manager of Sea Spell Diving, one of the businesses Maksym had taken away from Noll.

"Hey, Jon," she answered, her voice cheerful. "What's up?"

"Hi, boss. Just thought I'd give you a heads-up." Jon's voice carried a hint of concern. "Your boss was here this morning asking questions about the dive boats."

"Really? What did he want to know?" Lucy felt a slight unease creep over her.

"Mr. Byrne wanted to know if anyone had taken any of the dive boats out besides the regular outings we organize. He seemed pretty insistent about it. He also asked when was the last time you were at Sea Spell Diving."

"Thanks for letting me know, Jon." Lucy tried to keep her voice steady. "Did you tell him anything?"

"Well," Jon replied defensively. "I mean, I told him the truth – that I only see you on Tuesday evenings with him. Is there a problem, Lucy? It's the first time I see him here outside of your night dives."

"Nothing to worry about, Jon," Lucy assured him. "I appreciate you looking out for me."

"Alright," Jon said hesitantly. "Just let me know if there's anything I can do to help. Take care, Lucy."

"Will do. Thanks again." Hanging up the phone, a subtle tension filled the room as Lucy realized Maksym was investigating her. His partners probably told him boxes were missing. "Well, good! The plan is working!" Lucy giggled. "Maybe they'll kill him!"

She left her office and slid into the driver's seat of her sleek, expensive Porsche. She felt a surge of adrenaline as she revved the engine and sped off toward an exclusive spa in Miami. The sun glinted off the smooth curves of the car, drawing admiring glances from passersby. It was hard not to enjoy this life, even if it wouldn't last forever.

Upon arriving at the spa, Lucy was greeted with the VIP treatment. A handsome young man who could have stepped straight out of a GQ magazine escorted her to a private massage room. "I'll be your massage therapist today," he said, smiling warmly. "Please undress and get under the cover sheet. I'll step out for a moment to give you some privacy."

Lucy smirked and nonchalantly pulled her tiny sundress over her head, revealing her nude body. She never wore panties or bras – it just wasn't her style, and she also found it more comfortable that way in Miami's heat and humidity. The massage therapist blushed but quickly recovered his composure. Lucy was well aware of the effect she had on men, and she enjoyed the power it gave her.

"Very well," the therapist said, clearing his throat. "Please lie down on your belly on the massage table."

Lucy obliged, stretching out on top of the cover sheet instead of under it. She let out a contented sigh and thought to herself; maybe crime does pay after all.

MAKSYM DROVE HIS GAS-GUZZLING, planet-destroying big pickup truck along i95 towards Miami. He was returning from his visit to Sea Spell Diving. As he drove, he spoke on the phone.

"I don't know if Lucy was involved, but I find it suspicious," Maksym said, his voice dangerously calm. "So do your job and keep her under control, or I will."

He didn't wait for an answer and expressed his anger at the red button on his smartphone's screen.

LATER THAT AFTERNOON, the warehouse loomed like a shadowy fortress, its secrets hidden behind steel walls. Lucy Grayson stood at the entrance, her heart pounding in her chest like a caged animal desperate to escape. The air was stagnant and heavy with the scent of damp concrete.

"Here we go," she muttered under her breath, pushing open the door and stepping inside. "Today, I become a corrupt agent!"

The dim light from the high windows barely illuminated the space, but it was enough for Lucy to see the trailer with the inflatable boat resting on it. She could feel the weight of Sierra's trust pressing down on her shoulders, a burden she carried willingly for her friend.

Lucy's eyes scanned the space for any sign of trouble. But there was none. It was just her, the boat, and what lay inside.

Climbing onto the inflatable, Lucy pulled the tarp aside and revealed the three waterproof boxes stashed within. Her fingers trembled as she opened one, revealing the bricks of cocaine that would change the course of their lives. She took a deep breath and grabbed three of them, shoving them into the backpack slung over her shoulder.

"Three bricks should do it," she thought. "It's all for the greater good."

Closing the waterproof box, Lucy jumped out of the inflatable boat, landing softly on the concrete floor. With one last glance around the warehouse, she replaced the tarp, concealing the evidence of her crime. The adrenaline surged through her veins, making her hands shake as she zipped up her backpack.

"Okay, Lucy. Time to get out of here," she told herself, taking a moment to steady her breathing. She couldn't afford any mistakes now, not when they were so close to striking against Maksym and the corrupt system that allowed men like him to thrive.

The warm Suth Florida air greeted her as she stepped outside, the weight of the backpack on her shoulders a reminder of the stakes at play. Lucy locked the door behind her, leaving the darkness and secrets behind.

"Sierra... Noll... I hope this works," she thought, determination and fear intermingling within her as she walked away from the warehouse, ready for whatever came next.

LATER THAT EVENING, the saltwater clung to Lucy's skin as she stepped off the dive boat and onto the wooden dock, the sky overhead punctuated by a smattering of stars. The air hung heavy with tension, the scent of ocean and gasoline mingling together. She glanced around at Maksym's group, their faces hard and focused as they went about their routine – a well-rehearsed dance of deception.

"Hey, Lu," one of the men called out, his voice gruff but kind. "Why don't you go get changed?" He jerked his head toward the parking lot, shadows obscuring his features. "You weigh less than the boxes!"

"Thanks, Eddie," she replied, her heart pounding in her chest. It was the same routine every week, but Eddie always wanted to sound like a gentleman. Her role was underwater where her size didn't matter, but her skills did.

She needed to play it cool, act as if this was just another night. Her life most certainly depended on it.

"Hey, Max!" another man shouted from the dive boat as he hoisted a waterproof box onto the dock. "The two boxes for your truck!"

"Got it," Maksym responded, striding over with an air of authority that sent shudders down Lucy's spine. His eyes scanned the scene, seemingly taking in every detail with ruthless efficiency.

She shivered as the cool breeze licked her damp skin. She stood next to her Porsche, fumbling with the zipper on her backpack. Her heart beat in rhythm with the waves lapping against the shore. "Get a grip, Lucy," she muttered under her breath as she pulled out a sundress and quickly slipped it over her head.

"Still enjoying fast cars, Lucy?" Maksym called from across the parking lot, his eyes lingering on her figure.

"Speed gets the blood pumping," she replied, trying to maintain her composure. As much as she hated Maksym's attention, she couldn't afford to alienate him. Not now, when she was so close to finishing her mission.

"True that," he chuckled, turning back to oversee the boxes being loaded into the cube truck.

Lucy scanned the area, her eyes finally settling on Maksym's pickup truck. The men had placed two of the waterproof boxes in its bed. She needed to act quickly – and discreetly.

"Hey, Max!" one of the divers called out, dragging him back to the dock. Seizing the opportunity, Lucy made her way to the pickup, her stomach knotting with each step.

"Please, let this work," she prayed silently. When she reached the truck, she glanced around, ensuring no one was watching her. With trembling hands, she lifted the corner of the vinyl cover just enough to slide the three bricks of cocaine in.

Lucy's heart pounded as she struggled to zip the vinyl cover on Maksym's truck, her hands slick with sweat. Her mind raced, searching for a plan, when she saw him walking toward her.

"Shit," she muttered under her breath, tossing the empty backpack beneath his pickup. With a forced smile plastered on her face, she met Maksym's gaze and waved.

"Hey, Maksym," she called out, trying to sound casual. "I just wanted to talk to you for a sec."

Maksym raised an eyebrow but sauntered over. "What's up, Lu?"

Lucy leaned against the side of his truck, crossing her arms. "Well, I've been thinking about our dive operations, and I believe I could help launder more money through them if you're interested."

Maksym's eyes widened, clearly surprised by her proposition. He studied her for a moment before shaking his head. "Just do your job, Lucy. I'll let you know if I need any more help from you."

"Sure, no problem, boss," she replied, masking her relief as best she could. Her stomach churned, thoughts of being killed or tortured haunting her. But she couldn't let that fear control her. Not when so much was at stake.

"By the way," Maksym added, leaning in closer. "You seem a little… off today. Everything okay?"

"Me?" Lucy laughed nervously. "Oh, I'm just tired. You know how these night dives can be."

"Right," Maksym said, his voice dripping with skepticism. "Well, get some rest tomorrow in your office."

She didn't know how to answer, but she forced herself to maintain eye contact. Maksym opened the driver's door and stepped into his truck without another word. She wanted to collapse onto the pavement, but she couldn't – not yet.

"Get it together, Lucy," she whispered to herself. "You've got this."

With each step away from Maksym's truck, Lucy's heart pounded harder against her ribcage. The taste of danger lingered on her tongue, a metallic tang that reminded her of just how close she had come to being caught.

"Hey, Lucy!" called one of the divers as she passed. "Great dive tonight, huh?"

"Absolutely," she managed to reply, her voice breathier than usual. "Always a thrill to mix fun into it."

"See you next week!"

"Next week," she echoed, nodding and forcing a smile. Her sundress clung to her damp skin, and sweat trickled down her spine, but it was fear – not the oppressive Florida heat – that caused her to shiver.

Finally reaching her Porsche, she fumbled with her keys before sliding behind the wheel. The leather seat felt cool beneath her, offering some semblance of relief after her near brush with exposure. She gripped the steering wheel tightly, knuckles turning white and hands shaking.

"It's the coffee! I need to drink less Cuban coffee."

Her mind raced through the possible consequences of her actions: Maksym discovering the bricks, confronting her, or worse, handing her over to his connections in the underworld. The thought of what they might do to her sent waves of nausea roiling through her stomach.

"Get a grip," she whispered to herself, taking deep breaths to steady her nerves. "You've made it this far. You can't fall apart now."

Lucy glanced back at Maksym's truck, where he was now chatting with some of his men with his window rolled down. From a distance, he seemed almost approachable, a regular guy enjoying a conversation with friends. But she knew better – knew the darkness lurking beneath his friendly exterior.

"Max doesn't suspect a thing," she told herself, trying to quell the frantic beating of her heart. "Just play it cool, and you'll make it through this."

"Play it cool" – words that seemed to mock her as she sat trembling in her car. But she repeated them like a mantra, forcing herself to believe them.

"Play it cool," she whispered one final time. With a deep breath, she started the engine and pulled away from the dive center, leaving behind a cloud of dust and the echoes of her own fear.

At a red traffic light, she took her smartphone out of her purse and switched off the silent mode. An urgent text message blinked on the screen: her D.E.A. boss ordering her to meet him "NOW."

"Where?" she replied, her fingers tapping quickly in response. Moments later, an address appeared on her screen. With the light turning green, she revved the engine and sped off, her mind shifting gears to focus on her D.E.A. boss.

Along the way, Lucy smirked as she pulled into the parking lot of a small, local Cuban restaurant. The scent of strong coffee and savory pastries wafted through the air, tantalizing her senses. She felt the need for caffeine and sugar before meeting her boring boss. Her less-caffeine resolution hadn't lasted long!

"Boss man can wait," she muttered to herself. "If he's gonna be a turtle with Maksym's case, I can afford to be a turtle picking up some pick me up."

"¡Hola!" the friendly cashier greeted her as she entered. The lilting melody of Spanish conversation filled the space, making it feel alive and vibrant.

"¡Hola! Un café cubano, por favor," Lucy replied with a smile, her voice confident yet relaxed. She leaned against the counter, feeling the coolness of the stainless steel under her fingertips.

"¿Azúcar?" the cashier asked, raising an eyebrow.

"Claro," Lucy confirmed with a nod. After all, today was about living on the edge and embracing the sweet decadence that life offered – even if only for a moment.

As she waited for her order, Lucy glanced around the café. The rustic wooden tables were filled with patrons lost in conversation and enjoying their snacks. A sense of camaraderie hung in the air, providing a stark contrast to the dark world of drugs and corruption that she navigated as part of her undercover job. Moments like these reminded her that there was still goodness in the world, that not every-thing had been destroyed by greed and selfishness — at least, not yet.

"Here you go, señorita," the cashier said, handing her a small cup of steaming Cuban coffee. The rich aroma tickled her nostrils as she thanked him and handed over some cash.

"Gracias," she said, taking a careful sip. The hot liquid burned her tongue slightly, but the intense flavor and sweetness were worth it. She closed her eyes for a moment, savoring the taste before reality came rushing back.

"Alright, time to face the music," Lucy murmured to herself, downing the last of her small, strong coffee. She placed the empty cup on the counter and strode out of the café, her steps purposeful and determined. Whatever her D.E.A. boss had planned, she was ready – coffee-fueled and invigorated by the stolen moments of pleasure that made life worth living.

MAKSYM GLANCED in his rearview mirror and noticed that the back end of the soft tonneau cover on his pickup seemed unfastened. Looking around, he realized there was no safe place to stop on the highway.

"Ah, what the hell," Maksym muttered to himself, deciding to keep driving despite the loose cover.

He exited i95 in Miami, the city's skyline looming before him like a fortress of glass and steel. Shortly after, a Miami Police car appeared behind him, lights flashing. "What the fuck is the problem now?" Maksym grumbled under his breath, yet his lips curved into a smile as the officer approached his window.

"Good afternoon, sir," the officer said with an air of authority. "Driver's license and vehicle registration."

"Of course," Maksym replied smoothly, handing over the documents. He knew better than to appear rattled in front of the law.

The officer examined the papers and then looked at Maksym. "You didn't come to a complete stop at the last intersection."

"Really? I apologize, officer. Didn't realize it."

Just as he spoke, the officer on the passenger side of his pickup yelled something that Maksym couldn't quite catch. The first officer's eyes narrowed. "Sir, step out of the vehicle."

"Is there a problem?" Maksym asked, striving to maintain his cool composure as he opened the driver's door and stepped out.

"Put your hands on the top of the truck," the second officer commanded, his voice tense. As Maksym complied, the officer called for backup, leaving Maksym stunned. What was going on?

"Officer, what seems to be the issue?" Maksym asked, trying to regain control of the situation.

"Looks like you've got a nice load of cocaine back there," the second officer informed him, nodding towards the flapping tonneau cover. Maksym's heart skipped a beat. He only had two closed waterproof boxes in there. "What the fuck?"

The policemen's expressions were a mix of disbelief and determination as they surveyed the illicit cargo.

With a metallic clink, the handcuffs snapped shut around Maksym's wrists. His heart pounded in his chest as two backup police cars screeched to a halt behind him, their sirens blaring and lights flashing. The officers surrounding him gawked at the three visible bricks of cocaine in the back of the pickup truck.

"One hell of a nice load you got there," one of them said gruffly, guiding Maksym to the back of a patrol car. "Maybe use the vinyl cover next time!" His buddies laughed.

Maksym gritted his teeth, knowing that someone had set him up but unable to do anything about it at the moment. As he climbed into the back of the police car, he vowed to find the person responsible for this betrayal and make them pay.

CHAPTER 25
SOCCER TICKETS

"Vivir mi vida, la la la la;
Vivir mi vida, la la la la."

LUCY PARKED near a cheap diner and strolled inside, spotting her D.E.A. boss sitting in a dark corner. He looked impatient and angry, his eyes scanning the room before locking onto her. Even before she reached the table, he began yelling at her for being an hour late.

"Where the hell have you been, Lucy?" he demanded, his face turning red.

Lucy sat down across from him, working hard to hide a smirk as she casually apologized without giving a reason. "Sorry, I got held up," she lied, feigning contrition.

Her boss grumbled something under his breath before taking a sip of his cheap coffee. "Just don't let it happen again."

"Of course not," Lucy said sweetly, her heart pounding with exhilaration. Her plan was unfolding perfectly, and no one seemed to suspect her true intentions – not yet, at least. The thrill of it all sent shivers coursing through her veins, and she could hardly contain her excitement. But for now, she had to maintain her cover and play the dutiful D.E.A. agent.

As she sipped her own coffee, Lucy carefully studied her boss's face, searching for any hint of suspicion or doubt. She knew she couldn't afford to make a mistake, not with so much at stake. Every move she made would have to be calculated and precise.

Lucy's boss rubbed his temples and scowled, clearly frustrated. The dark corner of the diner seemed to intensify his bad mood as he leaned closer to her. "So, any updates on Maksym's case?"

"Nothing new," Lucy replied, maintaining a neutral expression. "I'm still laundering money for him through the dive businesses."

"Has there been any change in his smuggling activities in the Florida Keys?" her boss prodded, his eyes narrowing.

Lucy shrugged. "Not that I'm aware of. I still help Maksym with placing and recovering the Blue Dragon waterproof boxes during our night boat outings, but I never see what's inside."

Her boss continued to press her for details about Maksym's operations in Key Largo, and Lucy couldn't help but wonder if he somehow knew about the three missing Blue Dragon boxes. But how could he know? Maksym hadn't mentioned anything about them to her, so she pretended to be oblivious.

"Like I said, I'm not involved in whatever is inside the boxes," she reiterated, trying to keep her voice steady. "Maksym handles that part himself. How do you even know it's drugs?"

Lucy's boss glanced at his smartphone as it vibrated on the table, cutting through their conversation. With a furrowed brow, he picked it up and answered without offering an apology or even acknowledging Lucy. She sat there, her hands folded on her lap, wondering if he would have shown more courtesy had he been with an older male D.E.A. agent instead of her.

"Who is this?" he barked into the phone, his tone betraying both surprise and frustration. Lucy strained to listen, but she could only make out one side of the conversation.

"Arrested? When? How?" Her boss's face reddened with each question, making Lucy's curiosity piqued.

The exchange was brief and tense; upon hanging up, he turned to

Lucy, his eyes blazing. "Maksym Byrne has been arrested. They found bricks of cocaine in the back of his pickup truck."

"Really?" Lucy feigned shock, trying not to let her satisfaction show. "So, it's really cocaine. Well, that's good news, isn't it?"

Her boss hesitated, his mouth opening and closing like a fish out of water. It was strange, she thought, that he didn't seem happy about the arrest. Was he expecting something else? Was he involved in some way? She couldn't be sure, but the thought nagged at her.

"I mean, I'm sure the D.E.A. would have preferred to take credit for taking down a smuggler," she continued, watching him closely. "But, oh well, either way, it's done."

He stared at her, still struggling for words. Finally, he managed, "Yes, I... suppose it's a good thing."

Lucy cocked her head, studying him with a mix of concern and suspicion. What was going on behind those eyes? What secrets did he hold?

"So I can go back to the D.E.A. office now?" Lucy asked, trying to gauge her boss's reaction. "My undercover job is over since Maksym has been arrested, right?"

Her boss hesitated, his expression inscrutable. "Wait a bit longer; see how it plays out," he finally said. "Besides, we wanted to find out more about... the guns..."

"The guns?" Lucy feigned ignorance.

"I meant... the money laundering..."

Lucy narrowed her eyes, noticing his evasiveness. He should be happy, she thought, but instead, he seemed almost... nervous. It was as if there was something he wasn't telling her.

"Alright, boss," she agreed reluctantly, feeling the weight of unspoken secrets between them.

As they prepared to leave the cafe, Lucy couldn't help but think of Noll and the two dive businesses Maksym had stolen from him. "What will happen with Maksym's shares of Nollaig's... Mr. Durand's businesses?" she asked. "Will he get them back?"

Her boss interrupted her, his tone cold. "I don't give a shit about Durand."

Lucy's heart sank at his dismissive response, but she held her tongue, unwilling to risk exposing any of her true feelings.

"Lucy," her boss continued, "just enjoy your life as an overpaid business executive for now. Wait for orders."

"Fine," Lucy muttered, feeling the sting of betrayal and disappointment. She clung to the hope that, somehow, she would eventually make things right – not just for herself but for Noll as well.

LATER, Lucy sat in her Porsche, the engine purring softly beneath her. The dark parking lot of an abandoned building loomed before her, its desolate atmosphere a stark contrast to her luxurious car. She checked her reflection in the rearview mirror, ensuring she looked nothing less than seductive. With a deep breath, she prepared for what was to come.

A Miami PD car pulled into the lot, its tires crunching over the gravel as it came to a stop beside Lucy's Porsche. The officer stepped out, his uniform crisp and imposing, exuding authority. Lucy opened her car door and stepped out, her hips swaying with an allure that seemed to draw the officer's attention. She smiled at him, her eyes sparkling with mischief.

"Thank you for coming," she said sweetly, running a hand through her blonde hair. "How did everything go?"

"Exactly as planned," the officer replied, his voice gruff but not unkind. "I don't know how you managed to have the flexible cover of the pickup truck unsecured so we could see the drugs in the back, but we did. Your Maksym Byrne has been arrested."

Lucy fluttered her eyelashes at him, then wrapped her arms around his neck and gave him a sensual hug. "Thank you again," she murmured into his ear, her breath warm against his skin.

The policeman shifted uncomfortably, clearing his throat. "One thing I still don't understand is why the D.E.A. couldn't have arrested him and taken the credit. It seems more like your territory."

Lucy disentangled herself from the embrace, smoothing down her dress and adopting a more mysterious air. "Some things are better left unsaid," she replied cryptically. "Just remember that no one in Miami PD or the D.E.A. can know that the lead to his arrest came from me."

The officer nodded. "Don't worry, even my partner doesn't know it was more than a routine traffic stop. Although," he added with a laugh, "he didn't seem to think it was much of a missed stop."

"Let's keep it that way," Lucy said, her eyes dark and severe. She knew the risks she was taking, but the thrill of it all was intoxicating. No one could ever suspect her true intentions. For now, Maksym was in custody, and the next phase of her life could begin.

"Before you leave," Lucy called out to the policeman, reaching into her purse. She pulled out a small envelope and handed it to him with a teasing smile. "I have something for you."

He raised an eyebrow as he took the envelope and opened it, revealing two front-row tickets for the next local game of Inter Miami FC soccer team. His eyes widened in surprise. "Wow, these are amazing seats. I'll get to see Messi up close!"

"Consider it a gift between friends," Lucy replied, her voice honeyed and flirtatious. "Totally unrelated to… you know."

"Of course," the officer agreed, still appreciative. "Thank you, Lucy. It's very generous of you."

"De nada," she purred in Spanish, wrapping her arms around him once more for another sensual hug. As they parted, she hummed, "Vivir mi vida, la la la la; Vivir mi vida, la la la la."

"You don't sound like Marc Anthony, girl!"

CHAPTER 26
CRYSTAL

THE HOT MIAMI sun cast a shimmering glow on the water of Sierra's private pool as if it were a scene from paradise. Nollaig lounged in a comfortable chair, clad in a boxer-style bathing suit and sun guard top. His salt-and-pepper hair and tanned skin radiated vibrancy and strength, though his eyes held a hint of lingering darkness. Sierra, her bikini-clad figure reclining nearby, seemed to be the embodiment of relaxation, her blue hair creating a striking contrast against the sun-soaked terrace.

As they basked in the tranquility of the moment, the sliding door to the penthouse terrace opened with a soft rumble. Lucy stepped out, her long blonde hair tied into a loose ponytail. Sierra called out to her, asking how her meeting with her boss went, but Lucy remained silent. She turned around and disappeared into her penthouse for a moment before re-emerging onto the terrace wearing only a micro bikini bottom, her top discarded in favor of the European freedom she preferred.

"Hey, how'd your meeting go?" Sierra asked again, concern furrowing her brow.

Instead of answering, Lucy dove headfirst into the pool, cutting through the water with practiced ease. She resurfaced, facing Sierra and Noll, droplets of water streaming down her body as she raised her arms triumphantly above her head.

"Let's break out the champagne and celebrate!" Lucy declared, her grin infectious.

Sierra and Nollaig exchanged glances, curiosity piqued by the sudden shift in mood. They couldn't deny that the idea of celebrating was enticing after all they had been through. The three friends had come together under the weight of their shared struggles, bound by a common goal: to bring down Maksym and make this society at least a tiny bit better. But even in the midst of their fight, they each grappled with their own internal battles.

Sierra studied Lucy's expression, searching for a clue about her meeting with her D.E.A. boss. "So I take it the meeting went well?" she asked, trying to match Lucy's enthusiasm.

"Actually, it was so-so," replied Lucy, her smile faltering slightly. "But that's not why we should celebrate. We should toast to Maksym's arrest last night!" Her grin returned in full force.

"Great idea!" Sierra agreed, her own excitement growing. She stood up and disappeared into the condo, returning moments later with three champagne flutes and a bottle of Cristal.

"Nothing screams overpriced Miami like Cristal," Noll laughed as he eyed the bottle.

With a practiced hand, Sierra removed the foil from the bottle and gripped the cork firmly. She tilted the bottle at an angle and applied pressure until the cork burst free with a satisfying pop. The friends cheered as bubbles frothed at the mouth of the bottle.

Sierra filled each flute with the sparkling liquid, then handed one to Lucy and another to Noll. They raised their glasses, the sun catching the effervescent gold, casting a warm glow on their faces.

"Here's to new beginnings and a life free from Maksym's evil," Sierra declared, her eyes shining with determination.

"Cheers to that!" Nollaig agreed, his voice resolute, as if he were steeling himself for possible battles yet to come.

"May we always be this unstoppable team," added Lucy, her own resolve unwavering despite the challenges they had faced.

The three friends clinked their glasses together, the sound echoing across the terrace like the ringing of a bell. As they sipped their champagne, the weight of their shared burdens seemed to lift, if only for a fleeting moment. In that instant, they truly believed they could conquer anything that stood in their way. And they knew, deep down, that their bond was unbreakable, forged in the fires of adversity and tempered by the strength of their loyalty to one another.

As they sipped their champagne, Sierra's eyes locked onto Lucy's. The laughter and celebration faded into the background as she asked, "So, how did it really go with your boss?"

Lucy's smile waned as she stared at the rippling water in the pool. She hesitated before saying, "I'm not really sure. I was ready to go back to the D.E.A., but my boss wants me to stay undercover for a while longer."

Nollaig leaned forward, concern etched on his face.

"Right now, I don't know what it means," Lucy admitted, her voice tinged with frustration. She turned to Nollaig, her gaze searching his. "Speaking of which, have you thought about what's next for you? How you'll get your businesses back?"

Nollaig rubbed his chin, deep in thought. He shifted in his chair, the sun casting shadows across his face. "To be honest, I haven't had much time to think about it. We were so focused on taking Maksym down, and now that he's behind bars... well, I just don't know."

"Even with Maksym in jail, he still owns fifty percent of Seize The Deep and Sea Spell Diving," Nollaig continued, his voice heavy with uncertainty. "He still has two out of three votes on the board of directors. Reclaiming my businesses might not be as simple as we'd hoped."

Lucy bit her lip, sympathy flashing in her eyes. She reached out and placed a hand on Nollaig's arm. "We'll figure this out, Noll. We've come this far together; we're not giving up now. I can't wait for you to fire me!"

Sierra raised a hand, cutting through the tense atmosphere that had settled over them. "Hold on," she said, her blue hair shimmering in the sunlight as she shook her head. "You both bring up good points about Noll's businesses and Lucy's future with the D.E.A., but let's focus on the positive for now. Maksym is in jail, and that's definitely good news for both of you."

"Sierra's right," Nollaig agreed, his eyes showing appreciation for her effort to lift their spirits. "We can't undo everything Maksym has done overnight, but we've made progress. Let's celebrate that victory."

Lucy nodded, her face breaking into a smile. "You guys are right. We deserve to celebrate." She glanced around the luxurious pool area, the hot Miami sun reflecting off the water's surface. "And I can't think of a better place to do it."

"Come on, let's cool down!" Lucy set her empty glass aside and gracefully dove into the pool, followed by Sierra and Nollaig. The cool water was a welcome relief from the oppressive heat, and they frolicked together like carefree children.

As they took turns splashing each other, their laughter filled the air, mingling with the distant sounds of the city below. For the moment, they were free from the weight of their responsibilities and the looming uncertainty of their futures.

"Who knew fighting crime and taking down criminal masterminds could be such fun?" Sierra teased as she swam up to Nollaig, water droplets glistening on her shoulders.

"Ah, but we couldn't have done it without our fearless federal agent," Nollaig replied, gesturing towards Lucy with a grin. "And our intrepid... rich... hacker extraordinaire."

"Teamwork makes the dream work," Lucy chimed in, grinning broadly. "But seriously, we're a hell of a team."

"For sure," Nollaig agreed, his eyes twinkling with genuine affection for the two women who had become his closest friends and allies. "Here's to us and whatever the future may bring."

Later that afternoon, Ne-Yo was playing on Sierra's sound system. "Yes, well, it's a beautiful day. It's gon' be a beautiful night. Break out the champagne. Everybody get a glass. Let's start it off sexy. Whatta ya say."

Sierra looked at Noll and Lucy with a thoughtful expression. "You know, this is just one more step toward getting your businesses back, Noll, and for you to return to the D.E.A., Lucy."

Lucy sighed, stretching out on her lounge chair. "Yeah, I guess I'll eventually have to get used to not driving an expensive car and actually working more than a few hours a week."

"Life can be so cruel," Sierra teased, earning a playful glare from Lucy.

"Speaking of life changes," Nollaig interjected, "I'm grateful that my cancer surgery was successful. It's been quite the rollercoaster these past few months, but things are finally looking up."

"About that," Lucy said, mischief glinting in her eyes, "We don't really know for sure if your operation was a complete success, do we? Maybe there's something we should... check?"

Sierra caught on to what Lucy was alluding to and smirked. Some men experience difficulties with erections after prostate removal operations. Nollaig raised an eyebrow, his face flushing slightly as he realized what they were teasing him about.

"Hey now," he protested, trying to maintain some semblance of dignity despite the laughter bubbling up within him. "I assure you, everything is functioning just fine; thank you very much."

The laughter still lingering in the air, Sierra and Lucy shared a look that signaled they had an idea. They both stood up, approaching Nollaig, who was sitting on a lounge chair by the pool. With a mischievous glint in their eyes, they leaned in and kissed each other deeply, their lips pressed together as if trying to convey more than just carnal desire.

"Hey," Nollaig protested weakly, his face flushed despite the sunlight that bathed them all, "I told you, I'm alright."

But the women ignored him, too focused on their playful exploration of one another's bodies. While they continued kissing, Lucy reached for the strings of Sierra's bikini top and pulled, releasing the fabric and revealing her nipple piercings. Their mouths pulled apart momentarily, only to reconnect as their chests pressed together, nipples brushing against each other in an intimate dance.

As the kiss grew more heated, Lucy moved her lips away from Sierra's mouth and began trailing them down Sierra's neck, between her breasts, and over her belly. Her hands worked to tug Sierra's bikini bottoms down her legs, leaving her completely nude under the warm Miami sun. Sierra returned the favor, undressing Lucy with equal fervor until both women stood naked before Nollaig.

"Look what you've done to us," Sierra teased, gesturing to their state of undress. "All this talk about your health and operation, and now we're here like this."

"Can't help it," Lucy replied with a grin. "We just need to make sure everything is working properly."

Nollaig's eyes darted between the two women, admiring their beauty but also feeling exposed by their attention. He knew they were teasing him, but he couldn't deny the stirring in his loins as he watched them interact so intimately.

Standing naked before Noll, Lucy, and Sierra eyed the bulge in his bathing suit with amused grins. They exchanged glances, mischief dancing in their eyes.

"Would you look at that?" Lucy said, nudging Sierra playfully. "Seems like our friend here is quite responsive."

"Indeed," Sierra chimed in, a teasing tone in her voice. "But do you think that's a reliable indication of Noll's recovery?"

"Hard to say," Lucy replied thoughtfully, her gaze locked on Noll's growing discomfort. "We might need some more evidence to be sure."

Noll shifted in his seat, trying to maintain an air of nonchalance despite the heat creeping up his neck. "You two are having way too much fun at my expense," he muttered, but there was no anger in his voice—only a hint of embarrassment.

"Aw, don't be like that, Noll. We're just curious," Lucy said innocently, though her eyes sparkled with mischief. "Besides, it's only natural for us to wonder how well you've recovered, given all you've been through."

"Exactly," Sierra agreed, nodding sagely. "And there's only one sure-fire way to find out, don't you think?"

With that, Lucy began to sashay towards Noll, her hips swaying seductively as she closed the distance between them. Sierra followed suit, mirroring Lucy's movements as they approached him.

As they reached Noll's chair, Lucy slid her hand under the elastic waistband on one side of his bathing suit while Sierra did the same on the other side.

"Alright, alright!" Noll exclaimed, his face flushing a deep shade of red. "I can assure you, everything is functioning as it should. Now, can we please drop this?"

Lucy and Sierra exchanged smirks before pulling their hands back, leaving Noll's bathing suit in place. "Fine..." Lucy said with a mock sigh of disappointment. "Your loss!"

"Remember, Noll," Sierra added, her voice dripping with playful sarcasm, "we're only concerned for your well-being. Friends look out for each other, right?"

"Right," Noll replied, his voice a mix of gratitude and mild exasperation. "And I appreciate your... thorough concern."

"Anytime, Nollaig," Lucy said, winking at him. "Anytime."

CHAPTER 27
BLUE HERON BRIDGE

"*Come on down to the bottom of the sea;*
Come on down here."

SIERRA PULLED the F150 she had recently purchased into the parking lot next to the Blue Heron Bridge in West Palm Beach. The hot South Florida sun beat down on them. The air was thick with humidity, and the scent of saltwater filled their nostrils. Noll leaned over from the passenger seat and playfully nudged Lucy in the backseat.

"See, your fancy Porsche would've been useless today," he teased. "So typical of CEOs."

"Hey, I like my Porsche," Lucy pouted, but she couldn't help smiling at Noll's banter.

Sierra parked the pickup truck in a spot not too far from the water, her eyes scanning the area around them. She noticed the position of the sun and observed, "We're 60 minutes before high tide, as you requested. Perfect timing."

"I can't believe you guys have never dove here before," Noll commented. "This is one of the greatest scuba diving sites in the USA for shore diving. The only thing is… you must dive at high slack tide."

The three friends crawled out of the truck, each lost in their thoughts as they looked out at the beautiful scene before them. The turquoise water sparkled under the sun, and the breeze carried the distant laughter of scuba divers enjoying their day.

Noll insisted on setting up and carrying Sierra and Lucy's dive gear, a small gesture of gratitude for all they had done to help him. "You two have saved my life more than once," he said, his voice sincere. "The least I can do is carry the gear."

As Noll busied himself with the scuba diving equipment, Sierra and Lucy stripped down to their bikinis and waited. The air was thick with humidity, and sweat beaded on their skin as they watched Noll work.

"Are you sure this dive is a good idea?" Sierra asked hesitantly, her blue hair clinging to her damp forehead. "What if Maksym's goons find out Lucy was here with us... or her D.E.A. boss?"

"Fuck'em," Lucy spat, her green eyes flashing with anger.

Sierra frowned, clearly not convinced. "Maksym was certainly not alone in his organization."

Lucy shrugged, gesturing around them at the other divers preparing for their own adventures beneath the waves. "We just look like normal divers among all these people. And he can rot in jail!"

"Normal? Us?" Sierra laughed, even though she couldn't shake the nagging worry that they were taking unnecessary risks.

Noll chuckled, shaking his head as he glanced around the dive site. "You know, there's nothing normal about the three of us here," he said, gesturing around with a wry smile. "Scuba diving is still, unfortunately, an activity for old men. Do you see any other old men here with two beautiful young women?"

"Hey, don't confuse me with facts," Lucy responded playfully, brushing a strand of her long blonde hair from her face.

Sierra laughed along with them, her piercing dark brown eyes sparkling in amusement. "Well, it's a good thing we're in South Florida then, where beautiful young blonde bimbos are a dime a dozen."

"Hey, there!" Lucy objected.

"Does that make me a sugar daddy?" Noll asked, joining in their laughter.

Lucy giggled and glanced around at the other divers who were busy preparing their equipment. "To them, maybe you look like a sugar daddy or an uncle with his two nieces. If they only knew that it's Sierra who's the filthy rich sugar mama..."

"Ah, the things people don't know," Sierra mused, her lips curving into a sly grin. She adjusted her bikini top, feeling the weight of their shared secrets – from her hacking activities to Lucy's under-cover work – binding them together more than any family ties ever could.

For now, though, they would focus on the beauty surrounding them, enjoying this rare moment of peace amid the chaos of their lives. They would leave Maksym and his criminal thugs behind, submerging themselves in the tranquil waters below, where their worries couldn't follow.

With their dive gear on their backs and fins in their hands, Sierra, Noll, and Lucy walked across the small beach under the bridge to the dive entry point. The sand was warm beneath their feet as they navigated among the dozens of other divers milling about, preparing for their own dives.

"Wow, it's pretty busy here today," Sierra commented, glancing around at the clusters of people dotting the shoreline. She adjusted the straps of her buoyancy compensator with practiced ease, the weight of the equipment familiar and comforting.

Noll nodded. "As I said, it's one of the best shore diving spots in the country. People come from all over to experience it."

Once they reached waist-deep water, the trio paused to put on their fins. The cool water felt like a refreshing balm against their sun-warmed skin. As soon as they were ready, they exchanged thumbs-down signs, which is a signal among scuba divers that meant they were ready to descend into the depths below.

Underwater, the beauty of the dive site at Blue Heron Bridge unfolded before them like a living painting. As they descended, a kaleidoscope of vibrant colors greeted them, with sunlight dappling through the water and casting dappled patterns on the ocean floor.

Schools of fish swirled around them, darting in and out of the coral reef that stretched out as far as the eye could see.

Sierra marveled at the intricate coral formations, some resembling delicate fans and others gnarled branches reaching for the surface. Tiny creatures peeked out from hiding places within the coral, their eyes following the divers curiously as they swam past. An eel slithered by, its sinuous body weaving effortlessly through the water.

Noll led the way, pointing out elements of various marine life to Sierra and Lucy as they swam along. Each new discovery was communicated through an elaborate dance of hand signals, their excitement palpable despite the silence of their underwater world. At one point, Noll gestured towards a large sea turtle that glided gracefully overhead, its massive flippers propelling it effortlessly through the water.

Lucy's eyes widened in wonder as she watched the turtle, her mind momentarily set free from the weight of her undercover work and the looming need to testify in court against Maksym's criminal activities. For a brief moment, she allowed herself to be lost in the tranquility of the ocean and the companionship of her friends.

About an hour later, the three friends reluctantly signaled to each other that it was time to ascend. As Sierra, Noll, and Lucy broke through the water's surface, they filled their BCDs with air, making them positively buoyant. The sunlight danced on the tiny waves around them, reflecting off the droplets clinging to their masks.

"Wow, that dive site is gorgeous!" Sierra exclaimed, her eyes still wide with excitement. "Thanks for introducing us to this place, Noll."

"Absolutely incredible," Lucy agreed, smiling at Noll. "I never knew a place like this existed so close to home."

Noll grinned, pleased by their reactions. "It's one of my favorite spots. I'm glad you both enjoyed it as much as I do."

Once they stood in waist-deep water, they removed their fins and began walking towards the shore. They carried their fins in their hands, feeling the weight of the waterlogged gear but not minding it. The sun warmed their faces, and the saltwater left trails of evaporating moisture behind.

Once back at the vehicle, they slowly removed their dive gear and placed it, dripping wet, into the bed of Sierra's pickup truck. Lucy, still grinning from the exhilaration of the dive, turned to Noll and jokingly asked, "Is it a requirement to own a pickup when you're a scuba diver?"

"Actually," Noll chuckled, "I once knew a gal who went diving with her Smart car – you know, those tiny little cars sold by Mercedes. She only carried her own dive gear, though. No gear for dive buddies."

"Wow," Lucy laughed. "That must've been quite a sight!"

"Definitely turned some heads at the dive site," Noll admitted with a grin.

AS THEY WERE ready to leave after their exhilarating dive, Noll hummed Matt Nathanson's song. "Too many cars drinking too much gasoline; There's no good news on my TV screen; There's a hole up in the sky so come on baby dive; And live life at the bottom of the sea."

Lucy's phone rang. She glanced at the screen before answering with a puzzled expression.

"Hello?" she said, her brow furrowing as she listened to the voice on the other end. Noll and Sierra exchanged glances as they caught snippets of her responses. "Yes... Are you sure? How can that be? What does that mean for me?"

When Lucy hung up, she was silent, her face pale and her eyes wide. Her sudden shift in demeanor unnerved Noll and Sierra, who immediately sensed something was wrong.

"Lucy," Noll probed gently, "what's going on? You look like you've seen a ghost."

"Guys," Lucy began hesitantly, swallowing hard, "Maksym Byrne has been released."

"Released?" Sierra echoed, her voice tense.

"Probably out on bail until trial," Noll mused, trying to make sense of the news.

"No," Lucy interrupted, shaking her head. "It's not bail. All charges have been dropped. He said something about the evidence being unacceptable."

"Unacceptable?" Sierra exclaimed, her disbelief apparent. "What the fuck?"

Noll, Sierra, and Lucy stood by the F150, speechless and stunned. The weight of this unexpected revelation hung heavy in the air, casting a shadow over their previously carefree day. Their success now seemed fleeting, and the future uncertain. The world above the waves suddenly felt suffocating, a stark contrast to the peaceful beauty they'd experienced below the surface.

CHAPTER 28
TEFLON

s I walk through the valley of the shadow of death;
I take a look at my life and realize there's nothin' left."

THE MID-AFTERNOON SUN cast long shadows on the diner's checkerboard floor as Lucy slid into the booth across from her boss. Her still-damp hair clung to her neck, a reminder of her recent scuba diving excursion.

"Where were you today?" her boss asked, his eyebrow raised in curiosity.

"Scuba diving," Lucy replied, a hint of defiance in her voice. "You told me to enjoy the life of an overpaid wealthy executive, remember? Letting the poor people do all the work for me. Living the American dream."

Her boss didn't find her sarcasm amusing. His eyes narrowed.

She sighed. "Fine, let's get serious. Why the fuck is Maksym back in business?"

"That's above your pay grade. And I'm the one asking questions. And giving orders."

Lucy shut up. There was definitely something weird with her boss.

Nollaig sat in his corporate lawyer's office, the familiar scent of leather and mahogany bringing back memories of when he managed his dive businesses. The lawyer leaned back in his chair, hands clasped behind his head as he delivered the news. "There are no criminal charges against Maksym. And even if there were, it doesn't change the fact that he owns fifty percent of Seize The Deep and Sea Spell Diving."

Nollaig frowned, gripping the edge of the table. "What if he was convicted as a criminal? Couldn't we force him out then?"

The lawyer chuckled, shaking his head. "In that case, the feds could, perhaps, seize his assets as ill-gained. You'd be dealing with bureaucrats instead of Maksym, but believe me, having any kind of logical discussion with the government is a lost cause. You're better off trying to hold water in your hands."

Noll could feel the weight of defeat pressing down on him, but he refused to accept it. He needed to find a way to reclaim his life and earn a living. But with every door slamming shut in his face, it felt like an insurmountable task.

Noll clenched his fists, doing his best to remain composed as the lawyer continued. "To make matters worse, with the divorce, your ex-wife now controls 50% of your shares... 25 % of Seize The Deep and Sea Spell Diving. And she's given a proxy to Maksym's lawyer for her shares, so now Max effectively has control over 75% of the shareholders' votes."

"Are you serious? Why the fuck would she do that?" Noll couldn't help but feel like he was being pushed further and further into a corner.

"Divorce, Noll... It brings out the worst in people," the lawyer replied, his expression somber. "And you know, even if Maksym were really arrested, it could take years for the legal process to do its thing, and even longer before the shares are sorted out. And let's not forget that he could very well sell the company for next to nothing to someone else tomorrow morning."

Noll's heart sank as the lawyer's words echoed in his head. All the fight he had left inside him seemed to evaporate, leaving only despair behind. He knew that getting his dive businesses back was a long shot, but hearing the cold, hard truth from his own lawyer was devastating.

"Then what am I supposed to do?" Noll asked, his voice barely above a whisper. "I've lost everything."

"Look, Noll," the lawyer said, leaning back in his chair and clasping his hands together. "You've been through a lot... a divorce... a bankruptcy... I know it's not easy to pick up the pieces, but you have to move on with your life."

Noll stared at the floor, teeth clenched as he tried to contain his frustration.

The lawyer continued, trying to inject some levity into the conversation. "Hey, at the very least, you are now qualified to be President of the United States, right? Maybe start a MUGA movement – Make Underwater Great Again." He chuckled at his own joke, but Noll didn't find it funny.

"Thanks for the advice," Noll spat out, his patience wearing thin.

LATER THAT EVENING, Noll, Sierra, and Lucy sat around the dining table in Sierra's luxury condo. The atmosphere was tense, and Noll couldn't shake the feeling of defeat weighing heavily on him.

"Come on, guys," Sierra said, her voice firm but compassionate. "So what if your lawyer, Noll, and your boss, Lucy, only had bad news? Welcome to planet Earth, where only bullies become billionaires." She glared at both Noll and Lucy, who were staring blankly at their plates.

"Stop being so depressed," she continued, her words punctuated by the clink of silverware against porcelain. "The world is fucked, and we need to stop being naive. Let's focus on what we can do with our lives instead of wallowing in self-pity."

Noll looked up at her, his eyes filled with a mixture of anger and resignation. Sierra was right, he knew, but it was hard to see beyond the injustice of it all. Lucy glanced between them, her expression unreadable.

Noll leaned back in his chair, staring at the half-empty plate of food before him. With a sigh, he said, "At least you'll continue to have a fat salary to launder Maksym's money, Lucy. You'll have a nice car, spa treatments a few times a week... but me? I've got nothing."

"Are you fuckin' kidding me?" Lucy was mad at Noll's comment. "Max will probably reach the conclusion I was behind the coke in his truck... If he hasn't already. I'm a walking dead!"

"Enough with the pity party, Noll, Lucy," Sierra interjected, her voice firm but not unkind. She placed her fork down and looked directly at them. "Listen, guys. I had some fun hacking into Maksym's nightclub... a few times... trying to figure out how he launders his money and maybe find out where it goes."

"Yeah, so?" Noll muttered, rubbing his temples as if trying to alleviate a headache.

"The money trail ended up on a lot of dead ends, sure," she continued, her eyes narrowing slightly, "but there was a lot of money moving around, and... well... I managed to divert ten million dollars."

Noll and Lucy were stunned by Sierra's revelation.

Noll stared down at his clasped hands. Glancing around the luxurious condo, he took in the sleek, modern furnishings and state-of-the-art technology. It was clear that Sierra already had no shortage of wealth.

"Sierra," Noll said, his voice tinged with frustration, "I know you did all that to try to get Maksym in trouble, but how is it going to help me get back on my feet?"

"Who was that criminal known as the Teflon guy?" Lucy interjected, out of nowhere.

Nollaig sighed, running a hand through his short-cropped hair. "John Gotti," he replied. "He was called the Teflon Don because charges against him never stuck."

"Then Maksym is the Teflon thug," Lucy mused. "He lost $10 million in his money laundering activities, two full Blue Dragon boxes of US dollars, one full box of cocaine, got arrested with three bricks of cocaine, and yet, he has no issue with the law. And he doesn't seem to have problems with other criminal organizations he deals with, either."

They fell silent, each contemplating Maksym's seemingly untouchable nature and the uphill battle they faced in trying to bring him down. The weight of their situation settled heavily upon them, and Noll felt a sense of despair creeping back up on him.

Lucy started humming 'Gangsta's Paradise' by Coolio. "As I walk through the valley of the shadow of death, I take a look at my life and realize there's nothin' left."

"Enough, both of you," Sierra interrupted, her voice softer as she tried to bridge the gap between them. "We've spent a lot of time trying to bring Maksym down, but that wouldn't even get your dive businesses back, right, Noll? That's what your lawyer said. So instead, for now, let's focus on what each of us needs in this fucked up life."

Noll nodded slowly, acknowledging the truth in her words.

"Staying alive would be a good start." Lucy was still concerned about Maksym. "Money ain't gonna keep that mother fucker from killing me. Even though I'm not a mother..."

Silence hung heavy in the air, the tension between them palpable. Sierra sighed and leaned forward, her blue hair falling over her face as she locked eyes with Lucy. "If Maksym knew it was you, Lucy, you'd be dead already," she said firmly. "Maybe you can make one of his goons take the fall for the three bricks?"

"Maybe," Lucy mused, running a hand through her long blonde hair. "By the way, I've confirmed that the bills in the waterproof boxes at the warehouse aren't fake or tracked. I guess we have resources to work with."

Sierra took a deep breath, her dark brown eyes determined. "So let's focus on what we can do. Based on what your lawyer told you, Noll, you're not getting your dive businesses back... maybe ever. So, again, we should focus less on Maksym and more on what each of us wants in our lives."

A heavy silence settled over the room again as they each considered Sierra's words. The weight of their situation pressed down on them, but Sierra's resolve remained unshakable.

"Besides," she added after a moment, her voice tinged with cynicism, "even if Maksym was gone, another thug would take his place. Our entire society is a lost cause."

Noll frowned, his salt-and-pepper hair shifting as he shook his head. "That may be true, but we can't just give up without trying, can we?"

"Maybe not," Sierra agreed, her tone softening slightly. "But we need to make sure we're fighting for the right reasons – our lives – and not just out of anger or revenge."

Lucy nodded, her expression thoughtful. "True. Fine. Okay. We have the means to make a difference, even if it's just in our own lives. I'll manage to get off the hook for the cocaine in his truck. And the missing boxes. Then, let's use what we have to build something better for ourselves, and maybe, in the process, we can make an even bigger dent in Maksym's operations."

Noll slumped back in his chair, his expression pensive as he considered Sierra and Lucy's words. The soft hum of the air conditioning in Sierra's luxurious condo added to the quiet atmosphere, making the silence between them feel more profound.

"Fine," he finally said, breaking the silence. "So what do we do?"

Sierra leaned forward, her blue hair framing her face like a vibrant halo. "The $10 million I hacked from Maksym is sitting offshore in an account officially owned by the SNL Foundation. But we can't just withdraw money for you to live on – there has to be a legitimate source for your revenues on U.S. soil."

Noll's jaw tightened as he considered the situation. His mind raced, searching for a solution that would allow him to access the money without drawing unwanted attention. Slowly, an idea began to form in his mind.

"Wait," he said, his voice low and measured. "I think I have an idea of how to use that money."

CHAPTER 29
FLORIDA CITY

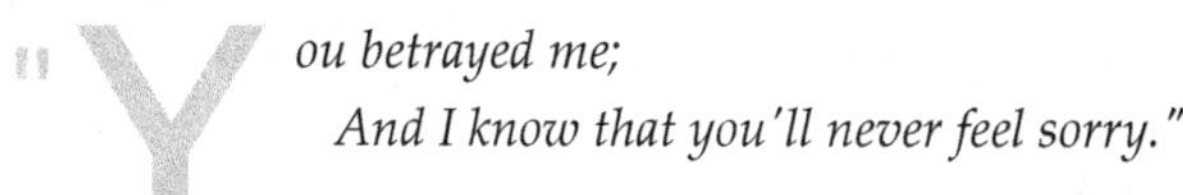

"*Y*ou *betrayed me;*
And I know that you'll never feel sorry."

HEATWAVE LOUNGE PULSED WITH ENERGY, the hypnotic beat of music drawing Lucy in as she crossed the threshold. The vibrant lights cast sensual shadows over her barely-there dress, hugging her body like a second skin. Her heart raced, torn between the thrill of dancing and the terror that Maksym would discover her betrayal.

As she moved through the crowd toward his office, Lucy allowed herself to be swept up in the rhythm, her body swaying to the music. Despite the danger, she couldn't deny how alive she felt in these moments, lost among the writhing bodies and pounding bass. But beneath her temporary euphoria, the ever-present fear gnawed at her insides, the feeling of impending doom never too far away.

Lucy reached Maksym's office door and paused. She took a deep breath, trying to calm her nerves as the music continued to throb around her. Her body was trembling, but she willed it to stop, knowing that she had to appear natural in front of him.

The door swung open abruptly, revealing Maksym. His intense gaze met hers. He'd clearly seen her approach through the one-way mirror in his office. His eyes narrowed as he scrutinized her, making her heart race even faster.

"Lucy," he said, his voice low and dangerous. "What do you want?"

She swallowed hard, fighting the urge to back away from him. She knew she had to be clever, to throw suspicion off herself and onto someone else. It was a risky move, but she had no choice. "Maksym, I... I need to talk to you about something," she began, her voice barely above a whisper.

Maksym signaled her to get in, and he closed the door behind her. She was at his mercy. The pulsating beat of the music was now muffled through the door and no longer enveloping Lucy's body.

Her eyes locked onto Maksym's, a mixture of anxiety and resolve swirling within them. She hesitated for a moment before speaking up. "There's something I noticed during our last night dive... It might be nothing, but I thought you should know."

"Stop dancing around the topic, Lucy," Maksym ordered, his voice cold and stern. "Just tell me what you want to say."

Drawing in a shaky breath, Lucy's fingers fidgeted at her sides, betraying her unease. "I saw Eddie messing with your pickup truck," she admitted, the words tumbling out of her mouth. "I don't know what he was doing, but it didn't seem right."

Maksym scrutinized her, his gaze sharp and penetrating. Lucy forced herself to hold his stare, refusing to let her fear show. She knew that if she faltered now, it could be the end of her.

"I didn't think anything of it at the time, but... The more I replay it in my head, the more... It was strange."

The dim lights of Maksym's office cast shadows across Lucy's face as she stood before Maksym. His piercing gaze bore into her, searching for any sign of deception.

"We can't have untrustworthy people in our team," he said slowly, each word dripping like venom. "And anyone who breaks my trust will pay the price."

Lucy swallowed hard, her throat suddenly dry. She couldn't shake the feeling that Maksym might suspect her. Her heart pounded in her chest, threatening to burst out at any moment. She forced a smile, hoping it didn't come across as forced as it felt. "Of course, Max. I completely agree."

"And thank you for telling me, Lucy," Maksym added, his tone unreadable. "Don't mention this again. If there's something going on, I'll take care of it. Understood?"

"Understood," Lucy replied, relief washing over her like a tidal wave. She had managed to plant the seed of doubt onto somebody else–at least, for now. Maybe.

As she left Maksym's office and faded into the crowd, Lucy couldn't help but feel the weight of her decisions bearing down on her. If her ruse worked, it could mean death for Eddie. The consequences, like the music enveloping her, were inescapable. And as she allowed herself to dance among strangers, her mind raced with thoughts of what might come next–questions of loyalty and betrayal, love and deceit, all entwined in a complex dance of their own.

But she eventually convinced herself that it was fine since Eddie was just a thug. And she left the HeatWave Lounge.

A COUPLE OF DAYS LATER, under the oppressive Florida sun, Maksym met with Lucy's boss in the parking lot of an abandoned building in Florida City. The D.E.A. boss leaned against his car, arms crossed defensively over his chest.

"Couldn't find anything on Eddie or that picture you gave me," the D.E.A. boss said, his voice gravelly and tired. "Checked the FBI, ATF, Secret Service, D.E.A. databases. Nothing."

Maksym exhaled slowly, his jaw clenched as he considered this new information. "So either he's a ghost, or he's not involved."

"Seems that way." Lucy's boss shifted his weight, the scorching asphalt beneath them radiating heat. Sweat beaded on his forehead, but he made no move to wipe it away.

Maksym leaned against the hood of his McLaren. The abandoned building's parking lot in Florida City was bleak. He studied Lucy's boss for a moment, noticing the sweat on his brow and the nervous energy in his stance.

"Look," Maksym said, his voice edged with menace. "Let's say Eddie isn't the rat. What if it's Lucy? She's been acting strange lately, and now perhaps she's trying to pin this on someone else."

The D.E.A. boss scratched his jawline, silent for a beat. His eyes seemed to search for answers in the shadows that played across the cracked asphalt. "I doubt it," he said at last. "Lucy is young, inexperienced. Reckless, even. But planting cocaine in your truck while you were there? That'd be crazy. She knows the value of an alibi."

"Is that so?" Maksym muttered, his gaze never leaving the other man's face. "Well then, you better find out who's screwing with my business. Money hacked from my accounts, guns and coke stolen, and now someone trying to frame me? If I don't get answers soon, I'll assume it's you."

He released a low growl, the sound rumbling through the still night air. It echoed in his chest, the visceral manifestation of his anger and frustration. In his mind, he could almost feel the weight of the threats he'd issued–crushing, suffocating.

"Alright," the D.E.A. boss replied, his tone subdued but resolute. "I'll find out who's behind this, Max. Just give me some time."

"Time," Maksym snorted. "That's something that's running out fast around here."

As they stood there, surrounded by darkness, Maksym couldn't shake the feeling that he was being watched–by unseen eyes, hidden in the shadows. A shiver ran through him, and for a moment, he wondered if it was the fear of betrayal that chilled his bones or the simple fact that trust was a luxury he could no longer afford.

"Look," Maksym said, his voice low and dangerous, "it could've been anyone hacking my accounts or stealing those boxes. But no criminal would try to get me arrested like that. They'd just kill me if they wanted me out of the way. I'm telling you, it's someone in the government."

Lucy's boss met Maksym's steely gaze, his eyes flickering with unease. "You think?"

"Listen," Max replied, the corner of his mouth curling into a sardonic smile, "only someone who knows how the system works could pull off such a stunt without leaving a trace."

"Or someone who's very skilled at covering their tracks."

"Exactly." Maksym's eyes narrowed, his suspicion creeping closer to conviction. "Either way, it's your job to find out who's messing with my business. And if you don't..."

The unspoken threat hung heavy between them, a storm cloud ready to burst.

As they prepared to part ways, the D.E.A. boss looked around at the desolate surroundings and asked, "Why did we meet here, anyway? This place gives me the creeps."

Maksym chuckled darkly, a sinister gleam in his eyes. "It's the perfect place for our little rendezvous. If you don't find the answers I need..." He let his words trail off before adding, "Well, I won't have to do anything. I can just leave you here, all alone in this godforsaken city."

The D.E.A. boss swallowed hard, the gravity of Maksym's words settling like a weight in the pit of his stomach. He knew that finding the answers Maksym sought was not just a matter of professional duty–it was a matter of survival.

"Alright, Max," he said, nodding. "I'll find out who's behind this."

Lucy's boss stepped back into his SUV, and as if on cue, Olivia Rodrigo's song "Traitor" played on the radio. "You betrayed me, and I know that you'll never feel sorry."

"Could it be Lucy?" he wondered.

Meanwhile, Maksym's thoughts also drifted back to Lucy. The young woman who had once been so full of passion for life now seemed different.

"Time's running out," Maksym whispered to himself, the words a reminder of the precarious balance that held their lives together. Time was indeed running out, and with it, the hope of ever finding solace in the shadows of a city gone mad.

CHAPTER 30
ONE DIVE AT A TIME

"*Like a small boat on the ocean;*
Sending big waves into motion."

NOLL HOVERED WEIGHTLESSLY in the clear water just below the surface, the Blue Heron Bridge looming nearby. Instead of a traditional scuba unit, he breathed through a regulator connected to a surface-supplied air system. A hose led from his mouthpiece to a small electric air compressor floating above. He carefully watched the four teenagers who accompanied him, each using their own surface-supplied air systems. Though Noll couldn't speak underwater, he communicated with them through a series of hand signals, making sure they were safe and enjoying themselves.

On the other side of the group, a female diver mirrored Noll's actions, also relying on a surface-supplied air system. Every now and then, Nollaig and the woman exchanged hand signals to confirm that everything was running smoothly. In between those brief moments of checking in, their attention turned to the breathtaking underwater world surrounding them.

The ocean floor was a mesmerizing tapestry of vibrant corals and swaying sea fans, teeming with marine life. Schools of iridescent fish darted around the divers, their scales shimmering as they caught the filtered sunlight piercing the water's surface. The teenagers marveled at the sight of a majestic sea turtle gliding gracefully nearby, its ancient eyes seeming to hold the secrets of the deep.

Even Noll, with his years of experience, couldn't help but be captivated by the beauty of the undersea world. It was in these moments that the weight of his recent tribulations seemed to lift, if only for a little while. As he watched the living colors of the coral reef undulate around him, he was reminded of why he had fallen in love with diving in the first place.

Despite the hardships of his recent past, Noll found solace and purpose in introducing these young people to the wonders hidden beneath the waves. This was where he belonged, immersed in the ocean's embrace, guiding others through this ethereal underwater realm. And as he exchanged another reassuring hand signal with the female diver, Noll knew that he was not alone in his mission. Together, they would fight against the darkness that threatened to swallow them, buoyed by the hope and inspiration found beneath the sea.

Noll and the female diver eventually signaled to the four teenagers that it was time to head back. The group swam slowly underwater back toward the shore while continuing to take in the breathtaking sights around them. A curious stingray glided by, its undulating movement captivating the young divers. They couldn't help but marvel at the delicate balance of life and beauty teeming beneath the surface.

As they continued their underwater journey back to shore, a school of yellowtail snapper weaved among the divers as if playfully escorting them along. The awe in the eyes of the teenagers was evident, even behind their dive masks. Further on, an intricate formation of brain coral caught their attention, its labyrinthine structure a testament to the complexity and resilience of marine life.

Eventually, the water began to shallow, and Noll motioned for the group to stand up. Rising to their feet, the teenagers broke the surface, their faces alight with excitement and wonder. Waist-deep in the water now, they could hardly contain their enthusiasm as they gushed about their underwater adventure.

"Yo, that was insane!" one boy exclaimed, his voice dripping with exhilaration. "Did you see how close that sea turtle got? It was like, right next to me!"

"Seriously, I can't believe we were actually swimming with all those fish," a girl chimed in, her eyes wide with disbelief. "And the colors! Everything was so bright and beautiful."

"Man, I thought I knew what the ocean was like, but this was a whole new level," a third teen added, shaking his head in amazement. "I never knew there was so much going on down there."

"Right? I'm definitely doing this again," another girl agreed, grinning broadly. "This was like, the best day ever."

Noll and the female diver exchanged knowing smiles, their hearts warmed by the teenagers' evident joy and a newfound appreciation for the underwater world they both loved so deeply. They couldn't help but feel a sense of pride and accomplishment, knowing that they had opened the door to something incredible for these young people. And as they stood there in the sun-dappled surf, surrounded by the laughter and excitement of their charges, Noll felt a renewed sense of purpose and determination take root within him.

For all the darkness and struggle that he had endured, moments like these were what truly mattered – connecting others to the hidden wonders beneath the waves and igniting a passion for the ocean that would, hopefully, last a lifetime.

With the warm water lapping at their waists, Noll gestured for the teenagers to remove their fins. "Here's a little trick," he said, demonstrating how to slide his hand between the fin and strap, securing it around his wrist. "Keeps your hands free and makes carrying everything easier."

"Sweet!" one of the boys exclaimed, following suit. The others mimicked the action, laughing as they worked out the technique.

"Nice. Now grab your air systems by the handle on top, and we're good to go," Noll instructed, watching as the teenagers balanced their equipment with one hand while keeping the other free.

"Man, this is so cool," one of the girls gushed, her enthusiasm apparent in her voice. "I can't wait to tell all my friends about this!"

"Right?" another boy agreed. "This was seriously the best thing we've ever done."

As they walked towards a van parked nearby, Noll couldn't help but smile at their excitement. It felt like he was making a real difference in their lives, and that thought filled him with renewed determination.

The van itself was a sight to behold – a vibrant, colorful canvas covered in underwater scenes and marine life. Bold lettering read "Scuba: No Limits," and smaller text identified it as a non-profit organization. The female diver who had been assisting Noll opened the back doors to reveal small, stacked boxes designed to hold each surface-supplied air system.

The group chatted and joked among themselves, their youthful energy contagious. Noll glanced at his female companion, who shared his grin. Both of them basked in the happiness of the moment.

The four teenagers, still buzzing with excitement from their underwater experience, quickly peeled off their wetsuits and tossed them onto the asphalt behind the van. Almost simultaneously, they whipped out their smartphones and began scrolling through social media feeds or posting about their dive adventure.

"Can you believe how beautiful that coral was?" the girl gushed to her friend while she tapped away at her screen. "I'm gonna get so many likes for these videos on my GoPro!"

"Right?!" her friend agreed, equally absorbed in his phone. "This was seriously lit!"

Noll and the woman exchanged knowing smirks as they observed the teenagers, their enthusiasm for the underwater world quickly eclipsed by their addiction to technology. "Well," Noll mused, "at least we managed to pull them away from their screens for a little while."

The woman chuckled, nodding in agreement. "Yeah, it's nice to see kids connecting with nature. But I guess the call of the smartphone is just too strong."

The two diving instructors started removing their own wetsuits, revealing the woman's toned, muscular physique. "Hey, Kim," Noll said, wiping the salt water from his face, "I just wanted to thank you again for helping me out with Scuba: No Limits. It means a lot to have you here on your days off."

Kim flashed him a genuine smile, her green eyes warm and sincere. "Of course, Noll. Honestly, I love doing this. And besides, I couldn't teach part-time at your former dive businesses anymore. The vibe there has changed so much since you were gone."

Noll felt a pang of sadness when his lost businesses were mentioned, but he pushed it aside and focused instead on the positive impact they'd made on the lives of these kids today.

With their own wetsuits removed and the teenagers busy on their smartphones, Nollaig and Kim began carefully storing the diving gear in the back of the colorful van. The boxes were lined up neatly, each one ready to hold a surface-supplied air system. As they worked, Noll glanced at Kim.

"Hey, are you still available for the SNL Foundation's board meeting tonight?" he asked, wiping his brow with the back of his hand.

"Absolutely," Kim replied, smiling. "I wouldn't miss it."

"Great," Noll said, satisfied. He returned his attention to the task at hand, securing the last of the gear before closing the van's back doors.

"Alright, guys," Kim called out to the teenagers, who reluctantly looked up from their phones. "Let's get inside the van and head back."

The teens murmured their assent, some more enthusiastic than others, as they climbed into the van through the side door. Once they were all seated in the middle section, Noll and Kim joined them, and the van pulled away from the dive site.

LATER THAT EVENING, Noll found himself sitting in the corner of a Starbucks with Kim and Harper. The three of them were gathered around a small table, coffees in hand, as Noll welcomed them to the first official board of directors meeting for the SNL Foundation.

"Welcome to our official boardroom," Noll joked, gesturing around the coffee shop with a grin. "Starbucks: where all the important decisions are made."

"Overpriced coffee and all," Harper quipped, smirking as she sipped from her cup. Noll laughed, but then his expression grew thoughtful.

"Maybe we should find a local café next time," he mused aloud. "You know, support a local business and save some money for the foundation. I guess old habits die hard, huh?"

As they shifted their attention to the future of the SNL Foundation, Noll felt a renewed sense of purpose. Surrounded by loyal friends like Kim and Harper, he knew that together, they would overcome whatever challenges lay ahead and help make the world a better place—one dive at a time.

As the board meeting officially started, Harper leaned forward, her eyes serious. "We need to choose our positions on the board. I think it's best if Kim takes on the role of President. It'll look better if someone without bankruptcy in their past holds that position. No offense."

"None taken!"

"Fine," Kim chimed in, nodding. "And you, Harper, should be secretary-treasurer. Considering Noll is the only one receiving a salary from the foundation, it wouldn't look good for him to handle the finances."

Noll nodded his understanding. "Alright, I'll be the vice president then. We've got a lot of work ahead of us, but I know we can make a difference."

"Absolutely," Kim said, smiling reassuringly.

Harper placed a supportive hand on Noll's shoulder. "We're here because we believe in what you're doing, Noll, and we're committed to helping these kids connect with the underwater world."

Noll took a deep breath, feeling a renewed sense of purpose surge through him. "Thank you both for being a part of this project."

"Of course, Noll," Kim said, her voice warm and sincere. "Helping underprivileged kids is an important mission, and we're honored to be a part of it."

Harper raised her coffee cup in a toast. "To the SNL Foundation and to the future—we're going to change the world, one dive at a time."

"Cheers," Noll and Kim said, clinking their cups with Harper's. The familiar sounds of the coffee shop hummed around them, but at that moment, all Nollaig could focus on was the bond between them and their shared vision for a better future.

Kim raised an eyebrow and inquired, "So Noll, what about fundraising for the foundation? Do we have a plan for that?"

Noll leaned back in his chair, his mind racing with thoughts of the future. "For now, we've received a generous $8 million donation from an anonymous donor. It should sustain us for quite some time. However, eventually, we'll need to consider raising more funds from other sources, yes."

"Sounds like we're off to a good start then." Harper nodded thoughtfully. "The anonymous donation is a great safety net, but it's smart to think about long-term financial stability."

Noll agreed, feeling optimistic about the future of the SNL Foundation as they made their plans.

AFTER PARTING ways with Kim and Harper, Noll arrived at Sierra's condo, his thoughts swirling around the events of the day. As he entered the penthouse, he noticed that Lucy and Sierra were on the terrace, seemingly unaware of his arrival. To his surprise, he caught them in an intimate embrace, kissing each other passionately.

Noll was shocked, not because he had any issues with their relationship, but rather because he realized how little he knew about his friends Lucy and Sierra. He had been so consumed by his personal troubles that he hadn't taken the time to truly understand them. The realization stung, and he felt a pang of guilt for his self-absorption.

Clearing his throat, Noll stepped onto the terrace, interrupting Lucy and Sierra's intimate moment. They broke their kiss at once, eyes widening in surprise. Sierra brushed a strand of hair behind her ear, her face flushed.

"Hey, Noll," she said, trying to sound casual. "How'd the day go?"

"Uh, good." He struggled to maintain eye contact, still processing what he had just seen. "The dive at Blue Heron Bridge was incredible for the kids, and the board meeting with Kim and Harper went well."

"Nice!" Lucy chimed in, clearly trying to lighten the mood. "I bet Kim and Harper thought SNL stood for 'Scuba: No Limits,' but really, it was originally 'Sierra, Nollaig & Lucy.'"

Noll couldn't help but smile, remembering how the foundation had been created, even though his mind was racing with questions about his friends' relationship. He shook off his lingering shock before continuing, "You know, I wish you both could be more involved with the foundation."

"Trust me, so do I," Lucy sighed. "But, as you know, I'm still under-cover as President and CEO of your former dive businesses, and Maksym can't find out that I've been helping you."

Noll nodded. "I get it, and keeping Sierra hidden makes sense, too. It's just... I miss having you both around when I'm working with the kids at Scuba: No Limits."

"Believe me, Noll, we'd be there if we could," Sierra added, placing a reassuring hand on his arm. "But for now, our roles need to stay sepa-rate for everyone's safety."

As they spoke, Noll couldn't shake the feeling that he barely knew his friends anymore. Their secret relationship had thrown him off balance, and he wondered what else he might have missed while consumed by his own personal struggles. He needed to rebuild those connections, not only for their shared mission but also for the strength of their friendship.

"Alright," Noll agreed, his voice taking on a determined tone. "We'll make it work and be there for each other in any way we can."

"Absolutely," Lucy and Sierra echoed in unison, their eyes meeting with a newfound understanding.

Sierra slipped away from the terrace, leaving Noll and Lucy behind as they continued their conversation. Moments later, she reemerged, carrying a bottle of Cristal champagne in her hands. Her blue hair glinted in the soft light of the evening, and her eyes sparkled with excitement.

"Damn! Do you buy these by the dozen?" Noll joked.

Sierra shrugged. "Alright, guys, it's high time we celebrate. Noll, you're back diving and helping people connect with the underwater world without worrying about profits or dive stores. That's definitely worth a toast."

Nollaig looked at the champagne and then at Sierra, a warm smile crossing his face. He had to admit that his life had improved significantly in the last couple of weeks. The weight of Maksym's betrayal still hung heavy on his heart, but helping others experience the magic of the ocean filled him with a sense of purpose and joy he hadn't felt in months.

"Thank you, Sierra," Noll said, accepting a glass of champagne from her. "You're right. Life is pretty good nowadays, as long as I don't dwell on Maksym and what he's done to my former businesses."

"Let's focus on the positive," Lucy chimed in, raising her own glass. "To new beginnings, and to making a real difference in the lives of others."

"Cheers!" they all agreed, clinking their glasses together. The sound of their toast was like a symphony, a harmony of hope and friendship that played out against the backdrop of the crashing waves below.

As they sipped their champagne, Noll allowed himself to feel a moment of contentment. He couldn't change the past or erase the pain Maksym had caused, but he could choose how to move forward from it. Surrounded by friends who believed in him and supported him, Noll felt more determined than ever to make a difference in the world, one dive at a time.

"Let's make this new chapter count," Noll declared, his voice steady and resolute. "For ourselves, for the kids we help, and for the underwater world we love."

"Absolutely," Sierra and Lucy agreed, their eyes shining with conviction.

On that, Lucy started humming Rachel Platten's 'Fight Song.' "Like a small boat on the ocean; Sending big waves into motion."

Sierra joined in. "Like how a single word; Can make a heart open; I might only have one match; But I can make an explosion."

And Noll, eager to prove he knew some recent songs, continued, trying to sing high but failing. "This is my fight song; Take back my life song; Prove I'm alright song; My power's turned on; Starting right now, I'll be strong; I'll play my fight song."

As they stood together on the terrace, the sun dipping below the horizon, they knew that they were bound by more than just friendship – they were bound by a shared purpose, a fierce determination to fight against the darkness and transform it into light.

CHAPTER 31
KIM & HARPER

SIERRA'S FINGERS danced across the three keyboards in front of her, her eyes darting between the multiple computer monitors on a gigantic desk with electrically adjustable legs. Her blue hair framed her face as she leaned closer to one of the screens, squinting at the data displayed. Kim and Harper flanked her, sitting on chairs on each side of Sierra, their attention equally focused on the task at hand.

"Lucy's boss at the D.E.A. is highly respected," Kim said, breaking the silence that had enveloped the room. "He's done numerous arrests and busts in South Florida. But what I can't wrap my head around is how all the charges against Maksym were dropped."

Kim sighed, looking uneasy. "I couldn't dig too deep without raising suspicion. Being a U.S. Marshal has its limitations, you know? People would start asking questions if I started poking around a suspect who got released with no charge by Miami PD."

Harper's brow furrowed, and she jumped into the conversation.

"Well, I'm here because Lucy asked, and I trust her, but... I don't know about this."

"Well," Kim replied, "I'm here because you asked, and I trust you. So..."

"In any case," Harper interrupted, "through my own contacts, I found out that Lucy was actually fired for cause by the DEA. I haven't told her yet."

Kim turned to Sierra, concern etched on her face. "Are you sure Lucy isn't part of Maksym's organization?"

The mere thought of Lucy being involved with Maksym sent a shiver down Sierra's spine. It was a possibility she didn't even want to entertain, but the question lingered in the back of her mind, gnawing at her like an itch she couldn't quite reach.

"Impossible," Harper insisted. "She got us here, for fuck's sake!"

"Well," Sierra said quietly, her voice wavering just slightly. "At least, I don't think so. But we need to find out more about Maksym's operations."

Sierra leaned forward in her chair, her fingers drumming on the edge of her massive desk.

"Lucy regularly mentioned meetings with her D.E.A. boss," Sierra began, her voice steady despite the uncertainty churning inside her. "She said it was him who asked her to leave her job at the D.E.A. and take up the money-laundering position for Maksym. Lucy's now the President & CEO of Noll's former two dive businesses, but she's only really laundering money for Maksym. Some old man actually manages the businesses."

Harper frowned, her blue eyes narrowed in thought. "Lucy is not a criminal. But even if she were, it wouldn't explain how Maksym's charges were all dropped. He was caught red-handed with three bricks of cocaine, for God's sake."

The three women exchanged glances, each lost in their thoughts, trying to make sense of the seemingly impossible situation. The room felt heavy with silence, the weight of the unanswered questions hanging in the air.

"Maybe your friend Lucy got us here..." Kim thought out loud. "Maybe it's her insurance policy? She's playing you."

"Or, maybe..." Harper was clearly annoyed, biting her lip as she considered her words. "Could Lucy's boss be the one working with Maksym? I mean, it's a long shot, but..."

"But why would he send Lucy undercover in Maksym's organization if he works with Maksym?" Kim countered, her brow furrowed in confusion.

Silence fell once again, the question lingering like a dark cloud over their heads. There were no easy answers, and the frustration of being so close yet so far from understanding the truth gnawed at each of them. Each possibility seemed more unlikely than the last, but they couldn't afford to dismiss any potential leads. The stakes were too high.

"In any case, Kim, the trackers are in place, right?" Sierra asked as she adjusted the height of the legs of her gigantic desk with a touch of a button.

"Confirmed," Kim replied, her voice steady and reassuring. "They're up and running."

"Good," Sierra said, her fingers flying across one of her three keyboards, pulling up three screens on the computer monitors. On each screen, there was a map with a red dot on it. The tension in the room seemed to heighten as the group became acutely aware of the stakes at hand. Sierra's eyes narrowed, focused on the dots. "I'll monitor the trackers and let you guys know what I find out."

"Thanks, Sierra," Kim said, though her mind was still racing with questions.

ON THE OPEN SEA, Lucy and Maksym stood near the captain on the Hammerhead, one of Sea Spell Diving's dive boats. Six rough-looking men sat in spots normally used by clients during dive outings. The waves crashed against the side of the boat, creating an unsettling rhythm that matched the tension in the air.

"Lucy," Max began, his tone serious, "you won't be diving today. You've graduated to being the boss."

Lucy glanced at the water, then back at Max. "Why? Don't you want to do the smuggling runs yourself anymore?"

Maksym looked at her for a long time, suspicion flickering in his eyes. Finally, he spoke. "Three boxes were stolen a while back."

"Damn! I see," Lucy replied, uncertainty creeping into her voice. She couldn't shake the feeling that there was more to the story than what Maksym was telling her. But for now, all she could do was play along.

As the boat continued to cut through the waves, a sense of unease settled over Lucy like a heavy blanket. She knew that the task ahead would be dangerous, but she was determined to see it through — for Noll, for Sierra, and for herself.

Lucy shifted her weight from one foot to the other, trying to catch Maksym's eye. "Okay, but what's the relation between three boxes being stolen and you wanting me to take care of the smuggling boat rides from now on?"

Maksym remained silent, his gaze locked onto the horizon. Lucy racked her brain, wondering why he hadn't mentioned his arrest to her. Was there something more going on that she wasn't aware of? She couldn't shake the nagging feeling that there was a piece of the puzzle still missing. She noticed, though, that Eddie wasn't aboard for the first time since they started these runs.

"Look," Lucy said, assertiveness creeping into her voice, "I don't want you to blame me if I come back with missing boxes if more of them get stolen. And we need to find a way to prevent that from happening."

Again, Maksym didn't respond. The tension in the air grew thicker, and Lucy felt like she could almost taste it. She took a deep breath and tried another approach.

"Is there an easy way to communicate with the people you smuggle for?" she ventured.

Maksym's eyes narrowed as he turned to face her, suspicion etched across his features. "Why are you asking?"

"Because," Lucy replied, exasperated, "if we want to make it more difficult for thieves, we shouldn't run the smuggling boat outings on the same night every week. That makes it too predictable."

As she spoke, Maksym's expression softened, and she could see him considering her suggestion. "Alright," he conceded, "you have a point. Just let me know at least 48 hours in advance of the day you'll pick each week."

Lucy nodded, relieved that Maksym had agreed to her idea. The risk that Maksym found out her role in the theft of the boxes was life-threatening, but at least now it looked like she wanted to address the issue.

"Maybe we should also change the underwater site where we pick up and drop the dry boxes underwater," Lucy suggested, trying to solidify her role as a committed member of Maksym's team.

But his eyes flashed with irritation. "You don't need to get involved in that part of the decision."

Lucy bit her lip, feeling her frustration rise at his dismissive attitude. She knew she was playing a dangerous game, but she couldn't let it go. "I'm just saying, if you want to keep things unpredictable, it makes sense to switch up the location too."

For a moment, Maksym looked like he might argue, but then his expression shifted, and he seemed to concede. "Fine, it's a good idea. But I'll be the one telling you which spot to use. We need to limit the risks of being noticed by coast guards or other government dogs."

"Okay," Lucy agreed, relieved that he had at least seen the logic in her suggestion. They continued on toward the dive site, the tension between them gradually ebbing away.

As they neared their destination, four of the tough-looking guys finished gearing up for their dive. Once the boat dropped anchor, they executed giant stride entries off the back of the boat. Soon after, they reappeared at the diving platform, each picking up an underwater dry box marked only with the logo of a blue dragon's head. Rigging the boxes with lift bags to slow their descent, the divers vanished into the depths.

Lucy watched from the deck, her heart pounding with a mix of anxious anticipation and longing for the beauty and peace she knew lay beneath the surface. As the divers disappeared into the water, she felt herself drawn to the edge, wanting to join them. Illegal activity or not, she wanted to be underwater.

As the boat swayed gently on the waves, Lucy leaned over the railing and frowned at the site below. The anchor had been dropped carelessly onto the delicate coral reef, a blatant disregard for the underwater world she so deeply loved. Turning to the captain, her voice was tinged with concern. "You've dropped the anchor right on the reef. We should be more careful."

Maksym, who had been observing the divers, caught wind of Lucy's comment and interjected, his tone authoritative. "From now on, you can direct how they drop the anchor since you'll be the boss."

"Alright," Lucy nodded, accepting the responsibility as part of her role in this dangerous game.

Time seemed to slow down as they waited. Eventually, the four divers resurfaced, bringing up four other dry boxes with the help of lift bags. The two remaining tough-looking men on board hauled the wet boxes onto the boat and handed off fresh dry boxes to the divers. This exchange continued for some time: four waterproof boxes went down, and four different ones came back up.

Lucy observed the operation, her thoughts racing. How many of these boxes were filled with US dollars? And how many contained cocaine? Guns? She tried to focus on the task at hand but couldn't shake the nagging questions that haunted her every move. As an undercover D.E.A. agent, she knew all too well the stakes involved in this deadly dance with Maksym.

Deep down, she yearned for the simplicity and beauty of diving, free from the treacherous webs of crime and deceit. But she also understood that playing her part was crucial in unveiling Maksym's secrets and ultimately dismantling his criminal kingdom. For now, she would have to bide her time, carefully navigating through the murky waters of deception and betrayal, hoping that the truth and justice would eventually rise to the surface.

As the underwater dry boxes continued to be swapped, Lucy's thoughts drifted towards the allure of the ocean depths that surrounded her, and she found herself humming The Shins' song, 'Sealegs.' "And we got sea legs; and we're off tonight."

Although the task at hand was part of a dangerous smuggling operation, she couldn't help but feel a longing for the serenity and beauty she found while diving. The clear blue water shimmered invitingly, teasing her with visions of vibrant coral reefs and the fascinating creatures that called them home.

Lucy sighed inwardly, understanding that for now, she would have to remain on the boat, watching the divers work from above. Her heart ached for the freedom that diving offered, an escape from the tangled web of crime and deception that enveloped her daily life.

Eventually, the four divers completed their task, resurfacing one final time with the last set of waterproof boxes. As they climbed back on board, one of the tough-looking men helped lift the anchor, giving the signal for the captain to head back to shore. Though no words were exchanged during the journey, the tension onboard was palpable, a silent reminder of the high stakes involved in this treacherous game.

While the boat sped through the waves, Lucy's gaze remained fixed on the horizon, her thoughts oscillating between the wondrous underwater realm she craved and the harsh reality of her current situation. The contrast between the two worlds seemed to grow more pronounced with each passing moment, fueling her determination to bring down Maksym and finally break free from the chains of deception that bound her.

The boat slowed down as they neared Sea Spell Diving's dock. Lucy glanced over at Maksym, who was leaning against the railing, his eyes scanning the horizon. She could see the wheels turning in his mind, likely already plotting his next move in this dangerous game they both played. She took a deep breath and approached him, determined to remain focused on her mission.

"Once we're ashore, is there anything else I need to do?" she asked, her voice steady despite the churning sea of emotions within her.

"Nothing's changed," Maksym replied, not taking his eyes off the horizon. "Load all the boxes into the cube truck in the parking lot of Sea Spell Diving, and that's it."

"I thought you usually took two of them in your truck?"

"Never mind, those!" Maksym seemed irritated.

Lucy nodded, but she knew that in order to keep Maksym's trust, she needed to appear serious about her job. "I'll need to know how many boxes are supposed to go in and how many to come back," she said firmly. "If you want me to tell you if any have been stolen, I need to be kept in the loop."

Maksym turned to face her, his eyes narrowing slightly as he assessed her resolve. After a tense moment, he simply nodded, acknowledging the necessity of her request. "Alright," he agreed before his gaze returned to the water before them.

As they reached the dock, Lucy steeled herself for the task ahead, knowing that each step brought her closer to her ultimate goal. And as the boat's engine slowed to a gentle purr, she vowed to persevere, no matter the cost.

CHAPTER 32
THE EX

NOLL WALKED into Sierra's condo, the soft hum of the air conditioning a subtle reminder of the luxuries he now enjoyed. He joined Sierra in the living room, still sweating from the hot and humid Miami climate. She looked up from her Darcy Kieran novel, her blue hair framing her dark brown eyes, and asked, "So, another day at the office?"

"More like one of the best days ever," Noll chuckled as he flopped onto one couch while Sierra reclined on another. He continued, "The dive at the Blue Heron Bridge with those underprivileged kids was amazing. I've never seen so much joy in people's faces."

Sierra smiled warmly, clearly affected by Noll's enthusiasm. There was an unspoken intimacy between them, their connection woven through shared experiences and mutual trust.

As they settled comfortably, Noll remembered his precarious situation. "You know, you should tell me when you want me out of here. I have a salary now, thanks to Scuba: No Limits. The SNL Foundation."

For a moment, Sierra just stared at him, her eyes piercing deep into his soul. Then she said softly, "This place would feel empty without you. I'd prefer if you stayed forever, but if you want to leave, that's totally up to you."

Noll felt a warmth spread through him, a sense of belonging he hadn't experienced in a long time. Shaking off the heavy emotion, he changed the topic. "Speaking of Scuba: No Limits, maybe everything does happen for a reason."

Sierra furrowed her brow, puzzled. "What do you mean?"

"Think about it," Noll explained. "I'm having more fun doing this than managing dive stores, and on top of that, we're making a real difference in these kids' lives. All with Maksym's dirty money. If he hadn't screwed me over, none of this would be happening."

Sierra giggled, her laughter like music to Noll's ears. "You're like a magician, you know? Turning bad money into good money."

Noll grinned, feeling a renewed sense of purpose. The world might have been dark and twisted, but he was fighting back with hope and love, one dive at a time. And Sierra was there, by his side, every step of the way.

The silence between Noll and Sierra stretched for a moment. Finally, Sierra broke it with a casual observation. "You know, if you dig a bit, all money is dirty money."

Noll nodded thoughtfully, conceding the point. "True enough," he said, taking a deep breath. "I love my current life, Sierra, except for one thing: not seeing my kids." He felt a pang in his chest, the pain of separation from his children never truly going away.

Just then, Sierra's computer room emitted a series of beeps, breaking the somber mood. "Excuse me a moment." She got up from her seat and disappeared into the room filled with monitors, each screen glowing with lines of code and data.

As Noll sat alone, his thoughts drifted to Susan and their children. He wondered what they were doing and if they ever thought about him, too.

Meanwhile, in a small town in New Jersey, Susan parked her car outside an office building. She stepped out of the vehicle, swearing under her breath as she navigated through the snow in her fancy shoes. "Why do my kids love this stuff?"

She entered the building, informed the receptionist of her arrival, and sat in the waiting room. As if on cue, Ayra Starr's 'Last Heartbreak Song' was playing. "I'll be better on my own; I'll be better on my own."

Soon, the receptionist approached her. "Mrs. Durand. Mr. Thompson will see you now."

"Thank you," Susan replied tersely, brushing past her. She was on a mission.

Seated across from her lawyer in his sterile office, Susan crossed her legs and leaned forward. "I heard Nollaig has a job with another dive business now," she said, her voice dripping with disdain. "I want you to go after his salary."

Mr. Thompson frowned, adjusting his glasses as he considered her request. "Mrs Durand, the divorce is settled. We'd need a good reason to convince a judge to reopen the case."

"Isn't taking care of his kids a good enough reason?" Susan snapped, her eyes flashing with anger. "He's off fornicating with young female dive instructors under palm trees!"

The lawyer sighed, rubbing his temples. "I understand your frustration, but it's not that simple."

"Make it simple."

"Alright," Mr. Thompson relented, clearly wanting to keep the peace with his client. "I'll look into Mr. Durand's new job and see what we can do to get more money for you and the children."

"Good," Susan huffed before launching into a rant. "And while you're at it, figure out why I'm not getting any money from the shares of Seize The Deep and Sea Spell Diving I got in the divorce. I've been in touch with Mr. Byrne, and he told me Noll was blocking the payment of dividends."

She clenched her fists, her voice rising. "I even gave Maksym a proxy for my shareholder votes to help him out, but I'm still waiting to see the first dollar out of these shitty businesses I never wanted to be involved with in the first place."

Mr. Thompson stared at her, momentarily speechless. He had never seen his client this furious. Finally, he cleared his throat. "I'll look into it, Mrs. I promise."

"See that you do," she said, her voice cold and clipped. "Because if Noll thinks he can abandon his responsibilities to me and our kids, he's got another thing coming."

Mr. Thompson sighed, trying to calm Susan down. "Alright, I'll investigate your ex-husband's salary and the two dive businesses to see if there's any way we can get money for you and the kids."

Susan's eyes narrowed. "And if you don't find a way, then I want you to sue Noll for any reason you can think of. Just to mess with his new job until he finally sends me the money I deserve."

"Okay, Mrs, but let's not jump to conclusions just yet," Mr. Thompson said cautiously. "I think it would be best for everyone involved if you and Nollaig could try to get along, at least for the sake of the children."

Susan's eyes flashed with anger. "Get along?!" she screeched. "That man doesn't even bother to visit his own kids!"

"Actually," Mr. Thompson interjected gently, "it was you who insisted during the divorce proceedings that Nollaig have no visiting rights."

Her face reddened, and she clenched her teeth. She couldn't believe the nerve of this lawyer, questioning her motives when she was only trying to protect her children from their deadbeat father.

"Just do what I ask," she spat out, struggling to keep her voice steady. "Investigate his salary, the businesses, and if necessary, sue him. I don't care how or why; just make sure he pays for abandoning us!"

Without waiting for a reply, Susan stormed out of the office, slamming the door behind her. Mr. Thompson sat back in his chair, feeling the weight of Susan's anger and realizing that despite the legalities of the divorce being settled, the emotional battle between Nollaig and Susan was far from over.

CHAPTER 33
GUNSHOTS

"*For a while there, it was rough;*
But lately, I've been doin' better."

THE OPPRESSIVE HUMIDITY clung to Lucy's skin as she sat in her car, parked in a dark, dirty back alley. The sun had long since dipped below the horizon, but the heat still lingered, leaving her feeling suffocated and uneasy. The smell of rotting garbage wafted through her open window, almost warning of the criminality lurking within the shadows of this forgotten place.

Beside her, her boss's car was parked with its front end facing the opposite direction, and his window rolled down so they could talk. In any other situation, Lucy would have found this comical, but now, with the weight of uncertainty pressing down on her, it felt like just another grim reality.

"Seriously," Lucy blurted out, unable to hold back her annoyance any longer. "What the fuck was wrong with a meeting at a diner? Were you too cheap to buy me a damn coffee?" She snickered, though the jab held more bitterness than humor.

Her boss's face turned cold. "I can't take the risk of being seen with you," he replied, his voice steely. As soon as the words left his mouth, however, his face paled as if he'd said more than he intended.

Lucy eyed him warily, unsure how to take this revelation. Was there something going on that she didn't know about? Or was her boss simply slipping under the pressure of their ongoing operation? She couldn't shake the creeping sense of dread that had settled in her chest, wrapping itself around her heart like a vice.

SIERRA SAT in her dimly lit computer room, bathed in the glow of numerous monitors displaying maps with red dots. Her blue hair, vibrant even in the darkness, framed an expression of intense focus as she studied the information before her.

Reaching for her phone, Sierra dialed a number with practiced ease. As the call connected, she allowed herself a small smile of satisfaction. "It's true," she reported in a hushed voice, her dark brown eyes never leaving the screens. "Lucy's meeting her so-called D.E.A. boss right now. They're side by side in some godforsaken back alley." She paused, taking a breath. "I'll call you if I notice anything else."

With that, Sierra disconnected the call and returned her full attention to the maps on the screens.

BACK IN THE DARK ALLEY, Lucy's boss was growing increasingly agitated. "You didn't do a good job, Lucy," he snapped, his frustration evident. "We still don't know who Maksym is trading guns and money with."

"Guns?" Lucy remembered that she had never officially received information about guns.

Her boss' face turned white.

Since he remained speechless, Lucy continued. "Look, with my new role taking care of the smuggling boat rides, I might be able to find something soon." She clenched her fists on the steering wheel, her knuckles turning white. Inside, she felt a growing sense of urgency – she wasn't just doing this for her own sake but for Noll and all the others affected by Maksym's machinations.

"Lucy, you're not moving fast enough," her boss growled in frustration, his patience wearing thin.

"Me?" Lucy shot back, anger flaring in her chest. "You're the one who's always been a turtle in this case!"

"Watch your tone," he warned, eyes narrowing. "Or..."

"Or what?" she interrupted, voice dripping with cynicism. "You can't fire me."

He barked back, "I could... 'not re-hire' you."

The air between them grew thick with tension, the silence oppressive as they stared each other down. Lucy struggled to find her next words, her thoughts racing through all the possible outcomes of their standoff. Finally, her boss broke the silence.

"Here's what I want you to do. Shake the tree. Disturb Byrne's operations so that he makes a mistake," he ordered, his voice cold and uncompromising.

"Alright," Lucy said slowly, trying to regain her composure. "I'll think of a way." But before she could continue, her boss cut her off.

"Go back tonight to the dive site where you exchange those blue dragon waterproof boxes and steal a bunch of them," he commanded. Lucy froze, remembering the night when she, Sierra, and Noll had done precisely that. She wondered if he knew about their previous theft, but she couldn't let that show.

"Okay... but it might not be enough to shake Maksym off," she suggested cautiously.

"Shut up and do it," her boss snapped, leaving no room for negotiation. Lucy swallowed hard, her heart pounding in her chest. She knew she had a dangerous task ahead of her, but it was her job.

LATER THAT DAY, Lucy's car's headlights swept across the storage facility's grim exterior, casting eerie shadows into the corners. Chain-link fences topped with barbed wire enclosed the property, reinforcing the sense that this was not a place for casual visitors. The air was heavy with humidity and the lingering scent of diesel, reminding her of the oppressive atmosphere in the alley earlier that day.

Lucy parked her car next to the storage unit Sierra had rented, where the pickup truck and inflatable boat were hidden from prying eyes. She glanced around nervously, but there was no sign of anyone else nearby. After a moment, Noll appeared from the darkness, his salt-and-pepper hair glinting in the faint light.

"Are you serious about this?" Noll asked, his voice tinged with disbelief as he approached Lucy's car. "Why do you want to steal more of those blue dragon boxes? Need cash for Christmas shopping?"

Lucy didn't find Nollaig's joke funny but still hesitated before answering, replaying in her head the tense conversation with her D.E.A. boss. "He wants me to disturb Maksym's operations so that he makes mistakes," she revealed, her tone reflecting her own uncertainty about the plan.

Noll raised an eyebrow. "But when we stole three boxes of cocaine and cash from him, it didn't seem to have any impact on his operations at all."

"Then we'll steal them all," Lucy declared, her determination overcoming her doubts. She looked into Noll's eyes, searching for any sign of hesitation or fear. But instead, she saw the same fiery resolve that had been driving him since they came back from Bonaire.

"Alright," Noll agreed after a moment, nodding with steely resolve. "Let's do it. If it can help bring the bastard down…"

SOON AFTER, the pickup truck's headlights cut through the darkness as Lucy and Noll drove along US1 toward Key Largo. The only sounds were the engine's thrum and the passing cars. The tension in the air was palpable, and they both knew they needed to lighten the mood.

"Remember when we first met?" Noll asked with a wry smile. "When you pretended to have been left behind by Vanilla Dive Center, and I came to rescue you."

Lucy laughed softly, recalling the memory. "Yeah, that was another request from my boss. But it was still a good thing you came along because Vanilla was gone for real. Who knows what would've happened to poor little me?"

"Speaking of that day," Noll continued teasingly, "I seem to recall you sunbathing topless on our way back to shore." He shot her a playful glance, his eyes twinkling. "Was that also ordered by your boss?"

"Hey, it was my way of thanking you," Lucy retorted, grinning. "Besides, you didn't seem to mind."

"Can't argue with that," Noll conceded, chuckling. The laughter dissipated, and they fell into a contemplative silence.

"Hard to believe how much has changed since then," Lucy mused. "Look where we are now." She gestured vaguely to the dark road ahead of them.

"Life has a funny way of turning things upside down," Noll said. "But it brought us together, and I wouldn't trade that for anything."

Instead of answering, Lucy gave him a sincere smile and started singing Benson Boone's 'Beautiful Songs.' "For a while there, it was rough; But lately, I've been doin' better."

ABOARD THE INFLATABLE BOAT, they arrived at the site where Lucy had hidden sixteen dry boxes underwater for Maksym the night before. The water was calm, reflecting the moonlight like a dark mirror.

"Maybe we should have brought help," Lucy suggested, biting her lip. "You'll be diving alone, and I'll be alone to lift the boxes into the boat."

"Relax," Noll reassured her. "I've done plenty of solo diving, even if it freaks out GASI. All my gear is redundant. And I can help you lift the boxes. We've got this, Lucy. We may have to do two or three trips, though."

She exhaled shakily, nodding in agreement. "Alright. I wonder how many boxes will have those white powder-flavored dollars."

Noll adjusted his scuba gear, securing the cylinder on his back and fastening the BCD straps. He glanced at Lucy, who was sitting on the edge of the inflatable boat, legs dangling over the side.

"Ready?" he asked, grabbing a lift bag from the floor of the boat.

"Ready as I'll ever be," she replied, worry lacing her voice. Noll gave her a reassuring smile before slipping on his mask and regulator.

With a splash, Noll disappeared beneath the surface, descending towards the first dry box marked with the blue dragon's head. He attached the lift bag to the box, added some air, and began his ascent. The lift bag buoyed the box effortlessly through the water.

Lucy leaned over the side of the boat, watching as the box broke the surface. She gripped it firmly, pulling with all her strength to hoist it onto the boat. Noll tried to help by pushing the box up from below but only succeeded in sinking himself into the water. Thankfully, Lucy was strong enough to lift the box on her own.

"Got it!" she called down to Noll, panting slightly from the effort. She untied the lift bag and tossed it back into the water for him to retrieve the second box.

"Thanks," Noll said, catching the lift bag and giving her a thumbs-down before submerging once more. As he reached the second box, attaching the lift bag securely, he heard the hum of a boat engine approaching. Confused, he looked up, wondering if Lucy had started their outboard engine prematurely.

Instead, the hull of a large vessel appeared above him, its propellers churning dangerously close. Panic surged through Noll as the boat loomed above him. He knew ascending now would be disastrous, placing him directly in the path of the deadly propellers.

"Lucy!" he shouted into his regulator, the sound muffled by the water and his own equipment. It was pointless. The large boat stopped next to their inflatable, casting a dark shadow over their relatively small inflatable boat.

Noll's mind raced as he hovered underwater, trying to come up with a plan. He couldn't risk surfacing with the large vessel so close, but he knew Lucy was alone on their inflatable boat above. Anxiety twisted in his gut, and he tried to calm himself down. It had to be the Coast Guard, he told himself. If that were the case, then Lucy would be fine; she worked for the D.E.A., after all. Noll was certain that her boss would be able to clear her name.

His own situation, however, could be more complicated. Noll wasn't sure how much leniency the authorities would show him, if any.

Eventually, the large boat's propellers stopped spinning, and Noll got ready to ascend. But then, a chilling sound reached his ears: the unmistakable noise of gunshots. Fear gripped him like an icy hand around his heart, and he realized that this situation might be far more dangerous than he initially thought.

CHAPTER 34
BROKEN WINDOW

SIERRA PACED BACK and forth in her living room, her blue hair swaying with each frantic step. The penthouse was dimly lit, casting shadows across the room and amplifying the tense atmosphere. The private elevator dinged, and Kim stepped out into the penthouse.

"Any news from Noll and Lucy?" Kim asked right away, her voice laced with concern.

"Nothing," Sierra replied, her dark brown eyes filled with worry. "I left them both a voicemail and a text asking them to cancel their boat outing, but I didn't get an answer."

Kim's brow furrowed. "Are you sure they're walking into a trap?"

"Come see for yourself," Sierra said as she led Kim to her computer room.

Her gigantic desk was covered with computer monitors. Sierra pointed at one screen where two red dots stood side by side. "Lucy met her boss in this dark alley," she explained, then moved her finger to another screen with a similar configuration of red dots. "And right after that, Lucy's boss met Maksym. And Lucy's car is at a self-storage space where I keep an inflatable."

"Shit," Kim muttered under her breath. Trying to remain hopeful, she added, "Maybe they got your message, and they're on their way back?"

"Then why aren't they answering my calls?" Sierra asked, her frustration evident.

Kim didn't have an answer. The weight of the situation settled over them like a heavy fog. They could only wait and hope for the best, knowing that their friends might be walking into danger.

NOLL'S LEG muscles strained as he swam further away from the inflatable boat and the vessel he assumed was a Coast Guard patrol boat. The water around him was dark, but his thoughts were darker still.

How could he leave Lucy behind? He chided himself, thinking that heroes in movies would never abandon their partners. But he was no Jack Ryan! And Lucy was an undercover D.E.A. agent. She should be able to handle herself with the Coast Guard. Meanwhile, what chance would he stand if he were caught with cocaine, guns, or piles of smuggled US 100-dollar bills?

His heart raced as he continued swimming in mid-water, neither too deep nor too close to the surface. Going deeper would consume more air, and he needed to conserve it for the long swim to shore. But he couldn't risk being spotted either, not with the unknown dangers lurking above. What were these gunshots about? He pushed his body to its limits, swimming as fast as he could while still pacing himself to limit air consumption.

"Damn it, Nollaig," he cursed inside his head, "you can't abandon her like this."

As his legs grew heavy, the internal battle raged on. Was he making the right choice? What would become of Lucy if she were in trouble?

The heavy weight of uncertainty and guilt gnawed at him with each painful kick of his legs.

"Stay focused," he told himself. "First, you have to get out of here."

As Noll continued to swim with the drag of his dive gear slowing him down, he knew there was no turning back now. He had to trust that Lucy could handle herself, even though every fiber of his being screamed otherwise. It was a decision that would haunt him, one way or another.

"Please, let her be okay," he thought desperately, pushing on through the water.

A BIT LATER, Noll stared at the pressure gauge, his scuba cylinder close to empty. Reluctantly, he ascended to the surface, breaking through the cloak of darkness that enveloped him. He scanned his surroundings.

"Where are they?" he muttered under his breath. No boats were visible in the pitch-black night. The compass around his wrist was his only ally, guiding him towards the shore as he swam on the surface, heart pounding with fear and guilt.

The shoreline came into view, a dark silhouette against the even darker water. Noll searched for a spot in the mangroves where he could make his exit and avoid private property. Pulling himself up onto the muddy bank, he quickly discarded his dive gear and wetsuit, leaving only his bathing suit clinging to his exhausted body.

"Damn it," he whispered, thinking about the distance between him and the end of the street where they had launched the inflatable boat earlier. Sierra's pickup truck held the key to his salvation – his phone. The Ford's keypad lock would grant him access, but he couldn't shake the sinking feeling that he might be walking into another trap.

Noll hesitated, weighing his options. If someone was after him and Lucy, they might have already looked for an inflatable launching spot. He glanced around, realizing he was relatively close to Sea Spell Diving, his former business. With morning looming, he decided he had to act fast.

As he approached Sea Spell Diving's premises, Noll trod cautiously, checking for any signs of unwanted company. The darkness provided some cover but also made it harder to spot potential threats. Relief washed over him as he found no trace of anyone lurking nearby.

"Alright, let's do this," he muttered under his breath, steeling himself for what he was about to do. He circled around a side door, knowing it would be less visible from the street in the back and the canal in the front.

Noll picked up a small rock and smashed the window, sending shards of glass dancing to the ground. He then reached inside, carefully unlocked the door, and slipped into the building. His heart pounded, and adrenaline surged through his veins.

"Please still work, please still work," he whispered, punching in his old password on the alarm system keypad. To his amazement, the code still worked – they hadn't removed it after ousting him from the business.

"Thank god," he breathed, relief mingling with renewed determination. Noll knew that he needed to act quickly, but the familiar surroundings brought back memories of happier times when Sea Spell Diving had been his pride and joy. Shaking off the nostalgia, he tried to focus on the task at hand – figuring out what happened to Lucy and, first, disappearing before getting caught.

"Lucy, I won't let you down," he vowed, thinking about the woman who had saved his life more than once.

Inside Sea Spell Diving, Noll's pulse raced as he scanned the room for a phone. He spotted an old landline on a desk covered in dive maps and hastily picked it up, dialing Sierra's number. He thanked god for always having been good at remembering numbers.

"Sierra, it's me," he said urgently when she answered. "I don't have much time."

"Jesus, Noll!" Sierra exclaimed. "I'm so glad you guys are okay. What happened?"

"I don't know if we're okay yet," Noll admitted, his voice tense. "But I can't talk now. I need you to pick me up at... the Key Largo community park. I don't have my phone, so I won't be able to communicate."

"Wait, what's going on?" Sierra demanded, her tone a mixture of concern and frustration. "Where are you right now?"

"Please, Sierra, just hurry," Noll pleaded, feeling the pressure mounting. He hung up the phone and rushed out of Sea Spell Diving, taking backroads and little-used pathways toward the community park. As he moved through the shadows, thoughts raced through his head. Was the park the right place to meet? Would he be exposed there?

"Nobody would think to look for me in such a public place," he reassured himself, trying to quell the rising panic in his chest. He thought of Lucy, possibly in danger, and clenched his fists in determination. He had to make it to the park and regroup with Sierra. Together, they could figure out their next move.

Darkness enveloped him as he moved quickly, fueled by adrenaline and the desperation to set things right. His every step echoed the beat of his heart — pounding, relentless, and driven by the hope that they could somehow turn the tide against darkness.

NOLL SAT under a palm tree in the dimly lit Key Largo community park, his body tense and his mind racing. The moon shadows cast by the trees overhead seemed to dance menacingly as he anxiously awaited Sierra's arrival. His heart hammered in his chest, each beat echoing the urgency of the situation.

The more he thought about Lucy, the darker his thoughts became. He couldn't shake the feeling that something terrible had happened. Why would the Coast Guard fire a gun when Lucy was alone in an inflatable boat with no weapon? His imagination conjured up numerous scenarios, each more horrifying than the last. Maybe it wasn't the Coast Guard.

"Damn it," he muttered under his breath, clenching his fists. "She saved my life twice, and now I'm not there for her." The guilt gnawed at him, intensifying his desperation.

He replayed their last moments together in his mind – the brief exchange of words, the lingering touch of her hand, the softness of her skin. The memory of her smile haunted him, and he felt a crushing weight settle on his chest.

"Focus, Noll," he whispered to himself, trying to pull his thoughts away from the abyss. "You need to be ready for whatever comes next."

As he waited, he noticed the sound of a car approaching. Alert, he scanned the darkness, searching for the source. Relief washed over him as he recognized the driver.

"Sierra," he called out, his voice strained with emotion. "Thank God you're here."

"Where's Lucy?" she asked as soon as Noll slipped onto the passenger seat, her eyes wide with concern.

"I don't know," Noll admitted, his voice cracking.

To make things worse, The Band Perry was playing on the radio. "If I die young, bury me in satin; Lay me down on a bed of roses; Sink me in the river at dawn; Send me away with the words of a love song."

CHAPTER 35
IN THE NEWS

 *"*omma, I got bad news, bad news;*
I've been rolling with some bad dudes, bad dudes."

SIERRA EMERGED from the reception area of a run-down motel tucked away in the shadows of a seedy part of town. She caught Noll's gaze and motioned for him to follow her. They moved cautiously towards the end of the building, farthest from the front desk, where their presence would be less noticeable. Sierra unlocked the door to their room, swung it open, and stepped inside, with Noll following closely behind.

"Look," she said, her voice low and cautious, "I don't think they can link me to you and Lucy, but it's better to keep you away from my penthouse for now. Just in case."

"Who's 'they'?" Noll asked, scanning the drab interior of the room.

Sierra hesitated, her dark brown eyes narrowing as she considered her response. "I don't know anymore who's who," she admitted. "But Lucy's D.E.A. boss is connected to Maksym. And so, then, anyone else could be an enemy too."

"Her boss? Shit! Maybe it was him on the boat, then."

"Are you sure Lucy isn't also part of Maksym's operations? That her so-called undercover activities weren't actually about keeping an eye on us?"

Noll was speechless, his mind racing at the thought. He didn't want to believe that Lucy, the woman who had saved his life more than once, could betray him like that.

"I don't believe it. I mean... If Lucy and her boss were on the same side, then... Who was on the boat?"

But Sierra was right – they knew nothing for certain. Their world was crumbling around them, the lines between friend and foe blurred beyond recognition. The only thing they had left was each other. The fight against Maksym's twisted empire now seemed like a pipe dream.

"Stay here and don't leave this room, Noll," Sierra instructed firmly, her eyes filled with concern. "I'll go out and see what I can find."

With that, Sierra slipped out of the motel room, leaving Noll alone in the dimly lit space. He sat down on the edge of the worn bed and grabbed the remote, turning on the TV. The local morning news was airing, and he settled in to watch, hoping to glean some information about what was happening outside their safe haven.

"Last night, the D.E.A., in cooperation with the U.S. Coast Guard, made a major bust on an international drug smuggling ring," the newscaster reported, his voice steady and composed. "Among those killed in the operation were former D.E.A. agent Lucy Grayson and former Miami and Key Largo dive store owner Nollaig Durand."

The color drained from Noll's face as he stared at the screen, speechless. A picture of him and Lucy flashed across the screen alongside images of their alleged criminal activities: a pile of cocaine bricks.

"Authorities believe that Grayson and Durand were the masterminds behind this extensive smuggling operation, hiding under scuba diving activities," the newscaster continued. "It's unfortunate they were killed in the process; the D.E.A. would have liked to learn more about their operations."

Noll felt his stomach churn with anger and disbelief. They were dead? How could that be?

He turned off the TV and paced the small room, his mind racing.

He needed to clear his head. With a heavy sigh, he stepped into the bathroom and turned on the shower, letting the hot water beat down on him as he tried to make sense of the news.

If he was supposedly dead, then maybe Lucy was alive too. It was possible that the news had gotten it all wrong – or maybe there was something else going on, something they hadn't discovered yet. Who managed to declare him dead without his body? And if Lucy was alive, where was she? And why hadn't she contacted Sierra?

As the water cascaded over him, Noll tried to push aside his fear and focus on what he knew for certain. He couldn't trust anyone but himself and Sierra now. The world they had known was disintegrating around them, and they were left to navigate the treacherous waters of betrayal and deceit.

Determined to find answers, Noll stepped out of the shower and dried off, donning fresh clothes. He had no idea what lay ahead, but he would not rest until he uncovered the truth about Lucy.

MEANWHILE, in a federal building in Miami, Kim sat in a cold, sterile interrogation room, her hands clasped on the table in front of her. She tried to maintain a calm demeanor as she faced the two stern-looking men who had been grilling her for what felt like hours.

"Look, I've already told you everything I know," she said with suppressed frustration. "I don't know anything about drug smuggling."

One of the men, his face a mask of impatience, asked, "Then why are you involved with Durand in a non-profit organization? Precisely in scuba diving..."

Kim sighed, trying to hold onto her patience. "Because doing good deeds for society can be rewarding; you should try it sometime."

"Ms. Banks, this is not a joke," the man snapped back, his eyes boring into hers.

"Well, if you're done with me, I'd like to go – no joke," Kim replied firmly, holding her ground.

NOLL SAT in bed in the dingy motel room, the flickering glow from the television screen casting shadows on the walls. He switched between news channels, hoping for some new information, but it was all the same: he and Lucy were supposedly dead, their reputations tainted by false allegations. But wait! Were allegations against Lucy false?

He tried to sleep, but the adrenaline coursing through his veins made it impossible. Despite having gone without sleep for the past 36 hours, his mind was too active, too worried. He couldn't help but wonder what Sierra was up to and when she would return.

Giving up on sleep, Noll propped himself up against the headboard and turned his attention back again to the news. His heart ached for Lucy and the uncertainty of their situation.

"Where are you, Lucy?" he whispered, his voice barely audible over the drone of the newscaster. "And what are we going to do now?"

MEANWHILE, in New Jersey, Susan parked her car in the office building's parking lot, cursing under her breath as the biting cold nipped at her cheeks. Snow crunched beneath her fancy shoes that were clearly not meant for this kind of weather. She trudged towards the entrance, desperately trying to shield her face from the icy wind.

"Damn this weather," she muttered, pushing open the door to the warmth of the building. She approached the reception desk, her cheeks flushed from the sudden temperature change.

"Mrs. Durand? You're right on time. Mr. Thompson is waiting for you," the receptionist said with a friendly smile, gesturing towards her lawyer's office.

"Thanks," Susan replied, striding purposefully into the room. The moment she entered, she wasted no time in getting straight to the point. "So what's going on with my ex-husband being killed in this D.E.A. drug operation I saw on the news."

Mr. Thompson sighed and leaned back in his chair, his expression somber. "Mrs. Durand, that isn't why I called you in yesterday. There's another matter we need to discuss, but I understand your concern."

"Then what's going on?" she demanded, her frustration evident.

NOLL'S ATTENTION was still glued to the television screen when he heard the faint sound of paper sliding across the floor. A folded note had been slipped under the door, making his heart skip a beat. He realized how sensitive his nerves had become, given his current situation.

He got out of bed cautiously and peeked through the curtains, scanning the area for any sign of movement. Finding none, he picked up the note and unfolded it. The message read: "Sierra: back tomorrow. Stay hidden. Food outside your door."

Noll hesitated before opening the motel room door, his mind racing with thoughts of potential traps or danger. But as the note had promised, a bag of fast food sat waiting for him just outside his room. The scent of hamburgers wafted through the air, and he was suddenly struck by how famished he was – he hadn't eaten anything in the last 36 hours.

"100% natural... chemicals. Better than nothing," he mused, bringing the bag inside and bolting the door behind him. He sat on the edge of the bed, tearing into the meal with urgency. As he ate, he couldn't help but wonder what Sierra was up to.

BACK IN NEW JERSEY, Susan remained in her lawyer's office, growing increasingly frustrated. "What do you mean, a one-million-dollar fund for each of my kids?" she demanded, her voice strained with disbelief.

Mr. Thompson sighed, trying to maintain his professional composure. "As I already explained, I received notification about two funds having been created, one for each of your children with Mr. Durand. There's one million dollars in each fund."

He paused before continuing, emphasizing the restrictions placed on the money. "Until they turn 25, the money can only be used for educational purposes or for buying their first house. At 25 years old, they receive any remaining balance, if there is any."

Susan clenched her jaw, her anger rising. She couldn't believe that Noll... who else could have done that? So, Noll... had left their children such a substantial amount of money while leaving her with nothing.

Susan slammed her hands on the lawyer's desk, her face red with anger. "How could that bastard not leave me anything? Did you hear the news this morning? They're saying my ex-husband was killed in a drug smuggling operation! If that's true, then these funds for our kids are probably dirty money!"

Mr. Thompson frowned, adjusting his glasses. "There's no clear indication of where the money originated from, Susan. But I understand your concerns. The fact remains that making waves around these funds could draw unwanted attention from the authorities. The feds can seize assets earned from criminal activities."

"Think of your children," he continued, trying to calm her down. "Let things play out and focus on providing a stable life for them."

Susan stared at him incredulously. "I need money to live, too! Damn him, and damn you! I'll call Mr. Byrne." She yelled before storming out of the office, her footsteps echoing angrily in the hallway.

***

BACK IN MIAMI, Sierra sat in a rental car in a dark, filthy alley, the front window rolled down. Across from her, Kim's silhouette was visible inside a large black SUV with tinted windows. Their vehicles were positioned so they could speak through their open windows without drawing attention.

"Here," Kim said quietly, passing a large brown envelope to Sierra. "I'm taking your word on this, but it sure is fishy. And listen, we shouldn't meet again until I let you know it's safe. Things need to cool down for Harper and me. We're being watched. But she quickly dropped him food and your note."

Sierra nodded, her expression unreadable. "Understood."

As if on cue, they both pressed electronic buttons, rolling up their windows simultaneously. With a final nod, they started their engines and drove away in opposite directions, disappearing into the night like shadows.

Sierra shook her head as Madchild's 'Bad News' started playing on her car radio. "Momma, I got bad news, bad news; I've been rolling with some bad dudes, bad dudes."

CHAPTER 36
MOJITOS

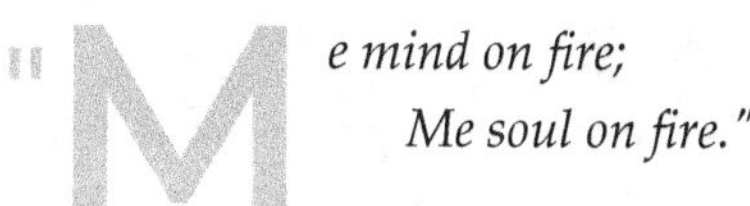

e mind on fire;
      Me soul on fire."

THE OCEAN STRETCHED out before Noll, its vastness a reminder of how small he was in the grand scheme of things. As he swam with determination, a white mooring buoy kept his attention. He pushed himself harder, feeling the water resist his movements as he approached it. Below him, the dark shape of a wreck loomed, an artificial reef frequented by local dive operators. The Pacific Ocean held many secrets, and the wreck was just one of many that this underwater world possessed.

He circled the buoy, taking note of the angle back to the shore. As Noll began his swim back towards land, his muscles started to ache from exertion, but he refused to slow down.

"Be prepared, Noll!" he told himself, pushing through the pain. "Be prepared."

The tide had shifted, and Noll found himself swimming against the current. It would have been easy to give in, let the water carry him away, but he gritted his teeth and forged ahead. He had faced much worse in his life, and he wasn't going to let the tide's pull defeat him.

As he battled against the current, memories of his past struggles surfaced in his mind – the divorce, the bankruptcy, the prostate cancer. Each obstacle, a reminder of the man he once was, and the man he was determined to become. He had tasted despair and survived, emerging stronger and more motivated than ever. The ocean might have tried to claim him once, but not today. The guy who had contemplated suicide was not him. He couldn't relate anymore to that prehistoric version of Noll, a man who was depressed and relied on others to make progress.

"Be prepared," Noll repeated, his breath laboring as he fought his way through the water. "Be prepared."

His heart pounded in his chest, a steady rhythm that echoed his mantra. He drew on every ounce of strength he had, refusing to quit. The shore grew closer, inch by inch, as he swam with unwavering resolve.

"Be prepared," he whispered one last time, gasping for air. As he staggered onto the beach, his legs wobbled beneath him, but he stood tall, victorious against the current that had tried to pull him under.

Noll knew he had a long way to go, but he also believed that if he could face the ocean's relentless current, he could face anything life threw at him.

***

WITH THE SUN still high in the sky, casting a warm glow on everything it touched, the dive boat was filled with excited chatter as tourists prepared their gear. Some were seasoned divers; others were taking their first plunge into the underwater world. Noll stood among them, feeling a familiar thrill that had never waned since his early days of scuba diving.

"Hey," a woman in her late twenties called out to him, a friendly smile brightening her face. "Are you our dive guide today?"

"Wouldn't miss a chance to be underwater," Noll replied with a grin, the energy of the group infectious. The boat rocked gently over the calm waves, and he couldn't help but notice how perfect the conditions were for diving.

"Great! We're really looking forward to exploring this new site," she said, her enthusiasm palpable. Noll felt a surge of nostalgia, remembering the excitement that had coursed through him when he'd first embarked on this journey years ago.

"Excuse me," another tourist, a man in his sixties, chimed in, "What's your name, son?"

"Ryan," Noll responded, pausing for a beat before adding, "Jack Ryan." He smirked at the skeptical look that crossed the tourist's face.

"Alright... Jack Ryan," the man said, clearly amused by Noll's choice of alias. "I'm sure you'll show us a great time underwater."

"Attention, everyone!" Noll called out, raising his voice to address the entire group. The tourists fell silent, all eyes turning expectantly towards him. "We're approaching the mooring for the dive site. Please make sure your gear is set up correctly, and remember to buddy check before entering the water."

As he scanned the faces of the eager divers, Noll felt a renewed sense of purpose. He might not have been able to change his past, but he could make a difference in the lives of others – one dive at a time. And as long as he had the ocean by his side, Noll knew he was where he belonged.

"Alright, everyone," Noll continued, his voice carrying a sense of authority that held the tourists' attention. "Before we dive in, I need to talk to you about our impact on the ocean and its fragile ecosystem."

The group listened intently as Noll continued, "This dive site is home to a delicate coral reef, so it's crucial that we all stay above it without touching or hitting it with our fins. I know you're all capable of doing that because you did a fantastic job hovering in mid-water during our pool session this morning."

A wave of pride washed over the divers' faces as they recalled their successful practice session.

"Being able to hover like that while removing, replacing, and emptying your mask, as you did this morning, makes you better than ninety-nine percent of scuba divers who got their certification cards on the cheap and fast," Noll added, his eyes scanning the crowd. "Heck!

That makes you better than ninety percent of scuba diving instructors out there."

The tourists exchanged excited glances, clearly thrilled by Noll's compliment. Their sense of accomplishment fueled their eagerness for the upcoming dive, as they understood their responsibility to protect the marine life that called the reef home.

Noll could see the spark in their eyes. It brought him a sense of satisfaction, knowing that he was helping these tourists not only enjoy the beauty of the underwater world but also understand the importance of preserving it for future generations.

"Keep in mind," he continued, "we're visitors in the ocean, and it's up to us to ensure that we leave no trace behind. And finally, remember there are only three speeds in scuba diving: slow, slower, and slowest. If you can go slower, you're going too fast. Enjoy your dive, and let's show the ocean the respect it deserves."

With that, the group of divers nodded in agreement, determined to make the most of their experience while honoring their commitment to protecting the fragile ecosystem they were about to explore.

As Noll led the group of tourists into the vivid underwater world, he couldn't help but marvel at the vibrant colors and diverse marine life surrounding them. The reef was teeming with activity, a stark contrast to the more subdued hues he had encountered in the Caribbean. Fish of all shapes and sizes darted in and out of the coral formations while marine creatures gracefully swam past the divers.

They communicated through hand signals, exchanging wide-eyed looks of wonder.

Noll smiled beneath his regulator, proud of how well the group was controlling their buoyancy and respecting the environment they were exploring. He continued guiding them through the dive site, pointing out intriguing creatures and unique coral structures that captured their attention.

ON THE WAY back to shore, the boat was filled with excited chatter as the tourists recounted their experiences from the dive. Each of them took turns filling out their paper dive logbooks, eagerly scribbling down details of what they had seen and experienced. Jack signed the page for today's dive, confirming their successful underwater adventure.

Watching them carefully preserve these memories, Jack mused about the value of the paper dive logbook. It was one of those items that hadn't quite translated well into digital form. There was something special about having your dive buddy sign a logbook page after a memorable dive.

"Thanks again, Jack," one of the tourists said, extending the logbook for him to sign. "This was the best dive I've ever had."

"Happy to be a part of it," Noll replied with a genuine smile. "The ocean has so much to offer, and I'm glad you got to experience it firsthand."

It was moments like these that made him remember why he had fallen in love with scuba diving in the first place.

"Hey, Jack," a scuba diving tourist said as she handed over her logbook for signature. "What's your real name?"

Jack smirked. "Why don't you believe it's Jack Ryan?"

"Come on, that's from a movie," she insisted. "Seriously, what's your name? I want to tag you on social media."

With a chuckle, Noll replied, "I don't do Facecrap, TikThroll, Instafake, or any other ego-trip antisocial platforms." The tourist stared at him, speechless, while Noll continued signing her logbook.

LATER, in a small apartment with bunk beds for the staff, Noll peeled off his wet bathing suit and changed into shorts and a T-shirt. Another guy who had been napping on one of the beds sat up and looked at Noll.

"Chasing pain instead of enjoying drinks with sexy tourists at the bar, again?" he asked rhetorically.

Noll chuckled. "I miss having regular mojitos, but I've got to be prepared."

"Prepared for what?" the guy questioned, but Noll stayed silent.

His mind was focused on the tasks ahead: staying fit, staying sharp, and figuring out how he could make a difference in this world full of corruption and greed.

He didn't want to let his guard down. "There are Maksyms and dirty D.E.A. agents in every country!"

And though he didn't want to dwell on his past or his enemies, he couldn't help but feel the weight of responsibility – both for his own life and for those he wanted to help. Noll was determined to rise above it all, to find a way to truly make a change, even if it meant facing pain and sacrifice head-on.

Noll walked out of the apartment, the lingering conversation with his fellow staff member still echoing in his mind. He couldn't afford to get too comfortable. He did not want to be too comfortable. As he stepped onto the beach, he took a deep breath, inhaling the salty air that mixed with the scent of palm trees.

He dropped down onto the warm sand, his hands sinking into the soft grains as he started doing push-ups. The shade from the nearby palm trees provided some relief from the heat, but he could feel the sweat beginning to form on his brow. Behind him, the calm ocean lapped at the shore, its rhythmic sound a soothing backdrop to his workout.

In his earbuds, The Merrymen were singing his favorite song lately. "Me mind on fire; Me soul on fire; Feeling hot hot hot."

The paradise around him stood in stark contrast to the internal turmoil that plagued him. He had lost so much – his business, his marriage, contact with his kids, even part of his health – but he was determined to rise above it all. He wouldn't let himself be defined by his past mistakes or the enemies who sought to bring him down. With the pain of each push-up, Noll felt his resolve hardening.

Just as he finished a grueling series of push-ups and got back on his feet, an old man with white hair approached him. Noll wiped the sweat from his brow, trying to catch his breath as the old man spoke.

"Jack, I've been hearing a lot of good feedback from the tourists who went diving with you this afternoon… again," he said, a hint of admiration in his voice. "Seems like you're quite the professional."

"Thank you," Noll replied casually, his heart rate beginning to slow.

"Ever thought about being a manager of a dive resort?" the old man asked, his eyes narrowing slightly. "We badly need more dive professionals who are professional for real, not just in name."

The question hung in the air, and Noll considered it for a moment. It was tempting to think about taking on a leadership role again, but he knew that his focus needed to be elsewhere. He couldn't afford to let himself get attached to any one place and even less to be in a position that could attract unwanted attention.

So Noll chuckled, beads of sweat dripping from his forehead as he wiped them away with the back of his hand. "Tell me," he asked the old man, his voice calm and steady, "how often do you go diving these days?"

The old man's eyes flicked to the ocean and lingered there for a moment before returning to Noll. He hesitated, his weathered face creasing into a frown. "Not very often anymore, I'm afraid," he admitted, a hint of melancholy in his voice.

The sound of waves lapping against the shore filled the silence that followed, mingling with the rustle of palm leaves swaying in the gentle breeze. Noll could feel grains of sand clinging to his damp skin, the grit between his toes a reminder of the paradise he now found himself in.

"I rest my case," Noll simply stated, his gaze unwavering as the old man reluctantly nodded solemnly in agreement.

CHAPTER 37
CYPHERWAVE

NOLL'S EYES fluttered open before the first light of dawn crept into the small apartment. His three roommates lay scattered around the cramped space, snoring softly in their bunks. Careful not to disturb them, Noll slid out of his top bunk and reached for his backpack on the floor. As he rummaged through it to find a t-shirt, a familiar item slipped out and fell onto the cold tile with a soft thud.

He picked up the passport, opening it to reveal the name "Jack Murphy" printed inside. A wry smile crossed his lips as he recalled Sierra's words when she had handed it to him in that dingy Miami motel: it was a good fake passport because she had gotten it from the best criminals in the world. He still wondered what she meant by that. Shaking off the memory, Noll tucked the passport back into his bag and pulled on the t-shirt.

Stepping outside the apartment, Noll breathed in the salty air of the Pacific Ocean as he started jogging along the beach. The rhythmic pounding of his bare feet against the sand melded with the crashing waves, drowning out the world around him. His heart thumped wildly in his chest, but he refused to slow down. Sweat soaked through his t-shirt and dampened parts of his shorts, yet he pushed onward. It was a beautiful day in this tropical paradise, and he needed to stay focused.

"Be prepared, Noll!" he muttered to himself between labored breaths. "Be prepared." The mantra fueled him, driving him forward through his exhaustion. Each step, each gasp for air, was a reminder of the life he had left behind and the one he now pursued. He would never be that broken man again – not if he could help it.

As Noll continued his run, his thoughts wandered to the SNL Foundation, Sierra, Lucy, and everything they had been through together. The pain of his past – the divorce, the bankruptcy, the cancer, the suicide attempt – was still fresh in his mind, but so too was the hope that they had given him. He was finally becoming the man he wanted to be.

"Be prepared," Noll whispered one last time before turning back toward the apartment, determination burning in his eyes.

THE OCEAN BREEZE cooled Noll's sweat-slicked skin. The salty air filled his lungs, invigorating him.

His breath came in short, rapid bursts as he jogged toward the small apartment where he and the resort staff were housed. Sweat dripped down his tanned face, a testament to his relentless determination to regain control over his life. He had fought through dark times, and now, with every pounding stride, he felt stronger.

As he neared the building, he noticed a figure standing near the entrance, looking around cautiously. From a distance, the silhouette reminded him of Sierra, but this person had bright green hair, while Sierra's had been blue. His heart started to race – was it really her? The woman who had helped him start anew?

He continued jogging, his excitement building with each step. As he got closer, he recognized the piercings and defiant posture that belonged to none other than Sierra herself. She had changed her hair color, but there was no mistaking her. Noll stopped dead in his tracks, staring at her while she remained oblivious to his presence. Memories of their last encounter in a cheap, dangerous motel in Florida City began to resurface, mixing with his current emotions.

"Sierra," he whispered to himself, his voice barely audible. Just as he was about to call out to her, Sierra's dark brown eyes locked onto him, still standing frozen a few feet away. A smile slowly spread across her face, and she walked toward him with a measured pace.

"Is Jack Murphy ready?" she asked when she finally stood in front of him. Her voice was sharp and confident – just as he remembered it.

Noll nodded, his own smile growing. "Yes, the son of a gun had a year to prepare himself."

There was a pause, and then Noll asked in return, "Is CypherWave ready?"

"Yes, sir!" Sierra answered with a hint of pride in her voice. And with a tilt of her head, she gestured for Noll to follow her.

As they walked, Noll couldn't help but think about the journey he had been through: the struggles with his divorce, bankruptcy, and cancer; the vacation in Bonaire that had nearly ended in tragedy; and ultimately, the renewed sense of purpose that now drove him. All of it had led him to this moment, standing beside Sierra on a Pacific Island.

THE SMALL PICKUP truck's tires crunched on the gravel road as Sierra navigated through a part of the island that was clearly meant for locals rather than tourists. Noll stared out the passenger window, taking in the simple houses and lush foliage that lined the narrow path. The ocean was still visible in the distance, a constant reminder of the world beneath the waves that had become his sanctuary.

Though they traveled in silence, Noll couldn't help but sneak glances at Sierra every so often. Her focus was on the road, her hands gripping the steering wheel with a quiet determination. At stop signs, their eyes would lock for brief moments before she returned her attention to driving. Each time their gazes met, Noll felt a surge of gratitude mixed with apprehension.

As if on cue, Carrie Underwood was singing in the car stereo. "I dug my key into the side of his pretty little souped-up four-wheel drive; Carved my name into his leather seats; I took a Louisville Slugger to both headlights; Slashed a hole in all four tires."

"Vengence..." Noll mused. "I never thought it could feel so good."

After they left the main road behind, the truck bounced over even more potholes and uneven terrain. Noll held onto the door handle, bracing himself against the jolts.

Sierra finally brought the truck to a stop in front of a dilapidated building with four separate doors reminiscent of an old motel. Noll looked at it skeptically but said nothing. In silence, he grabbed a suitcase and a backpack from the back of the truck while Sierra hoisted two dry boxes emblazoned with blue dragon heads on a dolly with wheels. He couldn't help the memories that resurfaced at the sight of those waterproof boxes, a swirl of emotions churning within him.

They entered the small apartment, Noll setting the suitcase and backpack near the door while Sierra carried the Blue Dragon boxes into the bedroom. As she threw them on the bed, Noll took the opportunity to explore her new home. It was far from Sierra's luxurious Miami penthouse, but it would serve its purpose.

The tiny apartment was barely large enough to move around in, its worn and peeling wallpaper a testament to the passage of time. Noll finished his quick inspection and joined Sierra in the cramped bedroom. She was kneeling by an open Blue Dragon box on the bed, carefully laying out various pieces of underwater photography equipment.

"Only one bed?" Noll remarked, taking in the limited sleeping arrangements.

Sierra glanced over her shoulder at him, smirking. "I figured we should look like a normal couple. Sort of. Maybe you'll officially meet me on the dive boat tomorrow? And then, we'll fall in love, and soon enough... We'll be living the dream, traveling the world while scuba diving. It's a perfect cover."

Noll couldn't help but chuckle at the thought. It was true; they needed to blend in, to appear as nothing more than enthusiastic dive professionals chasing adventure.

He approached Sierra, watching as she expertly unpacked the waterproof boxes. Once all the equipment had been removed, she pulled out the cut-out foam with holes that had held the underwater photography gear in place. Underneath, a second layer came into view: stacks upon stacks of crisp hundred-dollar bills.

Noll's eyebrows shot up, and he nodded toward the second Blue Dragon dry box. "Two for one special?" he asked rhetorically, his voice tinged with amusement.

Sierra grinned, her dark brown eyes twinkling with mischief. "You could say that."

Noll's gaze shifted from the stacks of hundred-dollar bills to Sierra. "What took you so long?" he asked, his voice low and steady.

Sierra shrugged, her dark brown eyes never leaving his. "Had a lot to do to be prepared," she replied simply, but there was an intensity in her eyes that told him it wasn't as easy as she made it sound.

Noll's gaze returned to the Blue Dragon waterproof boxes, their logo prominent on each one. The head of a blue dragon seemed to stare back at him, a symbol of dark power and influence. He traced the outline of the dragon with his index finger. "I'm coming for you," he mumbled under his breath, determination hardening his features.

"We are coming," Sierra interjected, her voice firm and resolute, with an accent on the 'we.'

For a moment, they stood in silence, locking eyes, their shared values resonating between them. In silence, they found strength and solidarity, ready for whatever challenges awaited them in their quest for justice.

KEEP an eye out for the second part of this adventure under the title "Operation Blue Dragon" at darcykieran.com, where you will also find a playlist for the chapter songs. And please subscribe to learn when "Operation Blue Dragon" becomes available.

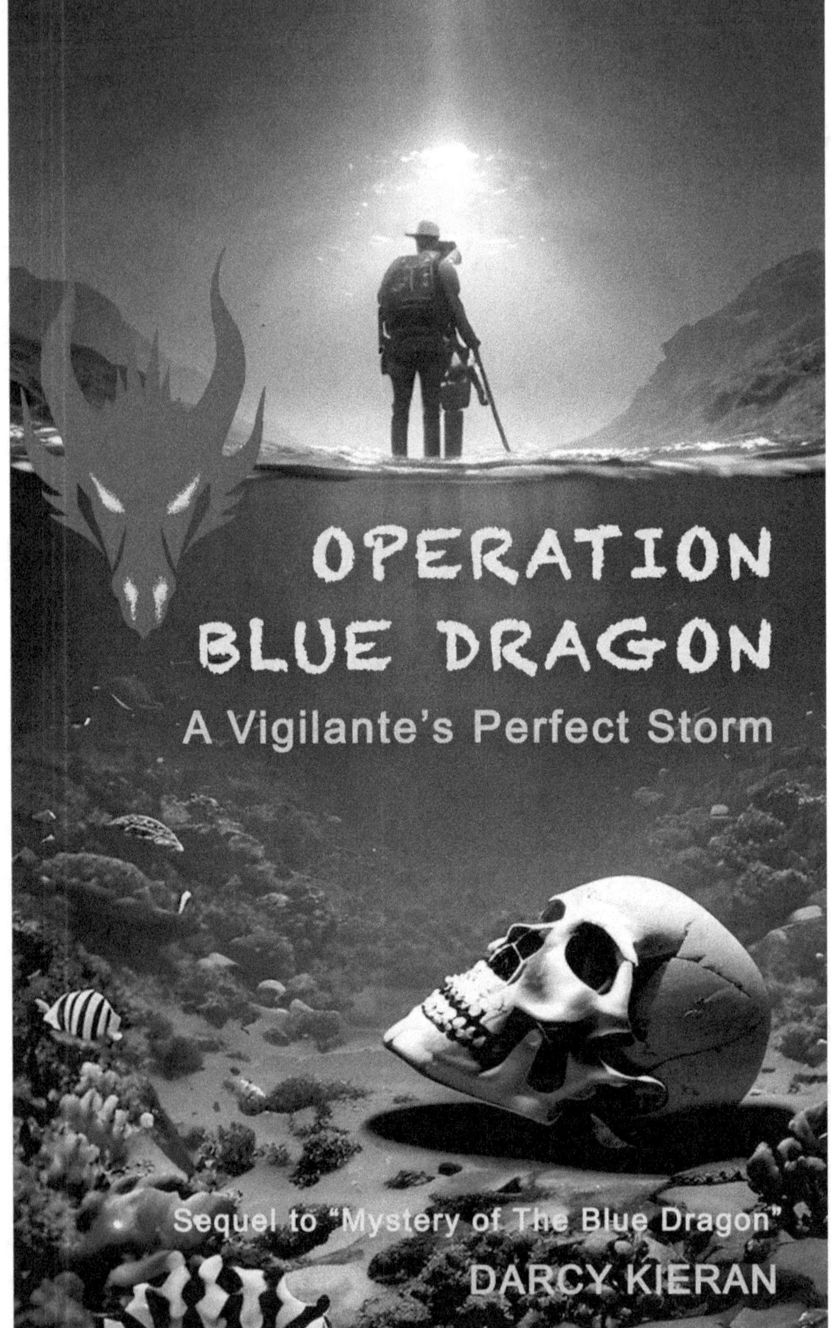
OPERATION
BLUE DRAGON
A Vigilante's Perfect Storm
Sequel to "Mystery of The Blue Dragon"
DARCY KIERAN

LEARN TO DIVE

If you want to learn to dive with the type of high-quality and safe scuba diving skills and practices Nollaig has been championing in this story, have a look at the following work by Darcy Kieran:

- "<u>The Ultimate Beginner's Guide To Scuba Diving</u>: How to Increase Safety, Save Money & Have More Fun!"
- <u>Logbooks</u> based on safety, performance & fun with mastery of buoyancy and continuous improvement.

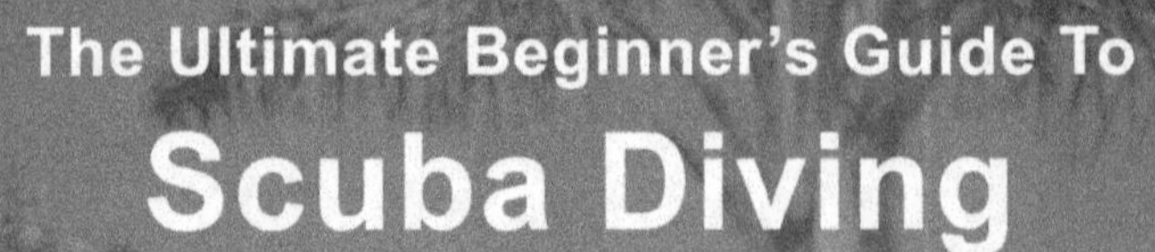

businessofdiving.com/books

The
Evolved
SCUBA DIVER
LOGBOOK

businessofdiving.com/books

ALSO BY DARCY KIERAN

- Other novels: darcykieran.com
- Non-fiction books for scuba divers: businessofdiving.com/books
- Scuba Diver Press: scubadiverpress.com
- Non-fiction books for dive professionals: businessofdiving.com/books
- Scubanomics: scubanomics.com
- Business of Diving Institute: businessofdiving.com

CONNECT WITH DARCY KIERAN

Please subscribe to know when new novels become available:
scubanomics.com/subscribe

GIVE ME FEEDBACK, PLEASE!
A SPECIAL REQUEST

YOU CAN MAKE MY DAY!

First of all, thank you for reading this story. There are million books, but you picked *this one* and for that, I am extremely grateful.

If you liked it, I'd love to hear from you and hope that you could take a few seconds to post a positive review wherever you purchased it. You'll find useful links at darcykieran.com .

On the other hand, **if you did not like this book**, could you please give me anonymous feedback at businessofdiving.com/contact so that I can improve?

Either way, I wish you all the best, a lot of pleasurable readings, and safe diving!

ABOUT DARCY KIERAN

In the dive industry, Darcy has been a Course Director and Instructor Trainer with multiple dive training agencies for recreational scuba diving and tech diving. He owned/managed dive shops, dive gear distributors and wholesalers, dive resorts, and charter boats in Canada and the USA.

He's been on the Board of Directors of the Diving Equipment & Marketing Association (DEMA), a dive industry trade association based in California. And he brought with him valuable experience from other industries, including sporting goods manufacturing, radio & TV broadcasting, transportation, digital marketing agencies, and education.

Darcy is an engineer, radio announcer, public speaker, and author.

Stay in touch at:
darcykieran.com

linkedin.com/in/darcykieran
reamstories.com/scuba
bsky.app/profile/darcykieran.bsky.social
x.com/darcykieran
goodreads.com/darcykieran

www.ingramcontent.com/pod-product-compliance
Lightning Source LLC
Chambersburg PA
CBHW071418200726
48294CB00002B/432